FAMILY FORTUNES

Books in
The Fairfields Chronicles Series

by Sarah Shears

THE VILLAGE
FAMILY FORTUNES
THE YOUNG GENERATION
RETURN TO RUSSETS

Published by Bantam Books

FAMILY FORTUNES

Sarah Shears

BANTAM BOOKS

NEW YORK · TORONTO · LONDON · SYDNEY · AUCKLAND

FAMILY FORTUNES

A BANTAM BOOK 0 553 40262 5

Originally published in Great Britain by Judy Piatkus (Publishers) Ltd

PRINTING HISTORY
Judy Piatkus edition published 1985
Bantam edition published 1991

This book is set in Times Roman

Bantam Books are published by Transworld Publishers Ltd., 61–63 Uxbridge Road, Ealing, London W5 5SA, in Australia by Transworld Publishers (Australia) Pty. Ltd., 15–23 Helles Avenue, Moorebank, NSW 2170, and in New Zealand by Transworld Publishers (N.Z.) Ltd., Cnr. Moselle and Waipareira Avenues, Henderson, Auckland.

Made and printed in Great Britain by
BPCC Hazell Books
Aylesbury, Bucks, England
Member of BPCC Ltd.

Part One

Chapter 1

When young Carrie Simmons stood on the station platform at Fairfields that day, in the Spring of 1918, and saw the man she was to marry step carefully off the train, she was shocked and dismayed. She had last seen her cousin, Albert Blunt, in 1914 when he volunteered for the Merchant Navy. In those four years, she had matured. At twenty-one she was ready for marriage, but was not prepared for the ghost of the man who went away. In the gaunt figure, with his cropped head and scarred face, ragged and dirty from long weeks of travel from the prisoner-of-war camp in Turkey, she could see little resemblance to that healthy, good-looking farmer's son, for even his eyes, so intensely blue in his tanned face, were blank. But he was her Bertie even though he stared back at her as though she were a stranger as she walked slowly down the platform. He was due to-day, but why was there no one from Russets to meet him?

Beyond the budding hedges, the fields stretched away to the steep slope of the hill and the village. The silence was broken only by the rattle of the porter's truck, and the clear voice of the child asking, 'Is that Carrie's Daddy?' and the doctor answering his grandson, 'No, it's a poor wounded soldier home from the War, and Carrie will look after him.' 'Then he will soon be better.' She would always remember the child's quick response. He had such confidence and trust in his Carrie, the young village girl his mother had engaged as nursemaid to her baby son; his grandmother would have preferred a trained nurse from London.

'Hello, Bertie.' She hesitated only for a moment, then her arms enfolded him. She could feel the bony skeleton of his weak, emaciated body through the worn jersey. Corduroy trousers and canvas shoes had gathered the dust and dirt of the long journey. His thin arms clutched her compulsively. He was crying and sobbing, 'Carrie – Carrie – Carrie.' Now she could hear nothing but that once familiar voice calling her name, out of the past; but even the voice was no longer familiar – or had she forgotten?

She knew already, at this sad, crucial moment of her young life, that from henceforth she was utterly and completely enslaved, and that there was no escape. But she had her mother's warm, impetuous nature, and her mother's resilience. Born and bred in the village slum of Richmond Row, Carrie Simmons was a product of the working class. For a brief period she had enjoyed the comfort and luxury of an upper-class society as nursemaid to the doctor's grandson. She had shared the temporary home of an Army officer at Tidworth, travelled with the child and his parents to India, helped to nurse the child through typhoid fever, and brought him back to England on her own, all before her seventeenth birthday. Child and nurse had been inseparable companions, and now they were to be parted.

The same train that had brought Bertie back had also brought the child's mother home from India. But she was a stranger to her small son, as this man in Carrie's arms was a stranger. They both had been thrust into a situation they had to accept, for there was no alternative. The grandfather would be the go-between in the difficult days of adjustment, and the old-established, family servants were kind. In another year or so, Carrie's Jimmy would be swallowed up in a world of small boys at preparatory school. His future was ordained, and he would follow the same pattern as his father and grandfather – preparatory school, public school, university, followed by a career in the Army, the Church, or the Civil Service. Unless it happened that young James Saunders was destined to be a rebel against society, like his Uncle Dennis, who, so they said, had murdered a pretty school teacher from the village school, and had fled to a family tea plantation in Ceylon.

At the moment, young James was being led away in the opposite direction, not unduly disturbed because his devoted Carrie was not coming home with them. He had been promised a ride back in the front seat of his grandfather's car, and he had met on the station platform his hero, twelve-year-old Philip Martin, a daily pupil at the Grammar School. Altogether it was an eventful and exciting day for a small boy getting a little bored with the nursery routine. There were no tears or tantrums. He would miss Carrie, and ask when she was coming back, but it would be fun getting to know the lady who was his mother, riding the new bicycle she would buy, having meals in the dining-room, and spending his first pocket money. The sadness of parting was not for the child but the nursemaid, and her heart ached as she exchanged the child for the man in her warm arms. She knew her duty lay no longer with the small boy.

'Are they expecting you home today, Bertie?' she asked gently, as the train puffed slowly away along the branch line on which her father had once worked as a ganger.

Bertie looked puzzled. 'I don't know,' he admitted, after some reflection.

'Aunt Lucy would be here to meet you, wouldn't she, if she knew you were coming on this train?'

'Yes.'

'Never mind, don't worry. Sit down on this bench. I'll go across to the station hotel. The porter drives a cab now. I'll ask him to take us to Russets. You didn't have any luggage?'

Bertie shook his head. He was still looking puzzled, so she smiled reassuringly, left him sitting on the bench, and hurried away, to tell the doctor she would be going with her fiancé to his home. Looking back from the level crossing, she could see the hunched figure staring after her, and she was choked with tears. He was like a child, so she must be a mother as well as a wife and nurse. The prospect was not too daunting, she reminded herself, because she would not be alone. His mother and his brother Tom would be there to share the burden, and Russets was a dear, familiar place she had known since early childhood. Aunt Lucy was her own mother's twin sister. They both were widows. They both had lost a son in the War, and both now had second sons who had come home broken in body. But Albert suffered not only from his physical wounds, it seemed; it was doubtful if he would ever be completely restored. 'Time would heal' the women would say with brave optimism, but many of the returning soldiers were defeated. They had suffered too much, and there was a limit to their endurance. One by one the wounded men were coming back to their village. Men who went away as boys, answering the call to fight for King and Country with patriotic fervour, seeing only the glory, not the terrible carnage.

Carrie had been sustained by a single postcard from Turkey. 'Only a few battle scars,' Bertie had written cheerfully. 'Wait for me, sweetheart.' And she had waited, hopefully, for another two years, not knowing what he must endure in that prisoner-of-war camp before they would meet again. Hope had kept his memory alive, and hope would sustain her through the long, difficult years ahead.

Aunt Lucy was crossing the yard from the dairy when the station cab drew up at the gate with a screech of brakes. She stared, surprised, for cars to the farm were a rarity. She often caught a glimpse of an ambulance on its way to the Big House, since Marston Park had been converted into a hospital for wounded officers in 1915. Visitors would arrive by train and hire the station cab, for few had their own cars.

When Carrie had paid the driver, a gaunt figure, with a scarred face, stepped carefully down on to the cobbles. Carrie offered a helping hand, but it was pushed aside with rough impatience. The woman who was his mother, and the girl who would soon be his wife, stood watching in helpless pity and love, while he picked his way across the yard. His brother, Tom, stood hesitating in the doorway of the Dutch barn, shocked into an awareness of the contrast between the two brothers. Suddenly overwhelmed by a sense of guilt for his own rude health, he could not face the inevitable question in those faded blue eyes.

Katie, the young servant girl, hovered uncertainly at the kitchen window, waiting to be told what to do next, for she could not remember her duties from one day to the next, and had to be reminded. She was a big, strong girl, not very bright, but a hard worker, and her mistress was kind. Katie had never known kindness at the Orphanage, only tolerance and a harsh discipline. She gaped at the little group in the yard, her roughened hands smoothing the clean white apron she was instructed to wear in the afternoon. She was proud of those white aprons. The morning aprons were rough hessian. When she had arrived at the farm at the age of thirteen, on the carrier's wagonette, she had been dumped in the yard with her tin box just as her predecessor, a dark-eyed orphan with gypsy blood, had been dumped. The trunk contained three of everything, according to the normal regulations for orphaned servant girls. Her wardrobe consisted of three print dresses, three white aprons, three hessian aprons, three caps, three pairs of black shoes, three pairs of black stockings, three sets of calico underwear, and three flannelette nightgowns. All but the shoes and stockings had been stitched laboriously at the Orphanage. A Winter coat of dark serge, with a felt hat, completed the wardrobe. No provision had been made for 'Sunday best', and it was assumed a servant girl had no time or opportunity to wear 'Sunday best' clothes. Her new mistress soon remedied the omission, however, and Katie was taken to Tunbridge Wells on her first free day, and allowed to choose two dresses from a big department store, half the cost being deducted from her wages during the first year of service. Lucy Blunt would be amply rewarded in the years ahead with a loyal, devoted servant. But now that mistress was holding a strange-looking man in her arms – a man who looked like a tramp. Katie shivered. She was very frightened of tramps since one had molested her in the wood where she gathered faggots for the kitchen stove.

With an arm about her son's shoulders, Lucy held out a welcoming hand to her future daughter-in-law, and asked anxiously, 'You've come to stay, haven't you?'

'Yes, Aunt Lucy.'

'But you've brought nothing with you?'

'I didn't expect to be meeting Bertie. I had taken Jimmy to the station to meet his mother, and Bertie happened to be on the same train. It was a nice surprise.'

'The child didn't mind being left?'

'I don't think so. His grandfather was there and Teacher. I expect he will soon get used to doing without me.'

'Will they send your things on or shall you have to collect them?'

'I expect they will send them. I would rather not go back. It wouldn't be fair.'

'No. Better to make a clean break.'

They were walking slowly towards the house, and Lucy was holding the girl's hand in a warm clasp. She could feel her trembling, and knew she was fighting back her tears. It was such a sudden parting from the little boy, such a drastic step for her young niece. Carrie was so like her, they would have passed for mother and daughter – the daughter she had hoped for to complete the family. But it was too late now.

'This is Katie,' she said, introducing the servant girl.

Katie backed away, fumbling with her apron.

'Lay two more places for tea, please, Katie,' her mistress reminded her.

'Yes, Ma'am.' Her willing hands were clumsy. She was very conscious of the man who had collapsed in the rocking chair. He was staring at her with those strange eyes, and in her nervousness, she dropped a cup. It lay at her feet, shattered on the brick floor, and her lips quivered. She still expected to be punished but there were no punishments in this house. It was not her fault. Lucy knew the cause was Albert upsetting the girl. It would take time to adjust. They all had to adjust, not only Katie.

'It's all right. Don't cry. I'm not cross with you. Pick up the pieces and put them in the bin,' she told the girl kindly, and set the kettle to boil for tea. She always made the tea, since she could not trust Katie with boiling water. She still missed Emma, who had been so quick to learn her ways, but unreliable. Her wildness had been quite a hazard, for she would run off to the woods when the spirit moved her, without a by-your-leave. Then Emma had run away for good when she heard Harry had been killed. Lucy's eldest son had loved her in his rough fashion. It suited Emma. She had not wanted a gentle lover.

Albert's tongue licked his cracked lips, and his mouth watered in anticipation of the food on the table. Home-baked bread, dairy butter and cheese, jam and cake. He drank the hot, sweet tea gratefully, and asked for more, but when his mother laid a plate on his knees as he sat in the fireside chair, he stared at the buttered crust and the generous portion of cheese and his stomach revolted. He shook his head, and Lucy took the food away. Why couldn't he eat when he looked so thin and starved? she asked herself. But when his cropped head slumped on his chest, she realised it was sleep he needed more than food, and she gathered him in her strong arms, carried him to the parlour, and laid him gently on the sofa. His shrunken body shivered, and she covered him with the shawl that had covered all her boys when they felt poorly, and the body of Bert, her husband, when he fell off the hay-wagon, and her nephew, Freddie, after the accident in the park when he lay unconscious for three days. Now that same nephew was a patient at the hospital for wounded officers in the Big House.

Freddie had married Cynthia, the second daughter of Sir Neville Franklin who owned the big estate, including Russets Farm, and the other farms. They all were his tenants. They all were subject to his autocratic authority. And she herself more than any other, should know the extent of that authority. Sir Neville was a law unto himself. He had lusted after the plump pretty farmer's wife long before her husband fell off the hay-wagon.

Twelve months later he had taken her. When her fourth son was born, the squire claimed the boy, but did not claim his mother. It was not another mistress he wanted, but a mother to bear a longed-for son. Cursed with four daughters, and envious of his tenant farmer with three healthy, good-looking boys, it seemed reasonable to expect Lucy Blunt would produce another boy. Sir Neville was not disappointed.

As she tucked the shawl around Albert's thin shoulders, she sighed for those early years before her 'fall from grace', when life had seemed so simple and pleasant. Young Charles had divided the family. She loved Harry, Tom and Albert dearly, but she adored the boy so ridiculously like his father. Now Charles was at Eton, and she would see him at Easter unless he decided to spend the vacation with the friend with the pretty sister. Like father, like son!

Before she could sit down to her own tea, she had to go in search of Tom. She had last seen him hovering in the barn, reluctant to show himself to his younger brother. Tom had always been the most gentle of her sons, a sensitive, creative boy, who had grown into a man on whom she could depend during the War years. The two land-girls had left to be married only recently, and since it was impossible to find a substitute male or female, they had managed on their own, working long hours in a happy partnership. They were tired, but everyone was tired in this last year of the War, and they were expecting Albert home. With Carrie to lend a hand, the four of them would manage fine, Lucy and Tom had decided. Hard work was no novelty at Russets. Lucy was strong and capable. There was no job on the farm she could not tackle. Her husband and sons had relied on her for everything in those early years before the tragedy of that hot Summer afternoon. Harry had stepped into his father's shoes overnight. 'Don't worry, Mum. We'll manage!' he had told her – and started giving orders to his younger brothers who resented it, to the servant girl, Emma, who laughed mockingly and tossed her black hair, and to old Walter, who came to help out immediately after the tragedy. He used to spit on his hands, dry them on his dirty corduroy breeches, and ask, slyly, 'So you be the boss 'arry, lad?'

There had been so much friction because of Harry's bossiness, and it seemed that peaceful days with Bert at the helm had gone for ever. Yet the friction had been nothing compared to the shame and resentment when the boys discovered their mother to be pregnant, and her lover to be none other than Sir Neville Franklin. Who could expect them to welcome the beautiful baby who grew so quickly into a replica of his father, and was so proudly acknowledged by him? It was too embarrassing. Someone in their own class of society might have been accepted eventually, but not Sir Neville Franklin, who did no more than raise his riding whip when passing by on that handsome black stallion.

Lucy found Tom propped against the doorpost of the Dutch barn, his dog at his feet. With his lissom body, tanned face, vivid blue eyes, and sun-bleached hair, he presented a picture of perfect health, and the kind of beauty made perfect by sun, wind and rain. It was a face as changing as the weather, reflecting his every mood, and his mother read the changes because she knew him and loved him. They had grown very close since Harry and Albert had gone away, and all the resentment and jealousy had been forgotten. Young Charles was no longer a threat, or even a contestant in the battle for their mother's favours. He came to visit her for an occasional day in the holidays, when he claimed her full attention with his light-hearted charm and teasing affection. Then he was gone. 'Like a cuckoo in the nest,' Tom had observed, and it was true.

'Come and get your tea, Tom.' She spoke calmly, yet all her quivering senses had been alerted to the dangers and the difficulties that awaited them in the near future. She had been an emotional creature in her younger days, with a quick temper, but Bert had been placid, so they suited each other. She could see herself in Carrie, and was sorry for the girl, embarking on the unaccustomed role of wife to a farmer's son so obviously unfit to be a farmer. Behind the picturesque façade of seed time and harvest, and grazing cows on green pastures, lay the heavy drudgery and the tedious routine. It had taken her a long time to adjust and Carrie would also know the tears of frustration in her unfamiliar environment. One had started her life as a house-parlour maid, the other as a nursemaid. It was different for Bert and their sons, born and bred at Russets. It was in their blood. Only love and loyalty could surmount all the strangeness and the hardship, and her niece was no weakling..

'Where is he?' Tom was asking.

'Fast asleep on the parlour sofa. He was too exhausted to eat his tea.'

'He looks terrible, Mum. What have they done to him?'

'Those scars on his head and face look to me like burns. His ship was one of several torpedoed in that convoy, if you remember.' Tom nodded. 'But he drags his feet, and seems to be in pain. There must be a more recent injury on his body.'

'You mean from the prisoner-of-war camp?'

'Yes. The Turks are cruel, Tom.'

He shuddered, and she laid a comforting arm about his shoulders.

'I feel guilty,' he muttered.

'Why?'

'I stayed at home.'

'But one of you had to stay. You were doing essential War work. I couldn't have managed without you, Tom. You need have no regrets.'

'But I do, and I shall. I am shamed by my younger brother. It's no use, Mum. I dread the moment when we come face to face. What can I say to that pitiful wreck who once looked like me, and hadn't a care in the world? What can I *say*?' His voice was choked.

'Come and get your tea. Carrie is waiting. You can help her, Tom. She's very young, and shocked.'

Then he dropped his mother's arm from his shoulders and walked briskly across the yard. He was very fond of Carrie.

She was spreading home-made gooseberry jam on a slice of crusty bread, thinking of Jimmy. He would be having tea with his mother and grandfather in the drawing-room. No more nursery meals. She was frightened and confused by this sudden plunge into a new environment, and not yet ready for marriage to that grim stranger asleep in the parlour. In that short time they had been together, she had known it was not only his appearance, but his whole personality that had changed. What had she expected?

When Tom stood in the doorway, she ran to him for comfort, instinctively, and he held her close because he saw her as a sister, not as his brother's sweetheart. Carrie had been visiting at Russets since she was three years old, and had endeared herself to all three brothers. She was so plump and pretty, so much like the little sister they had been promised. Now she was shoulder high, and her curly hair tickled his chin.

'Why are you wearing your nursemaid's uniform?' he asked her, when she had dried her tears on his grubby handkerchief, smelling strongly of silage!

'I came straight here from the station to bring Bertie

home. I hope I don't have to wait too long for my other clothes.'

'I'll telephone after tea and ask to speak to Jimmy's mother,' Lucy promised as she poured Tom's tea.

He did not ask to see his brother, and she did not suggest it. Albert must not be disturbed. She had never called her youngest son Bertie because it seemed disrespectful to the old Queen's Albert, after whom he was named. Her twin sister, Ruby, had named her firstborn Albert. It was more popular than any other name in working-class families, as was Victoria in the upper class. There was no reason why Carrie should not fly into Tom's arms for comfort. It was natural, and Albert was asleep in the parlour. But circumstances had changed so drastically in the past hour or so, it now seemed that a little caution must be practised to avoid any further trouble in the family. She must warn Carrie not to be too demonstrative. Albert must be protected against that demon of jealousy that was not unknown to him. It was Albert who had been so jealous of his half-brother, Charles, at one time. Feeling neglected, he had accused her of spoiling the child. It was true, of course.

'You never had time to make toffee for us when we were little,' he had grumbled, sulkily. It was still Charles' favourite sweet, and she always filled a tin with her home-made toffee for his school tuck box. Albert had wanted to sit on her lap when he was quite a big boy because he could not bear to see her cuddling Charles. So that old demon of jealousy could be resurrected unless they were careful and kind. It would be unkind to tempt Providence. As his mother, she could now see the danger, and they must be warned.

'Surely the carrier could collect Carrie's trunk if one of the servants at the doctor's had it ready packed?' Tom suggested. 'Then we needn't trouble anyone to deliver it.'

Carrie sighed with relief. She would feel both glad and sorry to break the last link with that house, and her young charge, but until she did so, she would have no sense of belonging permanently to Russets. Aunt Lucy was no stranger, and she loved her dearly. Tom was like a dear elder brother. Only Bertie was a stranger, and it was Bertie who would soon be her husband. She hoped he would sleep all evening. His own room and his own bed would be ready to receive him tonight, after he was bathed and fed. In the morning she would feel more able to cope. Tomorrow was another day.

When they had finished tea, Katie was reminded to clear away and wash up. Tom went out to the wash-house to boil peelings for the pig swill in an old copper kept for that purpose. Tom was a quiet, methodical worker, and knew exactly what must be done at any hour of the day. Yet the routine was never monotonous, for animals have a way of disturbing the pattern with unpredictable behaviour in the same way as humans. A cow in calf, or a mare in foal can be a very temperamental creature if she is nervous or frightened. But Tom could handle them gently and soothingly. There was nothing he loved better than to watch a suckling newborn calf or foal. The miracle of birth was all around them, and death was no stranger. Tom had lived so close to nature all his young life, he would be lost in any other place. The changing seasons of the year were all the change he needed. There were no holidays, no respite from the daily round, the common task, but he wanted none.

As he fed the copper fire with faggots, he thought of his brother laying asleep on the old sofa, and his heart ached with pity.

Albert was still sleeping at midnight, and Lucy decided she must wake him. Until she saw him bathed and fed, and tucked up comfortably between the clean sheets on his own bed, she could not retire. The emotional events of the day had wearied her. The joy she had visualised with Albert safely home had been sadly marred by his pitiful condition. She would have to keep reminding herself this was actually her son, and she would hope and pray that he would eventually recover some semblance of his former self.

The big zinc bath, half filled with hot water, was waiting in front of the kitchen fire. Bathing at Russets was still a major operation. The water was heated in the wash-house copper – not the one used for the pig's swill! – and ladled out into buckets. The same procedure with a ladle and a bucket had to be used to empty the bath, and the water used on the kitchen garden. A big bath towel and striped pyjamas warmed on a line over the stove, and a fresh tablet of Lifebuoy soap stood ready in a dish on a kitchen chair. A screen encircled the bath to keep off the draughts. It looked very cosy, very inviting, but Albert was sleepy and sulky at being disturbed, and had to be coaxed off the sofa and into the kitchen.

'I'll wash your back when you're ready, dear. Drop your clothing over the screen. You won't need those dirty old rags any more. They are only fit for the bonfire!' she told him, cheerfully, and carried them away.

But when he called her to wash his back she could not prevent the gasp of horror or the tears that pricked her eyes. His emaciated body was so thin, she could count the ribs, and his back and chest so terribly scarred, very little of the original skin remained.

'Not a pretty sight, is it, Mum?' he muttered, gruffly.

But she was too choked to speak, and she soaped and rinsed his back with a soft piece of flannel because her hands were rough.

'I can manage now.' She was dismissed curtly as a servant, and he had not thanked her for her loving ministrations. Perhaps he was embarrassed? Perhaps he had forgotten how to say thank you?

Now she was shy of her own son, and that was ridiculous, she told herself. It was a miracle that he had survived, and it was proof of his courage and endurance. But what if his mind were permanently embittered by this terrible experience? Would it be fair to Carrie? Because she was suddenly so shy of him, she did not offer to dry his back, and the grunts and groans reminded her he was not finding it easy.

'Finished,' he told her, eventually, and she took the screen away and dragged the bath aside. Tom would help Katie to empty it in the morning before breakfast. Now she helped him into the new dressing gown and the slippers she had bought ready for his return. She had tramped all round Tunbridge Wells one hot day last Summer to find what she wanted, but both the dressing gown and the slippers were much too big, and he told her so in a gruff, disgruntled way, and asked for a cup of tea.

'What would you like to eat, dear? We had macaroni cheese for supper, but I didn't save any because it dries if it's warmed up.' Albert pulled a face. 'Bacon and eggs and fried bread?'

He nodded, and watched her covertly as she moved about the kitchen, making a pot of tea, slipping a plate in the oven, placing a cloth and cutlery on the end of the kitchen table, fetching bacon, eggs, bread and butter and lard. All her movements were quick, and her clean white apron crackled with starch. His eyes followed her, unsmiling, with a curious kind of intentness. It made her nervous, and her hands trembled as she handed him a cup of tea, hot, strong and sweet, the way he had always liked it.

'You look more like my Albert now,' she lied, and patted his damp head affectionately.

He recoiled as though he had been struck. 'Don't touch my head,' he snarled.

'I'm sorry.' She turned away, saddened and hurt, to cook his supper.

The grandfather clock struck the half hour, an owl hooted in the barn, the bacon sizzled in the pan. All familiar sounds, but her son was remote from all familiar things, and she could not reach him.

Only Katie slept at all that first night, in the attic room that had once been Emma's. Her clothes still hung in the wardrobe, and the little treasures that Harry had bought at the Michaelmas Fair still had pride of place on the chest of drawers, for Emma had run away in her print dress when the Mistress had read the telegram, and she hadn't come back. Harry was dead.

The door of Albert's room stood wide open all next day, and he slept exhausted. From time to time Lucy, Tom or Carrie would stand silently beside the bed, gazing down with wet eyes on that scarred face and cropped head. Katie went about her work quietly. Carrie was initiated into the solemn rites of the dairy, after she had fed the hens and collected the eggs, but her mind wandered to the little boy in the doctor's house in the High Street, and she had no sense of belonging to Russets. That would come later, much later.

The lovely month of May seemed even lovelier this year – or was it because they noticed it more? Each in turn, Lucy, Tom and Carrie, wandered away from that silent, morose figure on the bench in the yard, to enjoy a brief half-hour or so in the wood. It was bluebell time, and the beeches were green with fresh leaf – a fitting backcloth for the blue carpet. Nature was seldom disappointing, and the bluebells could be relied upon to appear each year in due season.

Lucy snatched a little time in the late evening before supper when the sinking sun cast slanting golden rays between the green branches, picking out small brilliant patches of blue, leaving the rest in shadow. Once upon a time, Lucy and Bert had walked in the wood together, hand-in-hand, then, a little later, Bert had carried Harry to see the bluebells. The following year they had both carried a child, and when Harry was able to run on ahead, they had Albert. Both parents taught their sons to recognise and appreciate the beauty of nature, and had time in their busy lives to answer the boys' everlasting questions when they were young. The boys looked alike, with their flaxen hair and blue eyes, but were totally different in character and temperament – and their differences were apparent at an early age.

So when Lucy hurried away to the wood that first evening, after the eventful homecoming, nostalgic memories came flooding back, and she longed for Bert with a desperate and futile longing, leaning her aching back against the bole of a tree. The voices she heard in the wood today were the shrill voices of children, and when she closed her eyes, she could see them darting between the trees in their bright, hand-knitted jerseys. If only she could put back the clock! If only Bert had been spared to share this second devastating shock, and the responsibility she must carry single-handed. It was not only Nature that was tempting her with memories. She was feeling that urgent need she always felt at this season of the year, to lie with a man – and not just any man. The man who had fathered her fourth son had taken her roughly in his urgency. He had waited a year, for decency's sake, after Bert's death, and patience had never been one of Sir Neville's virtues. The memory of his strong, virile body and sensual magnetism could be recaptured as easily as the memory of Bert, her dear, stubborn, unemotional husband, who took his pleasure with conventional regularity every Saturday night! Only once had she known the exquisite excitement of her demanding lover. He had visualised her 'quiver' nourishing the male seed, and rejecting the female. There was proof enough in those three healthy boys fathered by his tenant farmer.

Lucy was still an ardent woman, sexually starved. Her widowed sister, Ruby, had confessed she felt the same way, and young Carrie was just such another. It was cruel to watch her strange 'courtship', with Albert dropping crumbs of affection into her lap when he was in the mood, and often ignoring her. Yet he was firmly determined to marry Carrie, and was only waiting to recuperate enough strength to put up the banns – or so he announced.

Carrie had found her own way to the wood because she remembered Albert had taken her there as a little girl, to pick bluebells. She was still young enough to gather a bunch, knowing it was a mistake, for they wilted so quickly indoors. She hadn't the same feel about Nature as her cousins, born and bred at Russets, and she was ignorant of all but the commonest species of bird and wildflower. But then her Aunt Lucy had had to discover so much that was familiar to Bert, after her marriage at the age of sixteen.

Tom would have taken Carrie to the wood. Tom would have taught her to recognise the difference between a blackbird's song and a thrush's. Tom would have shown her the badger's sett, where the swallows nested in the eaves of the big Dutch barn, and the best place to catch minnows in the stream. He would have introduced her gradually to an environment she had known only for a short happy time in childhood. But Tom had been warned to be careful, for his brother was already suspicious. So Tom went alone to the bluebell wood at the break of day, when the cows had been milked, and thought of Carrie, but kept his thoughts to himself.

They were married quietly three months after Albert's return, and only the two families, and Teacher and her son, Philip, were present. Albert was wearing a dark suit borrowed from his cousin, Freddie. It hung loosely on his shrunken body.

Lucy had not set foot in the church since the day of the funeral, when blinds had been drawn in the village as the impressive cortege went past. Bert's coffin, massed with flowers, had been placed on a wagon, freshly painted and scrubbed, for the solemn occasion, and the two magnificent Shire horses, with gleaming harness, had performed their unaccustomed role with admirable decorum. The upper servants from Marston Park, and the other tenant farmers, with their families, had all attended to pay their last respects. Sir Neville Franklin had followed the cortege on his handsome black stallion. It had been a memorable occasion with 'old Parson' officiating, and choirboys reverently singing 'Abide with Me' and the 23rd Psalm. But Lucy had wished that Bert's body could have been laid to rest in his own soil at Russets.

The wedding, in comparison to that impressive funeral, was a drab affair, and would be remembered only for its drabness. Carrie had visualised her wedding day as a glamorous affair of white satin and orange blossom, with her young nieces as bridesmaids and a peal of bells as they left the church. For Carrie, her wedding day passed like a bad dream. 'Those whom God hath joined together let no man put asunder,' echoed in her tortured mind. She felt trapped. Hopefully she had waited for Bertie to release her from the bond of marriage, but he had not done so. Ashamed of such disloyalty, it had to be excused only because the man who claimed her for his wife was not the man who went away. In the long separation, she had woven their fond relationship into a dream of romantic love. Every girl had her own particular hero, fighting for King and Country. Carrie had had her cousin. She had no need to look elsewhere. 'Wait for me, sweetheart' – she had shown that card to everyone, so proud and happy. But fondness was not enough. Only a deep, mature, unselfish love could sustain such a marriage – the kind of love that Cynthia had for her brother, Freddie. She was there at the church in her nurse's uniform with Freddie in a wheel chair. Cynthia's young husband had come back to her with one leg amputated, and internal injuries. He was being nursed in the Hospital for Wounded Officers at her old home, Marston Park, and she was a nurse at the Hospital for Women in Marylebone Road, London. Their marriage had been regarded as a sad mistake by all who knew them. According to tradition, working class had no place in upper-class society, only as servants, but Sir Neville Franklin's second daughter had confounded all her critics when she fell in love with Freddie Simmons from the village slum, Richmond Row. He had been riding his bicycle in the Park of Marston, and had narrowly missed colliding with her horse. During the three days that he lay unconscious at Russets, suffering from concussion, Cynthia had sat beside the couch every afternoon to relieve the family who were busy hay-making. Their courtship had been conducted in a London tea-shop, and it was Cynthia who had proposed to Freddie. She had endeared herself to Ruby, Freddie's mother, that hard-working charwoman, so firmly convinced that her son should know his place. Generations of children had been singing lustily at the village school:

> The rich man in his castle,
> The poor man at his gate,

God made them high or lowly,
And ordered their estate.

There was no excuse for Freddie or for Cynthia! Tradition dies hard, but it was not the ex-charwoman who first accepted that traditions could be broken by a determined young woman. It was Sir Neville. Cynthia had no doubts when she was faced with a crippled husband and an uncertain future. She knew her love was strong enough to carry the burden. It would take all of two years to recuperate from the internal injuries, and to learn to manipulate an artificial limb. Roehampton was the next stage. But Freddie was proud of his wife, and he had his own particular brand of quiet courage and no bitterness to mar their relationship.

Like so many other couples faced with a long separation, possibly for ever, they had married hastily in a register office. Freddie had left for a training camp on Salisbury Plain the following day, and Cynthia hurried back on duty at the hospital, determined not to weep in front of her formidable Sister Harper! Now she was a guest at Carrie's wedding, and her heart ached for her young sister-in-law who had waited three years for this poor, emaciated, embittered man at the altar. The twin sisters, Ruby and Lucy, bore the stamp of suffering that was almost universal in this last year of the War. It had changed all their lives, and they listened to the solemn words of the marriage service with saddened hearts and grave doubts.

Chapter 2

The fields were ripe for harvest on Carrie's wedding day, and the village preparing for another hop-picking season. From the forecourt of 'The Three Nuns', the publican and his wife waved at the wedding party in the farm wagonette as they went past.

'It seems only yesterday that little Carrie was trotting around the place with her rag doll while her mother got on with the scrubbing. Now she's married.' The publican's wife sighed for those early days, for the pretty little girl had been a great favourite with the customers, and no other charwoman had ever worked harder than Ruby Simmons.

Cook and Parsons waved to the young ex-nursemaid from the forecourt of the doctor's house, and Carrie smiled a greeting and tossed out her small bouquet of pink roses. There was no sign of Jimmy, but his mother had deliberately removed him for the afternoon. He was still missing his beloved Carrie, and a tearful scene had to be avoided at all costs on her wedding day. Still on friendly terms with Teacher and the boy Philip, she could keep in touch with events at Russets indirectly, and knew a wedding had been arranged for this particular day.

The village was teeming with memories of happy pre-

War years for each one of that wedding party in the wagonette – all but Katie, the excited servant girl in her Sunday best, who was bowing and waving to everyone to the manner born. They passed the house of the local solicitor where young Freddie Simmons had started his long apprenticeship as an office boy at the age of thirteen.

'If I had sixpence for all the mornings I had polished that brass plate, I should be quite a rich man!' he told them, with a chuckle.

'I always knew he would succeed. Freddie was my brightest pupil, and always one step ahead of the rest of my Infants,' Teacher reminded them.

Freddie blushed with embarrassment as the office window filled with clerks and typists calling his name. He lifted a hand in salute, though several were strangers. The head clerk was grey-haired now, and the young apprentices too young for military service.

It was an uncomfortable ride in the wheelchair in the jolting vehicle. The stump of his amputated leg was throbbing painfully, and an old shrapnel wound in his arm was slow to heal. But Freddie was determined to keep cheerful for the sake of that pretty little sister who seemed to have got herself into a sorry situation that should never have been allowed to develop. Waving to her old associates, she was holding Albert's hand, trying not to cry. The baker and his wife were busily nailing up a barricade of wire netting over their counters in readiness for the Cockney invasion for hop-picking. They hurried to the door to call 'Good luck, Carrie!'

'Remember how she used to bring that little boy into the shop every Saturday afternoon since the start of the War? A crusty cottage loaf and two sugar buns. Regular as clockwork,' the baker's wife reminded her husband.

'Aye, and she got herself into a load of trouble over that cottage loaf when Doctor's wife discovered they was feeding the swans with the bread and butter what Cook had sent up for tea. It were a fine old row, and Doctor's wife took the bread-knife to Carrie, so they said.'

'There were some truth in it, Bob, for she was took away to that clinic in Tunbridge Wells that same day. Not much peace in that house, I reckon, for that poor man. She was always such a snob, and she never took to Carrie, that I *do* know.'

'There ain't much you don't know about other people's business in this village, old girl!' the baker reminded his garrulous spouse. 'Come on, let's get this 'ere netting fixed or we shan't be ready for the buggers.'

More nostalgic memories were revived as the wedding party passed the grocery. It was here that Carrie's brother Jack had served his apprenticeship, sweeping the shop and the forecourt, and pedalling a heavily laden bicycle round the country lanes until he was promoted to assistant behind the counter. Jack was a steady, reliable husband to his wife Elsie, and a good father to his children. He had never acted impulsively in his life until the day he was confronted by that glaring poster of Kitchener, pointing a commanding finger – 'YOUR COUNTRY NEEDS YOU!' Then Jack was caught up in the fever of patriotic recruitment. He went away, but he did not come back. So Elsie stepped into his shoes. She was still there, and she was out on the forecourt helping the grocer with a huge roll of wire-netting.

'Nice to be some people!' she screeched, as the wedding party went past.

'She's got real common since the War,' her mother-in-law told them, scathingly. 'They do say she's 'anging up 'er 'at to the grocer. My Jack would turn over in 'is grave!'

Back at the farm, Lucy and Katie slipped on the clean white aprons over their best dresses, and bustled about the kitchen. Tom stabled the horses and wagonette with the help of young Philip, while Ruby and Teacher spread starched cloths over the trestle table already set up in the orchard, with benches for seating the small wedding party. Lucy had promised Carrie the wedding breakfast should be eaten outdoors if it was a fine, warm day, and Carrie had welcomed the idea. The same meal eaten in the parlour would seem so much more formal.

Only on a farm could such bounty be provided in this last year of the War that had so depleted the shelves of the grocery, and the butcher's cold storage. They had their own produce and were practically self-sufficient. Ruby and Teacher had contributed what they could spare from their meagre rations of tea and sugar and dried fruit. Lucy had baked a fresh batch of loaves in the bread oven that morning before breakfast, and Carrie had used the other oven for her apple pies and Bakewell tart – a great favourite at Russets. Carrie had taken to cooking like a duck to water, Lucy told her mother, and she was gradually getting familiar with the dairy work.

'I don't expect miracles, for I remember my own clumsiness in the diary when I was first married to Bert. As for milking, she has to lose her nervousness of the cows before she can make a good milker. But Tom is so patient with her, as Bert was patient with me all those years ago.'

'One of these days your Tom is going to make some lucky girl a good 'usband,' Ruby reflected as she piled crockery on a tray. 'Don't Tom never mention a girl, Luce?'

Lucy shook her head.

'Never 'ad a sweet'eart?'

'Not to my knowledge. I used to think I should see our Tom married to your Carrie, but Albert claimed her first. Tom was always the last to claim his share of anything, I remember, even as a child.'

'But if 'e were so fond of Carrie, why didn't 'e make sure of 'er when Albert was away? That were a good opportunity, sure to goodness.'

'Tom is much too loyal to take advantage of such an opportunity. He has very high principles, Rube. He was the one to be most upset when he discovered I was carrying Sir Neville Franklin's child. Harry was downright disgusted, and Albert was jealous, but Tom simply avoided me. I lost their trust, Rube, all three of my boys, and I had only myself to blame, for to tell the truth, I *could* have refused to lie with him. I didn't want to refuse. He had always attracted me, physically, and I knew it had to happen one day,' she sighed, as she arranged a paper frill round the big joint of home-cured ham. 'If I had my time over again, I would refuse, but then we don't get a second chance, do we? Tom won't get a second chance to court Carrie. It's too late. I have warned them both to be careful. Albert is so jealous. He can't bear to see them together. Where are they now? Have you seen them since we came back?'

'Yes, they are down in the orchard. Carrie offered to 'elp, but I told 'er we could manage.'

Katie was waiting as usual to be told what to do next.

'Take that basket of cutlery to the orchard and lay a knife, fork and spoon to each place. Don't forget the carvers and the tablespoons. Then you can come back for the bread,' her mistress instructed.

'Yes, Ma'am.' The girl bustled away.

'She's so willing, but she can't seem to grasp what has to be done. Emma was so quick. How she would have enjoyed her own wedding breakfast if Harry had been spared.'

'You think 'e would 'ave married 'er, Luce?'

'She told me he had promised to marry her after the War, but Emma was not always truthful, and it was probably wishful thinking. Poor Emma. I wonder what became of her . . . Remind me to give you a few slices of this ham to take back, Rube, and a jar of that tomato chutney. How's Mr Carter these days?'

'Contrary. I can't seem to do nothing right these days. I feel like telling 'im to find 'isself another 'ousekeeper.'

'Maybe it's a wife he wants, Rube? You're still a very attractive woman.'

'Then 'e can whistle, for I'm not looking for another 'usband,' said Ruby decidedly.

Cynthia pushed Freddie's wheelchair carefully through the long grass in the orchard. Apples were ripening on the trees, and bees humming in the branches.

'Are you getting tired, darling?' she asked, anxiously, and she stopped to peer down at him.

Freddie reached up, took her face between his hands and kissed her gently. 'I'm all right, Cynthie. Don't worry about me. I've been thinking how lucky they are, these two, to have their future settled and a home provided when so many will be unemployed and homeless when the War is over. Between you and me, I would have liked to see Carrie married to Tom. I have always liked him the best of the three brothers, though I've not seen a great deal of my cousins in the past. Since I left school, I have been too busy for visiting relatives, and they didn't visit me at Richmond Row when we were children. We were the poor relations, remember!'

'Did you envy your cousins?'

'No, never. I suppose we were self-sufficient as a family.'

They had reached the hedge, and Cynthia turned the chair round, sat down in the grass and took Freddie's hand. They could see Ruby, Katie and the woman Carrie called Teacher, bustling about between the trees. There was no sign of Carrie and Albert.

'Have you thought any more about Father's proposal?' Cynthia prompted, for she had been waiting for Freddie to mention it.

'You mean the farm bailiff's job?'

'Yes.'

He turned his head to look at her, his dark eyes giving beauty to his lean face. 'I can't honestly see myself as a farm bailiff, dear.'

'There would be a rent-free cottage, and some kind of conveyance for your use. I thought it seemed a good suggestion.'

'You're disappointed that it doesn't appeal to me?'

She nodded. She *was* disappointed, for she had visualised the two of them in the ex-bailiff's cottage on her father's estate. 'You don't have to decide right away, darling. There's loads of time, and I don't want you to feel under an obligation because the proposal came from my father. He was only trying to help.'

'I know, and I'm deeply grateful, but what prompted the suggestion, I wonder? I am a solicitor by profession. It's the one job I know from A to Z. I spent ten years of my life slogging away in that office in the High Street. Then I passed my finals and opened up my own little office in Soho. Nothing very impressive, 'tis true, but it suits me, and somebody has to represent the working class. You know how I feel about it, and you've seen the place. I have been paying the rent, so the rooms are still available after I have finished with Roehampton. I'm sorry, dear, but it didn't occur to me that your father would make such a generous offer. I was under the impression that he strongly opposed our marriage.'

'He did, but he's mellowed. He is not nearly so dogmatic as he used to be. We get along quite well, actually. I get invited to dine at his club once a week when I am off duty. He doesn't bully me any more. Poor Papa. As a family we are not very united.'

'I still don't understand what prompted him to suggest the bailiff's job. After all, there is no damage to my mental capabilities, thank goodness. It's only a physical disablement and I am learning to cope with that.'

'I know, and I think you are wonderful, my darling.' She was so disappointed she could have burst into tears, but this was no time for tears. Why had she felt so certain he would accept her father's offer? The old independent spirit was slowly emerging. Medical care, good food, and hours spent outdoors every day were all contributing to his recovery. His face had a healthy tan, and his eyes were clear and bright. No, she must not deprive him of the natural assumption to take the initiative. This man she had married was no weakling. She admired and respected his independence. His working-class background was something she had accepted, and she had no regrets. The prospect of making a home in those poky little rooms in Soho was not very pleasing, but she was so thankful to get Freddie back safely, she would make the best of it. In the meantime, she would carry on with her nursing, and visit Freddie once a week. She smiled reassuringly, and squeezed his hand.

'You are absolutely right, my darling. Of course we must go back to Soho, as soon as you're fit. Do you suppose your landlady would consider renting those rooms *un*furnished? If we had the two floors over your offices it would make a marvellous maisonette, and it still wouldn't disturb your landlady since she lives in the basement. While you're at Roehampton, I could spend my free time decorating, and picking up some furniture from the second-hand shops. It's going to be fun! I feel quite excited!'

'Bless you, Cynthia. That's a weight off my mind.'

'You were worried?'

He nodded.

'My poor darling. You mustn't worry about a thing. Just concentrate on getting well and strong before you have to report to Roehampton.' She kissed him affectionately.

Somebody was ringing a handbell to summon the wedding guests to the meal.

'Hallo Mother!' a boy's voice interrupted.

'Charles!' Lucy put down the carving knife and hurried across the yard. Her handsome youngest son vaulted easily over the gate and hugged her exuberantly.

'You are looking very beautiful, Mother,' he told her, and she blushed like a girl. Only Charles had acquired the easy charm of the upper class. Only Charles brought her flowers and kissed his mother's mouth. They adored each other.

'Sorry I couldn't get to the church, Mother. I have only just arrived back from Scotland. Been on holiday at Duncan Carmichael's place in the Highlands,' Charles was explaining as they waited for the family to assemble.

Tom and Philip were washing their hands under the pump, Cynthia pushing Freddie's wheelchair towards the laden table, Ruby was crossing the yard with a heavy tea-tray, followed by Katie with a big dish of baked potatoes. Philip's mother was staring at the boy whose birth had caused such a disturbance at Russets. He, too, would carry the stigma of 'bastard' like her own son, for Philip had been conceived just before his father was posted to India with his regiment, and the child was five years old when his parents were eventually married. She stood back in the shade of a tree, waiting to be introduced, for she was not a woman to push herself forward. Her second marriage to the schoolmaster at the village school had fully compensated for the few wretched years she had spent with her first husband. Married to the scholarly

Andrew Robinson, back teaching in the Infants' classroom for the duration of the War, and her son at Grammar School, Martha was quietly happy and content. She had known Carrie since her brother Freddie had brought her to school at the age of four. They had met again at Tidworth when Carrie had been engaged as nursemaid to Captain Saunders' baby son, Jimmy, and travelled to India with the regiment some three years later. Both had expected to spend a term of five years in Peshawar, and both were back in the village within twelve months – Carrie to escort her young charge to his grandparents following a bout of typhoid fever, and Martha to return to her old home at the wheelwright's after the death of her husband in skirmishes on the Frontier. Now her young friend was married to her own first-cousin, and Martha was troubled and deeply concerned for the girl. In the three months since Albert had arrived home from the prisoner-of-war camp in Turkey, his behaviour had been so strange and unpredictable, on her last visit to the School House before her marriage, that Carrie had confessed to being frightened.

'Don't tell Mum or Aunt Lucy that I'm scared of Bertie, will you, Teacher?' she had pleaded. 'I had to tell someone, and you always understand.'

'My dear, you know you can always confide in me. I understand all too well what it means to cope with an unpredictable man, and I hope you won't have to put up with the same sort of treatment that I had from Dick. I found myself completely dominated, physically and mentally, and that's bad. Don't let him turn you into a doormat, Carrie, just to keep the peace.'

Carrie had burst into tears, and Martha had folded the girl in her arms. At today's brief ceremony, her heart ached with love and pity.

Charles had stepped forward to take the heavy tray

from Ruby.

'Allow me, Madam,' said he, with a little bow, and Katie giggled.

The twin sisters exchanged a meaningful glance, for both had the same thought as so often happened when they were together – 'Thank God for Charles'. His lively personality would keep the party gay.

'A feast for the gods!' he declared, when he had dumped the tray on a small table under the tree. 'But where's the champagne?'

His mother shook her head. 'There's cider and elderberry wine, and tea for the teetotallers.'

'A pity. I could have asked Father for the champagne.' He shrugged and greeted his half-sister with a hug and a kiss.

'How are you feeling, Sir?' he asked Freddie, as they shook hands.

'They tell me I am mending very nicely, thank you Charles,' his brother-in-law answered cheerfully. They had not met since before the War, when Charles was at prep school.

When Carrie and Albert arrived some minutes later, the boy was suddenly confronted by a half-brother he hardly recognised. But he smiled disarmingly and offered his hand. 'Congratulations, old chap. May I kiss the bride?' He did not wait for permission, and his kiss was surprisingly adult, as his mother and sister had also discovered. 'Like father, like son,' Lucy would say.

Albert was frowning with disapproval. 'Break it up!' he growled, and they all laughed. Then the grammar school boy and the public school boy were shaking hands, and Tom was waiting his turn with a shy smile. He could not honestly admit that he felt any bond of affection or relationship with his mother's bastard son, but this was a family occasion, and he would not disappoint her.

'I suppose we should have invited Elsie and the children, shouldn't we, Rube?' Lucy suggested as she served the apple pies and the guests handed round the cream. Tom was serving the men with cider, and Ruby poured tea for the women.

'That would 'ave meant inviting Albert's family from Monks Farm. Couldn't 'ave one lot without the other, and you said you wanted to keep it quiet,' her sister reminded her.

'So I did, and we don't really know the family at Monks Farm. They keep themselves to themselves.'

'They wouldn't 'ave come anyway, not with 'op-picking started, and Elsie would be too busy in the grocery to get time off.'

'Don't be surprised to see Penelope later, with the current swain,' Charles interrupted. 'That naughty half-sister of mine has got herself quite a reputation at Marston Park!'

'Penny – a reputation? But she used to be so demure?' Cynthia reflected.

'Not any more. You've not seen very much of her, have you, since the War? Or Sylvia, either. Your little sisters have grown up.'

'I suppose the War has changed the pattern of their lives completely. They would have missed out on the London Season, and what we used to call the Marriage Market, but they have probably had a lot more fun. We older girls, Beatrice and myself, were so restricted and couldn't move without a chaperone.'

'Sylvia and Penny have to toe the line like all the other VAD girls when they are on duty, but they do have quite a lot of fun by all accounts, especially Penny, who has them queueing up for her favours! Sylvia seemes to have fallen for one in particular, a Canadian captain with one arm, but with Marston Park swarming with presentable young officers, all the girls can pick and choose.'

'Not all so presentable, Charles,' Freddie reminded him, quietly.

'It doesn't seem to matter, old chap. Wounded men invariably fall in love with their nurses, I've noticed. I wish I had been a few years older and seen some active service. As it is, the girls don't look twice at a fellow still at public school.'

'Don't talk such utter drivel!' snarled Albert, glowering at his young half-brother.

Freddie made no comment, but they all knew what he was thinking.

It was Cynthia who had the good sense to change the subject. Accepting a cup of tea from her mother-in-law, she asked, brightly, 'Could you get the day off next Saturday, Mother – and meet me in London? I have been given two tickets for a matinée, and Marie Lloyd is the star of the show. I think you would enjoy it. We could have lunch at Lyons before the show. I would meet you at Victoria and see you off. What do you say?'

'Bless my soul! Fancy that! I feel proper flummoxed!' Ruby declared. 'I'll get the day orf if it's the last thing I do! They do say that Marie Lloyd is a proper scream. All them cockneys what's down from London for the 'op-picking is singing 'er songs. And a meal at Lyons, my, my! But you're spoiling me, love.' Flushed and excited, she suddenly looked very young again. It had been a long War, and her elderly employer, even though he was Teacher's father, was a gruff man with a surly temper, who regarded any kind of pleasure as sinful. She wouldn't tell him why she wanted the day off. Keep him guessing, the old misery! She hugged Cynthia and kissed Freddie. She was so excited, she picked up her skirts and twirled around in the long grass. Charles leapt over the bench, clasped her round the waist – or where her waist should be! – and swung her round. They pranced round the table, panting and laughing, and when Ruby sank exhausted on the bench, it was Carrie's turn. Now everyone joined in the fun, clapping and laughing. Even Albert was grinning.

But it was Penny who stole the show in her neat VAD uniform. Dragging a reluctant young man by the hand, she suddenly arrived in their midst, darted about the table, kissing everyone, and finally sat down on Tom's knee. With her short bobbed hair cut in a fringe, wide grey eyes, and small features, her face had an elfin quality that was very attractive. Cynthia stared in amazement at the young sister who had developed so surprisingly from a plain, rather dull child into this pretty, vivacious young woman, perched on the knee of an embarrassed farmer! The shy young man she had dragged to the orchard was rescued by Lucy, offered a seat and a drink, and soon lost his shyness in such homely company.

Penny introduced him with a careless wave as Lieutenant David James Montague-Smythe – Monty for short. Charles served them with elderberry wine, and they drank the health of the bride and groom, and accepted a slice of cake.

'We are kind of related, aren't we, Mrs Blunt?' Penny suggested, meaningly.

Lucy smiled and glanced at the boy who was growing to manhood in two such widely different worlds – Marston Park and Russets.

'Shall we allow her to claim a relationship? What do you think, Mother?' he asked her.

'We already have Cynthia in the family, so why not Penelope?'

'I could marry Tom, couldn't I? Then I should really belong,' Penny suggested, coyly, stroking his blond head.

But such blandishments were wasted on Tom, who had

no desire or intention to marry into the upper class. If he couldn't have Carrie, he would stay single. It was as simple as that. He would be glad to get the day over. Nobody would ever know what he had endured when the girl he loved was united in marriage to his younger brother. Why hadn't he courted Carrie in those three years Albert was away? What a blind fool, with his high principles and strong sense of loyalty. They were not even engaged before the War. It was only what Carrie had called 'an understanding'. But Albert had claimed her, and Albert could not be trusted. With his bad moods and sulky temper, he had to be considered and cossetted. It was pathetic the way his mother and his new little sister-in-law were falling over backwards to please him. Was it love or pity that Carrie was feeling now that she was actually married to this poor wreck of a man who could hardly bear to let her out of his sight? And what had still to be revealed, to-night, in the marriage bed? Whey did Albert walk with a limp?

Penny was still perched on his knee, but he was repulsed rather than attracted to the girl. Putting her gently aside, he explained, 'You must excuse me, Miss Penelope, but cows have to be milked even on my brother's wedding day!' And the boy, Philip, glad to escape, followed him through the long grass.

After they had left, the party started to break up. The women cleared the table, and Charles helped to carry the heavy trays to the kitchen.

'You coming, Monty? I'm back on duty in half-an-hour,' Penny reminded him. They called 'Cheery-bye!' and hurried away.

'We must be getting back too, my darling.' Cynthia was bending over Freddie, gently tucking the blanket round the tender stump. When she had delivered him safely to Sister, she would take the short cut across the Park to the station to catch a train to Victoria, and then a bus to Marylebone Road. She would be tired. She was always tired these days, but who wasn't?

Philip and his mother would walk back to the village with Ruby, after supper. Lucy would make more tea to prolong their departure, dreading the anti-climax that must inevitably follow. She would kiss them goodnight, these two just starting on their married life, and watch them climb the stairs. Her heart ached for the girl, and the shock that awaited her. Lucy knew why Albert was limping. After tonight, Carrie would know, too.

Katie had been sent up with a can of hot water, and instructed to cover it with a clean white towel, to turn back the quilt, and turn down the bed. She had been allowed a glass of wine, and it had gone to her head. She was still giggling. A dainty nightgown was folded neatly on one pillow, striped pyjamas on the other. The mistress had moved into the bedroom where Carrie had been sleeping for the past three months. She had to call them Mister Albert and Missus Albert now they were married, respectful like. Mister Tom was her favourite. She stood beside the marriage bed wondering if she would ever lie with a man on her wedding night. Girls from the Orphanage, sent out to service at the age of thirteen, soon got themselves into trouble and had their babies in the Workhouse. Because they had been segregated from the opposite sex in their short childhood, they were ignorant and fearful of the consequences of 'getting into trouble', but an easy prey to the whiles of unscrupulous masters or their spoilt sons. Katie had nothing to fear in this household, for Mister Tom was in love with his brother's wife. Katie had offered herself and been refused, politely but firmly, so her avid curiosity was still unsatisfied and sex was just a naughty word whispered secretly in the bare dormitory at the Orphanage. She was not very bright about a lot of things, but she knew instinctively that sex was important because all her day-dreams revolved around Mister Tom, and she trembled with excitement as the dampness wet her thighs. She could feel it now, this trembling in her private parts simply looking at the marriage bed, and thinking of Mister Tom. They had told her in the market that the last servant girl at Russets had been lain by Mister Harry, the eldest son, who was killed fighting for his King and Country.

Market days were the highlight of her quiet life at Russets. She helped the mistress load the wagonette with eggs, butter, cheese, vegetables and fruit. Sacks of potatoes sold like hot cakes. Some poor families had to live on vegetable stew, bread and margarine and fat bacon. The mistress drove the wagonette to the manner born. There was nothing she couldn't tackle on the farm, and Katie worshipped the ground she walked on. Kindness and good food, her own little attic bedroom, Sunday best clothes and market days. What more could she ask or expect of life? Yet there was something more. To be lain by a man was the hallmark of maturity, and the risk of pregnancy would be no deterrent when the opportunity offered itself.

'Katie!' the mistress was calling. Supper dishes had to be washed up in the scullery before she could retire to her own lonely bed.

'Coming, Ma'am,' she called back, and ran downstairs.

The guests had gone. Only Master Charles was still hanging around his mother, but he would soon be on his way to Marston Park. They said in the market the boy was a chip off the old block, but Katie had not yet met his father. The mistress had been lain by a real gentleman – imagine that! Master Charles was upper class, for he called his mother 'darling' and that was an endearment never heard in the working class. Plain living and plain speaking. 'Know your place and keep to it. Be humble and grateful to your betters,' the superintendent had instructed the orphans.

But here, at Russets, on this wedding day, there had been only fun and friendliness, with the upper class enjoying themselves with the working class. They said in the market that the War was responsible for mixing up the classes. After the War it would be the 'new rich' living in the big houses and sending their sons to public schools and their daughters to colleges for young ladies, but they would never be gentry. Everyone seemed quite certain on that point. Private soldiers who had been promoted to officers would find themselves in upper-class society, like Lieutenant Simmons from Richmond Row, married to Miss Cynthia Franklin from Marston Park. And now her sister was flirting with Mister Tom.

''T'ain't right. Class is class,' Katie reckoned. The superintendent knew what he was talking about.

To be shy of her cousin Bertie was stupid when she had known him all her life, Carrie told herself when the bedroom door closed. But this man she had married was still a stranger. For three months she had been trying desperately to convince herself that he was the same person, but everything he said and did contradicted that recognition. It was not the scarred face that frightened her, but the unpredictable moods of depression and bitterness, when he turned away from her into himself, and sat huddled by the fire, or stayed in bed.

In one of his worst moods he had threatened to kill himself. It was his mother, not his future wife, who had sat beside the bed, cradling his head to her breast. The girl was too young, too vulnerable. 'Time will heal,' Lucy insisted. He must not be hurried. He would probably drain them dry, emotionally, and she herself must carry the blame if the marriage was a failure. For Albert's sake she had kept Carrie at the farm and not sent her away. It was a risk she had to take. Her son needed a wife. He had suffered enough. So she had sacrificed her niece.

When the bedroom door closed, she shivered with a sense of guilt and a dreadful finality. She covered her face with her hands and wept.

He looked at her with troubled eyes and she smiled reassuringly, her warm arms about his neck.

'It will be all right, love,' she told him, but he shook his head.

'That's what you say now, but you wait till you've seen it – it's repulsive – horrible!' He shuddered convulsively and she held him close, her heart pounding. What did he mean? What horror?

Over his shoulder she could see the bed turned down, nightgown and pyjamas neatly folded on the pillows, and a can of hot water standing in the bowl. When she first came to live at Russets, she had missed a number of things she had enjoyed for several years with her young charge. It seemed like putting back the clock to bath only once a week in front of the kitchen fire, when she had had her own bathroom on the nursery floor and bathed every night. Oil lamps and candles belonged to her childhood in Richmond Row, so did the hand-made rag mats scattered on the bare floors. Only the parlour had a carpet, but that room was seldom used. To have the servant girl, Katie, sitting down to meals at the same table had been a surprise, and to have her own plate piled with vegetables, served direct from the pots and pans on the stove. She liked to help herself from vegetable dishes. Things she had taken for granted would be regarded as luxuries at

Russets. Hard work had roughened her hands. She had no time to read the few books she had discovered in the glass-fronted book-case in the parlour, or to finish hem-stitching the new underwear that Teacher had made on her treadle sewing machine. It would be different in the Winter, Aunt Lucy had promised, with the long evenings, but not yet. It seemed to Carrie in that first Summer at Russets that the work was never finished.

'Will you wash first, love, or shall I?' she prompted gently.

He seemed surprised. 'I washed this morning. I'm not dirty.'

She wriggled free of his clutching arms and went over to the wash-stand. 'Don't look at me, *please*! Turn your head away,' she pleaded.

But he sat on the edge of the bed watching her. 'Get on with it,' was all he said, with gruff impatience.

She stepped out of her dress and stood in her petticoat to wash her face and neck, her arms and hands, with the new tablet of lavender soap her aunt had provided.

'Come here,' Bertie ordered, authoritatively. He had recovered his self-possession, and she went to him, automatically, because it had become a habit to do as he asked. She stood in front of him, shivering with apprehension, not knowing what he intended to do with her on their wedding night.

'Did you wait for me, Carrie? Are you still a virgin?' It was not the first time he had asked that question, and she answered him truthfully.

'I waited, and I am still a virgin.'

'I must take your word for it, for I can't prove it.'

'What do you mean?'

'Exactly what I say. I can't prove it. Stand still. I am going to undress you.' When he had stripped her naked, he looked at her with gloating satisfaction. 'Lovely.

That's all I need to compensate for my own ugliness.' He ran his hot, feverish hands over her breasts, her stomach, and her thighs with lingering sensual pleasure. 'My God, Carrie, I've waited a long time for this moment. It saved my reason in that bloody hell!'

It was the first time he had mentioned the camp in Turkey. They were still waiting to be told about his experiences in the three long years he had been away, but he flatly refused to talk about it.

'Get into bed. No, forget the nightgown. I want to feel you. You're mine, my lovely, all mine, and don't you forget it.' He smacked her bottom playfully, and she climbed into bed.

When he had pulled the curtains, he blew out the candles on the mantelpiece, dropped his clothes on the floor, and climbed in beside her.

'Now, let's get it over. Give me your hand.' He was breathing jerkily, and his hand trembled, but he did not spare her. There was a ruthless detachment in the gesture. When her hand closed over the stump of the mutilated penis she gasped and whimpered, 'What have they done to you, love?'

'I tried to escape. They punished me,' was all he said, but he did not release her hand. He wanted her to share the anguish he had endured alone for so long. They had destroyed his manhood, but now he had a wife, and he saw in her young virgin body an instrument for his sexual experiments. She was weeping, and her tears wet his scarred chest.

'I'll make it up to you, Bertie,' she sobbed – and his ego was satisfied.

Chapter 3

'I'm worried about Carrie,' Freddie told his wife, as she pushed him back across the park.

'So am I, darling. There is something very odd about your cousin, Albert, and your mother was not at all happy about this marriage, for she told me so. That's why I suggested the London show, to cheer her up. Actually, I didn't get free tickets. I queued at the box office,' Cynthia admitted.

'Bless you. She will enjoy it. It must be years since she had an outing of any kind. I have sometimes wondered if she made a mistake in leaving "The Three Nuns". Those were definitely the happiest years. She seemed to think it would embarrass Carrie, who had been engaged as a nursemaid to the doctor's little grandson, in the house across the road.'

'Why should Carrie be embarrassed?'

'Seeing her Mum cleaning the steps and the brass at the village pub. Anyway, Mum seemed to think the time had come to "better" herself for the sake of the children who were doing quite well in their respective situations, so off she went to "The Grove" as a daily working housekeeper, and from there to The Parsonage as cook when the old cook died suddenly of a heart attack. But there was no real enjoyment in either of these jobs, and she missed the lively company at the pub. She's a gregarious soul, our Mum.'

'Did *you* find it embarrassing to have your mother working as a charwoman almost next door to the solicitors' offices in the High Street?'

'No, it didn't occur to me.'

'Now she's changed her job again, and it's pretty deadly by all accounts. Why did she leave The Parsonage?'

'When the old parson died and the curate was appointed, he automatically inherited the house, but he and his wife were not at all popular, so the servants left.'

'Of course, I remember now. Father offered Mrs Wellington and Cecily a cottage on the estate, and that was the day I first met Cecily, and she told me of her plans to take up nursing as a career. She promised to speak for me at the Hospital for Women in Marylebone Road, and that's how it all started for me, I mean.'

'Is she still living there? We never seem to run into her.'

'Yes, she settled in quite happily after Cecily left. She has a resident housekeeper and a little dog, and her young grandson spends all his holidays there, so I understand.'

'What happened to Cecily? Didn't she volunteer for the Medical Corps?'

'Yes, we have lost touch, and *you*, my darling, must be held responsible for the end of that particular friendship.'

'Me? How did I get into it?'

'She accused me of disloyalty to my own class of society, and warned me if I married into the working class I should regret it for the rest of my days. I told her she was a snob, and a parson's daughter should rise above such ridiculous discrimination. I was furious! How dare she suggest the man I loved was some inferior kind of species! She has never apologised, and I have never forgiven her.'

Freddie was chuckling. He knew how fierce she could

be in his defence. Once upon a time he had tried to dissuade her from taking such a step, but she was determined. They married without the blessing of either her father or Freddie's mother, and she had proved her love was something more than an opportunity to break away from a society she found so stifling.

'And have you lived to regret it, my dear?' asked Freddie, turning his head to meet her candid gaze.

'Never! Not if I live to be a hundred!' she kissed him with warmth and tenderness that more than compensated for his crippling disability. Without her the future would be bleak, but she had encouraged him to look ahead hopefully. The class barrier no longer existed. They were equals. It had taken a War to break down so many class barriers on the home front. The gentry had given their sons. Their daughters were driving ambulances and nursing the wounded. Their servants were working in factories, manning the buses, milking cows, and digging potatoes. A skeleton staff of elderly servants, brought out of retirement, with two young girls fresh from the village school kept Marston Park functioning. Lawns had been dug up and planted with vegetables to feed the patients and nursing staff. Trees had been felled in the Park to provide wood for the fires. The late-parson's wife was back in her true element, with the Red Cross hut at her disposal, and a team of voluntary ladies happily engaged with rolls of calico and flannelette, to the rattle of tea cups!

The village grape-vine, ably assisted by the postmen, the school children and the customers in the saloon bar, spread the news that 'Old Parson's' daughter Marion had arrived home from foreign parts – some God-forsaken place in Africa, the Congo – and she was home for good with her two girls. They were making a temporary home in the cottage on Sir Neville's estate until after the War.

'When the War is over' we will do this, that, and the other, everyone was saying. Poor Marion. She was a widow now, and that nice young missionary had died of a fever. There she was, a plain pale ghost of her former self, with two plain, pale little girls, back in the village where she was born and bred. Everyone remembered that affair, for Parson and his family of three daughters had been public figures who enjoyed very little privacy. Everything they did was approved or disapproved by Parson's parishioners. Their upper-class status was much respected by the working class, and their servants were loyal.

The Parsonage pew, facing the choir stalls, attracted a lot of attention when the children were small. Cecily, Irene and Marion felt their importance, and their mother kept a strict eye on their behaviour. Everyone knew that little Irene was delicate and not expected to make 'old bones'. She was cosseted and spoilt in the nursery and schoolroom, the servants regarded her with loving concern, and her every wish was granted. The three sisters had nothing in common but adoration for a saintly father, as they grew into maturity. Cecily was the practical one, full of good works and very conscious of her duty. She drove the old mare in the governess-cart around the parish, in all kinds of weather. The Weald always reserved its worst weather for January and February, but Parson's daughter was not deterred by icy roads and country lanes deep in snow. The aged, the poor, and the sick were her main concern, and all of the working class, but her manner was inclined to be condescending, and she was not always welcome. Admired, but not loved. 'She do mean well' could be her epitaph when the time came to lie among the departed souls in the churchyard.

Irene, of course, was not expected to contribute anything but a brave smile and a little plain needlework for the Ladies' Guild.

Marion, the youngest, was lively and intelligent, and her father's favourite. The post of governess to Sir Neville Franklin's two elder daughters could not be refused, for the parson was appointed by the squire of Marston Park and they all depended on his generosity. And they had not expected the governess to fall in love with a sturdy young Scot from the mission field, on his very first visit. It was love at first sight, they said, and many who were present in church on that Harvest Festival morning remembered that she shared her hymn book with the young stranger in Parson's pew, and that their voices blended most beautifully in the well-known harvest hymns. 'We plough the fields and scatter the good seed on the land, but it is fed and watered by God's Almighty hand.' – 'Come ye thankful people come, Raise the song of Harvest Home. All is safely gathered in, ere the Winter storms begin.' How they sang, those two young lovers, as though their lungs would burst! They said she had actually proposed marriage to the young man – a most unladylike gesture from Parson's favourite daughter! It broke Parson's heart when she went away for five long years, and he did not live to see her again.

There would soon be trouble in that cottage, it was predicted, for mother and daughter had never been close, even in the old days at The Parsonage. The rooms were small, and the cook-housekeeper had made herself comfortable in the attics, and must not be inconvenienced. Marion's son, Richard, would be home from boarding school for the Christmas holidays, and his two sisters would be going to boarding school in the New Year.

So Marion came back to a country still at War, and a village peopled with old men, women and children. She had no status, for her mother was the mistress of the house, and no sense of belonging in a community she had discarded in her youth. Agnes and Harriet were sent out with the dog to walk in the Park. They were miserably cold and unhappy. Daddy had gone to Heaven. It was mean of God. They could have spared Mummy, but not Daddy.

On their first walk in their strange surroundings, they discovered Russets, and nobody seemed to mind if they sat in the kitchen with Susy, their feet on the fender, and cried. A nice young woman with pretty curly hair and blue eyes – how they envied her! – gave them a cuddle and a mug of hot cocoa. An older woman, who looked like her mother but turned out to be her aunt, was baking bread.

'You can come here whenever you like. Just make yourselves at home,' she told them.

It was all very comforting.

'We won't tell Mummy or Grandma. We will keep it a secret,' Agnes decided, and Harriet agreed, because she always agreed with Agnes.

They were a little afraid of the strange man with the scarred face they sometimes found in the kitchen, smoking a cigarette in the rocking chair. They would bid him 'Good-morning' politely because they were well-bred little girls, and run off with Susy to play in the big barn. One end was packed with sweet-smelling hay, and a ladder led to a loft where the apples would be stored when they were picked in October. Mrs Blunt had promised they should help when the time came, but the apples were not yet ready for picking. There was a proper season for everything on a farm, she explained, kindly, and Mother Nature would not be hurried. Mr Blunt, who said to call him Tom, was a nice man with hair the colour of straw and blue eyes. After all the dark faces they had known in the Congo, it was a change to find a family so fair.

Every day they made fresh discoveries in their fascinating new world, but had to hide their pleasure on their return to Grandma's cottage for fear of being forbidden this earthly paradise called Russets.

'Did you have a nice walk?' Mother would ask, automatically, from a sense of duty, not noticing whether they had been away for an hour or two. She was not really interested. She missed Daddy terribly, and Grandma was not very sympathetic.

'You must pull yourself together, dear. You are not the only woman to lose her husband. We are still busy with our War work, here in the village, and every pair of hands is needed. You could offer your services to Matron. It's only a short distance across the Park, and you would meet Cynthia again. She comes down from London once a week to visit her husband who is a patient at the hospital. It would be like old times to be back at Marston Park,' she added, meaningly.

How could she bear to be reminded of a chapter long since closed? Marion wondered. You cannot put back the clock. Her ex-pupils were grown up and married. The house had been converted into a hospital for wounded officers, and only one wing was reserved for the use of the few remaining members of the Franklin family. Sir Neville lived at his London club, his invalid wife had died. The two younger daughters, still in the nursery when Marion was in charge of the schoolroom, were working as VAD nurses in the hospital. There were no horses in the stables, and no servants in the servants' hall. Marion had gleaned all these facts from old Jarvis, the ex-coachman, when he pushed a barrow load of sawn logs to the cottage one evening – a good excuse to further his honourable intentions to marry that natty little woman whose pastry melted in the mouth! It was lonely in the converted stables without his wife, and six months of widowhood was enough. But it would take more than a load of logs and a few well-chosen blandishments to tempt the cook-housekeeper from her comfortable post.

It was sad to see the gaps where trees had been felled in the Park, and a field of potatoes where once there had been a green lawn as smooth as velvet. Such a homecoming after the tragedy in Africa, and the long, uncomfortable voyage was quite unbearable. Only one small gleam of light still shone in the dark tunnel of her grief – she would see her son at Christmas. The years of separation had robbed her of his childhood, but she knew by the photographs she had received that he was like his father. To have her son growing up in the likeness of her beloved Malcolm would compensate for her present state of apathetic indifference to her new surroundings, and the two little girls she left to their own resources. They had each other and Susy. They did not want her on their walks or in their private world of make-believe. She wondered vaguely where they spent their time and if they met anyone on their long walks, but was too tired to bother.

Mother was right, of course. Hadn't she always known what was best for her family? Only Marion had not conformed to her mother's wishes in those early years. It had been such a close relationship between father and daughter, but all the precious years of childhood and the bonds of family loyalty and unity were swept away in that other devastating relationship between a man and a woman. She was obsessed by the new love. There was no other life for her, no future, only with Malcolm.

She set off across the Park on a chilly Autumn morning, to offer her services to Matron; her sparse figure wrapped in a tweed coat of pre-War vintage she had borrowed from Cecily's wardrobe, a scarf tied over her lank hair. She was just a nonentity, drifting on a tide of memory.

* * *

'Tell us about the cuckoo,' Agnes demanded, as they watched Tom stirring peelings in the old copper. She was not really a demanding child, only curious, but her voice had the sharpness of authority, rather like her grandmother's. Tom seemed surprised by the question. His mind followed the seasons with automatic regularity, and it was Autumn now. He supposed a child who had grown up in the Congo had no sense of the seasons as they knew them at Russets, but his limited knowledge of geography did not stretch far over that vast country they had called Darkest Africa in the village school.

'What do you want to know?' he asked the child kindly, for her eager questions and lively interest in his own small world was a welcome break in the morbid thoughts that worried him since his brother's return.

'Is it true that a cuckoo doesn't build a nest, and the mother cuckoo lays an egg in the nest that belongs to another bird?'

'Quite true.'

'Then what happens?'

'When the young cuckoo is hatched out it is so much bigger and stronger than the other little birds, it eats the biggest share of the food the parent birds are providing, and pushes their own offspring out of the nest.'

'That's not kind,' said Harriet, tearfully, for she was a very sensitive child.

'Then what happens?' Agnes prompted.

'The parent birds go on feeding it till it is ready to fly away. Then they have to start all over again to raise another family, but not in the same nest. Nature has taught them a lesson. Have you never heard anyone described as a cuckoo in the nest?'

'No. What does it mean?'

'It means that child doesn't seem to belong to the rest of the family. It's odd one out, so to speak.'

'I don't want to be a cuckoo!' wailed Harriet.

'Don't be silly. You belong, doesn't she Tom?'

'Most certainly,' he smiled reassuringly.

'Is there a cuckoo in your family?' Agnes persisted.

'Yes.'

'Is it Albert?'

'No, definitely not.'

'Who, then?'

'Charles.'

'Where is he? Why haven't we met him? Tell us about Charles.'

'Charles is the youngest. He is still at school. You will meet him sometime in the Christmas holiday. He has dark hair and dark eyes – very handsome, so they say!'

'Will he like us?'

'Charles likes everyone, and everyone likes Charles.'

'Does he know he's a cuckoo in the nest?'

'Yes.'

'And does he mind?'

'It doesn't seem to worry him, but then nothing worries Charles.'

Harriet sighed enviously. 'It must be nice not ever to be worried. I worry about everything, don't I, Agnes?'

'You're a silly billy,' said Agnes, with rough affection.

The smell of the peelings was not very pleasant. There were bad smells and good smells on a farm, they had discovered. The pigs were fed with a horrible looking mess called swill, but then they wouldn't appreciate anything else for they were messy creatures with disgusting habits.

They did not offer to help Tom with this particular chore, but stood back, holding their noses, waiting for him to finish. They followed Tom everywhere, for they couldn't bear to miss anything, till he looked at his watch and reminded them it was time to go home.

'I wish we could stay here always. I like it better than Grandma's,' Agnes told Tom wistfully, as he harnessed Prince to the plough.

'Me, too,' Harriet echoed.

'Off you go now. See you tomorrow!' He waved and walked away, but they still lingered, holding Susy on a tight leash as instructed.

'They are going to plough Grandma's fields,' Agnes explained. 'The fields she was singing about on Sunday evening – you know, "We plough the fields and scatter the good seed on the land, But it is fed and watered by God's almighty hand."'

Grandma played hymns on the piano every Sunday evening. They did not go to Russets on Sunday. They went to church instead, and had to wear hats and gloves. It was nothing like Daddy's Mission Church in the Congo. In fact, it was deadly dull, and very boring. They knew all about God. He was their 'Heavenly Father'. But they still thought he was mean to take Daddy to Heaven. An earthly father is so REAL. He plays games and carries you on his back when you are tired. He takes you on his knee – one knee for Agnes, one knee for Harriet. He tucks you up in bed and kisses you goodnight after you have said your prayers. God could never take the place of Daddy. Grandma said they would meet again in Heaven, but it was an awful long time to wait.

'And I don't want to be dead!' Harriet had wailed.

Everything was strange in Grandma's church. There were no drums or cymbals, only a booming organ – and the congregation wore shoes. Once upon a time, they were told, when Grandpa was Parson, the family sat in the parsonage pew; Mummy and her two sisters, all wearing their hats and gloves, had behaved like three little ladies, never dropping their prayer books or turning their heads to stare at the Sunday School children, or shuffling their feet. They were good, obedient little girls. But Grandpa and Auntie Irene had gone to Heaven, and they laid flowers on their graves. Auntie Cecily was nursing wounded soldiers in France, and Mummy was too sad to sing. She only said her prayers.

When Lucy watched Albert holding the reins of Prince, their Shire horse, at harvest time, as he stood patiently in the stubble field while they loaded the wagon with the stooks of corn, she was choked with emotion. It was the first time he had volunteered to help in any way since his return. The first time he had shown the slightest interest in anything, apart from his own comfort.

'Thank God,' she breathed.

Seeing Tom atop the wagon with a pitchfork, she was reminded, yet again, of that other bright sunny day many years ago, with the wagon piled high with hay. She had watched with horrified fascination the sturdy figure of her husband, Bert, sway and fall. The three boys were young at the time, and too stunned and shocked to move. She ran to him, calling his name, but he was dead when she reached him. He had broken his neck. Every year since she had watched one or the other of her sons on top of the wagon at hay-making and harvest, first Harry, now it was Tom. She would never see Albert on that precarious perch. Perhaps he had remembered the accident had happened because a tiny baby rabbit had got tangled up in the huge, hairy hooves and the horse had moved forward a pace to get rid of it. But he did not seem to be concerned for his brother, balanced so precariously on top of the wagon.

Tom had not volunteered to serve his King and Country, so he had not suffered. Harry had died, and he, Albert, was a miserable wreck of a man, fit only to steady the horse and watch that tall, handsome brother of his showing off with the pitchfork. It was like a red rag to a bull to be confronted by this perfect specimen of young manhood, with his strong, healthy body, tanned face, and sun-bleached hair. The bitterness of envy was sour as gall, and Albert lost no opportunity in deriding the brother who had stayed at home.

'Bloody coward! No bloody guts!' he would snarl, suddenly and unexpectedly from behind his back when he was milking a cow, mending a fence, or sawing wood. Tom would blush, but not retaliate, and that in itself was aggravating to a man so embittered by hate. There was only one way really to get under Tom's skin, and that was in his treatment of Carrie. She was afraid of her husband, and she could not hide her fear. When Bertie was around she was nervous as a kitten, and often in tears when he bullied her for no better reason than that he liked to watch Tom's reaction. All their nerves were on edge these days, and only the two little girls brought innocent respite from the nagging anxiety. Surely there must be a limit to Tom's patience and forbearance? Lucy wondered. Why should he be blamed for doing his duty on the Home Front? For her sake he had stayed at home and worked like a slave, seven days a week. Even with the land-girls she could not have managed. He deserved to be praised, not scorned.

Now that Albert was a liability, they all worked harder than ever, including Carrie. Eat, drink, work and sleep, that was their life at Russets. Lucy was strong, but her strength was sapped by the discord, and the strain of trying to keep the peace. The weariness of her body was nothing campared to this constant nagging anxiety. Her heart ached for Carrie, no longer the pert little minx who had flirted with all three of her cousins before the War, but a quiet, serious young woman who had forgotten how to laugh. Her heart ached for Tom who loved Carrie and wanted to protect her. And her heart ached most of all for her poor, embittered Albert with his distorted mind and disfigured body. The scars were white now on his tanned face, for he had spent many sunny hours on the bench in the yard with *John Bull*, *Answers* and *Titbits*, amusing himself with crossword competitions. But nothing could hide or cure the terrible disfigurement his young wife had discovered on their wedding night. Only Lucy was aware of the torment and frustration they must endure for the rest of their days. For Carrie, there would be no babies to cuddle. For Albert, no escape from that crippling deformity, no fulfilment of a normal sexual relationship, no peace of mind.

'Please, Teacher, shall I wear my Sunday best to the Victory Party?' asked five-year-old Molly Stevens, looking up from her sand-tray in the Infants' classroom.

'Why, of course, dear. It's a very special party.' Teacher's homely face was flushed to-day, and her grey eyes bright as she gazed affectionately on the forty or so upturned faces, so young and trusting in their dependence.

She had sent Lottie Potter, aged seven, her eldest pupil, to buy twenty yards of red, white and blue ribbon from the haberdashery as soon as they heard the church bells pealing the glad tidings. Now all her girls had bows of ribbon in their hair, and her boys wore rosettes. The Infants had decorated their classroom with little paper flags. They were fluttering in the hot draught from the coke stove. The lower walls were plastered with pictures the children had drawn, but onlythe youthful artists could recognise the strange objects pictured on the brown paper with brightly coloured chalks. Now they were drawing pictures in the sand-trays on their tiny desks.

'Use your imagination, children,' said Teacher.

But supposing you hadn't any imagination? Then you just doodled in the sand with your finger till Teacher came round the class and peered over your shoulder, when you could explain it was a horse or a cow, a pig, or a mouse.

'Very good,' she would say, in that quiet, encouraging voice that had never been known to shout in all the years she had been teaching the Infants in the village school. Teacher had been loved and respected by two generations of children, for the early ones were grown up and married, and *their* children were sitting on the same tiny chairs at the same tiny desks, doodling in the same sand trays. Several of her boys had fought and died for their King and Country, and their names were inscribed on the parchment roll of honour hanging beside the schoolmaster's desk. Teacher had married and left the village for several years. Then she came back, and everyone was pleased to see her. They said she was a widow. They said her husband had treated her badly. Then she married the schoolmaster. They said it was the best thing that could have happened to that poor lonely man in the School House, with only an elderly housekeeper to look after him, who didn't even darn his socks! Now he had his old socks darned and new socks knitted. They said it had taken all of two years to make up his mind to propose marriage to Teacher. And all that time she was just waiting to be asked!

'Men are funny creatures,' said Ruby Simmons.

The flag was flying from the top of the mast in the school playground, and all the children had been marched out, class by class, to stand in circles facing the flag, with the Infants in front. A cold wind whipped the girls' starched pinafores, and cooled the boys' cropped heads. The poorer children shivered in their worn, ill-fitting garments.

'Why wasn't they wearing their 'ats and coats? They'll get their death,' grumbled one of the harassed mothers from a nearby cottage, looking over the fence.

The shrill voices of the children held a poignancy that was very moving. 'Land of Hope and Glory' and 'God Save the King' stirred the last feeble shreds of patriotism into fresh life and hope. Mothers who had lost their sons, and young wives with babies who would never know a father, huddled together behind the fence, crying quietly. Girls with bows in their hair, and boys with rosettes pinned to their jerseys, all were singing as though their lungs would burst. The Infants were too young to know the meaning of PEACE. But they all knew about that Victory Party in the village hall. The gentry would be there to wait on them. Parson would say grace, and give the signal to start. The plates of bread and butter had to be eaten before the cakes were put on the tables.

'It's real butter, not margarine,' they said, but it made no difference to children who lived on practically nothing but bread.

When the plates were empty, and the ladies of the upper class took them away and came back with more plates piled with cakes, sausage rolls and mince-pies, a chorus of 'Oohs' and 'Ahs', 'Gosh!' and 'Golly!' was sufficient appreciation for all the hours of preparation and all the hoarding of depleted rations. Small quantities of tea and sugar had been collected by Old-Parson's Wife together with sixpences, one for each child. All the tradesmen had contributed to the feast. Grocer had provided the ingredients for the cakes.

'I always knowed the old bugger 'ad plenty under the counter,' scoffed Miss 'Nosy' Parker irritably, as she hovered behind the scenes to help with the washing-up. Upper-class ladies enjoy playing the waitress, but shudder at a pile of dirty crockery!

Housewives had spared jars of their carefully hoarded Christmas mince-meat. Butcher had provided the sausages, and Baker stayed up all night in his bakehouse. Not a crumb was wasted. When small stomachs could take no more, pockets were filled. The conjuror had an appreciative audience, satiated with food, and hot, sweet tea.

'They was *live* rabbits what 'e pulled out of 'is top 'at. They wasn't dummies,' the eldest Baldock boy informed the tribe of seven brothers and sisters. It had been a debatable point whether eight victory mugs should be allowed to one family, but a show of hands at the committee meeting had voted in favour. Mum wasn't too pleased, however. The mantelpiece was already cluttered with mementoes of Michaelmas fairs. Toby jugs, and a tea caddy given away at the grocery on the occasion of Her Late Majesty's Jubilee.

'We could use 'em, Mum,' her eldest daughter suggested, helpfully.

'That you will not!' Mum retorted. 'These mugs is not for drinking, so don't let me catch you desecrating the memory of all the brave men what 'as died for their King and Country!'

'No, Mum,' they chorused, obediently.

'We 'ad a luverly tea, Mum,' sighed six-year-old Sarah-Ann, rubbing her stomach.

'I wanna be sick!' whimpered George.

'Then get outside, *quick*!' said Mum, smacking his backside with a hard hand.

There was a Victory Parade the following Sunday. Led by the village band, the few survivors of the Great War marched to church with flags and banners, followed by the Boy Scouts and the Girl Guides, and all the school children, still wearing their bows and rosettes.

'We ain't seen such a smart turnout not since the Relief of Mafeking,' old Josiah Jones informed the other inmates of the Almshouses, as they lined up to receive their victory mugs that same evening, from Sir Neville Franklin. First in the line was a chirpy little man with a wooden leg. 'Peg-leg' had served in South Africa, and also on the North West Frontier of India, as batman to the colonel of a famous regiment. He had some gruesome tales to tell to the customers at 'The Three Nuns'. The older generation turned a deaf ear, the tales had been repeated so often, but the younger generation and chance customers still listened attentively to the old man, and somebody would pay for a pint of beer. The younger generation was sadly depleted, however, and 'The Three Nuns' had its own 'roll of honour' of customers who had marched away to fight for King and Country, but would never again lean on the counter to listen to old Peg-leg. The children had christened him all those years ago, and only Old-Parson's wife called him by his real name, which was Obadiah Hobbs. The colonel had made a present of Peg-leg to Parson when he had no further use for his services. A batman with only one leg could become a bit of a liability in retirement. Yet he had survived his colonel for a number of years, and now had the honour to be the oldest inhabitant in the Almshouses. His loyalty and devotion had never wavered. They said he sat for hours at the colonel's bedside during his long illness, listening and recounting the tales of the famous regiment they both had served. They said he was there when the colonel had breathed his last, and Peg-leg cried like a child.

'It do seem strange to me, Sir, that all these victory mugs was already there, waiting to be 'anded out, and the Armistice only just signed,' Peg-leg was heard to remark, but he was only voicing the general opinion of the other inmates. The squire smiled benignly on the old man. The War had softened his hard, handsome features, and his arrogance was not so noticeable. They said he had decided Marston Park should be converted into a Holiday Home for poor Children from the East End of London when all the patients had been dispersed.

'My good fellow, you should know we British always win the last battle!' he said.

Peg-leg smiled a toothless smile. They said his gums were so hard he could chew the toughest bit of Butcher's wartime steak as easy as his neighbours, all boasting a set of false teeth.

'You're right, sir,' he agreed, saluted smartly, and received his mug.

The patients and staff at the Marston Park Hospital for Wounded Officers had their own memorial service. For many of the patients, the prospect of being sent home in the near future was not as wonderful as they had to pretend. Nearly all the men, of Canadian and American nationality, had been away from home for the best part of three years. Fathers would not recognise their children they had left behind, and the children would not welcome a stranger they must call 'Dad' or 'Pop'. Their wives would be strangers, and not all had been faithful to their husbands. As for the husbands, they were not expected to be faithful. It simply is not true that 'absence makes the heart grow fonder'. A normal man needs more than a photograph to kiss.

From Matron down to the youngest VAD recruit, all the staff had won the affection and admiration of their patients. It was a close community. Their own chaplain conducted the service, and many were moved to tears. They sang 'Fight the Good Fight', 'Oh God our Help in Ages Past', and 'Land of Hope and Glory'.

Penelope Franklin was detailed to accompany them on the piano – the schoolroom piano on which all four girls had practised their scales when they left the nursery. She looked very trim and boyish in her neat VAD uniform. Two of her sisters were present. Cynthia, with her husband, Lieutenant Freddie Simmons in a wheelchair, and Sylvia, with the young Canadian captain to whom she was engaged to be married. They would be married by the chaplain before the evacuation of the hospital. An only adored son of a widowed mother, he was already dreading the inevitable clash between the two women. Sylvia would be homesick and stifled in a small house, where neighbours walked in without knocking, and children ran free and unrestricted by gates or fences.

Of the three sisters, only Cynthia could see the way ahead clearly and objectively, with its eventual pattern of work and holidays, and the raising of a family. The path could be strewn with pitfalls, and Freddie would never be strong, but she was not afraid, and Freddie was not afraid.

For Penelope, it would soon be time to say farewell, for she had no desire to marry any of the men with whom she had been enjoying mild flirtations, even if one had been free. They were going home to wives and children, and widowed mothers, and they all faced up to their duty and their responsibilities with varying degrees of hope, fear and reluctance. The frivolous Penny was pensive as her small world started to disintegrate. She wished she could put back the clock. She wanted to cry, but she was a Franklin, and tears had been repressed in the nursery. What would she do without all the attentions of her admiring swains? Only her half-brother, Charles, would enliven the boredom during the holidays. Charles was great fun. They were two of a kind. They shared a light-hearted view of life, and the War years had passed over them, leaving no visible marks.

'Cheer up, old thing! The post-War prospects shouldn't be too gloomy, with swarms of Cockney brats all over the place!' Charles had written in one of his rare letters. 'Our fond parent has promised to retain the private wing of the house for the use of the family, and Hetty will be re-engaged as cook-housekeeper. You remember Hetty O'Brien? At one time the O'Briens and the Simmons were neighbours in that devilish unhealthy slum called Richmond Row – so Carrie tells me, and Carrie was a Simmons before she married that disagreeable half-brother of mine. Incidentally, I thought that poor girl was looking decidedly wretched when I last saw her. It can't be much fun tied to Albert. What do you think about it, Penny? – or don't you think about it? It doesn't really concern us, does it, not you and me? Mother is a darling, and I am terribly fond of her, but she is inclined to get her priorities wrong. To sacrifice that pretty creature for a son so embittered and war-scarred is no way to solve the problem in my opinion, for what it's worth. Have any plans been made for the Christmas vacation? I know Davenport would be glad of an invitation. His parents are getting divorced. He says it's absolutely beastly, and they haven't considered his feelings at all. He feels he is just an embarrassment to both. So I'll bring him along. With Cynthia and Freddie, Sylvia and Bob, it should be good fun. When are they getting married, those two? I must spend a day or two at Russets, but we three – Davenport you and I – could pop up to town to see a show. It would have to be Marie Lloyd. Do you mind? Dad raves about her. I think it's a kind of antidote to all the gloom at home. She's screamingly funny, and so delightfully vulgar! Cheery-bye, my sweet sister! Keep the flag flying, and the old chin up! Love, Charles.'

Yes, it would be fun, Penny was thinking, as she watched the last of the fleet of ambulances disappear round the bend of the drive. All the staff, including Matron, had been kissed and hugged, given small, handmade gifts, and thanked profusely. The atmosphere had been strained and emotional. The patients they had known so intimately had suddenly become strangers in the past few days.

Lieutenant Freddie Simmons would be transferred to Roehampton in the New Year. Cynthia would enjoy a long overdue leave to care for him in the meantime. Hetty had already been installed as cook-housekeeper in the private wing, with a young girl from one of the farms on the estate to train as housemaid. Hetty O'Brien was one of the few women completely dedicated to domestic service, and they were lucky to find one of the original staff so loyal to the Franklins.

Captain Robert McKenzie was staying behind to marry Sylvia. After a brief honeymoon, he would take his bride home to Canada.

Matron stood on the terrace surrounded by her nurses. She, too, would enjoy a long overdue holiday with a sister in Cornwall. She had no definite plans. Five years in a military hospital had spoiled her for a general hospital. Men were so much more amenable. The empty beds and the silent wards were depressing, but her nurses were not allowed to forget they were still on duty. Those empty beds and silent wards would soon be filled with noisy youngsters from London's East End, who would quickly adapt to their posh surroundings, but quite ready to return home after two weeks of running wild on the big estate. A game of cricket in the back streets of Stepney with a lamp-post for wicket and a bit of broken fencing for a bat, this was still cricket! It was all a question of where you were born and bred, and the War had not changed that fundamental issue.

Sir Neville would spend Christmas Day and Boxing Day with his family at Marston Park, then return to London. The big house-parties and the lavish entertainment of pre-War days would be remembered with nostalgia. The new chapter of post-War economy would seem barren in comparison, but that extravagant era had gone for ever. Death duties and heavy taxation would cripple the gentry, and upper-class ladies would find their attic bedrooms empty of servants, and their kitchens without cooks. The War had been responsible for a revolution in domestic service. Cooks and kitchen maids had been earning good wages in munitions factories. Housemaids and parlourmaids had been driving buses, manning the railway stations, serving in shops, learning how to use a typewriter. The scope had been varied and interesting. Caps and aprons had been discarded for ever. They would never go back to domestic service unless they could be hired by the hour, live at home or in bed-sitters, and have their evenings free. It was a form of slavery that only a War could bring to an end. Even Doctor's wife, on her return from the clinic where she had been recuperating from a nervous breakdown, was shocked to find her former parlourmaid installed as a booking clerk at the railway station, her former cook a manageress in a factory canteen, the simple-minded under-housemaid promoted to general factotum, and her daughter-in-law in the kitchen! Her immediate reaction of agitation was quickly soothed by her long-suffering husband.

'We are managing splendidly, my dear. Don't let it distress you. It's just a matter of adjusting to a new order. It is happening all around us. You will find the Forsters, the Hamiltons and the Bentleys all left with only one elderly servant. Now the War is over, I can retire with a clear conscience, for there will be no lack of volunteers to step into my shoes. But before I advertise in the Medical Journal, I will make it my business to speak to the Senior Consultant at Marston Park. I imagine the staff will soon be dispersed after the patients have left, and there may be a younger man interested in this practice.'

'You didn't tell me you were retiring, dear?' Dulcie was frowning in perplexity. She found so many changes confusing, after her quiet, uneventful sojourn in the comfortable clinic at Tunbridge Wells.

'I did, but you have forgotten,' he reminded her gently. He was glad to have her back. There had been so much time to think about the estrangement between them, and he now knew it was not solely the shock of discovering their middle son, Dennis, had murdered the young schoolteacher, but his own lack of understanding. He blamed himself for the inevitable breakdown, and was determined to make amends. Devoted to his practice, he had neglected Dulcie. She was a proud women, too proud to beg for his attention, so they had drifted apart. Dulcie was also fiercely maternal. She had loved her three sons passionately and foolishly, and when they left home for public school and university, and she realised she was no longer the most important person in their small world, she became depressed. It was not unusual for such a possessive mother to have little time for the husband, so perhaps the doctor, busy as he was, could be excused for neglecting her, in later years. Her daughter-in-law thought so, and so did the servants – the servants so happily engaged elsewhere on her return home!

There was no need to ask what had happened to Carrie, the young village girl her son's wife had engaged as nursemaid to her first grandson. She heard all the news from Eleanor Wellington – Old Parson's widow – and the first of her old friends to call on her. Carrie had married her cousin Albert and was living at Russets Farm. She was often seen driving the milk float in the village, with her own two grandchildren, Agnes and Harriet, perched precariously on the step, waiting to jump off to run for the customers' jugs! Their mother seemed to ignore the fact that her children spent more time hobnobbing with the Blunts than with children of their own class of society. Thank goodness they would be away to boarding school in the New Year, and would doubtless return home at Easter behaving like well-bred young ladies!

'Our world as we knew it has completely disrupted, my dear Dulcie!' the late Parson's wife declared in her forceful manner. 'Imagine it, all the ladies at my Red Cross sewing guild were obliged to make their own beds and cook their own meals!' She was trembling with indignation over such an extraordinary state of affairs, and ready to commiserate with Dulcie over her own depleted household.

When the doctor's daughter-in-law carried in the mid-morning coffee with a cheerful smile, both ladies gasped at her cleverness, and were obliged to admit it was an excellent brew.

Dulcie Saunders sighed and helped herself to a biscuit. 'You shouldn't be doing it, dear. You were not brought up to such duties.'

'I enjoy doing it, mother-in-law. I like being busy.'

'Shall you be joining your husband in India again?' Eleanor Wellington enquired of the younger woman, for she liked nothing better than to pass on all the tit-bits of information she collected on her travels round the village. It was the very breath of life. She *had* to know what was happening! It was *her* village, and she had kept her special place in the affections of her late husband's parishioners.

'No, the regiment is due to return home some time next year. I think we may be settled back in Tidworth for a time. I hope so,' Captain Saunders' wife explained, quietly. 'We have not yet heard. It is all in the lap of the gods. As my young son reminded me – "We follow the drum, don't we, Mummy?"'

'And how *is* James?' The older generation always insisted on calling a child by its baptismal name. It was

Carrie who had started the trend for 'Jimmy' in the nursery. Now the small boy, almost ready for prep school, would soon discover there would be no controversy over names in his new manly world. He would be re-christened 'Saunders Minor' – as a very unimportant junior. But there was one person in the doctor's household whose name was never mentioned, and not even Eleanor Wellington's thirst for information would be satisfied. The disgraced son, Dennis, had fled to his uncle's tea plantation in Ceylon, and it was assumed he was still there. A warrant had been issued for his arrest, but no extradition order had been obtained by the authorities. Then the War had intervened, and the case was dropped.

So they chatted on the safe topics of Christmas, and whether or not the butcher would oblige his regular customers with a nice piece of sirloin. Would they have to make do with a fowl for the fifth successive year?

There was no parlourmaid to answer the bell, and the doctor's wife had not yet adjusted to all these minor inconveniences – perhaps she never would. She was obliged to exert herself to show the visitor out, and after she had gone to replenish the drawing-room fire from the coal scuttle beside the hearth, she sighed impatiently, and sat back on her heels, staring into the fire, with a sense of utter futility. Never in her life had she been expected to show out a visitor or replenish a fire. An only daughter, of upper-class parents, her own private income had paid for her sons' education, their seaside holidays, their riding lessons, and all the little treats an indulgent mother loves to provide. A village doctor, especially one with so many poor patients, who could not pay their bills – indeed the bills were often not even presented – could ill afford to educate three sons in the traditional standard expected of their class of society. So Dulcie had paid, and her hold on the reins became so tight the boys hardly realised they had a father.

The drawing-room mantelpiece was crowded with photographs of Roger, Dennis and Lesley from babyhood to manhood, and in every one, her darling, her favourite was smiling. He had such a happy nature, such charm, everyone loved him. His naughtiness in the nursery had been excused. It was just high spirits. Only a nursemaid was employed, for Dulcie Saunders remembered that her early years had been ruled by a nurse with complete authority over her charge. A nursemaid had no authority, and no status. She could be supervised and scolded.

Among the professional portraits from the studio in Tunbridge Wells were framed snapshots she had taken with her camera – the boys on their ponies, the boys skating on the frozen lake at Marston Park, the boys splashing in the sea at Pegwell Bay, the boys lined up on the forecourt wearing their new suits on the occasion of their confirmation by the bishop, the boys in a boat on the river, the boys in their school caps and blazers, and finally three handsome young men, each in a silver frame, proudly garbed in cap and gown, holding their diplomas.

She was on her feet now, staring at these fond mementoes with anguished eyes. *They did not need her any more.* Roger and Lesley were happily married. A courtesy visit from Roger and his wife twice a year. Lesley she had not seen for four years, and Dennis? There was a time, before the War, when she had received several letters addressed to Brown's Hotel in London. She had stayed there, it was understood, for the purpose of attending celebrity concerts at the Wigmore Hall. But actually it was an excuse to get news of Dennis. She had accepted the fact that her son had lied to save his skin. She had even accepted the fact that her son was a murderer, but he was still her son, and her mother's heart still grieved. The empty years could never be restored. They were lost for ever. Yet, knowing his weak mentality, and his fondness for a pretty face, she had no doubt that he found the dark faces and slender bodies of those dusky maidens on the tea plantation even more desirable than the fairer ones he had wooed at home. Dennis could coax a bird from a bough with that charming smile, and any pretty girl who had taken his fancy in the village had been a willing accomplice. He quickly tired of the game once he had his way with her, and the excitement of the chase became nothing more than a habit. But he could easily escape. Public school and university, holidays abroad, and holidays at the palatial establishment of a favoured school-fellow all removed him from the village for much of the year. That note he had left, confessing he had strangled the young school-teacher had been flung into the flames of the drawing-room fire, but she remembered every word to this day. He hadn't meant to kill the girl, only to frighten her because she was teasing him about a former lover and he was jealous. He pleaded for his mother's understanding and forgiveness, and signed the note – 'Ever your loving and devoted son.' Dear God! What she had suffered during the long weeks of the police investigations after the body had been found in the bushes near the lake at Marston Park. Why hadn't the murderer disposed of the body in the lake? Nothing could have been simpler, they said. Why had that missing garment never been found? They said it was a sexual murder. They said there was no sign of a struggle, and the victim had been surprised into sudden death. They said – they said – they said . . .

She was weeping quietly, a photograph of Dennis pressed to her breast when the door opened and closed. Her proud head was bowed, her shoulders sagged, and the doctor's heart was touched into a tenderness he had not known since the early days of their marriage.

'My darling wife,' was all he said, but his arms were

strong and protective. He led her to the couch, and they sat down together, his arm about her waist, her head on his shoulder.

It was very quiet and peaceful, like a calm after a storm.

'I haven't forgotten what I promised,' he said at last.

She made no answer. Her eyes were closed and she seemed exhausted.

'Are you listening, my darling?' he asked.

She nodded.

'We are taking a long holiday, you and I, as soon as I can find a replacement. We are going to Ceylon to visit Dennis.'

Her eyes flew open. She lifted her head and stared at him. Now her wet eyes were shining, and her mouth trembling.

'Ceylon?' she whispered. 'Thank you, my dear. *Thank you.*'

Chapter 4

The wheelwright had allowed his housekeeper a free day, rather grudgingly, because he was a man accustomed to being waited on hand and foot all his life; first, by a doting mother, secondly, by a long-suffering wife, thirdly by a dutiful daughter, and finally, by a conscientious housekeeper. Ruby would leave his dinner in a low oven and his tea laid ready in the parlour, covered over by a clean cloth. The tea-caddy would be ready to hand beside the teapot, but she knew him so well by this time she could almost hear his gruff voice complaining – 'Drat the woman! I don't pay a housekeeper to go gallivanting off to London!' Considering it was only the second time she had asked for a free day – the other being the occasion of her daughter's wedding – Ruby considered, quite rightly, that she was not 'taking a liberty'.

Having decided on a firm line with the disagreeable old man, she fully intended to enjoy herself. Her employer's lack of co-operation did not really surprise her. The reactions of persons who paid your wages had always been unpredictable. Her stout working-class mentality was both sensible and shrewd. Sunday afternoon being her official free time, Ruby would escape as soon as she had washed up the dishes, and hurry away to spend a noisy but jolly few hours with her four grand-children. Jack's wife had intended a much larger family, but the War had robbed her of a good, steady, hard-working husband, and she had to be content with four.

The wheelwright's daughter – the indefatigable Teacher – would bring her schoolmaster husband and her son, Philip, to wait upon the crusty old man, but while he indulged in his customary 'forty winks' after the Sunday roast – he would insist that he only closed his eyes for ten minutes – they had ample time to explore the countryside on their bicycles. The new Raleigh models had been supplied so promptly at the end of the War by the dealer in Tunbridge Wells, and at such fantastic prices, it was assumed they had been stored for the duration in order to make a good profit. Nevertheless, the schoolmaster, normally a most careful spender, was determined they should enjoy a wider scope, and visit fresh fields. Walking was all very well, but they had long since traversed every lane and footpath within a five-mile area, and he could find nothing original on which to lecture his accommodating wife and stepson.

Ruby had found a new friend in her employer's daughter, and the formal mode of address considered polite was quickly dropped. She was Martha to her friends, she had insisted. Only Carrie and her ex-pupils still called her Teacher.

One of her several activities in the village was the local company of Girl Guides, who met for their weekly meetings on Tuesday afternoons, and went straight from school to the Village Hall. During the hop-picking season, when all the village children were picking hops with their families, the company was temporarily disbanded. The former captain, of upper-class society, had fled to the safety of California during the Summer of 1914, and Martha had been recommended by Old Parson's widow to fill the vacant post of leader.

'Such a sensible woman, kind but strict. The girls will love and obey her,' she prophesied.

Everyone still listened to Old Parson's widow. They had to, for her strong personality quelled all lesser mortals!

To raise funds for a week's camping holiday at Easter, the girls had borrowed the Boy Scouts' hand-cart to collect the jumble for a sale. Dutifully presenting themselves in their neat uniforms, they spent every Saturday for a whole month trudging round the village and outlying farms, including Russets, where they were offered refreshments and invited to sit down in the warm kitchen. The girls' industry and enthusiasm was contagious. Attics were turned out, and all manner of hoarded treasures discovered among the dust and the cobwebs.

On this particular Saturday morning, when Ruby was on her way to Victoria to meet her favourite daughter-in-law, Martha was busy in the Village Hall, sorting the piles of discarded clothing and household articles, assisted by a dozen pairs of willing hands. Shrieks of laughter echoed through the draughty hall.

'What's this, Miss?'

'Is this worth more than threepence, Miss?'

'Please, Miss, where shall I put this commode?'

'How about this rusty old lawn mower? Nobody won't ever give a shilling for that, Miss'.

Questions – questions – and such utter chaos until 'Miss' established the kind of order to which she was accustomed in the classroom.

'What do it matter, Miss, a bit of muddle? As soon as them doors is opened at 2 o'clock, we shall be sent flying, and everything turned upstairs down,' Rebecca Simmons – Ruby's eldest grandchild – reminded the captain reasonably.

'That is so, Rebecca, but we must have an orderly start. And whatever you do, don't put anything of your own property on the counters, even for a second, or you will lose it!' she added.

'My Mum could use that commode for our Gran, Miss. She often gets taken short in the night, Miss, does our Gran,' Freda Lindridge whispered, confidentially.

'Then put it to one side, Freda, and mark it sold.'

'But 'ow shall I get it 'ome, Miss?'

'Don't worry. We will find a way after the sale.'

'Yes, Miss. No, Miss.'

But Freda was always worried. Being the eldest of seven was a big responsibility.

''ow much is it, Miss?' Freda remembered to ask, rather anxiously.

'Sixpence.'

'I ain't got sixpence, Miss.'

'How much have you got?'

'Fourpence.'

'Then you can have it for fourpence.'

'Oh, *thank you*, Miss. Mum won't arf be pleased!'

When Cynthia admired her mother-in-law's coat and hat on her arrival at Victoria, Ruby was not ashamed to confess it had been intended for the jumble sale, and her good friend Martha had allowed her to purchase it from the stack of second-hand clothing in the attic at the School House.

'Charity begins at home, my dear, and you need not mention it to anyone outside the family if you feel a little guilty,' Martha had explained, kindly.

For five shillings she had purchased a good-quality coat, a velour hat, and a velveteen dress in a pretty shade of blue, and all in such good condition they could almost be described as new. Ruby hadn't intended to buy a dress. She thought to make do with a skirt and jumper, but Martha had pointed out, discreetly, that coats and hats were removed and left in a cloakroom at the theatre, and that the atmosphere at Lyons, where they would be having a meal, would be so warm and comfortable, she would be glad to discard her coat.

'I ought not to be spending money on meself, love, not with Christmas so near and presents to buy for the family. It do seem extravagant like.' Ruby had mused. 'But it's a fact I ain't got nothing decent enough to wear to London, for it's years since I bought anything for meself, and I can't 'ave Cynthia feeling ashamed of me, can I? Cynthia's upper class, and she's got good taste, not like Elsie, what always looks such a drab. Jew know, Martha love, I still can't get used to calling 'er by 'er Christian name. It seems like taking a liberty, yet she's so nice and natural, I ought not to feel arkard. Freddie tells me I've got a chip on me shoulder, whatever that might mean. But she's fond of me, and I feel the same way about 'er, that I do know. I mean to say, look 'ow she puts 'erself out to call on me on 'er way back to London after she leaves Freddie. It's a long walk to the station when you take the village road. And never missed a week in visiting our Freddie at Marston Park. There's nothing she wouldn't do for Freddie, bless 'er.'

'Yes, Cynthia has to be admired,' Martha agreed, as she searched for brown paper to make a parcel of the clothes. 'It must have been a terrible shock to see her young husband so sadly disabled. They only had a few weeks of married life together, I believe?'

'Not even weeks, love. It were only a matter of days. Then 'e went off to camp for training, and over to France ever so quick. Mind jew, our Freddie 'as to be admired too, for 'e's taken it sensible like, losing a leg and bits of shrapnel all over the place what 'as to be dug out. Makes yer shiver to think of it, don't it love? But Freddie always was the plucky one. Never made no fuss, not like Jack and Albert. As for young Carrie, she would yell blue murder if she just grazed 'er knee! Freddie was the delicate one. Colds and bronchitis most of the Winter, and often 'ome from school with a nasty sore throat. That used to worry me, love, for I was terrible scared of diphtheria. There wasn't much 'ope for a child not with diphtheria. Still, it wre a miracle they didn't all catch it with them stinking privies. I don't 'ave to tell you what Richmond Row was like, for your first 'usband, Dick Martin, was born and bred in the Row.'

Martha's eyes were clouded with memories of that unhappy period of her life. It had been a sad mistake to marry the father of her child, for Philip was already five years old when Dick came back from India with the regiment. This new chapter of her life, with her dear Andrew, and Philip a pupil at the Grammar School, and her own re-instatement in the Infants' classroom, was so peaceful and pleasant, she thanked God every day for her many blessings. It had taken a long time to adjust to the sexual relationship of a second marriage, but Andrew was gentle and patient. There would be no more children for she was past the age, but Andrew was not paternal, and quite satisfied with a stepson. As for Philip, he could have been jealous of a young brother or sister. Jealousy had been the main cause of his intense dislike of Dick.

When they had finished in the attic, they went downstairs and Martha put on the kettle for a cup of tea. Philip was busy with his homework at the kitchen table, but he stood up politely to say 'Good evening', 'That boy of Martha's 'as got lovely manners,' Ruby would tell Cynthia the following day.

There were so many memories for Ruby on that branch

line to Tonbridge, for Tom had been employed as a ganger. The cottages in Richmond Row, being railway property, at least one male member of every family was obliged to work on the line. It was a miserly wage because they had no rent to pay, so the wives went out charring, or took in washing, though how they managed to wash, dry and iron in such cramped conditions was nobody's business, least of all the upper-class customers who revelled in clean linen, with never a thought to the slavery. Ruby had chosen the charring in the early days of her marriage, and had always enjoyed her work. She counted herself lucky, with a regular wage, and useful perks in the shape of pies, stale bread and soup, and only five minutes walk from home. The publican and his wife at 'The Three Nuns' were kind and generous. Ruby had been allowed to take the children until they were old enough for school. At an early age they were taught to amuse themselves quietly.

'Now mind, I won't 'ave you being a nuisance!' Ruby would remind them sternly.

The customers liked to see young Ruby Simmons busy with her scrubbing brush and polishing rags. With her golden hair and blue eyes, plump as a spring chicken, she had many admirers. Her pert personality was deceptive, however, and those who mistook the warmth in her manner for an invitation to flirt were surprised to get their faces slapped. For Ruby, there was only Tom. Married at sixteen, like her twin sister Lucy, her small world had revolved around her husband and children. Looking back over those early years, as the branch line train chugged its way to Tonbridge – the terminus for Victoria and the South Coast – she was remembering, like thousands of mothers at the end of that terrible War, the son she had lost and the son who came home crippled.

Albert, the eldest of the three, had been conscripted, but Freddie and Jack had volunteered. Ruby was a little ashamed of Albert. A farm worker had no more right to avoid doing his duty than a budding solicitor or a grocery assistant. And it was Albert who not only survived, but came back unharmed, to find a tractor had been provided to make life easier, and his wife as eager as ever to get into bed! That she had enjoyed a liaison with one of the German prisoners-of-war employed at Monks Farm was no secret, but Albert was not a jealous man, and not particularly intelligent, so he saw no reason to chastise an unfaithful wife when the lover was probably back on his native soil and not likely to return.

Ruby sighed as the fields and woods slipped quietly past the window. Ruby had always been too busy to notice Nature's wonderland. Unlike her sister, Lucy, who had married a farmer, the seasons of the year had no particular significance, such as seedtime and harvest, haymaking and fruit-picking. She did not need a calendar to remind her to strip off the children's Winter clothing on the first day of May, and to wrap them up in coats and mufflers on the first day of October! Nature was something for the upper class to enjoy, not hard-working women like Ruby Simmons. Spring had to be endured rather than enjoyed, because of the orgy of cleaning that had followed her from 'The Three Nuns' to The Parsonage, The Grove, and finally to the wheelwright's. Summer was a time when you expected to sweat, windows and doors were flung open, and flies got stuck on the gummed fly-catchers suspended from the kitchen ceiling. Autumn was a noisy riot of Cockney invaders to pick the hops, but Ruby had always enjoyed the invasion. 'It do liven things up once a year and no mistake,' she would say. Winter came suddenly, sweeping across the Weald in gusty showers that caught out the unwary 'foolish virgins' with no oil in their lamps or coal in their cellars. Ruby always thought of her neighbours as 'foolish virgins' when they came to borrow from her own small stock of carefully hoarded oil and coal as soon as Winter set in. Biblical stories with a good moral had always been an important factor in the teaching at the village school. Scripture was a favourite lesson with the girls, but the boys were bored, unless the subject was some grand tale like David and Goliath, the mighty Samson who pulled down the Temple, or Jonah, swallowed by a whale.

Changing trains at Tonbridge was a hazardous affair for such an inexperienced traveller.

'Am I right for Victoria?' Ruby enquired anxiously of the guard and both porters before venturing into a carriage. All her confidence seemed to evaporate on the few occasions she had travelled beyond the boundaries of her own village, and she sat there nervously clutching her cheap handbag as the main-line train sped towards London. Her fellow passengers in the crowded compartment were a mixed bunch, and they paid no heed to the homely little woman in their midst. Children occupied the window seats, their mothers chatted loudly about their respective offspring, a prim-looking woman carried on with her knitting, and two City gents his themselves behind their newspapers. Ruby felt lost and lonely. It had been a mistake to accept Cynthia's invitation so readily, but it was too late now to change her mind. She leaned forward, her eyes darting anxiously towards the window every time the train stopped at a station, till the woman with the knitting remarked acidly, 'If you are bound for Victoria, you can't miss it. We don't go any farther.'

'Thank you, I'm sure,' said Ruby, much relieved, then added confidentially, 'I'm meeting my daughter-in-law.'

'Oh yes?'

'She's taking me to see Marie Lloyd. 'ave you seen 'er?'

'No, I don't care for music hall. I find it rather vulgar. I prefer a good play.'

'We shall be 'aving a meal at Lyons.'

'Which Lyons?'

'Is there more than one?'

'Good gracious, yes! They have the monopoly, of course, but I prefer Slaters.'

Somewhat dashed by her efforts to make contact with her right-hand neighbour, Ruby tried another topic, a safe topic.

'The weather's nice for the time of year, ain't it?'

'Do you think so? I personally find the onset of Winter rather depressing.'

'But there's Christmas just around the corner, and that's a luverly time, specially for the children. By next Christmas we ought to be able to buy a few more things to fill up their stockings. Now the War's over, I expect they'll have some nuts and oranges in the shops, and them little sugar mice. It all 'alps to fill their stockings. It ain't been easy lately, not since the War. By next Christmas we shan't 'ave to take our turn at the butcher's for the suet for the pudding, and the grocer ought to 'ave plenty of raisins and currants and sultanas. Jew know, I've been saving it up for most of the year, but I managed to get enough for a pudding and a cake, and a couple of jars of mince-meat. 'ow did you manage, if you don't mind me asking?'

'I have no need to bother. I always spend Christmas at an hotel.'

Ruby gaped. She could think of nothing more devastating than Christmas at an hotel. 'I should cry me eyes out, I'd be that miserable,' she said, with simple honesty.

The woman's tight lips twisted in a condescending smile. 'We are not all alike, thank goodness. Now, if you will excuse me, it's difficult to concentrate on the pattern if you persist in chattering.'

Ruby's face flushed with embarrassment. She had forgotten Martha's warning not to talk to strangers. A stranger could be a spy. Philip had also been warned, for he travelled by train to Grammar School. But now the War was over, and the danger past. Ruby closed her mouth. She felt properly flummoxed.

To see Cynthia waiting at the barrier at Victoria was such a relief, she hurried forward with outstretched hands, gasping thankfully, 'Am I pleased to see you, love?' and clutched at the familar figure as though she were drowning in the sea of strange faces.

'Hello, Mother darling. Have you had a difficult journey? Was it hot on the train?'

''ot and bothered, that's me, love. I got talking to a woman what was busy with 'er knitting and got carried away, like I always do. Then she got a bit snooty like. Said she couldn't concentrate on the pattern with all my chatter. It was my fault. I should 'ave kept my big mouth shut!'

Cynthia chuckled. 'Why should you? It's a free country still, thanks to our dear boys. Forget it, darling. She must have been one of those miserable spinsters crossed in love in their youth, and spending the rest of their lives in mourning for a dead romance.'

'She could 'ave lost 'er man in the War, couldn't she, love? But she weren't in black.'

'She could, and perhaps I am misjudging her, but she had no right to scold you. Now, let me look at you. How smart you are looking. Isn't that a new coat and hat?'

Ruby nodded. 'And I got a new dress, love. Martha said as 'ow you took orf your coats and 'ats when you went to the theatre, and left them in the cloakroom.'

'That's right. Am I being inquisitive, my dear, but has your mean old wheelwright increased your meagre wages? Tell me all about it.' She linked her arm in Ruby's and walked her down the platform.

'Jumble sale,' Ruby explained, importantly. 'Only

Martha gave me first choice the day before the sale. I got the lot for five shillings.'

'I can't believe it. It's such good quality. You couldn't have bought anything of better value at Harrods.'

'Thank you, love. I didn't want you to feel ashamed of me.'

'Ashamed? – of my husband's mother? Never! You're a darling and I love you.'

To have a daughter-in-law in the upper class was really most satisfactory, Ruby was thinking, as she stepped out proudly with the slim, youthful figure in her pre-War fur coat and matching cap.

The forecourt was crowded with buses, and they all looked alike, but Cynthia knew exactly which bus would take them to Marble Arch and Lyons. Sir Neville Franklin's daughter had long since outgrown the small exclusive world of Marston Park.

The ladies cloakroom was a dazzling palace, smelling of scent, not Jeyes Fluid! And it was free! Soap and towels were provided for a row of gleaming wash-basins, and the customers were reflected in the gilt-framed mirrors. Women of all ages were powdering their noses and making up their faces with rouge and eye shadow. Ruby stared, fascinated. Fancy that. And she thought it was only 'tarts' who made up their faces. She was learning quite a lot about human nature today and no mistake.

The majority of the women looked quite ordinary and rather shabby. Several of the younger women were dressed in black from head to toe – War widows no doubt. Ruby's heart ached for them as they reddened their lips. Perhaps it gave them courage. Cynthia was tidying her short, shining hair and she took a lipstick from her handbag.

'Can I be excused, love?' Ruby whispered, still a little intimidated by such grandeur.

Cynthia nodded.

'You won't go away?'

Her daughter-in-law smiled indulgently. 'Don't worry, darling. I won't budge an inch.'

An attendant in a white coat pulled the chain and wiped the seat. Ruby thanked her politely, but the woman's eyes were blank, her face a mask. What was she thinking? – or didn't she think? Imagine being confined to this glittering, scented palace all day!

'I wouldn't change places with that poor soul for all the tea in China,' Ruby confided, as they climbed the stairs to the restaurant.

'Who?'

'The lavatory lady.'

'Who knows, she may enjoy the job? It depends on circumstances. If she lives alone, for instance, in a furnished bed-sitting-room, where she hardly speaks to a soul, and has to economise on gas, then it could be quite a comforting place, especially in the Winter.'

Ruby was surprised at Cynthia's observations. What did the upper class know of furnished bed-sitting-rooms?

'Don't forget I'm a nurse in a women's hospital, Mother,' she reminded her, as though she read her thoughts. 'All our patients are working class, and one hears such sad tales of poverty and loneliness. But let's not dwell on other people's troubles today, darling. Let's be utterly selfish, just for once.'

'Right you are, love,' Ruby agreed, clutching Cynthia's arm.

They had left their coats and hats with an attendant in the cloakroom. Ruby's new dress matched her eyes, and her freshly washed hair had a golden sheen in the brilliant light. She was flushed with excitement, and eager as a child for the treat in store. A small orchestra in an alcove of palms played popular music. The tables were draped in starched damask cloths of snowy whiteness. (They must have used a lot of starch and blue-bags, Ruby was thinking.) The silver and glasses were polished to perfection. But only elderly waiters were left to serve the customers, assisted by trim, uniformed waitresses. The young waiters had marched away to serve their King and Country, but they hadn't come back.

'A table for two, Madam?' enquired a dapper, grey-haired man, deferentially.

'Yes, please,' Cynthia replied.

They followed him to a side table, where he pulled out their chairs and they sat down. Every little courtesy that surprised Ruby was familiar to her young companion. She had grown up with starched damask cloths and silver – real silver. It was no novelty to be waited on. There had been a butler, two footmen, and a parlourmaid, at Marston Park before the war. Her manner had a charming naturalness as she handed the menu to Ruby and invited her to choose.

'*You* choose, love. I'm sure it's all luverly.' She wouln't know where to start on such a menu. But where had all the food come from, and the War only ended a few weeks ago? Ruby asked herself. And where would all those street vendors at Marble Arch be eating their dinner? It hadn't escaped their notice that all the men were still wearing their faded, shapeless uniforms. Cynthia had paid sixpence for a box of matches, received a smart salute and a grateful 'Thank you, Miss'. But the rest they had carefully avoided feeling mean and guilty. Cynthia would be going short of essentials for the rest of the month after this spending spree, but it was worth it to see the shiny-eyed wonder in those cornflower blue eyes. She had sent Ruby's fare by post, to spare her any embarrassment.

Pushing the thought of that pathetic little group of survivors to the back of her mind, Ruby clasped her work-worn hands in her lap while her mouth watered in anticipation. Cynthia was ordering clear soup, and fillet steak garnished with onions, peas, mushrooms and tomatoes, served with chips and french beans.

'We will decide on the dessert later,' she told the hovering waiter.

'Very good, Madam.'

'And we would like butter with the rolls, please.'

'Certainly, Madam.' They exchanged a smile of complete understanding. It would be a pleasure to serve such a charming customer. The smile slid away to Ruby's flushed face.

'This is fun, isn't it, darling?'

'Luverly. I don't arf wish we 'ad young Carrie with us. She don't get no treats now she's stuck down at Russets.'

'Next time we will invite her. You're worried about Carrie, aren't you, Mother?'

'I can't 'elp worrying, love. What sort of marriage is that with a man what can't ever give a child?'

'I didn't know.'

'It's a fact, love, for she told me so the last time she come up with the eggs. Broke 'er 'eart, she did. "What shall I do, Mum?" she asks me. "It's not normal, it's not natural, I want to be a proper wife, and I want children." What could I say, love? What would you 'ave said?'

'It's a tragedy, Mother, and Carrie is too young to be so deprived. Why did that nice sister of yours allow it to happen? She must have known about her son's condition.'

'She did know, for she 'elped 'im to bath that first day 'e come back.'

'And Carrie, when did she discover the truth?'

'On 'er wedding night.'

'That was cruel.'

'It were a terrible shock.' Ruby sighed gustily, and

Cynthia could only repeat, 'Next time we will bring her. That's a promise.'

The soup was hot and savoury. Cynthia nodded approvingly. 'It's good,' she said.

But Ruby was watching closely, and quick to notice her mistake. There was a right way and a wrong way to sup one's soup.

'It's very good, love,' she agreed. 'I got the 'ang of it ever so quick,' she would tell Martha later in the day.

'Now, what shall we have for dessert?' Cynthia was asking, as they laid down their knives and forks. 'Let me see what they have to offer.' She consulted the menu once more. 'Lemon meringue pie, gâteau, peach melba, knickerbocker glory. What do you fancy, darling?'

Ruby was giggling. 'Knickerbocker glory, please, love.'

'A good choice. It's quite delicious. I had it on my birthday when Papa took me out to lunch.' She smiled at the memory of Sir Neville Franklin lunching at Lyons!

'Will your father go back to Marston Park to live now that the War is over?'

'Not permanently. Only for short periods to keep an eye on the estate. We shall all meet at Christmas, but not in the main part of the house. That is already being converted into a country Holiday Home for poor children from the East End of London. Your sister will have told you about it?'

'Yes, she did. It's a luverly idea. If your own mother 'ad lived, she wouldn't 'ave liked to see all them poor children all over the place. They said she were a very proud lady.'

'Not as proud as Papa. He can be quite insupportable, though he has mellowed quite a bit since the War. Mama always had her own private apartment, and her personal maid, so I doubt whether it would have affected her very much. After the birth of my youngest sister, Penelope –

you met her at Carrie's wedding – Mama took to her couch. She felt she had failed in her duty to produce a son and heir, and Papa lost interest until he thought of a solution. You know the rest of the story, darling. It was no secret.'

''e took my sister Lucy to bed, and only a year after she lost Bert. That were not nice. The boys was proper disgusted, I don't mind telling you, love. Why did 'e 'ave to pick on a nice respectable woman like our Lucy, when 'e could 'ave lain with any woman what took 'is fancy?'

'Because she was strong and healthy and beautiful, and had three sturdy sons of her own. He saw her as the perfect mother for the son he wanted so desperately. Don't be too hard on him, darling. It hasn't turned out too badly. Your sister adores Charles, and Charles adores his mother. He seems to accept the fact that his parents must live in two separate worlds, which is quite remarkable in a way. I am very fond of Charles. We all are. He's a delightful person. One just wonders what the future holds when he comes of age. He will probably surprise everyone. We shall see.'

When the tall glasses arrived, filled to the brim with ice-cream and fruit salad and topped with real cream, sprinkled with grated chocolate, Ruby dived in eagerly, but could find no words to describe properly such a delicious concoction, only the one word that came so readily to her lips – LUVERLY! It seemed a pity to spoil such a wonderful meal with coffee. A cup of tea that normally followed her mid-day dinner would have been most welcome, but this was no normal day. 'When you're in Rome, you do as the Romans,' Martha would say. So she dutifully sipped the strong bitter beverage. Soft music drifted across the restaurant – 'Roses of Picardy' – 'In a Monastery Garden' – 'The Moonlight Sonata' – all pretty tunes that Ruby recognised but could not name. Old

Parson's daughter, Cecily, had often played the piano in the drawing-room at The Parsonage when she was busy in the kitchen. Cecily had volunteered for the Medical Corps, and married a doctor, to everyone's surprise. The War had changed all their lives. They said she would be living abroad because her husband was American. They said the housekeeper would be leaving as soon as a replacement could be found. She didn't care for the job now Miss Marion had come home from the Congo with her two little girls. Children made a lot of work. But what else could the poor soul do when she was left a widow in a foreign land? Ruby asked Cynthia, and her daughter-in-law seemed to be very sympathetic to Marion's plight. The children appeared to spend most of their time at Russets, but they would be going to boarding school in the New Year.

'Quaint little girls with an old-fashioned charm,' she described them. 'Miss Marion used to be your governess, didn't she, love?'

'Yes, the best of the lot in my opinion, and we had quite a few, we four sisters. I think we must have been rather troublesome, of perhaps they found it rather dull. Marston Park is so isolated, and no transport available to Tunbridge Wells on their free day. Marion had a lively intelligence. We missed her when she left. I don't like to see her so quiet and sad. We often run into her in the Park on my free day when I'm pushing Freddie in his wheelchair, and I wish I had more time to renew our acquaintance, but I can't neglect Freddie. Poor Marion. If only her father were still alive. They were so close. Her mother is such a forceful character, and so dictatorial. I shouldn't care to upset her.'

'She means well, and she don't spare 'erself,' Ruby volunteered. 'Mind jew, she wouldn't allow no back answers from 'er servants. It was "Yes, Ma'am", "No,

Ma'am" or you was in trouble.'

Cynthia was looking at her watch. 'Darling, we must go, or we shall miss the start of the show.'

The waiter was hovering again, and she smiled her thanks and slipped a coin into his hand.

Ruby would remember that eventful day as long as she lived, because it was not repeated. For some reason or other she was always prevented from meeting Cynthia in London, and after a time, she ceased to bother, for she was not a woman to expect such treats as her due. She could live on memory, and recall with vivid reality that tremendous ovation from the excited audience when Marie Lloyd stepped on to the stage. All the acts had been wonderful – at least, Ruby thought so – but Marie came last and stole the show, as she did every night. They said it was Marie who gave the men the courage to go back to the Front after their leave. They said that men had died with her name on their lips. She was everyone's sweetheart.

When they came out of the theatre, the shock of finding herself in the street struck Ruby with the force of a douche of ice cold water, and she shivered as they waited for a bus to Victoria.

'Back to earth with a bump, eh, love?' She clung to Cynthia's arm.

'You did enjoy the show, didn't you, darling? You were laughing so heartily people were turning round in their seats to look at you.'

'You wasn't ashamed of me?'

'Of course not. Music-hall is meant to be enjoyed that way. But you mustn't catch cold. We shall have time for a quick cup of tea in the station buffet. That will warm you up.'

'I never catch cold, and I never get an 'eadache, only a bit of rhumatics in me poor old knees, and that's to be expected, love, when I've been kneeling on 'em for a good many years.'

They parted with warm hugs and kisses, closer than ever after today.

'Goodbye, Mother darling. Take care.'

The plump little figure, framed in the doorway of the moving train had become very dear to the elegant young woman in her fur coat and cap. She would have much to tell Freddie on her next free day, and Freddie would listen quietly, smile his patient, fleeting smile, and thank her for giving his mother such a rare treat. He loved her for the way she had captured the older woman's stubborn heart, for his Mum had not approved of his marriage. She thought it was taking liberties for a lad from Richmond Row to marry the daughter of Sir Neville Franklin of Marston Park, but Cynthia had proved her wrong. Love had broken down the class barrier that had divided them for generations, and the War had completed what love had started.

It was a long journey back, and Ruby climbed the steep road to the village between wind-swept fields in almost total darkness. When her eyes had grown accustomed to the darkness, she picked out several twinkling lights away in the distance – remote farms and cottages where the lamps still burned. At the top of the hill, she passed the little grey stone school and the School House, and now she could see a lantern swinging from the porch of the 'Adam and Eve', and she was nearly back. She could not think of it as home-coming. It was just a place of work, and a roof over her head. There would be no welcome from that gruff old man. He would be sitting in the parlour, waiting for his supper with the table still laid for tea, and the scuttle empty of coal. He was not a man to do a woman's chores, especially a woman to whom he paid a wage. She sighed as she pushed open the gate, and her footsteps dragged as she crossed the yard and made her way to the back of the house. She was surprised to see a light in the kitchen, then the door opened, and Martha stood there.

'Is anything wrong, love?' she asked, tentatively.

'Father–he's dead.' She was crying quietly. Martha did everything quietly.

'Dead?' Ruby whispered, and reached out with her warm arms. 'When? What 'appened?' She was trembling with shock.

'I came along after school to make tea, and found him dead in his chair. A heart attack, Doctor said, and so sudden he wouldn't have suffered for more than a few minutes. I didn't know his heart was weak, but Doctor had known for some time it would end like this. He said he was sorry, but a doctor had to respect the wishes of his patient.'

'Where is he?'

'On the couch in the parlour.'

'So 'e didn't 'ave 'is tea then? And I made the dough cake special. It were always 'is favourite.'

'Never mind, dear. You were not to know this would happen. You mustn't blame yourself. You couldn't have prevented it even if you had been here. I'll put the kettle on. You will be ready for a cup of tea.' She was more concerned for her friend than herself. She had a home, a husband, a son. Ruby would be homeless again. What next, she wondered, for this gallant little woman? Life was hard for women like Ruby Simmons.

She had taken off her coat and hat and draped them over a kitchen chair. She sat down, feeling drained and exhausted. She was sorry the old man had to die alone, but tears would be a mockery. She sipped the hot tea gratefully.

'Will you mind staying here on your own until we decide what is best? Andrew will advice me. He is so good in an emergency,' Martha was saying.

'I don't mind, love.'

'I suppose it will have to be sold, the business and the property? The two men were due for retirement anyway, and Father was so methodical, I'm sure he has left instructions for their pensions in his Will. Philip will be upset. He was very fond of his grandfather. It's the end of an era, Ruby. I don't suppose we shall see another wheelwright in the village. Times are changing. It's going to be a mechanical world, with machinery on the farms, and cars instead of traps and carriages for the upper class. It's sad, but I suppose it had to happen, sooner or later.' Her face was pale and strained, but she was so calm, and her mind already busy with arrangements for the funeral. Her father had been a staunch Wesleyan all his life. She must see the minister about the memorial service. The Chapel would be crowded. Father had been much respected. When she married Andrew, she had changed over to Church. It was her duty as a wife. But Andrew and Philip would pay their last respects at the Chapel. She could foresee every detail. It would be conducted exactly as her father would have wished. But she could not foresee a time when the house would stand empty and the yard cleared of its familar clutter.

She could not bear to ask her friend the vital question. 'What shall you do? Where shall you go?' There was no room at the School House, and no room at Russets.

'You must come to us for Christmas, Rube,' Lucy insisted. She had left Katie to hang out the washing, and walked up to the village. The postman had reported the wheelwright's sudden death as he went on his round the following Monday morning. She found her twin sister busily turning out kitchen cupboards and packing the contents into tea chests, ready to be collected by the Boy Scouts for their next jumble sale. They would need to make several journeys with their handcart, for Martha had promised them all the useful articles from every room in the house. The furniture would be sold in the Auction Rooms at Tunbridge Wells. Apart from a few personal treasures from childhood, and her father's Bible, Martha had no room at the School House; that was adequately furnished and comfortable.

Ruby climbed down from the step-ladder, pushed a wayward lock of hair out of her eyes, and kissed her sister's glowing cheek. Ruby was pale and anxious for the future. Lucy was anxious – who wouldn't be with Albert so contrary and Tom so quiet and unhappy? But her healthy life had kept her cheeks glowing, and her plump figure had grown matronly with the passing years.

'Thanks, Luce. Just for a couple of days. There's plenty to keep me busy here for several weeks after Christmas.'

'We shall expect you Christmas Eve, and you must stay over Boxing Day. You can have Tom's room. He won't mind sleeping on the couch in the parlour. Carrie will be pleased to have you. She hasn't been looking too well lately, but she doesn't complain. We both know what the trouble is, Rube, but I honestly don't know what else we can do. I suppose we are not the only family to be saddled with a problem that has no solution. It's something we have to accept, as Cynthia has accepted a crippled husband. We can only blame the War and be thankful that we have them back. You lost your Jack, and we lost Harry. And when Harry was killed, I also lost Emma. I still miss her. She was a good servant, for all her wildness, and she was not to blame for her gypsy blood. She was like one of the family. Katie is so slow, but she does her best.'

'So Emma 'as never been back, even to see you, 'as she?'

'No, and I don't expect to see her again. She only stayed for Harry's sake. I think she was hoping he would marry her eventually, but Harry had no such intention. It was selfish, but he knew he could take her when he wanted her. All men are selfish, Rube, even the best of them.'

'Not my Tom; 'e were always thinking of me and the children.'

'It surprised me that Emma hadn't caught Harry by having his child. Then he would have married her. He used to say she was cunning as a little fox. Poor Emma. I wonder who she is living with now, and whether she is still running away to the woods when the fancy takes her. She often tried my patience, but I should take her back gladly if she showed her face at Russets.'

'Elsie won't be too pleased, Luce, when I tell 'er I shall be spending Christmas at Russets, and the children will be disappointed, but I must say I don't fancy Elsie's 'ospitality. It's such a muddle. She don't never seem to get straight, and the children 'as been allowed to get out of 'and since they lost their father. You can't blame Elsie, for she's out to work all day, six days a week, and they come 'ome from school and 'elp themselves to tea. It's the War to blame again. My children was lucky. I was always there when they come 'ome from school. There's no comfort for those children in the Winter, 'aving to take their bread and bacon, of bread and jam to school for their dinner, and then 'aving to wait for their Mum to come 'ome from work to cook their supper. I'm fond of my grandchildren, Luce, but they're that noisy and tiresome, I feel like smacking their bums, and Elsie wouldn't stand for no interference.'

'Well, you're coming to us, Rube, and that's settled. It's up to you to make your excuses to Elsie.'

'She can 'ave the Christmas pudding and the cake what I made ready last month, and I'll take a few mince-pies.

I've already bought the little presents for the children from the sixpenny bazaar. They still 'ang up their stockings. Cynthia give me ten shillings to spend on the children. After all, they were Freddie's nieces and nephews, even if they seldom met, she reminded me. She's real kind, Luce. I shall miss 'er, when she don't come down to Marston Park no more, but Freddie will be going to Roe'ampton in the New Year.'

'And Cynthia's sister, Sylvia, will be off to Canada with her captain. It's not a very lively prospect fot the youngest sister, Penelope. She's had such a good time during the War with all those young officers. I know she had to work hard, and the VADs did most of the unpleasant chores, but they were all young together, and had time for fun. Penelope is not like her sisters. More like her father in a way, though she hasn't his looks. Only Charles has his father's features.'

'Yes, Charles is an 'andsome lad. You must be very proud of 'im, love.'

'Proud and sad, Rube. At one time he seemed to prefer Russets to Marston Park, but not any more. I've not seen him since Carrie's wedding. When he does come he seems restless, and he makes all manner of excuses to get away. They are two of a kind, Charles and Penelope, yet only half brother and sister with two different mothers – one upper class, and one working class. Charles pretends not to mind being a bastard, but I'm beginning to think he *does* mind. What a rod I made for my own back Rubė, that Michaelmas Day, when I allowed the squire to take me to bed. You see, I didn't realise he was just using me to carry the son he wanted so desperately. I thought he liked me for myself. It was humiliating when I discovered the truth. And I would have enjoyed being his mistress, for I'm a hot-blooded woman. It's different with you, Rube, for you never wanted any other man but Tom. Sometimes my body so yearns for sex I have to get up and go down to the kitchen and make a cup of tea. And I don't want to lie with just any man, Rube, only the one man I can't have.' She laughed mockingly at her own foolishness, and her blue eyes were sad.

Ruby looked at her twin sister with fresh understanding and affection. 'I'll put on the kettle, love. Take off your 'at and coat. We don't often get a chance for a chat these days, not private like, and there won't be no chance at Christmas. You might 'ave an idea where I could look for another job, for I do declare I be proper flummoxed.'

Sir Neville insisted on escorting his family to church on Christmas morning. It was traditional, and he was still traditionally minded. The upper class had a duty and an obligation to show themselves at church on three special religious festivals during the year – Easter, Harvest Thanksgiving and Christmas. For the rest of the year it was a matter of convenience. The gentry were often away in their other establishments, and excuses were made for them. The war had not prevented Sir Neville from adhering to this obligation, and although he would have preferred to spend Christmas in the company of the current favourite – a lovely young stage actress who was expected to equal the fabulous Siddons, he was determined to do his duty. They walked to church across the Park, after Hetty had cooked and served a breakfast of bacon, eggs, kidneys and mushrooms.

It was a step down the ladder for Hetty O'Brien, and she was not at all pleased to accept the post of cook-housekeeper-parlourmaid to the Franklin family after many years of good service and steady promotion. Before the War that changed all their lives, Hetty had been enjoying the prestige and privileges of housekeeper at

Marston Park. She bullied the one young housemaid into a semblance of pre-War efficiency. She was also training her to wait at table, and the poor child would be expected to change her cap and apron a dozen times a day during this short festive season.

Charles was pushing Freddie in his wheelchair, Cynthia and Penelope hanging on their father's arms, Sylvia on the arm of her Canadian captain. It was a crisp, sparkling day, and they stepped out briskly. The walk to and from church would give them an appetite for the dinner that Hetty was preparing, with the help of the young maid.

Covered in a hessian apron, she was busy at the sink with the vegetables. When she had finished the kitchen chores, she would discard the hessian apron and hurry upstairs to make beds and tidy bedrooms. The chickens had been plucked by Tom at the crack of dawn, and Carrie had driven over in the milk float to deliver them to Hetty, together with brussels sprouts, milk, cream, eggs, butter and cheese. She had also delivered a similar order to the cottage on the estate, for Mrs Wellington had a large family to cater for this Christmas. Her eldest daughter, Cecily, had married the American doctor and they were spending the holiday with the rest of the family. The grandson, Richard, was home on his Christmas vacation. With her widowed daughter, Marion, and the two girls, the cottage was bursting at the seams. But Eleanor Wellington found it a challenge, and she had everything organised, down to the last red berry on the holly the children had gathered with Carrie's help in the wood at Russets. Marion had been instructed to stop mooning about the place and to assist the overworked housekeeper.

'We don't want her walking out on Christmas Eve, and she might well do so, since she is only staying over

Christmas to oblige me,' her mother pointed out reasonably. It was only a small establishment now, but the ex-parson's wife had not lost her capability. She longed to be back at The Parsonage at this festive season of the year, and she had never quite adjusted to taking a minor role in parish affairs, or a back seat in church. The Parsonage pew was occupied only by the parson's wife these days, since they had no children. The parson, who was once the curate, suffered from a swelled head, and a poor delivery. His sermons weren't a patch on Archibald's, Eleanor Wellington insisted. But what could you expect from the son of a grocer?

The two families met up in the Park, and the two girls soon lost their shyness of Sir Neville, took the hands of Miss Cynthia and Miss Penelope, and chatted excitedly about their Christmas tree and the presents waiting to be unwrapped after dinner. Richard was a tall, serious boy, wearing spectacles, and his mother leaned on his arm with possessive pride in her clever son. She had missed so much of his early years by living in the Congo, and she would try to make amends by spoiling Richard from henceforth. His sisters found him poor company, and they stared at the handsome Charles with undisguised admiration as he manfully pushed Mr Freddie in his wheelchair.

Agnes decided there and then to marry Charles, and Harriet was so accustomed to her sister's domination – Agnes was like grandmother – she merely sighed and decided to be an old maid.

On this first Christmas after the War, the church was crowded, but many of the women were wearing widows' weeds, and the number of male members of the congregation had noticeably diminished. Only the disabled, the elderly, and the teenage boys were left. Yet the spirit of Christmas had not been lost. The children kept it alive, and for their sakes it would be a happy day. The choir boys looked angelic in their clean starched surplices, the carols soared towards Heaven, the holly and ivy draped the window sills, the pulpit, the font, and the choir stalls. A splendid Christmas tree, ablaze with candles, welcomed the worshippers in the porch. Nothing had changed.

Marion caught her breath and clutched Richard's arm. Last Christmas she had her darling Malcolm. She could not sing the familiar carols. She was too choked. Last Christmas they were wearing cotton frocks and straw hats, and surrounded by shining ebony faces. Last Christmas they had a real baby in the crib. He was black. Malcolm had been positively argumentative on the matter. Who had the authority to swear that Baby Jesus was white? Certainly not a missionary-teacher in the Congo!

With Christmas dinner successfully accomplished and the presents distributed, Eleanor Wellington, who never tired, and had never been known to take forty winks in the afternoon, rallied the family for a brisk walk across the Park, to get an appetite for tea. To appease her two young grand-daughters, who pleaded to stay at home to play with the presents they had received, she allowed them to walk in the direction of Russets. They raced on ahead with the little dog, while the rest of the family followed more sedately.

The family at Russets, drowsing quietly in the warm parlour – this being one of the few days in the year when the parlour was used – were suddenly aware of excited voices in the yard, and Lucy hurried out to welcome the visitors.

'We have come to wish you all a happy Christmas, Mrs Blunt, and to say thank you for the lovely sledge Tom has made for us,' Agnes chirped happily.

Tom had joined his mother in the yard, and the children flung themselves on him with hugs and kisses.

'Will it snow today?' Agnes demanded.

'No sign of it yet,' he told her.

'We want to use it, don't we, Harriet?'

'Yes, we do,' the younger child agreed.

'It's the best present we've ever had in our whole lives,' Agnes insisted.

'Yes, the very best,' Harriet echoed.

By that time, the grown-ups had joined them, and Christmas greetings were exchanged. An amused glance passed between their Aunt Cecily and her new husband since they had spent hours tramping round the London stores and money they could ill afford on dolls for the girls. Toys had practically disappeared from the shops during the War years. There was a time when Cecily would have been annoyed to have her gifts overlooked, but the married state had mellowed her. They were obviously a devoted couple, and Cecily glowed with health and happiness, in complete contrast to her sister Marion – a pale, silent ghost of her former self.

'Won't you come in and have a glass of wine?' Lucy invited, hospitably.

'No, thank you. We have promised our housekeeper to be back for tea at 4.30, so we mustn't keep her waiting. You see, Mrs Blunt, we are being a little bullied this Christmas, since she has already given notice to leave.'

Lucy thought it would have helped the situation if the housekeeper had been allowed to go off duty after she had finished cooking the Christmas dinner. Even with a little help with the washing up it must have been a major operation in a small kitchen. Surely they could have managed to get their own tea, and that poor overworked woman could have retired to her own sitting-room and fireside at the top of the house? But the ex-parson's wife was accustomed to good service, and still expected it. Lucy's reactions were quick, as always.

'Are you looking for another housekeeper, Mrs Wellington?' she asked.

'Indeed I am. I have advertised in the parish magazine, but not a single person has applied for the post. It's a sad state of affairs, Mrs Blunt, with servants so reluctant to take up their duties again. They have been allowed too much freedom during the War, and seem to prefer anything but domestic work. At one time I could pick and choose from half a dozen applicants. Alas, those days are past.' She sighed, and sent Richard to collect his sisters who had disappeared with Tom.

'Do you remember Ruby Simmons?'

The question surprised her. 'Of course I remember her. She came to The Parsonage to take over the kitchen when Cook died so suddenly. She was quick to learn our ways though her cooking was not up to the standards to which we had been accustomed. She did her best. Why do you ask? Ruby is your sister, is she not?'

'Yes, my twin. She is staying with us for Christmas. Her late employer recently died, so she is looking for another post.'

'The wheelwright? Of course. But how stupid of me. I should have made it my business to call on her and offer her the post.'

'Would you like to see her?'

'Indeed I should.'

When her sister appeared in answer to Lucy's call, she was flushed and sleepy from sitting over the fire, but she quickly rallied when the situation was explained, and accepted the post without a second's hesitation. After all, she knew from past experience that Mrs Wellington was a fair mistress for all her sharp tongue and bossy ways. 'The devil you know is better than the devil you don't know,' she would insist when Carrie had her doubts.

'Thank you, Ma'am. I shall be pleased to accept the

post, if you don't mind waiting a week or two. I can't just walk out on the muddle at Mr Carter's place. It wouldn't be fair to Martha, for she's been a good friend to me.'

'That would be quite agreeable, Ruby. Just send a message when you are ready, and I will come along to collect you in the trap.'

'Thank you, Ma'am.'

'Well, that's settled. How fortunate that we happened to walk this way or I should have missed you, and you would have been promised elsewhere.'

Ruby agreed, with a secret little smile on her lips. Times had indeed changed if the mistress was prepared to collect a servant and her baggage. Before the War it was customary to borrow a hand-cart, or wait for the carrier no matter the miles to be covered.

When the family had departed, Lucy turned to her sister, to ask, anxiously, 'You didn't mind, Rube? I don't want you to think I was interfering.'

'You were doing me a favour, love. Why, I shall be almost next door. I feel proper pleased to get it settled.'

It was time for milking, and Carrie went off with Tom to the cowshed. Albert had curled up on the couch after the heavy meal, and fallen asleep. Katie had been invited to tea at a neighbouring farm, where another young servant girl from the Orphanage was feeling homesick. Though how anybody in their right mind could feel homesick for the Orphanage, Lucy failed to understand.

'They give us a luverly time at Christmas Day, Ma'am. It were the best day in all the year. We was allowed to eat till we was fit to bust, and we all 'ad a present off the tree. It were something to wear, like a new pinafore or a pair of stockings,' Katie had explained. She wasn't homesick, though she did miss the company of the other children. She was lucky to have such a kind mistress and such a nice place. If it wasn't for Mister Albert, it would be even nicer. But there was always something to put up with in service, they had been warned before they were sent out into the world, at the age of thirteen. If it wasn't the master it would be one of the sons.

So she put up with Mr Albert taking liberties when he got her alone in the scullery. He liked to lift her long skirts and push his hand up her drawers.

'Open your legs, blast you!' he would growl.

When her thighs were wet he seemed satisfied, and dried his hands on her apron. Man were funny creatures.

Chapter 5

Tom and Carrie were glad to get away on their own for an hour or so, and the milking provided the only opportunity. Lucy was doing her best. The Christmas dinner had been up to its usual high standard, since they were not dependent on shops, and were practically self-supporting. But it was a strained atmosphere, and nobody really cared for the stuffy, over-crowded parlour. Tomorrow they would be back in the kitchen. Tom would walk to the village to watch the gathering of the traditional Boxing Day Meet in the forecourt of 'The Three Nuns'. Only a few of the original enthusiasts would be mounted this year, but it would still attract a crowd of villagers. Sir Neville would be there. He had never missed a meet since he was mounted on his first pony at the age of four.

Accompanied by Charles and Penelope on hired hacks, they would make a handsome trio. Sylvia and her captain, also on hired hacks, would be making their last public appearance before leaving for Canada. Cynthia would be a spectator with Freddie in his wheelchair. He had not managed to persuade her that he could be left at Russets for the day. Cynthia was a very determined young woman!

So Tom would meet up with them and push the wheelchair across the Park. They would enjoy a glass of sherry with the rest of the party before the long walk back. Carrie would be watching wistfully from a bedroom window as Tom walked away with Agnes and Harriet skipping along beside him. Why couldn't she accompany them? She knew why. Albert's jealousy. Whatever the cost to her own feelings, Albert must not not be thwarted in any way. They all feared his violent temper, and the disturbing influence that hung like a threatening cloud over the homestead that once had been such a pleasant peaceful place. Of course they had had their troubles. What family ever escaped? Joy and sorrow, smiles and tears. Life was a lottery. There was the tragedy on that bright Summer day when a devoted husband and father fell off the hay-wagon and broke his neck. And there was another kind of trouble the following year when a widowed mother confessed to her three astonished sons that she was carrying Sir Neville's child in her womb. Charles was the cuckoo in the nest. Sir Neville had claimed his son at the age of seven for the start of that traditional system of upper-class education as firmly established as the laws of the Medes and Persians. Lucy had accepted the ultimatum with the same fortitude that she had accepted Bert's tragic death.

From the age of seven Charles was a visitor to Russets. It was not his permanent home and he could not be blamed for a situation in which he was obliged to conform to rules at Marston Park and to please himself at Russets. To lose her eldest son, Harry, was another cruel blow for Lucy. He was her right-hand man after his father's death – a farmer in his very bones, who loved the land and followed in the steps of his forebears with the same sturdy independence. Yet he had to die in his splendid young manhood, like thousands of others, and lie alone in foreign soil.

Now it was Albert, and Lucy could see no end to his disturbing influence. She was already suffering the pangs of self-reproach in her treatment of Tom and Carrie. She was not being fair. To sacrifice two young lives for the sake of one had not solved the problem but only increased the tension. She had long since realised her mistake. Tom and Carrie should have been sent away to make their own life together. They could have emigrated to New Zealand or Australia. She had been selfish. Because she had lost Harry, she could not bear to lose Tom, and Tom would never go away and leave Carrie to face the future alone. The eternal triangle. How would it end?

She was afraid for these two who loved each other and had to steal a kiss furtively, as though they were ashamed. She had seen them in the cowshed, wrapped in a close embrace. She had seen Tom sneak into the wood, where Carrie and the children were gathering the holly and ivy for Christmas decorations, and watched the children running back across the field without Carrie.

It was dangerous. One day they would be discovered. One day their feelings would be too strong to control, and they would lie together and there would be another little cuckoo in the nest.

But now it was Winter, and work to be done seven days a week. There was Spring, Summer and Autumn to follow, and Nature did not wait for humans to be ready, but demanded obedience, duty and service in due season. Lucy had married a farmer at the age of sixteen. Whatever the claims of the family, the land had top priority.

Two weeks later, Ruby stood waiting to be collected by her new mistress. Looking about the deserted house and workshop, and the empty yard, she shivered at the desolation and tears flooded her eyes. Would she ever know the joy and security of her own home again, as she had once known it in Richmond Row, that despised slum? Of course she was grateful to be offered another post, and she had seen the two attic rooms. Comfortably furnished and a nice little retreat for a cook-housekeeper when her work was finished.

It had been decided that she would be paid the same wage that she had been earning at the wheelwright's. Mrs Wellington had decided and Ruby had accepted with nothing more than a sigh of resignation. She was too tired to argue. What did it matter? Living so far from the village shops, she would not be tempted to spend. She would have a roof over her head, three good meals a day, and as many cups of tea as she could drink. Could any working-class widow expect more at middle age? Then she remembered that her sister and her daughter would welcome her at Russets on Sunday afternoons. She would be free after she had washed up, set the tea trolley, and prepared a cold supper for the family. With luck, and a little help from Miss Marion, she could be out of the house soon after 2.30, and Tom would walk back with her at 10 o'clock. She would be nicely settled before the worst of the Winter weather. At 4 o'clock in the afternoon it was already dusk, and her new mistress would have a lantern on the trap.

A short dumpy figure was hurrying across the yard, and Ruby rubbed a hand across her wet eyes and called out cheerfully, 'Martha! What are you doing out at this time of day? You should be indoors getting tea for your man.'

'I came to wish you well in your new post, dear, and to bring you the good wishes of Andrew and Philip.'

'Thank you, love. That were a kind thought. I were feeling a bit sorry for meself, and that don't get you nowhere, do it?'

'It's going to be all right. With Russets so near you won't be lonely, and we all know Mrs Wellington's bark is worse than her bite. But we mustn't lose touch. We have our bicycles and we can often ride your way on a Sunday afternoon, weather permitting. Will your sister mind if we turn up at Russets?'

'She would be ever so pleased to see you, love. It's an open 'ouse, and Luce makes everybody welcome.'

The clip-clop of the mare's hooves reminded the two women that the time had come to close one chapter and start on another.

'Are you ready, Ruby?' an authoritative voice called from the trap as it rattled over the cobbled yard.

'Ready, Ma'am.'

'Who is that with you?'

'My friend, Martha Robinson, the schoolmaster's wife.'

'Ah yes, and the daughter of your late employer.'

They exchanged greetings, then Martha helped Ruby to lift the tin trunk into the trap, kissed her warmly, and watched her drive away. Yes, it was the end of an era, and she, too, felt the desolation, and hurried back to the School House to put on the kettle in her own warm kitchen.

'I've just seen Ruby off, and my heart ached for her. I think she had been crying,' she told Andrew, when he joined her in the kitchen and she handed him a cup of tea. He made no answer, and she asked anxiously, 'Are you not feeling well, dear?'

'Just tired.'

She pushed him gently on to a chair, knelt down to take off his shoes, and put on his slippers. He smiled his thanks, and she looked up at him with warm affection. She would fuss over him, as she fussed over Philip, and he reminded himself of the strange twist of fate that had taken Martha's first husband and left her free to marry again, yet they had waited almost two years. He was not a demonstrative man, or an impulsive one, and Martha had waited to be asked. After that short, tragic interlude with Parson Wellington's invalid daughter, Andrew Robinson had known a period when a guilty conscience gave him no peace. He blamed himself for Irene's infatuation. He should not have encouraged it in her precarious state of health. But she had always been spoilt from a small child when tuberculosis was diagnosed, and she had set her heart on a normal sexual relationship, and Andrew, knowing she was doomed to die young, could not refuse her. They had intercourse in the Summer house one Sunday afternoon. The following day she died. He still laid flowers on her grave in the churchyard, but Martha asked no questions.

Her marriage to Andrew made few demands. They respected each other's privacy, and shared the common interest of the school. Even now, Martha sometimes wondered whether her quiet, reserved husband was entirely severed from that umbilical cord. He was a man of forty when his mother died, and he moved to Fairfields to take up the post of schoolmaster at the village school. Perhaps there is a little of the child in every man.

'I have been thinking about Easter, dear. Could we not get away for a few days? We have our bicycles. We could get as far as Canterbury. I have always wanted to see the cathedral, and Philip would benefit by the experience. What do you say?' She was all woman, yet she had a childish pleasure in simple things.

'As you please, my dear,' he agreed, affably.

'Thank you, Andrew.' She touched his cheek with her lips, and went to the door to welcome her son home from Grammar School. He had grown as tall as his step-father. He was cold and hungry, and he crouched over the fire with a mug of tea, warming his hands. This was her family. She loved them both and she had never seen a sign of jealousy.

'I got full marks for maths today, Sir,' Philip was saying.

'Splendid – but you were going to call me "Uncle" if I remember rightly?'

'Sorry, Sir – I mean Uncle.' They all laughed.

'What's your name?' Agnes demanded of the new cook-housekeeper.

'Ruby, Miss.'

'I'm Agnes, and this is my sister Harriet.'

'Pleased to meet you, Miss.'

'Are you going to live with us for always?'

'I hope so, Miss.'

'Grandmother will be pleased. She doesn't like changes, does she Harriet?'

'No, she doesn't,' Harriet agreed.

'We are going to boarding school next week. Isn't it exciting? I can hardly wait. Harriet doesn't want to go. She wants to stay here and have Mummy teach us, like she did when we lived at the Mission with Daddy. Grandmother says the time hasd come to mix with other girls, *white* girls. You see, all the children were black at the Mission. Do you know any black children, Ruby?'

Ruby shook her head. What a chatterbox!

'Daddy told us they were all God's children. We had a black baby Jesus in the crib for Christmas. A *real* baby, wasn't it, Harriet?'

'It was sweet, and it didn't cry once.'

The two girls were much alike. They had the same small features, straight lank hair and grey eyes. The difference in their mentality could be read in their eyes. Agnes faced the world with bravado, and an avid curiosity, while

Harriet shrank from it.

'Grandmother says we have to leave Susy at home. They don't allow dogs at boarding school,' Agnes explained.

'I don't want to go. I don't want to leave Susy,' Harriet sniffed, miserably.

'Don't be a baby, Harry. You promised Daddy to be brave before he went to Heaven.'

'I know I did, but that was a long time ago. I didn't know about boarding school, and I didn't know about Tom and Carrie. They're my best friends. Oh, Angie, why must we go away? I like it here.'

It was a long speech for Harriet, who seldom got a word in edgeways, and was completely overshadowed by her sister's forceful personality – as Marion was overshadowed by her mother. Yet it was not always so, for Marion had been the most independent of the three sisters, with a strong will of her own, encouraged by her father. Parson Wellington had spoiled her, his favourite daughter, and when she fell in love with the young Scottish missionary-teacher, and he gave his blessing to their marriage, he knew they would be parted for five years, possibly for ever.

It hadn't taken Ruby more than a few minutes to recognise a broken heart, and she wished she could comfort the young widow with her own personal recipe for grief. Hard work, and loving concern for the living. That was her recipe. But a servant had little real contact with her employers. The War had not changed that fundamental issue. She had met all the family when her new mistress had taken her by the arm, thrown open the drawing-room door and announced triumphantly, 'Here she is! I told you she would not let us down!'

Ruby smiled. She was a little embarrassed by the introduction, and surprised when the two male members in the family group stood up and gave her a stiff little bow of recognition. 'Such luverly manners,' she would tell her sister on Sunday afternoon.

'It comes natural, Rube, with the upper class. Our menfolk would feel foolish. Can you imagine your Tom and my Bert standing up for *us* when we entered a room?'

They giggled at such an improbable situation.

'My Tom 'ad nice manners. 'E wasn't ever rude, and 'e never used a swear word,' Ruby insisted, for she would not have Tom's memory belittled.

'My Bert wasn't all that *polite*, and he often buggered me and the boys, if you can call that swearing. But we was lucky, you and me, Rube. How many widows can boast that their husbands never looked at another woman in all their married lives? *And* they gave us three sons,' she added as an afterthought.

The cottage was a hive of feverish activity for several days, after Ruby's arrival, with three trunks to be packed and three tuck-boxes to be filled, and Grandmother directing operations like a field marshal. There were tears from Harriet, excited impatience from Agnes, and superior shrugs from Richard. The dog yapped at the tin trunks, and Marion hung around her adored son with helpful suggestions that were either unsuitable or ridiculous.

'Mother, I've *told* you. I can't wear that muffler you knitted. I should feel a fool. The fellows would hoot with laughter. I should never live it down.'

'Very well, darling. But you will wrap up warmly on the playing field, won't you? The weather is so treacherous at this time of the year.'

'Yes, Mother,' Richard agreed, for it seemed the only way to appease her. Wrap up for rugger? What a fantastic notion!

It had been a worrying vacation, with his mother so

clinging and possessive, and his two young sisters feeling neglected and jealous. It was not his fault that Mother was trying to make up to him for all the lost years. As though it were possible. Grandmother knew it was not possible, but Grandmother was a sensible person. It would be a relief to get away. Families were such a bore.

Then they were gone, Harriet hugging her teddy bear.

'The girls will laugh at you,' scoffed Agnes.

'I don't care!' wailed the poor child – and ran to Ruby for a warm, consoling kiss.

'What's the matter, Penny? Why are you crying?' Charles asked, solicitously. His youngest half-sister was not given to tears as a rule. She was light-hearted and frivolous. He had been mooching about the place all afternoon, looking for some fresh diversion, and wishing it was time to go back to school. The Christmas vacation was dragging to a close, with Father back in London, Cynthia seeing Freddie settled at Roehampton, and Sylvia on her way to Canada with her husband. The main part of the house echoed to the clatter of workmen, busy on the conversion of a military hospital to a Holiday Home for poor children.

But Charles was not interested in the scheme, and bored with his own company. It was Hetty's free afternoon, and she had left soon after lunch to walk to the village and catch a bus to Tunbridge Wells.

He found Penny lying face down on her bed, weeping disconsolately.

'Leave me alone!' she shrugged off his hand and went on crying.

He turned her over and dried her face with rough concern, for he was fond of Penny. 'You may as well tell me what's wrong, darling, for I'm not leaving this room till you do,' he threatened.

'I'm so *miserable*!' she wailed. 'Everybody's gone and there's absolutely nothing to do. I wish I were dead!'

He pulled her into his arms. She weighed no more than seven stone because she ate sparingly and avoided fattening foods. Even at Christmas she had not been tempted to indulge in the normal practice of over-eating. Her head sank to his shoulder, and he felt very manly sitting there with a girl in his arms. It was not the first time. He liked girls. In fact, he liked everybody. Penny was wearing one of her new fashionable dresses that fitted her like a glove. He could feel the shape of her breasts and thighs, and he wondered if she wore any underclothes. It was warm in the bedroom. All the rooms in the flat had radiators, and the sitting-room also had a coal fire. It was really very comfortable, but comfort at their age was not the most important factor. They both saw life as a game to be played with careless disregard of the rules.

'Why do you stay here, darling? Why not go to London? I shall be gone in a few days. You can't stay here alone,' he reminded her, kindly.

'I don't know anybody in London, not since the War.'

'There's Aunt Augusta, Father's younger sister.'

'Younger? She must be nearly in her dotage. Aunt Augusta is fifty if she's a day.'

'But she does live in Mayfair, and she's not such a bad old geyser. I stayed there one Easter Vac, and she made a great fuss of me.'

'That's no recommendation. Everyone makes a fuss of you, even an elderly aunt. Hasn't anyone ever told you, Charles, that you could charm a bird off a bough?'

'No.'

'Well, I'm telling you now.'

'Darling, don't be silly.'

'It's not being silly. You're a born charmer, like Papa.

We girls haven't got it, and it can't be cultivated. I could almost wish I were not your sister.'

'*Half*-sister. What does it signify?'

'We *are* related.'

'Funny little Penny.' He kissed her mouth. It was not a brotherly kiss.

'Who taught you to kiss that way?' she demanded, opening her eyes. Her lashes were still wet. She had a wide-eyed innocence that was totally deceptive. Penny was not innocent. The War had changed all that. Being a VAD in a military hospital had completed her education.

'Kiss me again,' she said, and he kissed her again, and found her lips parted. Her tongue played with his own tongue with a tormenting sensuality that was new to his limited experience. He was a little afraid where it might lead. Yet she must have known that two exploring tongues could be dangerous. He tried to break away, but she pulled his face down closer, and he stopped worrying. He could feel the trembling of her slight body. Had she expected he would make love to her? He knew already that it was too late to stop. They were two of a kind, easily susceptible to sex, taking no thought for the morrow. This was not love. This was an urgent demanding sensation that had to be satisfied. Intercourse was nothing more than a natural climax of two young healthy creatures impatient for a new experience. There was no tenderness, but they didn't expect it. They were laughing when it was over. It was naughty, but it was fun! And it was an answer to boredom.

She didn't write to Aunt Augusta. She had a better idea, after Charles had gone away. She remembered that two of the VADs had moved back to London and were sharing a flat in the Edgware Road. They had exchanged cards at Christmas. She had no idea whether they would care to share with a third party. 'Two's company, three's none.' But it was worth a try. They could only refuse. After all, she could pay her way. She had a good allowance from Papa, and she would soon find a job.

She addressed the letter to Betty, the younger of the two girls, nearer her own age. She hadn't enjoyed a close friendship with any of the nurses because she preferred the company of men, and could pick and choose. When Betty wrote back agreeing to the proposal providing she took her share of the chores, including the cooking, Penny was thrilled, and lost no time in piling her clothes on the bed.

Hetty was worried. She could foresee a time when her services would no longer be required, and it was a comfortable post. It had taken a little time to adapt to such a small establishment, but it was no use wishing to put back the clock. The good old days of the servants' hall, and her own status in the servants' hierarchy were gone for ever. This was a new era.

'When can I expect you back, Miss Penelope?' she asked, anxiously, as she helped her to pack.

'I'm not sure, Hetty, but I'll let you know when to expect me and I'll leave you my address.'

'Thank you, Miss.'

'My sister will probably spend more time here when she has finished her work at the hospital, later in the year, and Papa will be here for Easter to meet Master Charles.'

Hetty sighed with relief. This was her home, and domestic service her life's work. She had few friends, and no intention of getting married. Marriage was purgatory for the working-class woman. She remembered all too vividly the poverty and the drudgery her own mother had suffered, with a husband who spent half his wages on drink every Saturday night, then had his way with his wife's weary, unprotesting body. Sex was something degrading and disgusting in that hovel they called home, and Hetty had no use for it. She liked her comfort. She liked order and cleanliness. She had a certain pride and respect in her own virginity. Hetty O'Brien was no fool!

Joan and Betty were working as salesgirls at Selfridges. They had no boy-friends, but enjoyed a freedom and independence they would never have enjoyed had they lived at home. The flat was a poky little place on the attic floor of a terrace house, crowded with second-hand furniture the landlady had picked up in the street markets. But the girls were inordinately proud of it, and it suited their mentality. The War years at Marston Park had not changed their fundamental attitude to life. They knew what they wanted – to marry a decent chap with a regular job in civvy street – a nice little house, near the shops – two children, a boy and a girl. Before the War, they might have achieved such a modest ambition, but it was doubtful if they would do so now. Men between the ages of twenty and forty were scarce and the competition was keen. At the Saturday night hops, there were a dozen girls to every man, so the girls danced together. To have an escort to the pictures was a rare occurrence now that soldiers and sailors no longer flocked to London for their home leaves. Betty and Joan had had ample opportunity to find husbands during the War, for they spent all their free time in London. But somehow they hadn't fancied any of the men so free with their favours, so eager to jump into bed. They were Londoners born and bred, and their working-class background had not prepared them for the opulence of Marston Park. As for the patients – all officers, but not all gentlemen – the two girls were not at ease with such superior escorts.

So Penny found herself a square peg in a round hole, for she hadn't Cynthia's capacity for adapting to a new environment so alien to the one in which she had spent all her early years. When she visited the hospital in which her elder sister had been working for some years, she was horrified.

'I could get you a job here, Penny, but you would have to be resident,' Cynthia suggested.

Penny shuddered. 'No thank you, darling. I'm in no hurry. I should like to enjoy myself for a few weeks. It's such a novelty. I know I shall adore living in London.' The West End was a fascinating place for a young woman with money to spend, and all the time in the world to savour its delights. She could eat a snack lunch at the counter of one of the new buffet bars, and afternoon tea in the lounge of a popular hotel in Piccadilly. It was all great fun!

But her heart sank as she climbed the stairs to thc poky little flat in the early evening, with the shopping she had collected. It was so sordid. With her usual light-hearted approach to any situation she had accepted the role of cook, and the girls expected a meal to be prepared on their return from work. Penny was too proud to confess the only culinary art she possessed was boiling eggs and making tea and coffee – one of her duties as a VAD at Marston Park!

'What's this?' Joan had demanded, truculently, that first evening when presented with a burnt offering, surrounded by half-cooked potatoes and a vegetable she failed to recognise.

'Lamb chops. I do apologise. I'm afraid they are a little overdone, but the gas oven was too high.' Penny's face was scarlet. It was her first encounter with a gas oven.

The tiny kitchen was cluttered with dirty dishes. She had no method, and the result was disastrous. How could she have used so many pots and pans to cook such a simple meal? Betty was wondering, but she kept her mouth shut.

'A little overdone,' sneered Joan, who had not wanted to share the flat with a third party, and was determined to prove it was a mistake. 'What's this?' She was jabbing at a soggy looking mess that looked like squashed leeks but had no smell.

'Endive,' Penny pronounced it the French way.

'Never heard of it,' snapped Joan, irritably.

'Hetty calls it chicory. We often have it at home, but I was not sure how to cook it. I must ask Hetty.'

'I shouldn't bother. We'd rather have cabbage, anyway.'

Penny sighed. How does one cook cabbage? 'There was such a fascinating variety of vegetables and fruit on the stalls in the street market in Soho. I bought a melon as well as apples, bananas and grapes. By the way, I talked to a man on the cheap-jack stall, or rather he talked to me. Talk about the gift of the gab! He said his name was Lennie O'Brien and asked me to give his love to his sister, Hetty. He hadn't seen her since before the War. I'm not surprised. He looked like a gypsy and was very cheeky He said he remembered me from the time when all the family from Marston Park attended the village church. He would hold the carriage horses while the coachman had a pint of beer in "The Three Nuns". He was paid sixpence. It was a lot of money in those days.'

Joan was not listening. She had been on her feet all day, and she was not interested in the doings of the gentry before the War. Snobs! The whole lot of them, including Penelope Franklin! Betty was eating the unappetising food without comment. She knew it had been a mistake to assume that because they had all worked as equals during the War, they could live together as equals now the fighting was over. Penny was upper class. It was not her fault that she couldn't climb down to their level any more than they could climb up to hers. Betty was a good-tempered young woman, however, and had accepted the fact that Sir Neville Franklin's daughter had never cooked a meal in her life quite cheerfully.

'Aren't you eating, Penny?' she asked kindly.

'I ate at midday, and I had a good tea,' she explained. She really was sorry for making such a mess of the meal, but she had apologised. She also realised it had been a mistake. She would have to move, but where? Perhaps she could use the rooms in Soho while Freddie was at Roehampton? She would phone Cynthia at the hospital and they could meet and talk it over.

'No pudding?' Joan interrupted her thoughts.

'There's fresh fruit and cheese,' Penny pointed out as she cleared the plates and stacked them in the sink.

'No thanks.' Joan liked her pudding. They had a choice of several in the staff canteen. They ate well and cheaply at midday, so it was not important this evening meal. But if Penny stayed, she must pull her weight. It was only fair.

Betty helped with the washing up while Joan smoked a cigarette, then both girls ran downstairs to wash in the bathroom they shared with the tenants on the second floor. Joan was in a better mood, her tiredness forgotten. They were going to see a film at the local cinema, where they paid ninepence for a seat in the stalls. They could afford to go twice a week, and they followed the fortunes of their favourite screen idols. They did not invite Penny, and she was too proud to ask. She would read, she told herself. She had bought several second-hand books from a stall in the market, including *Wuthering Heights*. She lit a cigarette and settled down in a creaky wicker chair and turned over the pages, her mind wandering. She found her new surroundings sordid and depressing. The acrid smell of the burned chops still clung to the small crowded rooms. The gas-fire flickered and hummed. She shuddered involuntarily. It seemed she would always be shuddering over one thing or another if she stayed here. Her spirits sank to zero. Papa would have a fit if he could see her now. Dear Papa. It was not often that she felt sentimental over Papa. He hadn't played a very important role in their lives. But tonight she would have welcomed a glimpse of that handsome, autocratic face. She supposed Charles's idea was probably the best – to get in touch with Aunt Augusta.

She sighed and closed the book. She would make a cup of tea and go to bed early. Tomorrow was another day. She would telephone Cynthia. Her elder sister was a sensible person, these days. She had made a success of her marriage, and broken down the barriers of class distinction. Cynthia lived and worked among the working class, and had never been so determined. Her whole personality had changed since she married Freddie.

In the tiny room that had once been the boxroom when the house was privately owned, Penny lay awake, listening to the unfamiliar rattle of the traffic on the Edgware Road. She had tossed her fur coat over the thin blankets, but she was still cold, and she felt peculiar.

She went on feeling peculiar for several weeks, and she couldn't blame the smell of cabbage or the greasy sink, or the penetrating stench of a blocked lavatory, for she had finished with all that and now lived in the furnished rooms in Soho. Cynthia had listened sympathetically, then reminded her young sister they were not allowed to accept private calls at the hospital.

'Meet me at the ABC in Oxford Street at 3 o'clock. We can talk there – and don't worry, darling,' she added, comfortingly, before she hung up the receiver.

What was the ABC Penny had wondered? – and was surprised to find it was a tea-shop.

'I'm on night duty and not supposed to be out, but

nobody checks on me now I'm a senior,' Cynthia explained. Staff nurses were allowed to live out, so she was using the rooms in Soho. Freddie had been paying the rent during the War years, and the landlady, who lived in the basement, kept the rooms clean. They were not much bigger than the rooms in Edgware Road, but surprisingly different. Cynthia had gradually discarded the old furniture, and re-furnished with the bare minimu, so the rooms were no longer cluttered. She had chosen carefully from second-hand dealers. It had given her an absorbing interest during the War, when Freddie was away. As each room became empty of furniture, she decorated and discovered she had quite a flair for paper-hanging and painting. The threadbare mats were discarded, and the floorboards stained. With a generous cheque from Papa, she bought rugs and curtain material. The transformation had amazed Freddie, and dclighted the landlady who had never know a tenant to actually improve the place. She thought Mrs Simmons was a lovely lady, and saw no reason why her sister should not share the flat.

'You'll be company for one another, duckie, while your poor 'usband is 'aving that new leg fitted at Roe'ampton,' she panted, after climbing the basement stairs. With her hair in curlers, her feet in carpet slippers, and a grubby apron wrapped about her ample figure, she was not a very good advertisement for her lodging house, but Cynthia was not concerned for her appearance.

'She's kind and warm-hearted, and she would do anything for Freddie. Actually, she thought it was Freddie's idea, all the renovating, when he hadn't even noticed it was so deplorably crowded and shabby. Aren't men funny? When he brought me home, after we were married, I nearly died. I was so appalled. Poor darling. I soon discovered there were more important things to worry about. I shall never forget our wedding night, Penny. We both were completely ignorant of sexual intercourse. Working in a hospital for women, the male anatomy was still clothed in mystery. I had seen Charles as a naughty little boy, running naked to the bathroom. Even that was a revelation since we had no brothers. Wasn't he a darling little boy? I do hope we can have children later, but we haven't discussed it.'

She had pulled the curtains and lit the gas fire. Now they were settled down comfortably, and she went on to talk about their wedding night – disclosures she had never shared with anyone.

'The sexual part solved itself, eventually, but that wasn't all. I discovered Freddie was desperately afraid to go back to the Front, and I had to boost his morale on our wedding night. You see, he had been promoted from the ranks, and sent to take a short course of training that hadn't really prepared him for the responsibility of leadership. Freddie is not a born leader, and he couldn't understand why his superior officer had recommended him for promotion. A subaltern had to make snap decisions that might prove fatal to the men depending on his initiative, and he was terrified of letting them down. Thank God I managed to convince him that he would not be found wanting when the time came, for we all know he nearly gave his life to rescue his sergeant – though he's rather embarrassed by the medal, poor darling.'

'Thank you for telling me about your wedding night, Cynthia. I think you were marvellous. Freddie is a very lucky man. I know he was offered the job of bailiff when he is fit enough for work, but he turned it down because Papa told me. To have a cottage on the estate and the old mare and governess cart for transport would seem an ideal job for a disabled man. Were you very disappointed?'

'Yes, but not unduly surprised, knowing how independent he can be. I could see his point. He had slogged away for years as a solicitors' clerk, passed his exams, and opened up the room on the ground floor as an office. He was barely established when War was declared, and he volunteered almost immediately. Once upon a time I might have tried persuading him to accept the bailiff's job, but not any more. I know when I'm beaten.' She smiled wryly, and changed the subject. They talked of their childhood and the good old days they had taken for granted would last for ever.

Cynthia had accepted her role as a working man's wife in the new era, but Penny knew her limitations. She hadn't the strength of character or the determination for such sacrifice. She would take what she wanted with no thought for the consequences, like Papa, when he had his way with Lucy Blunt. She was a little ashamed of that mad impulse with Charles, and wondered if he would feel embarrassed when they met again at Easter.

'Come along, I'll show you how to make an omelette. It's so simple,' Cynthia was saying, and Penny followed her to the kitchen. They had shopped in the street market, and their tastes were similar. No more cabbage!

'I shan't always be here to cook your supper, darling! So you had better take note of what I'm doing,' the elder sister teased, as she whisked the eggs and melted a small nut of butter in the frying pan. A crispy French loaf and camembert cheese completed the meal, and they carried it into the sitting-room on two separate trays. Coffee was brewing in a percolator on the gas-stove. No more 'Camp' coffee out of a bottle!

When Cynthia hurried away to catch a bus back to the hospital, and Penny found herself alone again, all the excitement and novelty of the past few hours quickly evaporated. She drank a second cup of coffee, lit a cigarette, and settled down, once again, with *Wuthering*

Heights, but soon lost interest in the surly Heathcliffe. The mushroom omelette had been delicious, and it was so easy to make, but now it lay heavy on her chest, and she felt sick.

'Damn!' she muttered, irritably, and flew downstairs.

The back scullery had been converted into a bathroom and lavatory, and here she found evidence of a man's unseen presence, in a razor and shaving soap. A well-worn dressing-gown hung behind the door. A small paraffin stove stood ready for lighting.

For her sister and her husband, these small rooms in Soho spelled Home. The brass plate on the front door would be polished again, in the not-too-distant future, and Freddie would be back in business. A working man's solicitor, he called himself, and there would be plenty of work with the trade unions.

Clutching her stomach, Penny crept upstairs. She was shivering and lonely – and she felt so peculiar.

The week before Easter, young Charles Franklin received a letter that would shape the destinies of a number of people. It was very short, and he read it three times before he had grasped its true significance.

> Dear Charles,
>
> This is going to shock you, but not half as much as it shocked me! I am going to have a baby, and you are the father. I have told Cynthia the father was one of the young American officers at the hospital, and she has accepted it, since I had a reputation for flirting. But it *was* only flirting, Charles, and I was still a virgin when we had intercourse, you and I. Nobody must ever know about *us*. Never! Never!
>
> Penny.

He was too stunned by the impact, his mind went blank. When he recovered, he began to plan what he must do. Poor little Penny. What dashed bad luck. He couldn't imagine her with a baby. He supposed she would have it adopted? Should he write back? What could he say? Supposing the letter fell into hands other than Penny's? He would never live it down. And Penny had emphasised secrecy. She would not wish him to get involved. But then he was already involved – the father! He remembered the sudden, sharp cry of pain at the moment of intercourse. So Penny had kept her virginity, and all the kissing and cuddling with the fellows was nothing more than teasing. Would it have made any difference had he known she was still a virgin? There was no time, and the impulse too strong to deny.

When he had finally convinced himself it would be a mistake to get in touch with her, and that it would be extremely embarrassing to meet again until it was all over, he began to think about the Easter vacation. There was still time to arrange to spend the vacation in London, with Gerald Levine. Gerry fancied himself as a man about Town. With a French father in the diplomatic service, and a mother who had once been acclaimed the prettiest debutante of the season, there was some justification in the claim. As for his own father expecting him at Marston Park for Easter, he could imagine his annoyance! But it was not the first time he had excused himself of recent years. Mother would be disappointed. He had only to pick up the phone to make his apologies, but was a coward. He would send a postcard and a telegram to Father, who strongly objected to postcards!

Cynthia was worried about leaving Penny on her own at the little flat in Soho, but there was no alternative, since she refused to go back to Marston Park, or to her elder sister in Norfolk. Now her off-duty days had to be shared between Freddie and Penny, and she was torn between the two.

Freddie was nicely settled at Roehampton, however, and very understanding. He had to be told about the baby, and he said he was not surprised. In all fairness, he supposed Penny had been too young to be suddenly let loose in a world of men so soon after leaving the schoolroom. Cynthia agreed. She was very conscious of her own indifference to the welfare of her two younger sisters. She had seen very little of them since she left home to start on her own nursing career. Sylvia could be trusted to behave herself. She had taken her VAD work much more seriously, and the Canadian captain had been her only escort during off-duty hours. It was just another wartime romance that followed the pattern of a thousand others – falling in love – a short engagement – marriage – and away to a life overseas. Since their Papa was still completely enslaved by the young actress, there was no need to worry him about Penny at this early stage. It still suited him to live at his London Club, and he gave little thought to his four daughters. The running of the estate could be left almost entirely to an efficient young bailiff – an ex-officer, and a gentleman. The War years had served as an enjoyable interlude, but he was not sorry to be released from the tedium of office hours. He had spoken to Cynthia on the telephone, and been told that Penny was sharing the flat in Soho. He had never seen the flat, and saw no reason to get involved in an arrangement that seemed to suit all parties. He did enquire if Penelope could manage on her allowance, however, and was assured it was quite adequate. When he had enquired after his son-in-law, and asked for news of Sylvia and Beatrice, Sir Neville felt a smug satisfaction in doing his duty, and hung up the receiver with a sense of relief that his four daughters had arranged their lives so sensibly. With three married, and the youngest in the safe custody of an elder sister, he could relax his parental authority. The important question of Charles's future still had to be decided. He was inordinately proud of his handsome son, but the boy had a strong will of his own under that charming façade. As if he hadn't recognised himself at the same age!

To find herself an expectant mother with time on her hands, in a strange environment, was a depressing state for the pleasure-seeking Penelope Franklin. She hadn't forgiven Charles for not answering her letter, for she had taken the precaution to give her address as 'Poste Restante', and had called at the post office every day for several weeks, then finally decided he was not going to reply.

Most afternoons were spent in the cinema, and she still ate a snack lunch at the counter of the buffet-bar, and her tea in the lounge of that popular hotel in Piccadilly. Like her half-brother, Charles, she could not abide her own company, and could hardly tear herself away from the scintillating atmosphere of the hotel lounge and the lobby, with its constant flow of cosmopolitan visitors, and the excited exchange of foreign tongues and gestures. Cynthia had made her promise to get back to the flat before dark, since she felt so responsible for a young sister in a district so often in the news. To be followed by an amorous Italian waiter and accosted by an elderly gentleman with a taste for attractive young women was rather frightening, but Penny kept such encounters to herself.

As the months went by and her condition became

obvious, she was no longer accosted, but regarded with interest and respect as a prospective mother. Cynthia had purchased wool and simple knitting patterns, and reminded Penny that she could start knitting for the baby, but she usually found her engrossed in a romantic novelette, and the knitting discarded when she called at the flat in the evening. Penny had no accomplishments and no feeling for the unborn child other than impatience, and a sence of injustice. Why had it happened? Why should she suffer such a harsh penalty because of a few ecstatic moments with Charles? It was not fair! Charles escaped, while she was burdened with a swelling stomach, and terrified of the mystery of childbirth.

'You mustn't worry, darling. Everything will be taken care of in the maternity ward at the hospital when your time comes,' Cynthia had assured her.

She was so kind, so sensible, but it made no difference to the unreasonable terror that swept over her whenever she sat alone on those Summer evenings, waiting for the sound of Cynthia's key in the lock. She was often disappointed, however, when some emergency at the hospital had cancelled all off-duty hours. Never in her short life had she known such desolation of spirit, or such physical discomfort – the morning sickness had passed, but now it was indigestion and swollen legs. She wept her self-pitying tears, and forgot all the early training in the nursery and the schoolroom. 'Control yourself, Miss Penelope!' But that was a long time ago, before that ghastly War had changed all their lives.

'You really should take more exercise, darling, and I don't mean on the streets. Why not take a walk in the park? It's such a lovely Summer,' Cynthia had suggested.

Was it a lovely Summer? Penny hadn't noticed. She had seen enough of parks anyway. All those boring walks with nurse, and later with a governess.

'Don't nag,' she told her elder sister, defensively.

There was no escape. Even her dreams were tortured fantasies, and she awoke with a headache and wished she were dead.

It was such a stupid thing to do – to miss a step and fall downstairs. She screamed and hit the floor and blacked out.

A cry for help from the agitated landlady sent a man hurrying to the nearest telephone, and a small crowd had collected when the ambulance arrived. She was just another casualty until her sister was notified, when she became a patient with an identity in the busy maternity department.

The baby was born within half-an-hour – a puny, wailing boy-child, thrust from his mother's womb into a cruel world at seven months, and not expected to survive.

But Penny had slipped away.

Part Two

Chapter 6

When the family vault was opened to receive its youngest daughter, the villagers stood back respectfully, remembering the elaborate funeral, with carriages and black-plumed horses, when Her Ladyship was laid to rest. This would be a simple affair in comparison, with the hearse meeting the train that conveyed the coffin, and the few mourners on the platform following in a slow procession of cars to the churchyard on the hill.

Only one daughter accompanied her father – a grave, silent figure in conventional mourning dress, lifting his silk hat to the familiar faces of the upper class, gathered in the doorway, acknowledging the rest with a stiff little bow.

Eleanor Wellington was there with her daughter, Marion, remembering the child Penelope in those early years at Marston Park. Doctor Saunders, his wife and daughter-in-law were there, and the two aged spinsters from The Grove. The schoolmaster was there with his wife and stepson. Lucy Blunt and Carrie from Russets, and all the tradespeople who had closed their shops and drawn their blinds. Hetty was there, dabbing her eyes with a wet handkerchief, also remembering those early years, and the pleasant pattern of their days. Beatrice was indisposed with influenza, Sylvia in Canada, and Charles spending the Summer vacation at Dinard with Gerry Levine and his parents.

They looked very lonely in the family pew, Sir Neville and Cynthia, but they stood proudly erect, and fastened their sad eyes on the massed wreaths of Summer flowers strewn over the coffin. The sickly sweet scent of the lilies on the elaborate cross in the centre was a little overpowering, but Sir Neville had insisted on the most expensive tribute from a florist in the West End. Shocked into contrition by the tragedy, he blamed himself for neglecting his duty as a parent. Yet he was not wholly to blame. Why was he not informed of her condition? Why had Cynthia accepted full responsibility when he was available but a short distance away? he had demanded of his elder daughter. But she was too upset to scold.

When Parson had pronounced the benediction at the graveside, he lifted his head and caught the sympathetic gaze of Lucy Blunt – the mother of his son – and knew what he must do to make amends for his neglect of Penelope. He had not seen his grandson, for Cynthia had explained he weighed only five pounds, and must stay in the maternity wing at the hospital until his weight had increased to that of a normal infant. He had been baptized Julian Neville Franklin. There remained only to find a good foster mother, and now he knew it must be Lucy Blunt.

When he rode into the farmyard at Russets the following day, the scene was unchanged from that Summer day when the farmer had fallen off the hay wagon. They were late in gathering the hay this year because of freak storms, and it would be a poor crop – one of the hazards of farming.

He sat there, on his hired hack, anxious to get the matter settled and return to London. There was nothing to keep him at Marston Park. Charles had disappointed him at Easter, and now he had gone off to Dinard for the Summer vacation. He would have to remind his wayward son that his allowance would be stopped unless he spent the last week of the vacation at Marston Park – one day of that week to be spent here, at Russets, for his mother had also been neglected this year.

When the buxom little figure moved away from the group in the hayfield and hurried towards the house, he wondered if she would comply with his wishes, for she was under no obligation to do so. As the mother of his son she had proved her worth, and demanded nothing for herself. He had taken her deliberately, and rather callously, he recalled, with no thought for the consequences of such a selfish action as far as her own feelings were concerned. He had wanted a son, and she had given him his heart's desire. Thereafter he had seen her, not as a very desirable woman, but as the mother of Charles.

He lifted his hat in greeting as she approached, and swung from the saddle with easy grace. She was flushed and breathless. Her shining hair was slipping from its combs, her eyes were still a bright gentian blue. She had hardly changed in all the years since that eventful day when he held her in his arms beside the stiff body of her husband. He wondered if she still smelled of earth and sweat, and whether he had made a mistake in not claiming her for his mistress as well as the mother of Charles. It was too late now for regrets.

Her heart was thumping as she recalled the urgency of his strong, virile body that Michaelmas Day. But he had aged. He was not the same man.

'Good morning, Lucy.' He was staring at her with such directness she felt uncomfortable. What did he want with her now? she asked herself.

'Good morning, Sir Neville,' she answered,

breathlessly.

'Could we talk indoors? I won't keep you from your work for more than a few moments.'

'Certainly.' She led the way into the kitchen, where Carrie was brewing tea and arranging mugs on a tray. Lucy introduced her niece, and Sir Neville looked surprised.

'She could be your daughter, you are so alike.'

'That is easily explained. Carrie's mother is my twin sister.'

'I see.' He refused a cup of tea, and ignored the kitchen chair Lucy pushed forward. When Carrie started for the door, he told her, 'There is no need to hurry away. What I have to say to your aunt is not a private matter.' Then he laid his hat on the table and asked quietly, 'Lucy, my dear, will you foster my little grandson?'

She gasped and shook her head. 'No, I'm sorry. I couldn't start all over again with another baby.'

'But this would not be the same. You would be in sole charge of the child. There would be no interference. This would be his home. He would not be taken away at the age of seven and sent to a preparatory school. I would leave it to you to decide on his education, I could promise you that. Cynthia tells me he will need a lot of care since he was born prematurely. Is it that you haven't the time, or that I am not deserving of your kind co-operation? I can understand your reluctance.' He sighed.

She stared at him with troubled blue eyes, no longer certain, hesitating before this man whose very presence made her body tremble and her heart ache with yearning. Yes, he was changed. The old arrogance had been replaced by a strange humility. There was pleading in his voice, and in his dark eyes.

'Excuse me,' Carrie interrupted, looking from one to the other. 'I could help. I could be the nursemaid. I've had a lot of experience, Sir, and I know what it means to care for a delicate child. *Please*, Aunt Lucy, do let us have the baby here. It would be so wonderful, for I can't have a baby of my own.' She was flushed with excitement. Lucy had not seen her so animated since she came to live at Russets.

'My niece was nursemaid to Doctor Saunders' little grandson before her marriage. She travelled to India with her charge, helped to nurse him through typhoid fever, then brought him back to England all by himself. She loves little children, and would have liked a family of her own. Unfortunately, that is not possible,' Lucy explained.

Sir Neville nodded, surprised and pleased at this new development. He braced himself for a final appeal. 'That would be an excellent arrangement, Lucy, would it not? With you as foster-mother, and Carrie as nursemaid. You could make her an allowance from your own allowance which would be more than adequate. Cynthia tells me it will probably be another three months before the child can leave hospital, and by that time all your seasonal work would be finished, and you would have time on your hands.'

Lucy smiled whimsically. 'Time is something in short supply on a farm, Sir Neville. Every season brings its own pattern of work.'

'Yet I envy you. It's such a healthy life. I can think of no better place for a child to grow up. Charles has hardly had a day's illness because he had such a good start in life. I was sorry it had to be interrupted when he was seven, but you did understand?'

Yes, Lucy understood. It had been a heart-breaking experience to part with a little boy of seven who must conform to the standard of his upper-class parent.

The big brown teapot stood ready on the hob. They

were waiting in the hay-field, and Carrie was waiting, expectantly.

'It will be like old times to have a baby's washing airing on the fireguard, and the smell of Pear's soap,' said Lucy, quietly.

'Then you will? Thank you, my dear.'

She thought he was going to kiss her. But Carrie was there, so he held her roughened hands and smiled into her eyes.

'Believe me, you will not regret it. This child will be as dear to you as Charles – and no separation. That's a solemn promise, Lucy, witnessed by your niece.' He bade her farewell with a stiff little bow, took up his hat and walked out. They watched him ride away. He turned to wave, then he was gone.

Lucy shook her head.

'He could still charm a bird off a bough. Father and son, they make a mickey out of me, Carrie,' she said. But there was no malice, only affection in the accusation. She took the girl in her arms, and kissed her.

Charles complied with his father's wishes and came home for the last week of the Summer vacation. He was tanned and handsome, and charming. To have his allowance stopped would be a hell of a nuisance, since he was heavily in debt to Gerry.

They went riding together, father and son, on their hired hacks, and Sir Neville hinted at opening up the stables and having their own hunters by the Christmas vacation. The old sense of companionship as they rode about the estate was missing, and conversation flagged over the meals, cooked and served by Hetty, who was delighted to have them back, for it relieved her mind of the earlier anxiety that her services might no longer be required.

By the third day, Charles was restless and bored, and glad to escape to Russets for the promised visit to his mother. He found her busy with preparations for the infant, though he was not expected for some weeks. The pram, the cradle and the cot had been brought down from the attic, toys turned out of the cupboards, and baby clothes were being aired on the fireguard. It was obvious to Charles that no expense had been spared when he was a baby. Now *his* son would be growing up at Russets. It was a solemn thought.

'Julian will grow up here. Russets will be his home. Your father has promised,' Lucy explained.

'So he should, darling. He was lucky to get your consent.'

'It was partly for Carrie's sake. She still misses that little boy.'

'What happens when she has babies of her own? Won't that complicate matters? I mean, it would take all her time. You would need to employ another dairy maid.'

'There won't be any babies.'

'Why not? She looks very healthy.'

'She is. But it takes two to make a baby, Charles.'

As if he didn't know!

'Albert is not up to it?'

Lucy shook her head, then changed the subject and refilled his glass with the lemonade he still preferred to the cider. He was looking at her with the same directness, the same intensity in his dark eyes. He was so like his father. They were two of a kind, and she had always known they would have their way with her. She was no match for them.

It was quite a relief when the two schoolgirls stood in the doorway with the little dog on a leash. Agnes and Harriet had spent most of the Summer holiday at Russets, and it seemed they had never been away. There would be more tears next week, however, for boarding school was a hateful place for the younger girl. They stopped on the threshold and stared, a little shy of their idol, since they had not met since last Christmas.

'Hello, Charles,' they chorused.

'Hello, you two. Come on in. Have some lemonade,' he invited.

Agnes sighed with disappointment. Charles had not noticed she had grown up, and she was so proud of her little pointed breasts! But Charles *had* noticed. He was not likely to overlook anything of that nature! He thought both girls had improved in looks in the past year. They were not so pallid, or so skinny. Boarding school was obviously the right place for them. He was perched on the table, swinging his legs, and Agnes was sure this would never be allowed in grandmother's kitchen. Mrs Blunt invited them to help themselves to lemonade and home-made biscuits. They were never allowed to help themselves. They were always helped. How they wished they lived at Russets! There was no scolding here, and no strict rules about wiping your shoes on the mat, and removing your gum boots on the doorstep.

Mrs Blunt was turning over tiny garments on the fireguard, and they stood watching her.

'Are those for the new baby?' Agnes enquired.

'Yes, dear.'

'He must be a very small baby?'

'He *is* small.'

'Shall we see him before we go back to school?' asked Harriet, eagerly.

'No, I'm sorry. You will see him at Christmas.'

'Did you know his name was Julian Neville Franklin?' Agnes asked Charles.

'Of course.'

'It was sad that his mother had to die, but he won't remember her, will he? Grandmother says babies don't remember. Has he got a father? Nobody has mentioned him.' Agnes couldn't bear *not* to know what was happening, she was so like her grandmother. But it seemed that neither Mrs Blunt nor Charles could enlighten her, and when she insisted on knowing, Charles told her to mind her own business, jumped off the table, and chased the little dog into the yard. They followed him and joined in the romp, and forgot about the baby's father. To be teased and chased by their idol, to be caught and hugged exuberantly, this was something to make their young hearts flutter. But when he swung them over the gate and laughed at their embarrassment, Agnes was mortified!

Julian Neville Franklin was three months old when his Auntie Cynthia brought him to Russets. She had watched his gradual progress in the maternity wing, and felt such a warm affection for the tiny scrap of humanity making its gallant fight for life, she was reluctant to hand him over to his foster-mother. Yet she had to admit it was a sensible arrangement, for Lucy Blunt had already proved herself a wonderful mother to Charles. Sir Neville had paid for the hired car, since the train journey would be tedious and hazardous for a child so accustomed to warmth and regulated temperatures. But Lucy would know what was best for him, and Papa had insisted there must be no interference. He was determined to trace the man who had seduced his youngest daughter, yet he had no clue to the man's identity, and neither had Cynthia. Penny had taken her secret to the grave. He felt only a mild curiosity about this particular grandchild, and none of that proud ownership he had known at the birth of his son. He found the nature of the birth a little sordid. Yet Charles had also been conceived out of wedlock. A law unto himself, his behaviour was condoned. In the safe custody of Lucy

Blunt, this child would never hear the word 'bastard', and there would be time enough to invent a father before he started to ask questions.

So he arrived on a sparkling Autumn morning, wrapped in shawls with a little knitted bonnet tied under his tiny chin, and was handed over to his new mother without a whimper of protest. Why should he, when those arms were strong and comfortable? He liked the gentle rocking of the old rocking chair, and when his bonnet had been removed, and he was released from the tight cocoon of shawls, he stretched his tiny legs and yawned.

'Bless 'is little 'eart,' Ruby murmured, and even Albert was lost in wonder and stood there clasping Carrie's hand, feeling the first real interest in any creature, other than Carrie, since his return home. Tom stood silent, glad to see his mother with a baby in her arms again. She was all maternal, and it seemed unlikely she would be blessed with grandchildren, so this little boy would fill the gap in the family. Katie peered more closely at the infant, then her big rough hand reached out tentatively to touch one of the wriggling feet, comfortably warm in knitted bootees. The baby's wide eyes slipped about the group of faces with solemn approval, then he waved his arms and smiled. It was Penelope's smile. Cynthia was choked with tears. If only she had been there, Penny would not have fallen on the stairs, and she would be here today, sharing in the baby worship.

The lowing of the cows reminded Tom it was time for milking, and he slipped away with Carrie, almost unnoticed. When Bertie tucked a finger in the baby's hand, it closed around it with surprising strength.

'Look at this, Mum. He's hanging on like a limpet.' He was obviously delighted and went on his knees, smiling his rare, twisted smile. The tiny hand unfurled like an opened bud, and touched his scarred cheek.

The twin sisters exchanged a meaningful glance. Was this the answer to the problem of Bertie's slow return to a happier frame of mind? Would a baby succeed where all else had failed? If so, it would be nothing short of a miracle. Neither his wife nor his mother with all their unselfish devotion, had changed anything. This was something so unexpected and so tender, the two women dared not trust themselves to speak. Nobody, not even Carrie, had touched that scarred face so gently. They smiled at each other in instant recognition of a loving relationship, or so it seemed to those who watched. Lucy and Carrie had been fearful of Bertie's jealousy when they devoted too much time to the child. Now it seemed their fears were groundless.

Cynthia slipped away to watch Tom and Carrie with the milking. She came upon them in the cowshed, wrapped in each other's arms, and Carrie was crying. She crept away. They had not seen her. The baby could be a blessing, but also a sad reminder of her own empty womb. Poor Carrie. Ruby had explained, only recently, about Bertie's cruel disfigurement, and Tom's devoted love for his young cousin. What a tragedy. The eternal triangle.

Cynthia was saddened by the day's events. She, too, wanted a child, and Penny's unwanted baby had slept in her arms, so innocent of her needs. Now he would be loved by this family, and she would have no part in his life, other than a rare visit to Russets, birthday and Christmas presents. His Auntie Cynthia would have no real significance.

The driver of the hired car was asleep in the hay in the Dutch barn. He would be driving her back to London after a late tea. She wandered to the wood, feeling lonely and neglected, but she did not belong here. She belonged in London, until Freddie had finished at Roehampton. He had changed his mind about opening up his office in

Soho, and asked her opinion on Tunbridge Wells.

'That would be wonderful, darling,' she told him.

A brave new chapter, away from all their former associations would suit them both. In the meantime, she would take her midwifery at the hospital, then find lodgings in Worthing in readiness for Freddie's arrival at the convalescent home. Patience and hope. Nothing could be hurried, and each stage was a step towards the future, a step away from the past and its haunting nightmares. There was peace here, in this quiet wood, and the beauty of Autumn was all about her in the brown and gold of the oaks and beeches. The red and black berries on the bushes were draped in old man's beard. Across the Park, in her old home, she could hear the children from London's East End enjoying their country holiday, but she had no wish to go there, not without Penny. Later, perhaps, for she had to see Charles occasionally. There would be no continuity of life at Marston Park any more. It was so disrupted by the War and the changing circumstances. It was here, at Russets, that one felt a sense of continuity. Yet they all had suffered and were still suffering. The mellowed farmhouse, the Dutch barn, the fields and orchards, the sheep, cows and horses, all reflected a permanency on this lovely Autumn day. Julian was a lucky little boy to grow up here. She wondered whether Penny was aware of it, and whether she could see what was happening to that poor disfigured man in the farmhouse kitchen. Her baby's tiny hand had touched that scarred cheek and seen nothing ugly in those scars.

She often wondered about the thousands of men who had been killed in the war, and whether their spirits were at peace, or tormented. In a split second a young life could be snuffed out like a candle. This was Death in all its horrific agony, as Freddie had witnessed it. She was no stranger to Death in her own environment. It crept up slowly and painfully in a hospital ward, or it came as a thief in the night and snatched away a patient they thought was safely on the road to recovery. As for Penny, she had slipped away so quietly, without a struggle, while the infant had drawn its first breath. This was the miracle of Birth challenged by the closeness of Death, and the will to survive in that scrap of humanity. Penny was gone. She still missed her intolerably in the empty flat, and found it depressing in her off-duty. Perhaps her obvious reluctance to spend a night there had prompted Freddie to change his mind about re-opening the office in Soho next year. He was very sensitive to her moods, and not at all selfish. Sometimes he seemed to read her thoughts, or was it her eyes that he read? She sighed wistfully, and shivered in the cool twilight of the wood. She must go back.

In that bright, warm kitchen, she found a homely tea had been spread on a starched white cloth. There was ham and cheese, and her favourite blackcurrant jam, home-baked bread, and dairy butter, gingerbread and biscuits. Lucy Blunt was slicing ham, her sister brewing the tea, and Bertie in the rocking chair feeding the baby. Her mother-in-law looked up to ask, 'Where 'ave you been, luv? We missed you.'

It was good to be missed.

'You're one of the family now,' Lucy reminded her, for she had felt Cynthia's reluctance to hand over the baby. It was true, of course, but she envied them the unity of a close-knit family. These twin sisters were closer than she had ever been to Beatrice and Sylvia. It was only in the last six months of her short life that Penny had clung to her, because she was afraid.

Katie was carrying willow pattern cups and saucers to the table, staring at the extraordinary sight. Mister Albert was feeding the baby! She knew that he would not need to lift her skirts at the scullery sink now that he had the baby. It was all she had ever known of sex, and her strong body had been willing to yield to him. Men were funny creatures. You couldn't depend on them!

When she was sent to fetch the driver to tea, she found him yawning and stretching in the hay.

'Tea's ready,' she told him.

His face was dim in the shadows, but she got the impression he was staring at her. In her clean starched apron she was a comely wench, he was thinking, and when she backed away, he sat up, and caught at her wrist.

'Give us a kiss,' he wheedled. He thought she would struggle to get away, but she stood there, passive, unresisting. He chuckled, and pulled her roughly on to the bed of soft, sweet-smelling hay. Because her thoughts were still with Mister Albert, she was ready and willing to be laid by this stranger. It was pleasantly comfortable, compared to standing at the scullery sink! He was a big man, much bigger than Mister Albert, and she was surprised by a sudden sharp pain, and a trickle of blood on her thighs.

'You should have told me you were a virgin,' he grumbled, pulling down her skirts. 'But you enjoyed it, didn't you? You can't say you didn't enjoy it. A man always knows!'

It was all over in a matter of minutes, but it had given Katie a taste for something more than Mister Albert's fumblings.

They walked back across the yard, still strangers. He hadn't even asked her name.

'Mum's the word,' he reminded her, and dropped a half-crown in her apron pocket.

She giggled. She had no need to be reminded, for now she had come to the conclusion that men were all alike!

* * *

'What's come over him, Carrie?' Tom whispered, as they washed their hands in the scullery.

'I don't know, Tom.'

Bertie was still in the rocking chair, nursing the sleeping child. Wrapped in a shawl, he had fallen asleep over his bottle. Sister Maternity had sent instructions for feeding a premature baby, up to the age of six months. It would worry Lucy to have a baby falling asleep over its bottle after rearing young Charles, who had yelled for more.

When Tom and Carrie walked into the kitchen after milking, they stared in astonishment when Bertie put a finger to his lips.

'It's all right. There's no need to whisper. He is accustomed to people talking and moving about, so it won't disturb him.' Cynthia had not lowered her voice.

'Shall I take him while you have your tea?' asked Carrie, tentatively. But he shook his head, so she handed him a cup of tea and placed a ham sandwich on a plate within easy reach.

'It looks as though the dear little fellow 'as found 'iself a nursemaid, don't it, luv?' said Ruby.

Carrie nodded. She was thinking the same. Would it be Bertie's arms, not hers, this child would grow to love? A faint tinge of jealousy and disappointment had to be quickly stifled. Hadn't they almost given up hope of finding some interest or occupation for those idle hands? Hadn't she hoped and prayed – yes, *prayed* – for help and guidance? It was only pity that she felt for him now, but she would never leave him. She had promised him faithfully on their wedding night, and nothing had changed. More than anything in the world she had wanted this baby to recognise her with the same trusting innocence as little Jimmy Saunders. She would never forget that wonderful moment when her new mistress handed over her charge. Now Bertie had claimed him. She sighed, and caught the kind glance of her Aunt Lucy across the table.

For three months they had been preparing for this day, and talked of little else. Now the older woman seemed to be pleading with the younger to be patient of this new, surprising development. She could feel the pressure of Tom's knee under the table. Dear Tom. What would she do without him?

Another season was slipping away, and still they were stealing a hug and a kiss in the cowshed. Even this was dangerous.

'I want you, sweetheart. What harm would it do?' Tom pleaded.

Once upon a time she was Bertie's sweetheart, but that was a long time ago. 'Wait for me, sweetheart.' She still kept the card from Constantinople. She had waited. She had visualised a future at Russets with their children growing up, strong and healthy, and their marriage vows sacred – 'For better, for worse, for richer, for poorer, in sickness and in health. Till death us do part'.

In the past year, learning to be a good farmer's wife, she had wept for the nursery. It had been such a short chapter of her life with Jimmy, and such a sudden parting that day at the station, when she looked up to see a ragged stranger, with a cropped head and scarred face, stepping carefully on to the platform. No time to say goodbye to that endearing small boy she had loved as her own child. They led him away, and he had not been allowed to visit her. 'A clean break. It was better,' they told her. What had happened to her young dreams? She felt the burden of her marriage vows too heavy to bear. She had no life of her own, torn between the demands of the two brothers, for Tom would not wait much longer.

'I want you, sweetheart.' That was Tom.

'I need you, Carrie. Promise you will never leave me.' That was Bertie, and she had promised.

'Would you like a jar of blackberry and apple jam to take back to London?' Aunt Lucy was asking Cynthia.

How funny! Carrie scolded herself for being so engrossed with her own solemn thoughts she had not been listening to the homely exchange of news and views between the other women at the table. Aunt Lucy was a tower of strength at Russets. She had suffered, but she had not lost her sense of values, or her sense of humour. Her rich laughter was a tonic in these troubled times, her warm kitchen a haven where weary bodies relaxed, and tired minds had an answer to their problems. She loved them all, these grown children who still depended on her to settle their disputes and keep the peace. Only Charles had grown away from them, but then he had always been the cuckoo in the nest. She had seen him only once this year, and nothing had been arranged at Marston Park for Christmas – the second since the end of the War. The Big House would be empty and silent, with only the caretakers. The children would be coming back in the New Year, but could not be tempted away from the crowded tenements of Stepney at Christmas.

Cynthia went off in the hired car with her jar of jam, and Tom walked back to the cottage with Ruby. She was fond of Tom, but she could see no future in his devotion to Carrie.

'You're making a rod for your own back, lad, and you know it,' she scolded. 'And it's not fair to Carrie. If you wasn't 'ere, my girl would settle down and make the best of it with Albert. There must be 'undreds of young wives with crippled 'usbands 'ome from the War.'

'Crippled, yes, but not *deformed*. It's monstrous! They

were devils, Aunt Ruby.'

'So you know?'

'Mum told me. You say I am not being fair to Carrie. Was Albert fair to marry her in all innocence? It was the meanest trick a man could play on a woman.'

'But they was *promised*, Tom.'

'Carrie was too young to be held to such a promise.'

'Supposing it 'ad been you, lad, what went to the War and came back only 'alf a man, what would you 'ave done?'

'I don't honestly know, but I do know it would have been better for everyone if he had not been saved when his ship was torpedoed.'

'It would 'ave broke your Mum's 'eart to lose Albert as well as 'arry.'

'But she's plucky, and time heals.'

'What do Carrie want, Tom?'

'She wants a family. You know how she loves little children.'

'There's that dear little mite of Miss Penelope's'. Ruby cold not persuade herself that another of Sir Neville's daughters would have taken a working-class man to father her child. It was still a mystery.

'You saw what happened, Aunt Ruby? Albert didn't even give her a chance to hold the child, yet he must have known how she feels. He's so darn selfish.'

'It might not last, Tom. Albert were just, well, so taken with the baby 'e couldn't bear to 'and it over to nobody.'

'It's just like him to ignore the fact that Carrie was standing there, longing to hold that little mite in her arms. She was near to tears, she was so disappointed. Aunt Ruby, how's it going to end? It seems so hopeless. If I had the courage, I would go away, but I haven't. Russets is my whole world. I love every stick and stone, every blade of grass. Not even for Carrie's sake could I tear myself away.'

'I'm sorry, lad, but I do feel that you made a big mistake in not telling Carrie that you loved 'er when Albert went away. She were fond of you both, and you wasted three years when you could 'ave been courting.'

'I was a fool, but it seemed disloyal to Albert. As soon as I saw him I realised my mistake, but it was too late.'

'You don't think you could change your mind about Carrie? There must be other young women what's only waiting to be asked. A farmer's daughter would be most suitable.'

'If I can't have Carrie, I shall stay single and live to be a crusty old bachelor!' he laughed derisively. 'What a mess, Aunt Ruby. What a bloody awful mess!'

Chapter 7

Once it was Charles who stole the limelight at Russets, now it was Julian. But no two babies are alike, and Penelope's baby made no demands on his foster-mother. He slept for hours in the warm kitchen, tucked snugly into the cradle that Charles had outgrown at six months. When he woke, he lay quietly, listening to the homely sound of baking, and the rattle of tea-cups, and voices, always voices. He was never left alone, and he was surrounded by love.

'He's awake,' someone would say, and he would be plucked out of his warm nest, and hugged. It was not always the same lap on which he found himself, and some were more comfortable than others, but he lay on a warm towel, stretching and yawning. There was no hurry. A warm napkin was waiting on the fireguard, and his bottle would be made ready while he yawned and stretched. He was like a little prince in the kingdom of Russets – Julian Neville Franklin.

The sense of warmth was his first conscious sense, and others followed – the taste of a finger in his mouth – not always the same finger – the smell of a clean starched apron, and the touch of a scarred cheek. He was carried up and down and shown things, and his tiny hands reached out for the shining copper pans, the red geraniums on the window sill, and Carrie's curls.

Julian was Sir Neville's only grandson, and the other grandchildren had not yet been seen at Marston Park because of their mother's delicate health. Since the birth of her third daughter, and her husband's consequent disappointment, Beatrice had lost heart. Sir Neville had paid a brief visit to Norfolk at the end of the War, but he was a difficult guest to entertain, and his host was a solitary man with strict Victorian principles, completely lacking in humour.

The tenants on the Marston Park estate brought presents for Julian's first Christmas, and the children acted a nativity play in the Dutch barn, with a *real* baby. Agnes claimed the leading role, though she wasn't a bit like the Virgin Mary. Harriet was allotted the role of the Angel Gabriel. Joseph got stage fright when confronted by an audience, for they had been rehearsing in the kitchen, so he climbed into the loft and was not seen again until supper time. Only two kings came from Orient Far – the third had measles.

'When we lived in the Congo with Daddy, our Baby Jesus was black,' Agnes explained importantly to the rest of the cast. They didn't believe her. Who ever heard of a *black* Baby Jesus?

It was Christmas Eve, and the barn was lit with lanterns. The audience sat on benches and kitchen chairs, with the sweet smell of hay in their nostrils, and the piping voices of the children a poignant reminder of other Christmases before the War had robbed them of their sons.

As the children finished their performance with a lively rendering of 'Away in a Manger', Tom walked into the barn with a new-born calf in his arms, and stood the little creature on its spindly legs. Seeing it standing there blinking and trembling, it seemed to young Harriet that they were actually in the stable at Bethlehem, and she burst into tears.

'What's the matter? Why are you crying?' her sister demanded.

'Be-cause it's so beau-ti-ful!' sobbed Harriet, and ran to Tom to be comforted. Tom would understand. He was like Daddy.

'Harriet is such a sensitive child,' Grandmother explained to the schoolmaster who was sitting beside her. But she was rather put out, since she expected her grandchildren to set a good example to the tenants' children, all working class. The parents were delighted with their children's performance, however, and Joseph's reluctance was understandable, since he was only six. There was no panic when the youngest angel lost her wings, and the shepherd boy forgot his lines. The baby calf staggered to the crib and gazed at the human baby with limpid eyes.

'It thinks it's Jesus,' Harriet whispered, chokingly, and Tom squeezed her shoulders. She was a very endearing child, he thought, when she managed to escape from her domineering sister. He could hear the cow calling for its calf, so he rescued it from the group of admiring children, and carried it away. It was a cold, frosty night, and he thought it would snow before the morning.

Hot cocoa and mince-pies were served in the warm kitchen. Richard and Philip, who had long since outgrown a Nativity play, carried the chairs and benches back across the yard. Only Charles was missing. He had gone to Switzerland with a party of school friends to escape the traditional family festivities they found so boring. Richard was bored, but he would do his best to hide it for his mother's sake. As for Philip, his own small world was complete, with his mother and step-father. All three had enjoyed the advantage of 'only' children, and had no envy of big families. They would enjoy their quiet Christmas, and he knew exactly what to expect for the day had been planned to the smallest detail. They liked it that way.

When they walked back from the midnight service, the church bells would be heralding Christmas morning. After a few hours' sleep, and his favourite breakfast of bacon and eggs, he would be back in church with 'Uncle Andrew' while Mother cooked the Christmas dinner. He was a tenor now, and would sing a verse of 'Once in Royal David's City' as a solo. They would sniff the savoury smell of roasting chicken as they hurried down the path to the School House. Mother would be flushed and anxious that everything would be ready on time and perfectly cooked. Uncle Andrew would offer to help, and stand about, getting in the way. He was not a domesticated man, and would make rather a hash of carving the chicken! Philip had picked the frosted sprouts before they went to church. Now he would refill the log basket and the coal scuttles, for that was his regular job. The smell of the boiling pudding would drift through the open window. They were alone, isolated from the rest of the world in their safe little haven.

'Will you lay the table in the parlour, please, dear?' his mother would call, and he would hurry to do her bidding. The mantelpiece was crowded with Christmas cards from the children, all handmade, with ridiculous robins. Mother thought her Infants were so clever! The presents would be waiting to be unwrapped after the washing up. He was hoping for a small box camera, and a book on photography. It was his favourite hobby.

'That was an excellent meal, my dear. I have never tasted a better,' Uncle Andrew would say – he said the same every Sunday!

'Fabulous!' Philip would declare. It was the lastest in his rich vocabulary.

Uncle Andrew would insist on washing up, with a lot of help from Philip, of course. It was funny to see him draped in one of Mother's aprons. It happened every Sunday. They had gathered the holly a week ago.

'Not many berries this year. That means a mild winter,' said Mother, who was quite an authority on country lore.

When they had unwrapped the presents, he would fold up the paper and save the string with meticulous carefulness. Nothing was wasted. Then he would settle down to read one of his new books while Mother played their favourite carols. She was not a very good pianist, for she had been thumping the keyboard for the Infants' marching and exercising for so many years, she had lost her light touch. What did it matter? Uncle Andrew had no ear for music anyway.

There would be dainty bread and butter, strawberry jam, and plum cake for tea. Then back to church for the evening service, leaving the adults by the fireside. For the benefit of the working-class congregation, he would sing another solo. It was only fair.

After doing his duty, he would hurry home to roast chestnuts and drink ginger wine. The day would not be complete without Dickens, and Uncle Andrew would read aloud for an hour or more in his clear, precise voice – the voice of a much respected schoolmaster. Then hot, sweet cocoa and mince-pies, a grateful kiss for Mother, and so to bed.

Even as he helped Richard to carry the chairs and benches across the yard at Russets, his thoughts flew on ahead to Christmas Day – and everything went according to plan.

* * *

A week later, he was catching the train to Tonbridge, and the village children were back at school, the boys with new peg-tops and the girls with skipping ropes from the Bazaar, already back to normal as The Haberdashery. The peaceful interlude was over. Some of the boys at the Grammar School were swanking about the shows they had seen in London, and the expensive presents they had received. Wristwatches were all the rage, Swiss made, the best in the world, they claimed. And why shouldn't they be, when the Swiss had escaped the War, and were ready to flood the market? it was argued.

Philip listened, but made no comment. He was no fool, and the smug satisfaction he felt in their own quiet celebration was his own affair. To have it questioned or ridiculed would be unbearable. It must never change, he told himself. But he reckoned without a girl called Harriet, and the heartache of unrequited love. Change was inevitable, as the years slipped away. He owed it to his mother and step-father to pass the entrance examination to Cambridge. Charles and Richard had no problem. They were upper class, and would graduate from public school. His own working-class background was a drawback, but it was also a challenge. Carrie's brother Freddie was a glowing example, he was reminded.

Those early years in Tidworth would never be forgotten. It was there that he discovered the meaning of the word 'bastard'. He carried the chip on his shoulder with dignity, and told nobody, for he was a loner, and had no close friends at Grammar School. Charles was a bastard, and made no secret of the fact that his father was lord of the manor, and his mother the widow of a tenant farmer on the estate. He found the situation colourful and amusing, but Charles was privileged. He enjoyed the best of both worlds. He was handsome, charming and popular.

On the rare occasions when they met at Russets, Philip had been too shy to make contact. They were worlds apart. Everyone loved Charles. Only three people loved Philip – his mother, his step-father, and Carrie. It was a solemn thought, but he had accepted the two facts that he was born out of wedlock and he was not popular. Being clever and getting full marks on his school reports was no recommendation to his sport-crazy contemporaries. Philip Martin was fumble-fisted. He dropped more balls than he caught on the cricket field, had no sense of co-ordination with a football, and lagged behind, puffing and panting like an old steam engine on the cross-country runs! He was accused of lacking the team spirit. It was true, but it was not his fault. How could one explain to the majority that an only child is an individual, not one of the herd? The team spirit had no significance for Philip or his step-father, but the schoolmaster observed, sensibly, 'Never lose sight of the fact, my boy, that you paddle your own canoe. It's better so.'

'Is it, Sir? But it's lonely,' he had pointed out respectfully.

'Loneliness is a small price to pay for independent thought. Be yourself, Philip.'

'Yes, Sir.'

That was a long time ago, before he discovered he was a misfit at Grammar School, but it still applied. What followed after Cambridge had not yet been decided – Civil Service – Banking – Teaching? His future was often a topic of conversation, but never stressed, for his views were respected. The generation gap was narrow, since Philip was old for his years, and had no young friends.

When they walked to Russets on the first Sunday in the New Year they trod on frozen snow, and the green valley was hidden beneath a white blanket. It was breathtakingly beautiful. They could see Richard and his sisters climbing out of the sledge at the bottom of a steep slope. The girls were wearing gay little knitted caps, with matching scarves and gloves. They were laughing, and their faces were glowing. They had never looked so pretty.

'Hello, Philip! Come and join us. It's a big sledge, and there's room enough for four,' Agnes invited.

Philip hesitated. It was the last thing in the world he wanted to do. Couldn't they see he was not dressed for sledging?

'Come on! It's fun!' Harriet was beckoning.

'I think you should go, dear,' said Mother, smiling at his reluctance. She knew exactly how he was feeling. It would be uncomfortable and undignified. He would probably finish upside down in a ditch full of snow.

He looked from one to the other, and there was no escape without losing face. Harriet was already pushing open the gate. Her grey eyes were teasing.

'Richard bet me sixpence you wouldn't dare!' she told him.

'Did he? Well, here I am!'

'Don't you like sledging?'

'I have never tried.'

'Neither have I, not till this week, I mean. Agnes and me. We didn't have snow in the Congo.'

'I suppose not.'

'Agnes is disappointed not to see Charles, but he is still in Switzerland. You could hardly expect him to come back for this, could you? I mean, there is no comparison.'

'He mightn't know it has been snowing in England.'

'That's true. To tell you the truth, I like it best without Charles. He *is* so self-important. If Charles were here, there wouldn't be room for you, and I would sooner have you.'

Philip blushed. He was terribly pleased.

'Come *on*!' called Agnes, impatiently.

Richard was most affable, and not at all superior. They pulled the sledge to the top of the slope, climbed on, and sped downhill. Harriet was hugging him round the waist, squealing with excitement. It was the loveliest sensation Philip had ever known – a joyous, exhilarating sensation. They landed in the ditch. It was wet and very uncomfortable. What did it matter? Harriet was still laughing.

Parson's wife was one of a number of people to die in the influenza epidemic the following year. It was a great shock to Parson, who had not fully appreciated his wife's sterling qualities. Following in the saintly footsteps of the much-loved Parson Wellington, he had made but a small impression on his flock, and the congregation had dwindled during the War.

On his appointment, he had chosen a wife as carefully as he chose the pet dogs that shared his hearth. A spinster, with no relatives to support, her private income had proved a useful addition to the small stipend he received from his esteemed patron at Marston Park. She had none of the authority or the personality of Parson Wellington's wife, Eleanor, and was always amenable to his wishes. She rode a bicycle to the outskirts of the village, to visit the poorest of his parishioners, with flasks of nourishing soup that she carried in the basket strapped to the handlebars. Her lordly spouse commandeered the trap for his own visiting, since it was more fitting to the upper class, to which he aspired, but into which he had not yet been accepted. It was a thorn in the flesh to be constantly reminded that stepping into Parson Wellington's shoes and residing at The Parsonage had not automatically changed his status. To some of his parishioners he was still the curate, and they forgot to show the respect to which he was entitled. His predecessor had also been blessed with a wife and three daughters of such natural dignity and refinement, there had been no need to apologise for the shabbiness of The Parsonage. As for the long-suffering wife of the ex-curate, he soon began to despise the very qualities he had once favoured.

Now she was dead, and her funeral service was one of several he had conducted in the past few days. Victoria Langtry had succumbed to the influenza, and her sister had died a week later. Both had been entitled to all the elaborate trimmings of their class of society, while a mother of six, from Richmond Row, was hastily committed to the earth, and her children collected by a severe looking female from the Orphanage. Three inmates of the Almshouses, including the indomitable Peg-leg, slipped away quietly, as befitted old servants.

Then Dr Saunders had stepped out of retirement to assist the overworked younger man who had taken over the practice. A week or so later, the church bell was tolling again.

'Two for a woman,' they said.

It was Dulcie Saunders, the doctor's wife. The church was packed on the day of the funeral. They came from far and wide, from upper class and working class, to pay their last respects to a woman whom they hardly knew, because, as Doctor's wife, she had had her place in the village. She was also the mother of a son who, it was said, had murdered the young schoolteacher, all those years ago, and country people have long memories. No tears were shed for Dulcie Saunders, however, by the working class, only for the ageing doctor, who had devoted all his working life to his patients. Only a few conscientious souls had insisted on paying for his services. The majority were grateful to be excused. It had always been a bone of contention between them, for Dulcie had little patience or sympathy for such unprofitable methods.

'The rich can afford to pay a bit extra. Don't worry, my dear. One will balance the other – well, almost,' he had told her, soon after their marriage.

Carrie slipped into a back pew in the crowded church, and caught a glimpse of *her* Jimmy in his neat school uniform, following the bier, with his grandfather, his own father – promoted to Colonel and stationed at Catterick – uncles, and boy cousins he met for the first time that day. Carrie was choked with tears at that glimpse of her Jimmy. So many memories, happy and sad. Those early years in Tidworth as a proud young nursemaid in a cape and bonnet, pushing the son of an Army captain in his smart pram.

'You are in the Army now, Carrie, and you must follow the drum,' she was told.

She would keep out of sight today. She must not embarrass him. Little boys at preparatory school, having their first lessons in manliness, would not wish to be reminded of nursemaids. The team spirit was already important to young James Saunders, who was a friendly boy, not a loner like Philip Martin. There would come a time when they would pass in the street as strangers – grown men, with only a hazy recollection of those early years. But not yet.

When the epidemic had passed, the village stretched and sighed, and settled down to a long period of peace, disturbed only by the invasion of the hop-pickers in late August, the Summer Fair, and the Christmas social. The gaps in the community were filled.

Parson married again, and lived to regret it. She was very pretty, very young, and childishly delighted in her role as mistress of The Parsonage.

'They do say she can twist 'im around 'er little finger, Ma'am,' Ruby told her mistress.

'I can well believe it. He obviously dotes on the silly

little creature. One has only to watch his eyes straying in her direction from the pulpit when he should be concentrating on his sermon. It's not dignified. The man's a fool!' Eleanor Wellington had never suffered fools gladly!

An American couple rented The Grove for two years, and startled their neighbours by their unorthodox methods of bringing up their children. In fact, they brought up themselves, as they would tell you, quite frankly. Not for them the formal pattern of education. The girls played havoc with a succession of English governesses, and the boys played truant from their day school. They had no inhibitions, were loyal and devoted subjects of Uncle Sam, and thought the natives of Freshfields a bit corny. Extravagantly generous and friendly, the whole family would converge on the village from time to time, looking for 'quaint' specimens of rural life to add to their collection. Toby jugs, candle-sticks, and chamber-pots, children's hoops and peg-tops, beer mugs, Victorian bric-à-brac, and Edwardian fripperies, found a ready market.

'Genu*ine* antiques!' they enthused.

'I be proper flummoxed,' old Joshua Rootes admitted, grudgingly. 'Them varses wasn't worth more than a couple of shillings, and them silly buggers give me five pounds!'

Then they were gone, and the trustees of the small estate had it converted into a Nursing Home.

Charles Franklin had kept Penelope's secret for more than two years, and he saw his son for the first time running across the farmyard at Russets, holding Albert's hand. He was a very small child, but he had no fear of the huge Shire horse that Tom was leading.

Charles leaned on the gate, his dark eyes reflecting the emotion that he had thought to hide on this first encounter with Julian. There was something so familiar about that shapely little head, and when Tom swung the child on to Prince's back, the shout of laughter was Penny's. The two brothers obviously adored the child, but had no love for each other. They had nothing to say as they moved away to circle the yard. It was Albert who steadied the child, and Tom who led the horse. The small boy was the go-between, and too young to be aware of the antagonism between the brothers. The situation had not changed, but life went on at Russets. The human element was important only in its relationship to the seasons and the soil. The baby had prevented the rift between the brothers from widening, but that was all. Neither Lucy nor Carrie could have healed the bitterness and frustration in that tortured mind. The miracle had been achieved by a baby. His tiny hands had touched the scars. His innocence had seen nothing ugly in the man who bent over him. It was sad for Carrie who had expected to be compensated for her own disappointment, but Bertie had claimed the child from that first day, and she was left with the crumbs – the chores, the washing, and ironing, and an occasional cuddle when Bertie had one of his severe headaches.

When they came face to face with Charles, the brothers greeted him coolly, for they both resented the way he could come and go as he pleased and treated their mother so casually. Albert still felt a twinge of jealousy when he remembered the little half-brother who had demanded so much of his mother's attention. Now this elegant young man leaning on the gate had all the advantages and none of the disadvantages. His handsome features had the stamp of the aristocracy, of Sir Neville Franklin. He was not a Blunt, and never would be. His mother had long since accepted the fact that his rare visits had become more of a duty than a pleasure.

But Charles was not concerned with the brothers' cool

greeting. He was staring into Penny's eyes. 'Hello, Julian,' was all he said, but it was a moment of such agonising revelation, he was quite incapable of more.

'Say hello to Charles,' Albert prompted.

'Hello.' He was a very obedient child, and had none of the Franklin temperament. But that unwavering stare was disconcerting, and would always be a reminder of the girl who had given herself with such light-hearted abandon, and his own part in the momentary passion in which this child was conceived. It had seemed so harmless and when it was over, they laughed. It was fun. Everything was fun. But not any more. Here was the child he had refused to acknowledge. Looking at his son for the first time, he wished he had not been such a coward. Now he could never claim him. Julian belonged here, at Russets, with this family. His foster-mother was a wonderful woman. Her plump body and warm bosom still ripe for love had found fulfilment in another boy child, and in her devotion to her own disfigured son.

'Have you seen Mum?' Albert demanded.

'Yes, she told me where to find you.'

'You've been a bloody long time making up your mind to pay us a visit. Where have you been? For God's sake, Charles, she's *your* mother as well as mine!'

'I know. She understands.'

'You take too much for granted. A chip off the old block, that's you.'

'I know that too, but I can't be blamed for it.'

'Bastard!'

Charles shrugged. 'I suppose the same could be said of this young man?'

'Not if I have anything to do with it. We haven't given up hope of tracing the bugger. All we need is a clue. Cynthia was the only member of the family to see Penny during that period. They shared a flat, but Cynthia was still working at the hospital. Besides, it must have happened when Penny was in lodgings. The poor kid was lonely, so she took a lover. We've been over it so many times with Cynthia when she visits Aunt Ruby, but so far we've drawn a blank.'

'Does it matter any more? After all, it only concerns the family.'

'*Both* families. Julian is a Franklin, not a Blunt. I suppose Mum could have his name changed to Blunt by deed poll.'

'Would my father agree to that?'

'I doubt it. He has the last word on major issues, but he doesn't interfere over Julian's upbringing. It was different with you. When you were born he claimed you as his son and heir. Pity it wasn't a girl, then she would have grown up here, and saved a lot of trouble for Mum,' he hinted, meaningly.

'I didn't know.' Charles seemed surprised.

'Well, you know now.'

Tom had not said a word, and the small boy on the horse was beginning to fidget.

'Goodbye,' he said – and wondered why they laughed.

As they moved away, Carrie came from the dairy to lean on the gate, and Charles slipped an arm about her shoulders, kissed her mouth, and asked, playfully, 'Remember me?'

She nodded. She wondered how many hearts he had broken since they last met. 'Isn't he a poppet?' The small boy on the big horse claimed all her attention.

'He's very like Penny.'

'I suppose he is, but you don't notice it when you are always with him. You are seeing him for the first time.'

'You love him very much, don't you?'

'We all love him.'

'Once it was me, now it's Julian.' He sighed for he

couldn't bear to play second fiddle to anyone.

'But there is no comparison, dear. You were such a demanding little boy. Julian is so undemanding, so good. And he really belongs here at Russets. We don't have to part with him when he is seven. He will go to the village school when he is five with the children from the other farms on the estate. In a way, Julian has changed all our lives for the better, I mean. His coming made all the difference in the world to me. I can cope now, Charles.'

'Can you?' He turned to look at her, and she met his direct gaze with her candid blue eyes. Yet he got the impression she had lost her youth since they last met. Carrie had the same shapely comeliness as the twin sisters of the older generation – his mother and her mother. There was a clean, fresh smell about her person. Sun, wind and rain enhanced the natural bloom of her cheeks. Her hands were roughened, and the nails broken, but her hair shone gold in the sun's rays. For the first time he really understood why his father had lusted after Lucy Blunt – and they had told him it was obvious, even before that fateful day when her husband fell from the wagon. Servants talk. In his father's heyday, the servants' hall was a hotbed of gossip. To-day, however, only two indoor servants were employed to maintain the one wing of the great house reserved for the family – Hetty O'Brien, and the young housemaid who knew more than it was good for her to know. So far, he had silenced her tongue, but it was a nuisance, and he felt he was being robbed.

Even as he watched the child, he was remembering the way the maid had followed him to the stable, the day he had intercourse with Penny – the sly little minx!

'Excuse me, Sir, can I speak to you?' she had asked, innocently enough.

'Go ahead,' he invited, amiably. Hetty had done a good job in training the girl. She was respectful, and she no longer dropped her aitches.

'I thought you ought to know that I know what happened, Sir.'

He had stared at her in utter astonishment – a trim little figure in her starched cap and apron, but so deceptively innocent. To deny it would be futile. He could usually bluff his way out of any awkward situation with his own sex, and the opposite sex had been easy prey to his charms. But this was different.

'Well, what are you going to do about it?' he demanded.

'I thought you might like to give me a little present, Sir?'

'To keep your mouth shut?'

'Yes, Sir.'

'How much do you want? I haven't any money on me at the moment. I'll send it.'

'There is no hurry, Sir.'

'How much?'

'Would five pounds be all right?'

'Very well.' He was always in debt, borrowing from Peter to pay Paul. It would be money well spent, to keep her mouth shut.

'Don't send the money here, Sir. There's Hetty. She would talk.'

'Where, then?'

'I could give you the address of my friend in Tunbridge Wells. She's a War widow, and she's got her own house. I spend my free Sundays there. She wouldn't talk, Sir.'

'Give me the address.' He took out the small diary Hetty had given him for Christmas. She still regarded him as a boy, still called him Master Charles. He had often borrowed half-a-crown from Hetty during the holidays from prep school, and she didn't expect to get it back! Now he wished it was Hetty who had witnessed their 'naughtiness' – for that would be her word for it – naughtiness. She was one of the old-fashioned type of servant who fully understood the upper class was privileged. She might condemn such behaviour in her own class, but would 'make allowances' for the children of Sir Neville Franklin. Hetty had been making allowances at Marston Park since she was thirteen.

But the girl was too young to belong to that select hierarchy of pre-War servants, and for all her civility, she was no fool.

'What are you waiting for?' he had asked, when he looked up to see her still standing there.

'Nothing, Sir.'

'Then get the hell out of here!'

'Yes, Sir.'

After she had left, he wondered why he had agreed to pay her the money so readily. There was another way to silence a girl, and it wouldn't have cost him a penny. The son of Sir Neville Franklin knew by instinct what others had to learn by experience! But it had been a shock, and his reaction automatic. Too late he had realised his mistake, for it was only the start, and he was still paying. From time to time an unsigned letter would arrive at his lodgings. It was still a mystery how she had discovered his address. He did not reply to the letters, but simply put the money into an envelope and posted it to Tunbridge Wells. So there was no incriminating evidence, only the resentment of being trapped.

Once she had asked for ten pounds. She said her mother had died, and she must give her a decent burial.

'What's the matter, Charles?' It was Carrie's voice.

His thoughts had wandered. A disarming smile loosened the grim set of his mouth, and he bent to kiss her.

'Nothing is the matter, darling. Shall we see if Mother is brewing more tea?'

They walked away, and Charles had an arm about her waist.

'Cheeky young bugger!' muttered Albert.

Tom shrugged indifferently. His young half-brother was no rival to Carrie's affections. She loved him. Everyone loved Charles. There were different kinds of loving. His love for Carrie was constant, as unchanging as the seasons. But there had been a limit to his patience, and his waiting. The opportunity for which he had waited so long came about quite unexpectedly last Michaelmas Day – the day of the Fair. Little Julian had been too young to accompany them, and Albert had stayed at home with the child. Katie had been invited to join a party from a neighbouring farm. She would have the company of another servant girl. Tom would take Carrie to the Fair in the wagonette. It was the first time they had enjoyed an outing together.

Leading the horse, circling the cobbled yard, Tom's thoughts were also wandering, and he, too, was conscious of a terrible mistake. To force the issue could never resolve the problem of their unhappy relationship. It could only worsen. It was not Tom's nature to act impulsively, or to take what belonged to another. Now he was shamed by a guilty conscience, for he had taken his brother's wife as roughly as any country yokel, coming home from the Fair, bemused by too much ale or cider, and too much excitement.

But it was not drink that excited him that day. It was the joyous delight in her company. For Carrie, it was sheer relief to be free of Albert for a whole day. She was like a child in her enjoyment. They sang all the old songs they remembered from the early years at the village school, accompanied by the clip-clop of the mare's hooves and the rumble of wagon wheels converging on the town from all directions, for Michaelmas Day was still one of the few days in the year to be recognised as a public holiday. The War had changed so much, but not the traditional Michaelmas Fair. Unattached girls would attach themselves to complete strangers, and were lucky to keep their virginity! It was noticeable that several unwanted babies would arrive on the doorstep of the Orphanage some nine months later.

Emma had been one of those unwanted babies. Once upon a time, the three brothers had taken Emma with them to the Fair. Farm hands and servant girls had a right to be included. They travelled in the big wagon in those days; the horses' heads and tails decorated with coloured rosettes and ribbons, the brasses shining and jingling. If they passed anyone on Shanks' pony, they stopped and picked them up. They sat on a mattress of clean straw in the bottom of the wagon, but Emma had always claimed the driver's seat beside Harry. She would fight for it, like a little wild cat, while Harry laughed. They knew exactly how the day would end, but it usually started with a scuffle. Farmers' sons and daughters would mix freely with servants and farm hands for that one day. On the morrow, they were back where they belonged in their rightful places.

It was a holiday from school for scores of children who ran wild at the Fair. 'Give us a penny, Mister!' they begged. Grubby hands would collect coins. In five minutes it would be spent, and they would be back among the crowd for more pennies. Only the meanest could refuse a penny, and Tom was generous. He emptied his pockets of the pennies he had been collecting on market day for some weeks, and Carrie, hanging on his arm, giggled happily. It was so long since Tom had seen her so happy and carefree.

On this mellow September day, they were surrounded by people who had worked hard for this free day. The hops were picked, the harvest gathered, and the children had cleaned the hedges of nuts and berries. It was a time to eat, drink, and be merry – a time for laughter and love.

With Carrie's head on Tom's shoulder, they jogged along towards home in the pale light of the moon. Tom's big, roughened hand clasped Carrie's small, roughened hand. She was feeling sleepy and quite unprepared for the sudden jolt when he pulled on the reins and stopped the mare on a lonely stretch of road at the foot of Beacon Hill.

'Why are we stopping, Tom?' she asked, yawning and stretching her cramped limbs.

He made no answer. Jumping down from the wagonette, he tied the reins to a tree and flung open the gate. His movements were quick and decisive. Then he was standing there, holding up his arms, and his face was stern and strange.

'Come!' he commanded, curtly, but she shrank away from a man she hardly recognised. She knew now what he intended.

'No, Tom! – No!' She was pleading and sobbing when he reached up and dragged her down. His arms closed about her struggling body in a vice of steel, but all her frantic struggles did no more than hasten his steps towards the craggy summit of the hill, silhouetted in the light of the moon. She was frightened now. This man was a stranger the gentle Tom would despise.

When he laid her down in the hollow betweeen the crags, he leaned over her, breathing heavily. She tried to push him away, but he was too strong for her. With a shuddering sigh she gave up struggling and closed her eyes. There was a desperate urgency in those big roughened hands, but when a trickle of blood wet her split thighs and she cried out with a pain, his taut body slumped and slid away. Then he was lying beside her, face down, sobbing distraughtly.

There was no other sound on this craggy hilltop, and Tom's strangled sobbing was part of the strangeness, the unreality. Carrie would remember this night for the rest of her days. It had happened so suddenly, and it was quickly over, yet they both would wear the scars. It went deep. It was no light-hearted affair such as Charles and Penny had enjoyed.

Carrie lay still, drowned in sadness. Was she never to be allowed a small measure of happiness without paying the price? She had loved and trusted Tom. Now it was over, and she was emptied of emotion and very lonely. This was something shameful that could never be divulged. The peaceful interlude they all had enjoyed at Russets since little Julian arrived to join the family was shattered, but only their two selves must know of the shattering. Bertie was no longer spying on them, no longer suspicious, so he hadn't objected to the outing. Perhaps they had been lulled into a false security?

Away in the distance an owl hooted, and some small creature screamed in the clutches of its captor.

Carrie shivered and sat up. Tom had stopped crying. His long, lean body was stretched on the hard ground, his face buried in his arms. She scrambled to her feet. Her body ached as though she had been beaten. She made her way down the hill, slowly, climbed into the back of the wagonette, and sat there, waiting for Tom. Presently he came, staggering like a drunken man, untied the reins, and climbed into the driver's seat.

They travelled the rest of the way in silence, then Carrie slipped quietly into the house while Tom stabled the mare. The house was in darkness, save for the glow of the kitchen fire. There was no sound as he passed the door of the room where Carrie had joined her husband in the marriage bed.

He closed the door of his own room and sighed. What

had happened was inevitable, but he was bitterly ashamed. Another man might have packed his bag and left, but not Tom. He belonged here. The fundamental truth had not changed because of tonight, because he had raped his brother's wife. If suffering and heartache had to be endured, and the future was bleak, it would be bleaker still in any other place but Russets.

Pushing wide the window, he stood there, staring out on the dear, familiar scene, bathed in moonlight. When he had stripped off his best suit and boots and put on his working clothes, he felt better. It was not sleep he wanted, but time to think. Noiselessly, he crept downstairs to the warm kitchen, made a pot of tea, and settled down for the rest of the night in the old rocking chair, nursing the cat.

When Lucy walked into the kitchen at 5 o'clock and found Tom dozing in the rocking chair, she stood there for a long moment, gazing down at her son's twitching face and knew for certain that something had happened. They had agreed not to disturb Carrie, but to let her sleep on late.

Julian was asleep in his cot in Lucy's room. She would keep him in her room till he started school at the age of five.

Her mother's heart ached for her son – the only son left to her with the health and strength to work seven days a week in all kinds of weather, through all the seasons of the year. Tom had never taken a holiday, and never courted a girl. It was so sad, so utterly impossible, this relationship with his brother's wife. She had warned them both and she could do no more. They were not children, and they were not unaware of its potential danger. Carrie had a wider experience than Tom, for she had travelled abroad, but Tom was no fool. Yet they skated on thin ice. It was frightening.

What next? Lucy wondered. Since she lost Bert, her life had lost its direction, and its familiar pattern. It was Charles who had disturbed the family unity, and it had not recovered, would never recover. Before the War had robbed her of Harry, her firstborn, and Bert's favourite son had been returned to her only half a man, the rift was there. Bert's sons had been shocked and disgusted, and Albert had been jealous of the handsome little boy who demanded so much of his mother's time and attention. She remembered his sulky temper, and his accusing blue eyes. Everything she did for Charles was resented by Albert.

The cat on Tom's lap was yawning and stretching, and Tom opened his eyes.

'Hallo, Mum,' was all he said.

'Hallo, son.' She kissed his warm cheek and squeezed his shoulders affectionately. She wanted to cuddle him in her arms to tell him she knew and understood, and he was not to blame himself. It had to happen sometime. But she dare not make a fuss of him because he was a grown man, and she mustn't interfere. So she pushed the kettle over the fire to make fresh tea, and asked, 'Did you have a good time?'

He nodded.

'I didn't hear you come in. I tried to keep awake, but I must have dropped off after Katie went upstairs. It was after 12, and they made a lot of noise in the yard, the Penfolds. I expect they had been drinking. Why shouldn't they enjoy themselves? It's only once a year. Katie won't be feeling much like work today, but it's got to be done. I wonder if she has behaved herself. You know what I mean?'

'Yes.'

'One of these days we are going to be landed with another little bastard!' she laughed, and Tom joined in with the laughter, but it was forced.

Carrie wondered why they were laughing. She had lain awake, listening to Bertie's steady breathing, glad he had not wakened when she climbed into bed. She had heard Tom pass the door and then return, some time later. Her body still ached. It was unlike anything she had ever imagined. Sexual intercourse with Bertie, compared to this, was nothing more than a parody. Reliving it in every detail was tormenting her senses. She was trembling now, not with shock, but a strong desire for a repetition of this act of violence. The shame was forgotten. She remembered only the extraordinary sensation of their two bodies locked together as one body. She remembered the feel of the hard earth, her skirts flung over her face, his big, impatient hands, and his gasping breath – and her own back arching. The climax was not the trickling of blood on her thighs, or the end of her virginity. It was something singularly precious and sacred to this one night, this one man. *For it must never happen again.*

Chapter 8

In a small, rented terrace house, just off the Common, Freddie and Cynthia had settled down happily in Tunbridge Wells. Cynthia was expecting their first child. It was a time of re-adjustment, the start of a new chapter, and both were fully aware of the precarious nature of Freddie's post-War profession.

During his long convalescence in Worthing, they had discussed it freely.

'My dear, nothing has changed, fundamentally. I am still a poor man's solicitor, and I intend to keep it that way,' he had told her.

She had smiled complacently. 'My darling, have I ever tried to dissuade you?' And added, with a hint of forbearance, 'What would be the use? You are such a stubborn old thing, once your mind is made up!'

He had patted the hand that rested so lightly on his artificial knee. She was still a little nervous of that leg, and seemed to expect it to collapse if she leaned too heavily! It was the same hand that had surprised and distressed him at their first meeting in the tea-shop, before the War. It was the hand of a working woman like that of his mother, who had worked as a charwoman at 'The Three Nuns' when they were growing up in Richmond Row. The daughter of Sir Neville Franklin was no snob. She had proved beyond a shadow of doubt that the barrier between the classes was not insurmountable.

During his convalescence, she had still been working at the Hospital for Women, but he had persuaded her to give it up as soon as he knew about the baby. He still had to attend Roehampton at regular intervals, and he still walked with a stick, but he was fully recovered mentally, and felt he could cope with his physical disability.

It was a red letter day when he opened the door to his first client, and showed him into the tidy office on the ground floor. It was sparsely furnished, indeed the whole house was furnished very sparsely from their rooms in Soho. Until his modest services were recommended, it would be a precarious living, especially with the baby on the way, but he did have a small pension.

'We shall manage, darling,' Cynthia had insisted. Hadn't they always managed?

Looking back over the years, she realised how quickly she had adapted to a new way of life so far removed from Marston Park. She had no regrets. Freddie was her dearest love, her *only* love. Their child would not disturb their relationship. It was too firmly established. Cynthia knew already that she would not neglect her husband for the child. Maternity was not her strongest characteristic. She loved children, but not extravagantly. Her little nephew, Julian, was a great favourite. She had taken him to see *Peter Pan* last Christmas. Carrie had brought him to London by train and they met at Victoria. With the combined excitement of his first train journey, at the age of four, and the flying Peter Pan, he had been sick on the return journey! It was surprising that Carrie was not sick with excitement for such outings were rare, and she was like a child in her enjoyment. Dear Carrie. She was such a darling, and made for motherhood.

For that first year in Tunbridge Wells they were isolated from the family at Russets, because of transport difficulties. But Cynthia was making plans, and for once she did not share them with Freddie who had not realised his wife was lonely and sadly missed the busy routine of the hospital wards. Taking her daily walk along The Pantiles, she would slip into the crowded tea-shop for a cup of coffee and a doughnut. It reminded her of London, and their brief courtship. Reluctant to return to the quiet little house, she would sit on a seat, watch the constant promenade of shoppers on this favourite rendez-vous, and talk to anyone who shared the seat. Now she visualised a time when the child could safely be left with a trustworthy, motherly woman, and she could travel to London to resume the long interrupted nursing career. She was a little ashamed of harbouring such thoughts while she carried the child in her womb, but she promised herself to feed him, for at least six months, before putting him on the bottle. She knew for certain her firstborn would be a boy, but Freddie was amused, and had no preference either for a boy or a girl. Indeed, like so many husbands, he would have been quite happy *not* to share his wife with a third party! On one thing he insisted, however – a daily cleaning woman was engaged. She came in for three hours, six days a week, and charged a shilling an hour. Freddie paid her a pound, to cover her bus fares as well, and felt exceptionally generous!

The church bell was tolling one Summer evening. 'Two for a woman,' muttered old Obadiah Kemp, leaning on the churchyard wall. There had been a wedding in the afternoon, and the path was scattered with confetti. When the aged sexton appeared with his broom, Obadiah accosted him with the usual question, ''oo be that then, Sam?'

'Old Parson's widder.'

'Never!'

'Aye. Ruby Simmons what's the 'ouse-keeper, was on the telephone all of a dither. Said as 'ow Madam 'ad dropped dead in 'er kitchen.'

'Well I be buggered!'

'Aye, and I reckon Old Parson's going to be buggered when 'e 'ears 'is Missus bossing them 'eavenly 'osts around. Drat me, this blasted confetti don't arf take some moving.'

Obadiah sucked on his foul pipe and reflected on the sudden departure of one of the most colourful figures in the village.

'Won't seem like the same place, not without 'er telling us all what we ought to do, will it Sam?'

But Sam was a man of few words, and had said enough on the subject.

Marion seemed surprisingly calm, under the circumstances, for the full responsibility of the funeral arrangements fell on her shoulders. Fortunately, for everyone concerned, she had acquired a measure of independence since the War, when dire necessity forced her into employment beyond the familiar acres of Marston Park.

'You have no pension. You are still a young woman, and there is nothing organically wrong with your health. You have only to pull yourself together,' Mother had pointed out in her usual forthright manner. To this Marion had reluctantly agreed.

She had been living in the past with her beloved Malcolm for too long. She adored her son, Richard, and awaited his homecoming for the holidays with the eagerness of a young girl awaiting her sweetheart. The girls had been fully aware of their mother's indifference to their welfare for some time, and had grown away from her, depending on their grandmother. Now Grandmother was dead, and all three grandchildren were granted a week's compassionate leave, and seemed completely stunned by her sudden death.

'Your grandmother was old. She had to die sometime,' Marion reminded her children, sensibly.

But they could not accept such a simple explanation. The bottom had dropped out of their world. That indomitable personality who had ruled the lives of the two girls since they came back from the Congo, had disappeared for ever, and they were broken hearted. Their brother, Richard, rounded on them severely on the day of the funeral, for he was tired of their noisy grief.

'How do you suppose *I* feel? I have known Grandmother for years. I knew her when she lived at The Parsonage, and Grandfather was the Parson. I was only six years old when I was sent home to be educated. For God's sake, be your age!'

'That's blasphemy!' Agnes retorted. 'You know how she always objected to taking God's name in vain.'

'Grandmother objected to a lot of things, including the time you spent at Russets in the holidays. If she hadn't been so busy with the Red Cross and visiting the bereaved, she would have prevented it. Grandmother was one of the old school. She believed profoundly in everyone keeping to their rightful place.'

> The rich man in his castle,
> The poor man at his gate,
> God made them high or lowly,
> And ordered their estate.

'Exactly.'

'There was no harm in it. Grandmother and Mother were too busy to bother with us during the War, so we went to Russets. They were busy too, but they always had time for us, and Tom let us help.'

'Shall we walk across and see them, or would it be disrespectful to Grandmother?' Harriet wondered.

'You'd better ask Mother. She's in charge now,' Richard reminded her.

Marion agreed. It would pass the time and take their minds off their grief. She would be glad when the week's compassionate leave was over and they could return to school. She, too, had been granted a week's leave of absence by an understanding boss. After only a few months, he was dependent on her absolutely. She was quietly efficient and ladylike, and that was more than could be said for her predecessor! Marion had enjoyed the year's course at the Secretarial Training College in Tunbridge Wells, and had been recommended for the post by the principal. Her new boss was a self-made man, with a working-class background. He was confident of his abilities, industrious and exacting. But his boyish enthusiasm was contagious, and Marion had formed quite an attachment of recent weeks – an attachment she would have thought impossible with such fond memories of her beloved Malcolm. She was genuinely sorry to be away from the office for a whole week. Even Richard could not compensate for the lively interest in her new world of commerce. To be away from her mother's dominating influence had boosted her morale.

It was Cynthia, one of her ex-pupils, who had recognised in this new, vital personality, the governess who had ruled over the schoolroom at Marston Park before that romantic meeting with the young missionary from the Congo. They had shared a plate of sandwiches and a jug of coffee in The Pantiles tea-shop, one day, and renewed their acquaintance, but it was Marion who kept an eye on the clock, and hurried back to the office, and Cynthia who wished there had been more time to talk over the old days and make a friend of Marion. That first encounter had not been repeated, however, and Cynthia was innocent of the fact that Marion was often invited to lunch with her boss in an exclusive little restaurant a short distance from the office.

It had been a heart-warming occasion, and Eleanor Wellington would have been most gratified to witness her own funeral!

The church was packed, the bishop officiated, ably supported by the proud parson. The choir moved slowly and reverently down the aisle in their clean, starched surplices, bursting their lungs with her favourite hymn! –

All people that on earth do dwell,
Sing to the Lord with cheerful voice!

The school children were marched to church in a long crocodile, supervised by the schoolmaster and the teachers. After the service, they were given a half-holiday, much to the inconvenience of their working-class mothers.

Obadiah Kemp, clasping his best cap in his gnarled hands, had the last word, however. 'She were a rare old bugger, with 'er interfering ways, but she always knowed what was right and proper!'

Sir Neville called on Marion the following week to discuss the tenancy of the cottage on his estate. He had written a letter of condolence, ordered an ornate cross of arum lilies from the most expensive florist in Tunbridge Wells, and attended the funeral. It was his duty as squire, but he had genuinely admired the late Eleanor Wellington, and had always made a point of calling on her when he came down from London.

Now it became his unpleasant duty to inform the daughter – the ex-governess who had once jeopardised her father's clerical 'living' by giving notice – that he required the cottage for his groom, who was living over the stables with a rather superior wife. When he had finally decided to settle permanently at Marston Park, the stables had been decorated, and he was once again enjoying the 'sport of kings' with all the enthusiasm of pre-War days. It had not been an easy decision to make, but he had long since realised his adored mistress was unfaithful, and to play second fiddle to a young actor half his age was insufferable.

'There is no immediate hurry, my dear. Shall we say three months?' he suggested, blandly, sipping the sherry the housekeeper had been asked to serve in the small drawing-room.

Marion agreed.

They chatted for half-an-hour or so, about their respective families, then they shook hands and he strode away across the Park.

When Ruby came to collect the tray, she found Marion in tears.

''as something 'appened, Miss?' she asked anxiously, for there had been no tears since the mistress died, unless she had cried privately.

'Sir Neville wants the cottage for his groom, Ruby. Not immediately. We have three months to make other plans. It has been rather a shock. I shall be all right in a moment.'

'It don't come as no shock to me, Miss Marion. That groom's wife 'as been 'ankering after a cottage ever since they was married, that I do know. She don't like living over the stables, Miss. Says it's not what she's been used to. She won't give that poor man no peace, I reckon, not till she gets 'er way.'

Marion dabbed at her wet eyes, and blew her nose vigorously. 'But how about you, Ruby? What will you do? On my salary, with three children coming home for the holidays, I can't afford to keep you. I must start looking round for a modest little house to rent in Tunbridge Wells, convenient to the office, and more agreeable to the children now they are growing up. Mother has left only small legacies for her grandchildren. She must have been living beyond her means for some time. It was selfish of me to take it for granted that she could afford to keep us all, when we came home from the Congo. She always spoke vaguely of her private means, and I had no idea her resources had dwindled so alarmingly until I saw her solicitor. You do understand the position, don't you, Ruby? I am so sorry.'

'Now don't you start worrying about me, Miss Marion. It's like I always said, when one door closes another one opens. Somethink will turn up.'

'Mr Micawber,' murmured Marion, smiling wanly.

'Beg pardon, Miss?'

'Dickens' Mr Micawber. It was his unshakeable conviction that something would turn up.'

'I seem to 'ave 'eard that afore today, Miss.'

'I expect you have, Ruby. Do you know what I fancy just at this moment? – a nice cup of tea. I was never very partial to sherry.'

'You shall 'ave it, Miss. I'll put on the kettle right away. There's nothing like a nice cup of tea to buck you up.'

Waiting for the kettle to boil, however, Ruby's heart sank at the dismal prospect of starting all over again – a fresh job, another mistress, a strange kitchen.

'I feel proper flummoxed, and that's a fact,' she told herself irritably.

After tea, Marion chatted cheerfully about the problems of moving house, and the reactions of her children, but her mind was only partially occupied by these mundane matters. Why shouldn't she accept the proposal of marriage in the letter she had received in the afternoon post, and had tucked into her pocket? It was the first proposal she had ever received, she reflected, since it was she who had proposed to her darling Malcolm! No man could ever replace that first love in her heart, and no two men could be more different. Mother had been right to remind her that she had lived too long in the past. The children were growing up, and would soon be independent. They would have their own plans and ambitions, but would be reluctant to discuss them openly for fear of hurting her feelings.

She had to face reality. Every widowed mother had either to marry again or spend long years in loneliness.

She thanked Ruby for the tea, promised to make enquiries about another post, and went up to her bedroom to re-read the letter that was burning a hole in her pocket:

My very dear Marion,

This seems a good opportunity to put on paper what I have been intending to say for the past few weeks. You may think it presumptuous. It *is* presumptuous, for a man from the slums of Newcastle to ask a lady of gentle birth for her hand in marriage. Even so, I have to risk a rebuff. Fools rush in where angels fear to tread! I love you very much, my dear. Will you marry me?

Yours ever,

Stephen.

She was blushing, and her heart was pounding as she took a sheet of notepaper from her bureau to answer the letter.

They were married by special licence two weeks later.

Stephen Grant had been living at the Victoria Hotel for the past twelve months or so, and would be glad to move into a home of his own. Marion travelled to and from the village by bus for several weeks after their marriage, till Stephen decided this was too exhausting and insisted that she leave the packing and dismantling of the cottage to her capable housekeeper, and join him at the hotel till a suitable house was found. He had engaged another secretary – an older woman, unlikely to disturb the harmony of his recent marriage!

It was no longer imperative to find a modest little house to rent. Stephen seemed to have unlimited funds to buy a house, and they spent several enjoyable weekends inspecting properties that Marion had seen and liked during the week, finally deciding on a Georgian house in two acres of garden.

Marion kept in touch with Ruby on the telephone, and they met one afternoon at Freddie's place for tea. Ruby was a proud grandmother again after many years of waiting and hoping, and the disappointment over Carrie. Even the dismal prospect of finding another job and starting all over again had been swept aside in the joy of her new role. It had been a difficult birth, and Freddie had sat for hours in the waiting room of the maternity wing at the hospital, sick with anxiety, determined it would never happen again. Other prospective fathers kept him company, and the nurses were reassuringly cheerful and served them with cups of tea at frequent intervals. Freddie felt quite ill. He had eaten nothing all day, and refused to leave the hospital until it was all over.

'It will be a long wait, I'm afraid, Mr Simmons,' Sister Maternity informed him, kindly. 'A first birth normally takes longer than subsequent births, but your wife is most co-operative, and very brave.'

'My wife never makes a fuss about anything, Sister. As for subsequent births, there won't be any!'

Sister smiled. She had heard that pronouncement a hundred times, but when the baby was safely delivered, he would forget about this ordeal of waiting.

Limping up and down to stretch his cramped body, he was filled with dread as the hours dragged by. He could see himself as a widower with a tiny motherless child. Cynthia was going to die! Perhaps she had already died, and they were reluctant to tell him. Her young sister, Penny, had died in childbirth, and her elder sister, Beatrice, had almost died after the birth of the last child. He remembered the mothers who had died in childbirth at the Hospital for Women when Cynthia was working for her midwifery exam. It had always upset her. She was so sensitive – too sensitive for hospital nursing, in his opinion.

'But, my darling, I adore it. It means as much to me as your work means to you. One must be dedicated to one's profession or one may as well be a dustman, or a lavatory lady!' she had insisted. He loved her cultured voice. She was so articulate. It was her voice and her wide, intelligent eyes that he had first noticed, that day in Aunt Lucy's parlour, when he recovered consciousness after the accident. It seemed a long time ago. She was so impulsive, so lavish in her endearments. She called him 'Darling', 'Dearest', 'Beloved', while he hesitated over 'My dear girl'. She was so embarrassingly frank, he was the one to blush!

'Dear God, don't take her away,' he prayed. But why should God listen now, when he had forgotten his prayers for so long? Cynthia still said her prayers, kneeling at the bedside like a child. She swore it was her prayers that had saved him from spending the rest of his life in a wheelchair. He hadn't argued over the issue, but he knew it was not God. It was her courage and her caring. Without her he could never have endured the suffering and the frustration. Even now, there were days when an old wound ached intolerably, or the stump of his leg throbbed like an aching tooth. There would be no purpose in life without her. If she died and the child lived, he would blame that child for the rest of its days. Male or female, what did it matter? What did anything matter if he lost Cynthia?

He was alone in the waiting room when the door opened and the nurse announced quietly, 'You have a lovely little daughter, Mr Simmons.'

'My wife?' he whispered.

'She is sleeping comfortably.'

'Thank you, Sister. Thank you very much.'

She was not even a staff nurse, but it pleased her enormously.

'You may see her just for a moment, but she mustn't be disturbed. She is very tired.'

He followed her out of the room. She draped him in a white gown, and tied a mask over his face. He felt rather foolish, but he would have worn a suit of armour had she insisted. Under the mask his mouth trembled, but his eyes were shining and black as onyx. She looked very young and frail, lying there. He was choked with his love for her, and very humble. The nurse touched his arm to remind him to look at his daughter. He looked down on a tiny, shapely head covered in a smudge of hair, a cheek as soft to his touch as a petal, and one minute ear, no bigger than the tiniest shell Carrie had collected on the beach at Hastings on a rare seaside outing.

'She's very small, isn't she?' he whispered.

'She'll grow. She is exactly forty minutes old, and she weighs six pounds seven ounces,' said nurse, as one would remind a rather backward child of an obvious fact.

She helped him to disrobe in the adjoining annexe. Then he thanked her again and walked away down the long corridor, down the steps, and out of the main entrance. He walked home through the silent streets, and let himself into his silent house. But the silence was impregnated with joy and hope and love.

They stood at the window, watching the proud grandmother pushing the baby in the new pram on to the Common. Everything was brand new, including the pink bonnet and bootees that Ruby had knitted so laboriously.

Freddie had his arm about Cynthia's waist. It was strange to see her so slim again. She had decided to call the baby Wendy. They had so enjoyed *Peter Pan*, it seemed to be appropriate, and Freddie didn't mind. He took his turn with the pram in the afternoons when Cynthia was resting, and limped along The Pantiles.

'May I look?' the superior Tunbridge Wells matrons would ask, for it was unusual for a man to be pushing a pram. 'Such a beautiful baby!' 'Isn't she adorable?' they cooed – and Freddie glowed with pride.

Cynthia was wondering how soon she could approach the subject of taking up her disrupted nursing career, and whether Freddie would think she was an unnatural mother. Looking at her mother-in-law's sturdy little figure, they both were reminded that only a couple of weeks remained of the three months that Sir Neville had allowed them before the cottage must be vacated.

'Poor old Mum. She does seem unlucky. I do wish she had a settled home. She has been moving around ever since Dad died,' Freddie mused.

It was too good an opportunity to miss, and Cynthia plunged.

'Why don't we offer her a home, darling, and give her a little pocket money? She could have the small bedroom we had intended for Wendy, and we can have the cot in our room.'

'Can we afford it, dear? I mean, we are not exactly prosperous, are we?'

'We could afford it if I had a job.' He took her chin in his hand and turned her face towards him. '*Please*, darling?'

He sighed. 'I suppose I should have realised what you had in mind, but I didn't want to think about it.'

'I was not going to mention it for another six months because I fully intended to carry on feeding Wendy, but I can't. I've explained to you about the milk. She's not getting enough nourishment, and I have already put her on to Allenbury's for the last feed of the day. She could be weaned off the breast gradually, and Mother could take over the bottle feeding, and she could do the cooking, then neither of you would be neglected. I would so love to go back. May I?'

His smile was a little wistful, but he knew it was the only way to keep her happy. Being a housewife, even with a young child, was not enough, not for Cynthia.

'I won't do full time. I can stipulate a certain number of hours, and no night duty. I promise. *Please*, darling.'

'All right. You win.'

She flung her arms about his neck. There were tears on her lashes. 'Thank you, my darling. Thank you! Thank you!' She was trembling with emotion.

'Shall we tell her today?'

He nodded, and kissed her radiant face.

An hour or so later, Ruby pushed open the gate and wheeled the pram to the front door. Freddie and Cynthia were standing on the doorstep, their arms entwined about each other's waist. Like a couple of young sweethearts, those two, Ruby was thinking. It was a real treat to spend a day with them, and she had caught the early train.

'Never closed 'er eyes not for a second, the little luv. She don't miss a thing! I never saw such a young baby so knowing,' she asserted.

'You're prejudiced in her favour, Mum, because she's your grandchild,' Freddie teased affectionately.

'Say what you like, but it's a fact.' Ruby's face was glowing with health, her blue eyes shining.

'You will be glad of a cup of tea, Mother. I'll put on the kettle. Leave the pram there. She might drop off to sleep now the pram has stopped rocking. Most babies fall asleep when they are rocked. *Our* baby wakes up!'

Our baby. Ruby was pleased. It gave her a nice feeling of being allowed to share this precious little mite in a special kind of way. She followed them into the kitchen, and Freddie pulled up a chair for his Mum. Such luverly manners! All her children was brought up to be polite and respectful to their betters, but Freddie had adapted his ways to the girl from the upper class, and now you would never guess he was born and bred in Richmond Row. She took the pins out of her hat and laid it carefully on the table. She always wore her Sunday best when she visited Cynthia and Freddie, and her working clothes when she called on Elsie and the children. That was only one of the differences she made between them, quite unconsciously, not intending to be unkind. Elsie had always been jealous of Cynthia. She thought she was stuck-up because she spoke proper.

'It's not 'er fault, luv. You and me would speak the same way if we was born and bred at Marston Park,' Ruby had explained, but Elsie was not convinced. They only met at family weddings and funerals, and Wendy's christening would be the next important event in the family. Cynthia would send out invitations to everyone on Freddie's side of the family, including his brother

Albert and his wife, who couldn't be bothered to dress up, and were downright dowdy. Ruby would feel ashamed of her eldest son and wish, not for the first time, it had not been her Jack that was killed in the War. She was ashamed of such thoughts, but it was true. That Eva was a slut and it was no secret that she had slept with one of the German prisoners who worked on the farm while her husband was away. Be that as it may, Albert was spared, and hardly a scratch to prove he had served his King and Country.

The kitchen window opened on to a small neglected garden with a patch of rough grass that could never be described as a lawn. Weather permitting, the baby would be pushed out in her pram, after her morning bath, and left there till lunch time, for Cynthia's hospital training could never be disregarded. She had method, and an easy assurance that so many mothers lacked. In no time at all the baby would be fed, bathed, and smelling sweetly of powder and Pears soap, and tucked into her pram. Then Cynthia would get on with the chores. She enjoyed cooking, but housework was sheer drudgery. It had to be done thoroughly, according to her strict principles.

'You tell her, darling,' she had insisted, as they stood waiting for Ruby's return. It pleased Freddie enormously. A man has his pride. He knew if he had objected, Cynthia would stay at home. But this was no time to play the dominant role in a partnership so mutually agreeable.

'How would you like to live here with us, Mum, permanently?' he asked, as they sipped the hot tea.

Ruby looked from one to the other with a puzzled frown. They both were smiling.

'You're teasing me,' she said.

'No, I'm not teasing. We need a housekeeper, don't we, dear?'

'And a nanny for young Wendy,' Cynthia added.

'But. . . but. . .' Ruby stammered helplessly, waiting

for further confirmation.

'Cynthia wants to take up her nursing career. She feels all the years have been wasted otherwise. She's right, of course, isn't she?'

'Yes, I reckon so.'

'Well then, how about it? Make up your mind!'

Ruby gulped. Tears streamed down her face. 'It would be luverly,' she sobbed.

'Don't cry, Mother, darling,' Cynthia begged, giving her a warm hug. 'You will be doing us a favour, and we should love to have you.'

'It's knocked me all of a'neap, and that's a fact. To think I don't 'ave to start all over again looking for a new job. Miss Marion won't 'arf be pleased. She were getting a bit worried. Said she felt responsible. Likely as not she'll be popping over to see me when I gets settled. 'ow soon would you want me to start, my luv?' she asked her daughter-in-law, eagerly. 'There ain't no call to 'ang around in that empty cottage once I got it all turned out, and that won't take me more than a couple of days, now I knows for sure what I be going to do.'

'Come as soon as you like, Mother. Just let us know when to expect you, and I will meet you at the station. The carrier will collect your boxes. Have you got a lot of stuff?'

'Not more than will go in the old tin trunk. I been getting rid of it. What with all the moving around, and such poky little rooms. No, don't you worry, my luv. I won't make no mess and muddle. I be too used to being tidy. Now, shall I peel them taties, and 'ow about a nice apple pie? After I've 'ad me dinner, I'll get that pile of ironing done, and give this floor a scrub,' she decided, and tied on her apron.

Marion was surprised and hurt at the reactions of her

three children to her second marriage. All three hoped she would be happy with Mr Grant, but there was no warmth in their felicitations. All three behaved like adults – perhaps they were adults? – and told her of the plans they had made for the future. Obviously they had already decided, and had not even consulted her. Since she had never been close to her daughters, it was not so hurtful and she had read their letters quite calmly and replied, by return post, that of course they must please themselves, and sent her love and best wishes.

Agnes had written that she had decided to share a flat in London with Barbara Heath-Jones. They had much in common. Neither intended to marry, and would like to follow a political career. Both had diplomas for shorthand, typewriting and book-keeping, and were reasonably intelligent. They had decided to approach several parliamentary candidates (Labour) and offer their secretarial services. Since Agnes had not once mentioned her political motives, or her secretarial accomplishments, Marion could only assume that this Barbara Heath-Jones had a very strong influence on her elder daughter. But – LABOUR! What next? Grandmother would be horrified. It was so far removed from the Liberal tradition, and her unswerving loyalty to the Party.

As for Harriet, she had simply stated, in her own particular way, that she had always regretted leaving the Mission, and would be going back to the Congo as soon as she had completed a short course of nursing, and studied the modern methods of treating tropical diseases. She hoped Mother would understand, and she hoped Mother would be happy with Mr Grant. That was all, and it was not too surprising, since Harriet, who had been Malcolm's favourite, had always declared she would go back one day.

But it was Richard's letter that was causing so much

heartache. To have her adored son so deceitful – and it *was* deceitful to keep her in the dark of his intentions, and then to spring it on her so suddenly, so soon after her marriage.

My Dearest Mother,

I am afraid this is going to be rather a nasty shock. I had fully intended to tell you during the few days I was home for Grandmother's funeral, but I funked it. I have been taking instruction from a Jesuit priest, and when I am acceptable, I shall be received into the Catholic Faith. I have been seriously thinking of the priesthood for quite some time. I suppose it's hereditary with Grandfather and Father both with their devout convictions. But it is the Roman Catholic Faith that appeals to me so strongly. It has been suggested that I enter a Jesuit College in Brussels for a three-year period of training after leaving University. This I have decided to do. I hope you are well, and I hope you will be happy with Mr Grant.

Ever your affectionate son,

Richard.

The letter dropped to the floor, and she burst into tears – angry, hurt, tears. Such selfishness! Such utter disregard of her feelings! She wept until she was quite exhausted. Yet Richard was only following a similar independent path to his destiny as she herself had followed in her youth. Hadn't the favourite daughter broken her father's heart when she married the young missionary, and went off to the Congo for five long years? So each new generation falls short of the aspirations of the older generation. It was part of the pattern, the suffering, and the bitter disappointment.

When she had calmed herself, she sipped a glass of

sherry and picked up the telephone. It was seldom that she bothered Stephen in office hours, but the need to be reassured that at least one person still cared was too strong to resist. He listened patiently, told her not to upset herself since her children were old enough to decide for themselves, and promised to be home early. His nice, ordinary voice had a down-to-earth directness that was very steadying to her nerves. Sometimes she found his lack of culture and refinement a little disconcerting, but then she reminded herself of his good qualities, and admired his achievements. Stephen had a positive genius for making money. She would not enquire into his methods; these did not concern her. The lean years were over, and she was enjoying the spoiling and the luxuries that had always been beyond her reach.

Stephen was not the only man to prosper during the War years while younger men had fought and died in their thousands. In the short period she had worked for him as his secretary, she had often heard him on the telephone, giving instructions to his broker to buy or sell certain shares, but he did not confide in her. She was such a novice in the world of business. Now they were married, he never mentioned the office, and again she did not enquire. He loved her ardently and protectively, but it was a physical love, and neither the intellect nor the spirit had any part in it.

Since that unforgettable day in the Christmas vacation when Philip had been invited to join the sledging party and fallen in love with the young Harriet, he had haunted Russets during each vacation with the vague hope that she might be there. Class consciousness was still an important factor, and Harriet's brother Richard and her sister Agnes never failed to insinuate that he was trespassing where he had no right. Whenever he met the three altogether, he became so inarticulate he appeared quite stupid. His serious expression and lack of humour was a ready target for teasing.

Another obstacle to his lack of progress with Harriet was the child, Julian. She adored the little boy as she adored all small children, and he would rush to meet her to be enfolded in her arms when she climbed over the gate at Russets, and thereafter clung to her hand. Even Albert and Carrie took second place to Harriet in the holidays.

Lucy watched the obvious signs of Philip's growing attachment to the girl with her usual sympathy and understanding, and Carrie was sorry for the lad she had known and loved since he was first pushed into the Infants' classroom in his pram. That was a decision to shock the school governors, and set the gossips' tongues wagging. When the schoolmaster not only invited Teacher to take over the classroom again, but to bring the baby – a child born out of wedlock – and then to act as godfather to the child . . . well . . .! It was more than a nine days' wonder in the village, and probably the start of that particular attachment between a teacher and her superior.

Philip had grown surprisingly like Andrew in appearance of recent years, and his influence was quite considerable. In the company of his academic step-father, the boy could hold his own, but not in the company of his contemporaries. The entrance examination to Cambridge could not have been achieved without the help and encouragement of Andrew Robinson.

The years had slipped away, and the young generation grown into maturity too quickly for the mothers who would have kept them for ever in the realms of childhood if they had their way. Both Martha and Marion had been shocked and distressed by the obvious signs that the umbilical cord had been severed, and their children held independent views, incompatible with their own. But it was only when Agnes had finished school and followed her brother to Oxford that Harriet emerged from under the dominance of the elder sister. Gradually, like a bud unfolding, she began to display an interesting and likeable personality, and to develop her own particular talents. That she flatly refused to be coached for the entrance examination to university – and wouldn't have passed anyway – was a big disappointment to Philip, who had hoped their friendly relationship might blossom into something more romantic under the dreaming spires of the famous colleges.

It was not to be. Harriet knew exactly what she intended to do, and how to set about it. Cynthia proved a useful ally. In no time at all she was enrolled as a student nurse at the Hospital for Women, and had to endure the same kind of drudgery. Cynthia had warned her, however, not to mention to anyone her intention to leave at the end of her second year. The laws of the Medes and Persians were as nothing compared to the rules and regulations of the nursing profession!

Once again a slim, neat figure in uniform would hurry from the station to meet her friends at Russets. Once again, Lucy would welcome a girl from the upper class as naturally as she welcomed Katie's friend – a servant at one of the farms on the big estate. Unlike her twin sister Ruby, she had long since decided that class barriers should be abolished.

'If I was considered good enough to be the mother of Sir Neville's son and heir, then I'm good enough for anyone!' she contended.

She was right, of course. In the cosmopolitan atmosphere of the hospital, Harriet had completely lost her class consciousness. Since the War, the wards were brightened by the cheerful chatter and pretty gestures of Belgian, French and Dutch nurses.

'She treats me like a brother,' Philip complained to Carrie, one day. 'Can't she see I am in love with her?'

'Perhaps she doesn't want to see? Have you told her you love her?'

'Not in so many words.'

'Then perhaps you should?'

'I don't know. It's all so unsettling and unsatisfactory. I like to know where I stand. I hate all this uncertainty.'

'But life is like that, my dear. I thought I knew what the future held when I was engaged as a nursemaid to Doctor's grandson, but I was mistaken, for nothing went according to plan. The War changed everything. You were too young to be directly involved. The rest of us had to compromise and come to terms with a new way of life.'

'But Harriet does like me, doesn't she?'

'I'm sure she does. I think she is just being sensible, not to get involved emotionally. Unless you would be willing to give up everything for the Congo, Harriet would never think of you as a husband. She is already dedicated to that Mission.'

'That's true. She talks of nothing else when we are together.'

'Well, then, it shouldn't be too difficult to make up your mind. If you love her more than your own career, then you should be willing to make the sacrifice – that is, assuming she would marry you?'

'Shouldn't it be the man to lead the way and the woman to follow, like Mother and Uncle Andrew?'

'Your mother had a very different reason to wait for a proposal of marriage. She had you. Harriet is her father's daughter, and his influence in those early years must have been very strong indeed to last this long. No two women are alike, Philip, and cannot be labelled to suit your requirements. Circumstances can change the whole nature of a person, for better or worse.'

'In some ways I wish I had never met Harriet, then I could settle down to my studies. If I am ever to pass those law exams I have to get down to it seriously in the next couple of years. Being in love is so darn distracting!' he sighed heavily.

'Poor Philip! You have all my sympathy.' Carrie's smile was wistful. Being in love with Tom was her own personal cross to carry. Philip wouldn't know about that. She kissed him affectionately, and promised to let him know when Harriet was due for her next leave.

Easter was late that year, and the primroses fading in the wood where the bluebells had spread their carpet under the beeches. The hedgerows were draped with hawthorn and catkins, shiny yellow celandine spread over the ditches and violets were there on the sheltered banks for those who were young at heart. The sweet-scented white violets had to be searched for, but the unscented blue grew more prominently and had no shyness.

For Carrie it was a time of enchantment, and she often escaped from the chores to pick the wild flowers that faded so quickly in the house. Every year Tom would tease her about her childishness, yet he loved to see she could still behave like a child for all the restraint she exercised when they were together.

For young Julian, however, Easter was a time of big chocolate eggs, arriving by post in cardboard boxes. The biggest came always from Uncle Charles who was living in America with Auntie Sylvia and her husband. For breakfast on Easter Sunday there would be a coloured egg, and now that he was seven he would be going to church with Auntie Carrie and Auntie Harriet, who seemed to think he was old enough to behave nicely for the long service, lasting for one and a half hours. But the walk across the Park was full of interest for a small boy so essentially a country child. He had walked to school in all weathers with the farm children since he was five, and he had grown into a sturdy boy on the nourishing food and loving care he naturally accepted as his birthright. He never asked to go to the village or expected a holiday. Russets was his whole world, and the village school but a compulsory interruption at certain seasons of the year. Uncle Tom was the supreme authority on cows, horses, sheep and pigs. Uncle Bertie had a preference for the feathered creatures that ran free as air in the orchard and the barns. There was nobody more gentle with the tiny chicks, or more upset when a fox or a stoat raided the hen-house and left behind a trail of severed heads and bloody feathers. There were ducks on the pond and fat geese waddling across the yard. Uncle Bertie tied strings of nuts on the branches of the oldest apple tree to feed the birds in the Winter months, and a tame robin hopped into the kitchen to pick up the crumbs that Katie scattered.

It happened so suddenly – the stinging blow on the face, he dropped the hoop and stood there, stunned by the blow, with an awful feeling that he was going to be sick. But Teacher came to the rescue, rounding on his tormentors with her ruler. They dropped the hoop and fled, and he was led away to the safety of the Infants' classroom, the smells of the coke stove, wet boots, chalk and plasticine.

'Sit down, dear, and drink this water,' said Teacher.

He drank the water and felt better. Teacher was nice. She reminded him of Mrs Noah in the picture book about the Ark that he had when he was a little boy. Now he was a Big Boy he could read *Black Beauty*.

'I wouldn't bring the hoop to school, Julian, if I were you. It's rather tempting to boys who have no money to buy a hoop, and no kind uncles.'

It was the first indication that other children were not so fortunate as himself.

'All right,' he agreed. And they smiled at each other, the teacher who understood that each child was an individual person in its own right, and the small boy who had just discovered there were enemies in the harsh world beyond the Russets' acres.

'Harriet will be here on Easter Sunday,' Lucy told Philip on the telephone. 'She is visiting her mother and step-father in Tunbridge Wells on Good Friday and staying overnight with Cynthia and Freddie and little Wendy. She said to expect her some time in the late evening. You are most welcome to join us for dinner on Sunday, Philip, and spend the rest of the day with us. I expect you will be singing something special in the choir for Easter Sunday, won't you?'

'Yes, Aunt Lucy. It's from Handel's *Messiah*.'

'That should be lovely, dear.' Lucy was not familiar with Handel or his *Messiah*, but she had no doubt that Philip would make a good job of it. They had all been surprised by the strength and quality of his voice at the carol concert in the village hall last Christmas Eve. His appearance was deceptive, and his speaking voice quite ordinary.

'Thank you for letting me know about Harriet, Aunt Lucy. Will she be coming to church on Easter Sunday morning, do you suppose?'

'Sure to. She never misses her churchgoing if she can help it. Harriet is a very good-living girl.'

'I know.'

'I expect Carrie and Julian will keep her company, then you can all walk back together across the Park.'

His heart sank. He could foresee the child demanding all her attention, and the family gathered about the kitchen table for dinner, then probably sitting out in the yard in the afternoon or wandering around the farm, inspecting the new-born calf, the litter of piglets, and a newly hatched brood of chicks. He was not very interested in the farm, but they had been visiting at Russets since he was no bigger than Julian. It was Carrie who had first introduced him to the farm and the family, and of later years, he had often cycled there with his mother and Uncle Andrew.

'There won't be a lot of time, Aunt Lucy. I have to be back in the choir for the evening service,' he explained, after she had finished chatting about this and that.

'Aunt Lucy and Aunt Ruby could talk the hind legs off a donkey,' Mother would say. And when they got on the telephone, they didn't know when to stop!

'What a shame, dear, I suppose you couldn't play truant just for once?'

'No. It wouldn't be fair. The evening congregation will be expecting a solo. You see, it's mentioned in the *Parish Magazine*.'

'You're getting to be quite a local celebrity, Philip. They tell me you have joined the Tunbridge Wells Choral Society, and sometimes they give a concert at the Albert Hall.'

'That's right.'

'Wouldn't you be terribly nervous it you had to sing on your own in that great place?'

'Yes, I should, but only in anticipation. One soon becomes too involved with the part to be nervous.'

'It's a wonderful gift. Your mother must be very proud of you. She will be there, of course, on Easter Sunday with your step-father.'

'Yes.'

'She won't mind you spending the rest of the day with us?'

'She understands about Harriet. I mean, she has known for some time.'

'You told her?'

'No, she guessed.'

Lucy chuckled. 'Mothers have a way of knowing!'

'I sometimes think Mother reads my thoughts.'

'That doesn't surprise me, dear. You are so close and so devoted. She's a wonderful woman, your mother, to be taking on yet another generation of children in that classroom. Now it's Julian's turn, and I have to listen to what Teacher says, and what Teacher has done, every afternoon when he gets home. She tells me he is bright as a button, but not particularly interested in school. My boys were the same. It seems a long time ago.'

There was a pause, but he didn't interrupt. For one thing, he had nothing more to say, and for another, he knew she was feeling nostalgic for those early years.

'Where are you going for your Summer holidays this year?' She was back in the present, as cheerful as ever. Her lively interest in everything and everybody was one of her most endearing qualities.

'The Isle of Wight as usual, I expect. We all enjoy it, so why change?'

'The same boarding house at Sandown?'

'I expect so.'

'It must be nice to have a warm welcome every year. Sort of home from home.'

'Yes.'

'But it's only for two weeks. What shall you do with the rest of the long holiday?'

'What we usually do, Aunt Lucy – potter about, go for

long cycle rides, have a look at the hop-pickers, and have a look at Russets. We are not much help with the harvest, I'm afraid, but Mother brews a good pot of tea!'

'You are always welcome, dear, you know that, and Harriet will be here whenever she can get time off from the hospital. She won't spend much time with her mother. She doesn't get on too well with her step-father. Charles has promised us a visit this Summer, and Sir Neville is quite a frequent visitor these days. Russets is an open house. The more the merrier as far as I'm concerned!'

'So you see quite a lot of Sir Neville now that he is back at Marston Park?'

'Yes. Julian is the main attraction, of course. He offered to buy the child a pony, but I refused.'

'Why?'

'Because it could be the thin edge of the wedge, Philip. Charles was seven when he was taken away and sent to boarding school, and thereafter I saw him for only short periods in the holidays.'

'But he wouldn't rob you of Julian, surely?'

'One never knows what Sir Neville might decide to do, and Julian is very fond of his grandfather, and very proud of him. Only last Saturday, when he had little Sammy Mercer here for the day and they were playing so happily in the big barn, Sir Neville suddenly rode into the yard and spoiled everything.'

'How?'

'Why, Julian ran out, very excited, and Sir Neville asked him if he would like a ride on his horse. Of course the child said he would. Then Sir Neville scooped him up and sat him in front. I saw what was happening and ran out. Sammy was crying, and Julian called out, "He's not *your* grandfather!" I was furious, but Sir Neville only laughed. "Where are you going? When will you be back?" I called after them. "Later. I'll take good care of him. He's safe enough with me," he called back. Then they rode away, and I was left to comfort Sammy and give him his tea. Tom took him home when he had finished milking. That's the sort of thing that makes me wonder what he had in mind for the future.'

'I shouldn't let it worry you too much, Aunt Lucy. It was different with Charles. He was the son and heir, and you knew what to expect as soon as he was born, so Mother told me.'

'If it happens again with Julian, it would break my heart. There is a limit to what a woman can put up with.'

Philip made no answer. From his own young memories of the War years, it seemed there was no limit to a woman's endurance. His own mother had suffered physically and mentally with her first husband. That was still a vivid memory.

'Well, dear, I suppose I must hang up. I hope I have not interrupted your studies? Give my love to your dear mother, and my regards to Mr Robinson. Till Easter Sunday!'

'Till Easter Sunday,' he echoed, and hung up the receiver with a wry smile. Next time the phone rang he would leave Mother to answer it!

When Lucy put the receiver on the hook, her face was flushed. She always enjoyed a chat. It kept her in touch with everyone, and she hadn't to write letters. Yet she remembered a time before Charles was born, when they had no telephone, and messages were conveyed by horseback or Shanks' pony. Those were the days when they had to wait hours for the doctor, and she had to cope with any emergency. A life could be saved by prompt first aid, and common sense.

She stood there, gazing at Katie staggering under the weight of a heavy basket of washing she had collected from the orchard. But she was thinking of Julian. Would he be weaned away from her as Charles was weaned away from Russets? And was it only the child that Sir Neville came to see? He still could make her tremble and blush like a young girl. It was ridiculous the fascination he still held for her. Apart from his greying head, he was the same man who had seduced her that Michaelmas Day. And apart from a few grey hairs in her own head and the extra pounds of flesh on her plump body, she was the same woman.

If he wanted to lay with her again, would she be willing? she asked herself – and knew the answer!

Chapter 9

She had just sat down for five minutes in the early evening on Easter Sunday, when the telephone rang.

'Who is that speaking?' asked the unmistakable cultured voice.

'Lucy,' she said, and shivered in the warmth of the sun on the oak floorboards.

'Are you alone, Lucy?' he asked.

'Yes.'

'Where is everyone?'

'Gone on a picnic to the river.'

'Good. Expect me in about twenty minutes, and don't run away!' He hung up the receiver before she had time to reply. His voice was like a magnet, drawing her irresistibly back into the past. She had no strength, no will of her own to oppose him. The years had changed nothing between them, yet she knew his history was one of infidelity and his arrogance insufferable. How many mistresses had he known and loved and discarded in all the years of his virile manhood? The young actress had been clever, so they said. She had a young lover for some time before Sir Neville discovered he was being made to look a fool. Now he was probably bored, back at Marston Park, and she was nothing more than a tenant farmer on his estate for whom he had neither affection nor loyalty.

The War years had changed all their lives, but it had not changed the fundamental principles of Sir Neville Franklin. He still could remove his grandson from Russets; he still could alter the lease in which her sons would take over the farm after her death. He still could use her as a convenient substitute till he found another mistress. She was shamed by a situation she had no means to resist, and she stood there, trembling and sweating in one of the clean cotton frocks she always turned out at Easter, whatever the weather. It was too tight. She had put on more weight in the Winter without the strenuous field work. The bodice was stretched tight across her full bosom. It was time she bought something new to wear, but there was little money to spare for clothes, and she never went anywhere, so why bother? He will not even notice what I am wearing, she reminded herself, for she had no illusions about this relationship, and she was more than ever convinced that his need of her now was in some way connected with Julian.

She had not moved, and was still standing on the sun-warmed floorboards when she heard the clatter of hooves in the cobbled yard. A few minutes later, a shadow darkened the door. It was like putting back the clock all those years, when he laid his hat and gloves on the kitchen table and smiled the same disarming smile that Charles had inherited. But this time she made no protest as the hot flush swept over her neck and face, and she stared at him with her wide blue eyes. She was leading the way upstairs when he stopped her.

'Wait. There is no hurry. Can't we sit down and drink a glass of wine? Let's be civilised over this, my dear.'

Still she made no answer, so he pulled up a kitchen chair and sat down. Then she went down to the cellar and brought up a bottle of elderberry wine. It was very potent.

Albert had drunk too much of it on Boxing Day and been put to bed on the sofa. She poured two glasses, and he sipped the wine appreciatively.

'Excellent! You must let Hetty have the recipe.'

When he had finished, he held up his glass to be refilled, and asked gently, 'What's the matter, Lucy?'

She shook her head. 'Nothing.'

'You don't trust me, do you?'

Her eyes flooded with tears, and she stood there, twisting her hands. Suddenly she fell on her knees and pleaded chokingly, 'Don't take Julian away. I couldn't bear it. You promised, Sir. You promised!'

'Who said anything about taking the boy away? And don't call me Sir!' He put down the glass on the kitchen table and took her face between his hands. 'Silly little Lucy. You imagine things. Just because I offered to buy a pony for the boy, and gave him a ride on the horse, you see some ulterior motive. He *is* my grandson, Lucy, and I am fond of the child. Would you deprive me of his company altogether because of that promise to let him grow up at Russets?'

'No.'

'Well, then?'

'I'm sorry.'

Looking into those wet blue eyes, he was reminded of the day when her husband fell off the wagon and broke his neck, and he was there to comfort her. She had wept in his arms, and he had never forgotten the smell of earth and sweat, or the softness of her warm, plump body. She was all woman still. In her sweet simplicity, she showed up the artificiality of all those other women. He supposed he had always been attracted to Lucy, even before that fateful day, but his pride forbade him to take a mistress on his own estate. But Lucy was the mother of his son, his only son, and was still a lovely and lovable woman. He wondered why she had not married again. There was Isaac Sillitoe, over at the Home Farm, a widower for some years with a grown-up family, and a fine upstanding fellow.

'Why are you trembling?' he asked. 'You are not afraid of me?'

'I love you. I think I have always loved you,' she whispered.

His dark eyes were as soft as velvet now. 'My dear.' He kissed her with a tenderness he had not felt for any other woman, only for Charles, as a baby and a little boy, when he had lifted him from his mother's arms into his own. 'I am a lonely man, Lucy. I need you.' He did not say he loved her, and she didn't expect it. Neither did she expect to be his wife. Their two separate worlds were too wide apart. But to lie with him, to satisfy the longing in her strong body, that was all she asked. Her maternity had been satisfied, but not this tormenting sensuality that often kept her awake at nights.

'After today, is there ever a time when I would find you alone?' he was asking, as he dried her tears with his clean handkerchief.

'There's Saturday, market day. Even Albert goes to market now, and he would take Julian. Katie has her free half-day to meet a friend in the village.'

'I shall be here.'

She sat back on her heels and gazed at him. Now, at last, he would be her lover. He took her hands and pulled her to her feet.

'Kiss me,' he said.

Her arms slid round his neck. His lips were hard. They had been hard that other time, and he had taken her roughly. She wondered if it would be any different today, and if this new gentleness would disappear when they stripped off their clothes.

They climbed the stairs with his arm about her waist. In the silent house there was no sound, but through the open windows came the twittering of the house martins in the eaves. Even the dog had gone on a picnic!

It was not often they all went on a picnic together, but it was Easter Sunday, and a special treat for Julian who ran about gathering sticks to start a fire, while Tom piled stones in a semi-circle to keep off the draught. A fresh breeze was blowing across the fields. To boil water in an old saucepan and make fresh tea was a novelty, and Julian had carried the saucepan. The tea would have a smoky taste that Tom called 'coochy' but it was a picnic, and better than having tea out of a flask, said Harriet.

She was helping Carrie to spread the food on the white cloth. Albert and Philip sat on the grass watching. It was tantalising for Philip who now realised there would be no time at all to be alone with Harriet. It was different for Albert, who was married to Carrie and had her company day and night, seven days a week all through the year.

They sat there, hugging their knees, while the child ran back and forth with twigs for the fire. Tom had brought paper and matches. Nothing was forgotten.

From behind a cloud of billowing smoke, he glanced at Carrie's bright head and bare legs. She had left off her stockings today, and her legs were white. Soon her arms and legs would be tanned a golden brown, her pale cheeks would be flushed, and her eyes as blue as the periwinkles she gathered in the wood. She was very pretty in the Summer, like his mother only younger. They seemed to bloom afresh each Summer, working outdoors, leaving Katie to do the household chores. Baking would be done in the early morning or the late evening. But now it was Spring, an enchanted season that held also a measure of heartache. The years were slipping away. Most of the time he was content just to see her about the place, and to know she belonged to Russets and would never go away. It made his day complete to share the milking, morning and evening, to lift the heavy cans of milk on to the float and watch her ride away to deliver them. Julian went with her now in the holidays. He liked to have a hand in everything. One thing was certain. Sir Neville would never get his grandson to leave Russets, though Mother was not so sure when she saw them together.

'How much more, Uncle Tom?' the boy was asking as he laid another handful of twigs on the small pile.

'We want enough to keep the fire going for a bit after we have made the tea. Can't you find something bigger? Have you looked everywhere?'

'I think so.'

'I'll help,' Philip called out, glad of an excuse to get away from Albert, who was in one of his black moods and disinclined to talk.

They went off together farther afield, and found a lot of chips in a clearing where trees had recently been felled.

'Give them to me. I'll carry them,' said Julian, who wanted everyone to think he had gathered them all himself. Philip filled the child's jersey and he ran on ahead. He was a nice little boy, but of course he had too much attention, being the only child on the farm, Philip was thinking as he sauntered back. In his best suit and shoes he was not suitably dressed for a picnic, but then he would be going to church again this evening.

They had walked back across the Park after the morning service, and Harriet had told him the solo was so beautiful she wanted to cry. It was a very nice compliment. Then Julian had interrupted. He wanted them to look at the cygnets that had recently been hatched on the island in the middle of the lake, and were sailing across the water with the proud parents like a flotilla of tiny ships. It was always the same. Both Carrie and Harriet simply doted on the child. He was their pride and joy, but a definite hindrance to a friendly relationship that was showing little sign of developing into a romance!

When he got back to the camping site, Tom was sprinkling tea into the boiling water, and Harriet and Julian standing by with milk and sugar. Julian was prancing with excitement as the fire blazed.

'My chips have made a lovely fire, haven't they?' he demanded.

'Yes, darling, it was clever of you to find them.' She brushed wood fragments from his jersey and smoothed his ruffled hair. Carrie was lining up the mugs. Philip was choked with envy of the child, and had no appetite for the food or the smoky tea. He wished he had gone home. Mother had been disappointed. She was cooking a chicken, and had made an apple pie for their Easter Sunday dinner. His favourite chocolate cake, decorated with walnuts, was standing on the sideboard ready for tea. It was mean of him not to tell her he had been invited to Russets until today. Over his boiled egg he had mentioned it quite casually. Uncle Andrew was annoyed and most indignant. He always seemed to be upsetting him lately.

'It's all right, dear. I don't mind.' Mother had soothed him, but she *did* mind. He had seen tears in her eyes. Now he was being paid out for his meanness, for he was bored and irritated. It was very uncomfortable and decidedly chilly.

Julian was too excited to eat much, and pestered Carrie to let him take off his shoes and socks. He wanted to run barefoot.

'Keep away from the river, dear,' she reminded him as he ran off.

There was a little pebbly beach at the bottom of the bank, and his mischievous laugh floated back as he ran straight for the river, down the bank, across the pebbly beach, and into the water, without stopping. One second he was there, the next he had disappeared.

'Julian! Julian!'

Carrie and Harriet scrambled to their feet, screaming simultaneously. Tom seemed too stunned to move. His reactions had always been slow in any emergency. Albert and Philip were pulling off their shoes, but Philip was quicker. Dropping his jacket as he ran, his long, loping stride took him across the grass, down the bank, over the beach, and into the water. It was icy cold, and took his breath away, but he found the child almost immediately, brought him to the surface, and carried him up the bank, a limp little figure with closed eyes and a chalk-white face. Had he died of shock?

Stretched face down on the grass, he knelt over him, pressing hard with his thumbs. He knew the drill, and had practised it a number of times at the swimming pool at Grammar School. Swimming and life-saving had been compulsory, like football and cricket and cross-country running. How he had hated it!

'There may come a time when a life will be saved because of your prompt action,' the swimming instructor had told the boys, but young Philip Martin had not seen himself as a hero.

Carrie and Harriet were crying quietly, their arms wrapped about each other for comfort. Tom and Albert were standing back, watching silently, very conscious of their own inadequacy.

He was such a little boy, stretched on the grass and so still. Yet only a few minutes ago he had been laughing and shouting. At the age of seven he was full of mischief and daring. He saw no fear, anywhere, in his small world since

Teacher had explained about the bullies in the school playground. Thereafter he was a favourite, for he shared with other boys his iron hoop, his peg-tops and marbles.

It seemed an eternity that Philip knelt there, the breeze cool on his clinging wet clothes. Then, at last, the child was whimpering and vomiting in the grass. Philip turned him over very gently, took him up in his arms, and handed him to Harriet. It was the most wonderful moment of his whole life, standing there, looking down at the girl with the child in her lap – a child who was alive, and would have been drowned had he not been here today. They were gathered round: Carrie, Albert and Tom, gazing anxiously at the child who was staring back with wide, frightened eyes. For the rest of his life he would remember the deep, dark water closing over his head. There would be no swimming in the river for Julian. He was shuddering with the memory, and Philip picked up his jacket and handed it to Harriet, who wrapped it round the child, but not before their eyes had met, and spoken, as eyes can speak when the tongue is tied. They sat there quietly for some time, then Tom moved away to smother the fire, and Carrie packed the uneaten food and unwashed mugs in the baskets. Albert seemed too shocked to do anything.

When they were ready, they started for home, Tom carrying Julian, still wrapped in Philip's jacket. Harriet and Philip walked back together, hand-in-hand, and when he had helped her over the stile, she kissed him shyly, and whispered, 'Thank you.'

They were back early, and Sir Neville had been gone only a few minutes when the sad little procession could be seen in the distance, walking slowly across the field. Lucy ran to meet them, her heart pounding.

'What happened?' she gasped.

'He fell in the river. Philip pulled him out,' Tom explained briefly.

She could see the child was deeply shocked, and she would have taken him, but Tom insisted on carrying him the rest of the way. In the warm kitchen, she took him on her lap, stripped off his wet clothes, and wrapped him in a warm towel that Carrie had fetched from the airing cupboard. Then she turned her attention to Philip.

'You must get out of those wet clothes, dear. You can borrow whatever you need of Tom's. You and he are about the same size.'

'Could I borrow a suit? I have to go to church.'

'But you are not in a fit state, lad. Surely they could manage without you for once?'

'I can't let them down. I shall be all right.'

'Come on up to my room,' Tom invited. 'You can borrow my best suit, my only suit as it happens, for I only wear it for weddings and funerals.'

'Thanks, Tom.'

Philip followed him upstairs.

'Give yourself a good rub down. Carrie will get you a towel,' Lucy called after him.

'Shall I make a fresh pot of tea, Aunt Lucy? I think we could all do with a cup,' Harriet suggested.

'I was just going to ask if you would.' Lucy smiled at the girl. They all called her Aunt Lucy. Her strong body was satisfied sexually at last, and now she was concerned only for the young ones, all looking pale and shocked, and the little boy, lying so quietly in her arms.

'How did it happen?' she asked Harriet, as she waited for the kettle to boil. And the girl told her how the child had almost died, and only Philip had known how to revive him. When they heard him coming downstairs with Tom, they changed the subject quickly to spare his embarrassment, and Lucy saw him, for the first time, as a grown man. He had always seemed so young and boyish, depending on his mother too much for his own good –

Albert had been the same until he went away to war. Now she could see a new strength and maturity in that pale, aesthetic face. He could not take his eyes off Harriet. Something vital had happened between them. A spark had been kindled. She had seen it happen before, with Freddie and Cynthia, Tom and Carrie, and many years ago with Harry and Emma, the young servant girl.

'Pull up a chair and sit down, dear. I wish you would change your mind about going to church. You really look quite poorly.'

'Don't worry about me. I shall be all right,' he insisted.

Harriet handed him the first cup of tea out of the pot, not too strong, and sweetened with three lumps of sugar, exactly as he liked it.

'I am coming with you,' she told him, decidedly, and his heart missed a beat.

'How will you get back? You can't walk back alone. It's not safe. I wouldn't dream of letting you.'

'What do you suggest?'

'You could come back with me for the night, then you would be much nearer to the station for your early train. You can have my bed and I'll sleep on the couch.'

'Will you?'

'Of course.'

So it was decided. His nerves were taut, and he felt quite sick with excitement, yet he knew he was going to sing as he had never sung before! The words would have a fresh meaning now that she cared. Anything was possible. 'Where thou goest I will go!' Yes, even to the Congo.

She was pouring tea for Carrie, Tom and Albert. He thought he had never seen anyone pour tea with such grace and delicacy. Of course, she was upper class, but she was not like Agnes and Richard. His dear Harriet!

Julian was sipping sweet tea from Aunt Lucy's cup, a

faint tinge of colour on his cheeks.

'Can I have my clothes on now? I want to play with my white mice,' he told her – and wondered why Carrie cried.

Philip escorted Harriet to the pew where his mother and step-father were already seated, then he slipped away to join the rest of the choir. They smiled at the girl, and moved up to make room for her. Martha stared at the suit her son was wearing. What had happened? He looked very pale and tense, but that would be nerves. He was always nervous on these occasions, though it was no new experience. He sang solo as a boy soprano, now his tenor voice was much admired. She was nervous too, and she would be glad when it was all over.

The church was filling up with a working-class congregation. It was one of the three important days in the church calendar – Easter, Harvest Festival and Christmas. Daffodils and sweet-scented narcissi decorated the font, the pulpit, the chancel and the choir stalls. Madonna lilies adorned the altar. Primroses were bunched on the window sills. The brasses shone and sparkled in the light of the hanging lamps. The first hymn was processional, and the clean, white surplices crackled with starch as the choir moved slowly down the aisles. Philip was so close he could have touched Harriet as he passed by, but he was looking straight ahead, completely absorbed in the joyous Easter hymn. For the evening service, the organist and choirmaster had chosen an anthem, and Philip to sing the first part as a solo, followed by the boys and the men, and finally the whole choir. They hadn't long to wait for the anthem, but for Martha and Harriet it was an anxious twenty minutes. The congregation always sat for the anthem, and their hands were clasped tightly in their laps.

Gradually, as the rich, vibrant notes echoed through the old church, they both relaxed with deep sighs of relief, and proud pleasure in the soloist. He sang with his whole heart and soul, and he was fully aware of his performance. It was good. It was so good he could have wept with the pleasure of hearing his own voice pouring forth the joyous Easter message. He saw the congregation as a blurred mass of humanity – for only one person was distinct from the rest, and to that person he sang as he had never sung before. She cared! He wanted the whole world to know that she cared. It was so much easier to sing of his love and devotion. He was still too shy, too inarticulate, to express his feelings in the normal way.

She had kissed him on the stile and thanked him – for what? For saving the child, or for loving her? But then he had loved her since she was a schoolgirl. Her cool detachment had often hurt his pride. A peck on the cheek in one of her teasing moods, that was all until today, when her lips were soft and her breath sweet. It was not his mother's face that he saw today in the shadowed nave, but the small, oval face of a young girl, calm and pure, and innocent. They both were innocent as babes, untouched by the normal cravings of youth, and separated from their fellows by an inherent goodness and piety most of the young found embarrassing.

As a day boy at the Grammar School, Philip had not been subjected to the communal bathing and masturbation practised at some boarding schools. Harriet, too, had escaped the emotional entanglements of adolescent girls with their favourite teachers.

He felt the stirrings and sighings of the packed congregation as they shifted in their seats, and caught the fleeting smile on her shadowed face. Then the boys' voices were soaring, like the angels at the Nativity. In their clean white surplices, with their shining faces, they looked angelic. But they were mischievous as monkeys, with no thought in their heads but the extra shilling they would receive as an Easter bonus after the service.

The men had their turn at last. He could hear the booming bass of old Fred Butcher. Fred was a cowman at Monks Farm, and very proud of that voice.

They were waiting in the porch. Martha could see at a glance that the tension had gone when he kissed her cheek and shook hands with his step-father. Then he took Harriet's hand and explained about the sleeping arrangements. There was a new authority in his manner tonight, and he did not ask for his mother's approval. The girl said nothing. Martha smiled pleasantly, and agreed it was a good idea, but the first indication that she was losing her son was hurting like a wound in the heart. She had Andrew, and was grateful, but she had not suffered for Andrew as she had suffered for Philip. Because he was born out of wedlock, she had to carry the stigma the village imposed on her, submit to the rough domination of the child's father five years later when he returned to England with his regiment, and they were married, and to watch the bitter jealousy between the man and the boy while she served the man's purpose with her body. It had been a hard struggle, but she had endured until Fate took a hand and Dick was killed. Even so, it was another two years before Andrew proposed marriage, and they moved into the School House. It was a step up the ladder in the social scale from working class to middle class, and she had enjoyed her new status.

What would the future hold without Philip? They had been so close, so devoted. They had shared everything, and had no secrets from each other. Of course she had known he was fond of Harriet, but had not regarded it as a serious affair. How mistaken can a fond mother be when she refuses to face the truth that her son is a man? Martha Robinson was asking herself, as they walked back to the School House that Easter Sunday.

They left the men to stoke up the fire and went to the kitchen to brew a pot of tea and make chicken sandwiches. It was a good opportunity to question Harriet about the borrowed suit, and the girl told the full story for the second time that day. Her companion's face expressed the same distress as Aunt Lucy's. Martha could imagine the scene so vividly – the riverside picnic, the camp fire, the little boy gathering sticks, and Philip offering to help – wasn't that just like him! She could see Carrie lining up the mugs for the smoky tea, then settling down to enjoy the good fare Lucy had provided. She could see that same little boy running bare foot across the grass, down the bank, and straight into the water, and her son after him in a matter of seconds. She was shuddering now at the awful realisation that both could have drowned, and her eyes were wet as the girl finished her story.

'I thought I knew my son, but I didn't know he could react so promptly to danger,' she said.

'He was very brave, Mrs Robinson.' The girl was buttering bread, and she looked up to see the mother's hands covering her crumpled face. 'Don't cry. It's all over,' she soothed, with an arm about Martha's shoulders.

'It's not all over, child. You don't understand. It has only just begun,' the choked voice was saying.

What did she mean? For a moment Harriet was puzzled, then she realised the full implication of her own involvement with Philip. To a fond mother, the thought of losing her only son could be more devastating than a near tragedy which, after all, had a happy ending. What could she say to this sobbing woman? Harriet asked herself. It was not her place. Philip must not be robbed of the initiative, or his new manliness. So often in the past she had been aware of his dependence on his mother as though that invisible umbilical cord still held him captive.

It was not her fault that their friendly relationship had not developed into a closer intimacy. A girl has her pride! It had taken a terrible shock, a near tragedy, to break that tightened bond, but it was irretrievable, and the mother knew it.

With her arm about Martha's shaking shoulders, Harriet felt she could better understand this close bond that existed between a mother and her son, a father and a daughter. Her own mother had been heart-broken when Richard told her of his conversion to the Catholic faith, and his intention to spend three years in the Jesuit college in Brussels. Since they came home from the Congo, Mother had absolutely doted on Richard, trying to make up for the lost years he had spent at boarding school and with his grandparents. But it was too late. Poor Mother. It was mean of Richard not to tell her face to face – mean and cowardly.

Here was a mother who must be told the truth, perhaps tonight, or there could be no lasting joy or peace in this sweet new relationship. Somebody had to get hurt in each generation, as the young spread their wings. It was a solemn thought. Personally, she had hurt nobody by her decision to return to the Congo Mission after she had finished her training. Mother had married again, so there was no problem. Her daughters had never been close to her.

It was very different for Philip. To choose between a future as solid and satisfactory as now, and to embark on a life of danger and hardship was indeed a step into the Unknown. Who had said – 'Put your hand in the hand of God and it shall be safer than the known way'? She had been a witness to his courage today. Could he, would he be prepared to sacrifice so much for her sake? There would be no turning back. It would be their life's work, their future, and their children's future. *She* knew the hazards that such dedication entailed, for she had spent her early years in her father's shadow, and only death had separated them. For Philip it would be a tremendous upheaval in his quiet, scholarly world; a challenge and a test of faith. But the challenge would be shared, and her love would support and comfort as her own mother's devotion had supported and comforted the man she had followed to those far distant shores. Her mother's love for her father had been one of those passionate 'love-at-first-sight' affairs. Her love for Philip and his love for her had grown and developed gradually from friendship, and the quiet religious observances they had shared in that old church on the hill.

Martha was drying her eyes. 'I'm sorry, dear. It's not often that I make such a fuss.' She smiled wanly at the girl and busied herself with the tea-tray.

'What should we do without tea?' she asked. 'My husband and Philip prefer coffee, so I always make coffee for breakfast.'

So Philip likes coffee for breakfast! That shouldn't be too difficult. From now on she would be storing up such titbits of information as a squirrel stores nuts. In so many ways they were worlds apart, but in the things that mattered most – deep religious convictions, books and music, they were mutually compatible. As an only child, Philip was self-important, but not unbearably so. He was essentially kind and gentle, and he had nice manners.

When Martha had bathed her eyes, asked 'Do I look all right?' and been assured that she did, she carried in the tea-tray, and Harriet followed with the plate of sandwiches. Andrew and Philip stood up immediately, Andrew to take the tray from his wife, and Philip the sandwiches. The young ones exchanged a secret smile, but Andrew was disturbed by the aftermath of tears, for Martha was not a woman who wept easily. What had upset her? All would be divulged in due course, he reflected. There was a time and place for everything, and the marriage bed was not only the place for intercourse. They invariably fell asleep without giving it a thought. Martha liked to talk over the events of the day, and to settle any grievances that may have arisen between them. Of recent months it was Philip who sometimes disturbed the harmony they had enjoyed for so long. The girl he had brought home tonight was probably at the root of this disharmony, Andrew was thinking. It seemed so strange to have a fourth person included in their three-fold relationship.

When they had finished the tea and sandwiches, and discussed Philip's contribution to the evening service – though not praised it profusely, for that would embarrass him – Martha excused herself, and went upstairs to strip off Philip's bed and remake it with clean linen. Philip had carried up the girl's small dressing-case. The room was so obviously a scholar's room, with so many books on the shelves, but nothing in the nature of sport. Philip had grown so like his step-father, she liked to imagine her second husband was actually the father of her son. But this was wishful thinking.

Looking about the room, she wondered how soon it would be empty, and her heart ached intolerably. Her son would not have brought this girl home unless there was some understanding between them. He was suddenly remote, and she was conscious of restraint. The secret smile they shared; the way their eyes met and held, and spoke. She was choked with dismay that her son would soon have no further need of her.

Sitting on the bed, she tried to come to terms with a situation she had deliberately avoided, by pushing it into the back of her mind. She could hear them washing up in the kitchen, and their happy laughter floated up to her and intensified the heartache.

Then they came upstairs together and stood in the doorway, hand in hand.

'May I come in?' Harriet asked, quietly.

'Come in, my dear. It's all ready. Have you got all you need?'

'Yes, thank you. It's very kind of you to take so much trouble.'

'Not at all. It's a pleasure. You must be tired. It has been an exciting day, one way and another, hasn't it?'

'Yes, it has, one way and another!' They were still holding hands, reluctant to part.

'Are you coming down, Mother?' Philip asked.

'Yes, I shall be down in a moment.' She knew she had to face it, now, tonight, and it couldn't be postponed. But she had Andrew's shoulder to cry on, later. She was not alone, she reminded herself.

'Goodnight, Philip. God bless you,' the girl dropped his clinging hand.

'Goodnight, Harriet. God bless you,' he echoed, and kissed her, very gently. Then he picked up the pillow and blankets Martha had left ready for the couch, and ran downstairs. He was whistling, and Philip only whistled when something important had happened, like passing an examination or falling in love.

'Good night, Harriet. Sleep well.' Martha kissed the girl's flushed cheek.

'Goodnight, Mrs Robinson. God bless you.'

There was so much they might have said to each other, but it was too soon and too sudden, and the restraint was there between them. So Martha closed the door and followed Philip downstairs.

He was standing on the hearthrug with his back to the fire, a tall, manly figure in a borrowed suit. He seemed like a stranger, more remote than ever from his own mother – his nearest and dearest, until today. Andrew smiled and reached out a hand, so she went to him and perched on the arm of his chair. He squeezed her hand reassuringly, and it gave her the courage to listen and to accept, without interrupting.

'Mother, Uncle Andrew – something wonderful has happened! Harriet has promised to marry me!' he blurted out. 'I am so happy, I don't know where to put myself!' he added, laughing at his own foolishness.

'Then I am happy too, my dear,' said Martha, bravely holding out her arms. For a brief moment she held him close. She could feel the pulsing of his young heart, and his whole body tense with emotion.

'Congratulations, my boy!' Andrew was pumping his hand, and teasing, 'Isn't this rather sudden?'

'Yes, that's why it's so wonderful. I didn't think I had a chance in a million. It must have been the accident.'

'What accident?'

'We were out on a picnic, all of us from Russets except Aunt Lucy. Julian fell into the river and I pulled him out.'

'I see, so that's why you're wearing a suit that doesn't belong to you?'

'Yes.'

'Is the child all right?'

'Perfectly. He was playing with his white mice when we left for church.'

'And you think Harriet suddenly realised your sterling qualities?'

'I suppose so.' He sighed, ecstatically.

'Does this mean a change of plans for you, Philip?'

'Yes, a big change. There is no point in any further study for those law exams. It's not law I shall need in the future, but as much useful experience as I can cram into the next twelve months, that is, if the Missionary Society will accept me as a candidate. I have to convince them I am suitable, and in earnest. I shall see about it tomorrow.

We can travel up to London together on the early train, then Harriet will report back at the hospital. She says she doesn't mind waiting till next year if we can go out together, though she had intended to go out in the Autumn.'

'Go where?'

'To the Congo.'

'I see. You would be married, of course?'

'Of course.'

'It's a very big step, Philip. Are you quite sure this is what you want?'

'I have never been more certain of anything, Uncle.'

'It's such a hazardous undertaking, and you know so little about the work and the climate.'

'I know enough. Harriet spent all her early childhood at the Mission, and she never lost touch with her father's colleagues. I only regret I have wasted so much time on those wretched law books. I was never very keen, I just seemed to drift into it. But that's not good enough, is it? There must be a sense of purpose, and dedication, Harriet says, and she's right. She has inspired me with her own enthusiasm for the work.' He was starry-eyed in his eagerness, and they both realised how strong was the girl's influence. They could only hope and pray that her confidence and courage would support him in that far-off land. Philip had always depended on their support. He leaned. He had to be propped up and chivvied along. But Harriet must know he was not a strong character. They had seen quite a lot of each other at Russets. He went on talking, and they listened with interest, but also with doubt, for he still hadn't convinced them. Could he be making the biggest mistake of his young life in discarding a future for which he had been trained? Hadn't he patterned himself for years on the schoolmaster? It seemed so alien to everything they had shared, but he had made up his mind – or Harriet had made it up for him. They had never seen him so determined.

Andrew tried to smother his hurt because he had not been consulted, and Martha's heart ached because her adored son had not even noticed she had been crying.

Philip would have gone on talking all night. They had never seen him so animated, but Andrew faked a yawn and declared it was long past his bedtime. When he had gone upstairs, Martha fixed the fireguard and made up a comfortable bed for Philip on the couch. He stood there watching her, but his thoughts were not with her, as his starry eyes testified. She kissed his cheek and bade him 'Goodnight, sleep well', and followed Andrew upstairs. She could hear him cleaning his teeth in the bathroom. Dear Andrew. If the heavens were falling he would still be cleaning his teeth! When they were first married, she found his meticulous attention to his toilet rather irritating, and she had to remind herself that Andrew had been a bachelor for so long, such habits had become automatic. There was something very comforting about such ablutions tonight, however. Then she remembered she had not shown the girl to the bathroom and felt guilty.

When Andrew had finished, she tapped on Harriet's door, but there was no answer, so she must be asleep. She would leave the light burning in the passage and the bathroom door open, but she was still blaming herself for being such a poor hostess. Harriet was the first person to stay overnight at the School House, so perhaps there was some excuse.

The comfort of Andrew's solid body and broad shoulder was such a relief after the disturbing events of the day. Martha wept quietly, with her arm flung across his chest. She could smell the toothpaste on his breath, and his clean pyjamas still smelled faintly of the lavender bags she kept in the airing cupboard. He would no more have thought of sleeping naked than flying to the moon! His modesty was old-maidish, and he always undressed in the bathroom and dressed after she had left the bedroom to prepare breakfast. She supposed she had spoilt them both, the way she waited on them, but it came natural because she had always waited on her father. Six mornings a week at precisely 6.30, they were sitting up in bed, drowsy with sleep, sipping their hot tea. Sunday morning it was one hour later.

All three were conservative in their habits, and had settled down since the War to a period of quiet contentment. They liked to spend the holidays together, and they enjoyed long cycle rides together, weather permitting. On wet Sunday afternoons, they would read, and on frosty days in Winter, they would take a brisk walk to get an appetite for the sumptuous tea that Martha would provide. When the snow lay deep on the country roads, the trio would be seen plodding along in gum boots. The gramophone provided their musical entertainments, and Philip had collected a good selection of classical records. Andrew had contributed largely to his step-son's taste for Beethoven, Mozart, Schubert and Handel. The pattern of their days was unaffected by international disasters or political strife. The War had left them blessedly intact as a family in their small world. Now that small world was rocking with the sudden impact of a shattering blow. Why did it have to be Harriet? Why not one of the nice girls Philip had met at University? Why the Congo? It had a sinister sound. An outlandish, frightening place, inhabited by heathens, mosquitoes and snakes!

'Why? Why?' Martha whispered in her misery and dismay.

'Because, my dear, your son is in love, and he has determined, like Ruth, "Where thou goest, I will go".'

'But can you understand it, dear? Philip has no sense of

adventure. He has never been farther than the Isle of Wight, yet he had ample opportunity in his student days to holiday on the Continent. Now he embarks on a perilous escapade to the ends of the earth. It's quite ridiculous!'

'Nevertheless, it is what he wants, and what he intends to do, though not immediately, my dear. We shall have him around for another twelve months or so.'

'Not if he stays in London. He will be living in lodgings. We shall not see much of him then.'

'Perhaps we have been too complacent, Martha, you and I, too ready to assume that Philip was satisfied with his chosen career when he was actually putting up with it for our sake. It certainly is a shock to discover we were so mistaken.'

Martha sighed. Her plump little body was warm, and her clean nightgown smelled faintly of lavender.

'Try not to worry, dear. We still have each other, and our work here. Your infants will keep you busy and happy,' Andrew reminded her kindly.

Then he kissed her cheek, stretched his heavy, ageing body, and slept.

It was Easter Monday, and Andrew and Martha had the rest of the week free from school duties. Martha had cooked a breakfast of bacon and eggs for the young ones, watched them running hand-in-hand down the path, and waved as they turned at the school gate. They would need to run all the way to the station to catch that early train, but Philip was lazy in the early morning, even with the bright-eyed Harriet to hustle him along.

When they had gone, Martha set about cooking breakfast for herself and Andrew. The house seemed strangely deserted and depressing. They had planned to take the train to Gloucester, with their bicycles in the luggage van, then tour the Cotswolds, stopping overnight at country cottages. Now, for the first time, Philip would not be joining them, and Martha had lost her enthusiasm for the trip. But for Andrew's sake she must resist any inclination to feel that nothing was worth while unless Philip were there. This sudden, unexpected parting from her beloved son was only a prelude to the final parting later. She knew the story of Old Parson's favourite daughter, Marion, falling in love with the young missionary from the Congo, and that she had left behind a heartbroken father when she married her missionary and went away for five long years. And Marion was Harriet's mother. So there was something to be said for heredity.

Now her son was deeply involved. It seemed that such love was capable of conquering all obstacles, to forge ahead with implicit faith in the unknown future. Martha had never known such a test of love. She had married her first husband to give her son a name, and she had married Andrew because she had a great respect and tender affection for the village schoolmaster. She knew they could have remained good friends, for Andrew was a confirmed bachelor, and had waited two years after Dick's death before he proposed marriage. It would be foolish to jeopardise their quiet relationship by comparing it to the ardent nature of her son's romance. Philip, too, might have remained a bachelor, but for the intervention of Harriet. As for Harriet, she might well have departed for the Congo and eventually married a missionary but for the near tragedy on Easter Sunday that had opened her eyes to Philip's worth. Only yesterday; yet so much had happened to change the course of their lives – Philip and Harriet, and her own life with Andrew. Martha could see the years ahead with convincing accuracy. They would grow old together in this quiet pattern of days and years. But without the stimulus of Philip's personality and his companionship, they would drift into a routine completely lacking in interest and enthusiasm.

The truth must be faced, not for the first time in her life, that she was essentially a maternal woman, and that her son held first place in her heart. If she had to choose between saving one or the other in some terrible eventuality, she would not hesitate to save her son. It was this overwhelming maternity in her nature that had made a difficult first marriage impossible, for Dick had been insanely jealous of Philip. With Andrew, there had been no need to hide her love for her son. Seeing her with infants over a long period of years, Andrew had accepted the fact that her love for little children was an essential part of her nature. Andrew would not have been comfortable with a passionate woman in his bed. So they suited each other very well, Martha would remind herself from time to time in the years ahead, when she found him getting absent-minded and more and more fastidious in his habits.

Philip had cleaned and oiled the bicycles, and looked up the trains in the time-table. He had also planned their route. They had only to start, and the strangeness would wear off, Martha insisted, with a brave smile, then she added, surprisingly, 'Shall we invite Carrie to join us?'

Andrew agreed. They would travel light, as they had originally intended. Andrew would strap a portmanteau on his carrier, and Martha would pack a flask of coffee, sandwiches and apples in the basket on her handlebars. It was a long train journey via London, and they would be glad of a little refreshment en route, after an early breakfast.

As they waited for Carrie on the quiet country station, Martha's thoughts flew to that other station where Philip and Harriet must part to go their separate ways.

Everything went according to plan. Carrie had been delighted to receive a telephone call from her beloved

Teacher, and Lucy insisted they could manage without her for a week. It was her first holiday since her marriage, and, apart from market day and an occasional visit to Tunbridge Wells, she had not left the farm, or Bertie, for a single night. She was surprised to find him so agreeable. He even offered to clean and oil her bicycle that had not been used since she was living at the doctor's house in the village.

Andrew had agreed, rather reluctantly, to wait for a later train, so that Carrie could join them. He was fond of Carrie, but inclined to think 'Two's company, three's a crowd'. However, he was trying to understand the feelings of a devoted mother so suddenly obliged to come to terms with her son's extraordinary plans for the future. He must not mind if Martha devoted too much time and attention to this young woman she had known since the early days in the Infants' classroom.

So when Carrie arrived, hot and breathless, at the station, she was warmly hugged by Martha, and Andrew greeted her cordially with a firm handshake, and handed over her bicycle to the porter. Her excitement was infectious, and he could see his dear wife responding to the lively chatter with her normal cheerfulness. All those tears in the night had dampened his own enthusiasm for the trip, but he made no mention of it on this bright Easter Monday. His surprise and disappointment over his stepson was no light matter. It seemed such a waste. So much time and concentration had already been spent on preparation for the Law examinations. To change course in mid-stream was to throw away all they had worked for together.

Andrew's thoughts drifted back to those early years, when he had acted as unpaid tutor to Martha's boy, and contributed very largely to Philip's success in obtaining a place at Grammar School. Education was important to a boy, and Philip had been an apt pupil. But a man cannot weep over life's trials and disappointments, he reflected. That was a woman's prerogative.

He listened to Carrie's excited chatter with some irritation, and hoped she would calm herself if other passengers joined them in the carriage. But they were left alone for the entire journey. It was the end of the Easter weekend, not the start, and the trains would be crowded this evening with returning travellers.

A long train journey was a novelty for Andrew, who had not seen anything of the West Country, even in his youth. As an only son, he had been content to spend the Summer vacations at his mother's favourite seaside resort, and the Easter vacations on day trips to cathedral cities, museums and art galleries. Now he watched the unfamiliar landscape slipping past the window with only a lukewarm interest. It was too early to see the cattle in the fields. The first of May was traditionally adhered to, when the cows left their Winter quarters for the green pastures. Early lambs had grown big and fat, and were no longer skipping on their spindly legs.

Andrew complained of a draught when the window was opened, so Martha closed it, to Carrie's dismay. Her training as a nursemaid had accustomed her to open windows, even in the Winter, and her life on the farm was a healthy, outdoor life she would not have exchanged for any other, in spite of the constant reminder of Tom's devoted love. The Spring was a time for lovers, but not for these two who dare not touch for fear of repeating that fateful hour as they travelled homewards from the Michaelmas Fair.

But this was to be a cycling holiday, so Mr Robinson could not complain of draughts, Carrie reminded herself. He was still the schoolmaster, and she was not at ease with him. Teacher often lapsed into thoughtful silence as she watched the budding trees and hedgerows slipping past, and Carrie knew she was thinking of Philip in London. It had not surprised her to hear of the climax to that unlucky picnic. Philip's new manliness, and Harriet's recognition of his courage and resourcefulness, was all too obvious.

'They could not keep their eyes from each other,' Carrie told Martha. 'It reminded me of Freddie and Cynthia. They are still so much in love, those two, one feels it all the time in their company. They are very fond of Wendy, but it hasn't made a scrap of difference to their own loving relationship. Cynthia is not particularly maternal, is she? Wasn't it a happy solution to have Mum take over as nurse-housekeeper? Now everybody is happy, including Freddie, who declares he hasn't been fed so well since he left the convalescent home in Worthing!'

'Family problems can usually be sorted out, given time and patience,' Martha observed, with a sigh of resignation.

'I like Harriet. She has shown herself in her true colours since her sister went away. Agnes was so dreadfully bossy. We never see her at Russets these days, but for Harriet, it's her second home. Yes, I like her very much. She's a good Christian, but she doesn't preach. She has always been a favourite with Julian. Now there's another woman who might love her children more than her husband. I wonder.'

'I hope not, dear. Philip could be jealous. He was very jealous of his own father, and Dick was not entirely to blame.'

'But you would like to be a grandmother, wouldn't you?'

'I suppose I should,' Martha answered doubtfully. It was all too sudden to visualise her son as a father and herself as a grandmother.

Keeping to Philip's original plan for the tour, they cycled only as far as Birdlip that first evening, and were given supper, bed and breakfast at the inn because it was too late to find a cottage offering accommodation. As they waited in the bar for the landlord's wife to conduct them to their rooms, they were entertained by the customers, mostly farm labourers, enjoying the last hours of their free Bank Holiday. On the morrow they would be back to work at 7 o'clock. With the light evenings prolonging their working day, they would be out in the fields till dusk. In the Winter months they finished work at 4 o'clock.

'One do balance the other, you might say,' they would tell you, philosophically. Wives would contribute to the meagre wages by helping with the hay-making, fruit picking and potato lifting. No hops were grown in this part of the country. In the Weald of Kent, the women could depend on a regular six weeks of hop-picking every year, and school holidays were arranged to coincide with the picking.

The strong smell of beer and the smoky atmosphere in the bar was displeasing to Andrew's fastidious senses. It was probably the first time in his life he had set foot in a public house. For Carrie, however, the atmosphere was nostalgic of those early days at 'The Three Nuns,' where her hard-working mother had been charwoman. She remembered the smell, the pennies from the customers, the rag doll that she trailed around, and the sticky peppermints always to be found in Mum's apron pocket. They were happy days, till she began to envy the school children racing down the High Street, then she gave Mum no peace till she sent Freddie to ask permission of Teacher for her to start school. She had just passed her fourth birthday, and she was the youngest pupil. It was the beginning of her long friendship with Teacher, and she squeezed her companion's hand in affectionate gratitude as they waited in the bar.

The landlord opened a door and bellowed 'Mabel!' for the second time, when a fresh-faced little woman bustled in, drying her hands on her apron, and led the way upstairs. They were lucky, she said, for the week-end guests had left at midday, and she had stripped off the beds and made them up with clean linen, and cleaned the rooms. It was all part of their trade to keep two rooms in readiness for travellers, and food in the pantry.

'They do say it goes right back to the Middle Ages when they was called pilgrims,' she explained importantly.

The schoolmaster exchanged a meaningful smile with his teacher.

When she had fetched two cans of hot water for washing, she reminded them that a cold supper would be waiting in the parlour with tea or coffee, whichever they preferred.

'We will have coffee,' Andrew decided. Martha and Carrie were not consulted. It was only the first of a number of occasions when his over-riding opinions would irritate Carrie, but it was a holiday, and Teacher must be excused for making herself' too agreeable to her husband's wishes.

As soon as they had finished supper, he was ready to retire to bed, but Carrie was not tired, in spite of the long, exciting day, and she sat alone at the open window of her bedroom, gazing out at the wooded hillside, so much like her own lovely Weald of Kent. She thought of Tom, her dear, devoted Tom. Would they ever be free to enjoy a holiday together? Her married life was a mockery, yet Bertie seemed satisfied. She felt condemned to a lifetime of repression, for all her natural impulses had been smothered in the urgent need to behave decently. Her young, healthy body ached with longing, as her thoughts revolved about that memorable evening in September, when she and Tom had travelled homewards from the Michaelmas Fair. All those years ago, yet it seemed only yesterday that Tom had lifted her down from the trap, and carried her, struggling and pleading, to the top of the hill. Her gentle Tom was a stranger that night – a stranger with arms of steel, who had taken her as roughly as any country yokel tipsy with cider. But Tom hadn't been drinking. He was sober as a judge, and just as ruthless. It was all over in a matter of minutes. Then he was stretched beside her, sobbing bitterly. The memory was so vivid, she could feel the pulses throbbing in her thighs, and desire was so strong in her, she could not resist the temptation to recall every second of that heart-rending experience. Yet it could only torment, and not ease the longing for Tom.

Dear God! It was so unjust. What had she done to deserve such a penalty? Even Aunt Lucy looked suspiciously flushed and radiant as Sir Neville rode across the Park.

To visit Freddie and Cynthia in Tunbridge Wells was a tantalising reminder of her own predicament. Their loving gestures and secret smiles only intensified her loneliness. They had battled through the years of waiting and suffering to reap their reward. The child was living proof of the intercourse they had enjoyed as soon as Freddie was discharged from hospital. But there could be no happy ending for herself and Tom. He had not shared her anxiety during those weeks that followed his unpredictable violence on that isolated hill-top, because it had never been mentioned between them. His strong body had been too demanding to resist. Her response had been natural and spontaneous. How could it be otherwise when they were in love? But she could have conceived, and that, for Bertie, would be the ultimate insult to his manhood.

Now it was the turn of Philip and Harriet. They had

found happiness, and would soon be married. Since yesterday, their relationship had been transformed by a mutual understanding. What did the future hold for them? Marriage was such a lottery. Who could predict what a man or a woman must suffer to keep those marriage vows sacred? Poor Teacher with that sadistic Sergeant Martin at Tidworth – Doctor Saunders with a mentally disturbed wife – Sir Neville Franklin, tied to an invalid wife for years, because of his status in society, but unfaithful, not once, but a number of times. There was no guarantee of lasting happiness, even when two people were mutually compatible. Love could turn to indifference. The lover could actually murder the beloved in a fit of jealousy. An unfaithful husband could torment a wife into committing suicide.

Carrie shivered. Where had her thoughts strayed on this first night of the holiday? She undressed quickly and slipped into bed, but she lay awake, listening to the rough country voices on the forecourt and the hob-nailed boots clattering over the cobbles. Then all was quiet. For the first time in her married life she would enjoy the luxury of her own bed. On her return, Bertie would use her body again for his own pleasure. She never knew what to expect from him. It was all part of the sexual excitement his poor mutilated body still craved.

The baby Julian had diverted his thoughts, and there had been an interlude of comparative peace while the little boy claimed his attention. Then it was time for school, and Uncle Bertie was no longer indispensable.

She turned her thoughts away from that dreaded marriage bed at Russets and nestled into the hollowed centre of the flock mattress.

'Goodnight, Tom,' she whispered, and fell asleep.

Chapter 10

It was not often that Julian strayed beyond the boundaries of Russets – only to attend the village school with the other children from the farms on the estate. At the age of seven, however, he was curious to see the Big House where the poor children from London enjoyed their country holidays. When Grandfather took him for a ride on his horse, they rode away from the house, and he did not question where they went, for it didn't matter.

It was Easter Monday, and yesterday he had nearly drowned in the river. He would have a good story to tell the boys next week. They were his heroes now, these boys who borrowed his hoop, his marbles and his peg-tops. They swore like troopers, but when he said 'bugger' at the tea-table and wouldn't apologise, Auntie Lucy sent him upstairs. The fact that it happened to be Good Friday and a holiday seemed to make matters worse.

'What's come over the child?' she asked.

'Boys will be boys,' said Albert, with a shrug.

Some time later, Carrie volunteered to run upstairs to see whether Julian was ready to apologise. She found him engrossed in his latest toy – a model aeroplane he had assembled without any help from his uncle. He was launching it from the top of the chest-of-drawers, his eyes bright with excitement. Carrie did not scold. She loved small boys, and in her opinion, Julian had always been abnormally good and obedient compared to her young charge of nursery days.

'It flies, Carrie!' he shouted, prancing about on a clean starched cloth in his gumboots. 'Pick it up. Give it me back.'

'Please,' she prompted.

'Please,' he echoed, impatiently.

They played the game until Aunt Lucy came upstairs to see what was happening.

'Get down, Julian! Get down immediately!' she scolded. Obviously the child had forgotten why he had been sent upstairs, and this was no punishment. On previous occasions, she had found him in tears. A hug and a kiss, and all was forgiven. But Julian had forgotten to mention he would not be crying any more now he was seven. Only girls cry. In the company of the big boys, he was learning things that would shock Auntie Lucy, so he didn't mention that either. When they peed behind the lavatories, he could nearly reach the fence! Once they dared him to kick the ball through the window, and it landed on the schoolmaster's desk! Three strokes of the cane for that offence, but it was worth it to be told by ten-year-old Jim Thorn, 'You're a plucky little bugger.' Nobody at Russets knew about the caning. He had to pretend he had touched the hot stove. And he hadn't told anyone he was going to the Big House.

The Park seemed to stretch for miles, but he had only a vague idea of distance. The trees were green and his jersey was green so everything matched. Auntie Lucy had knitted the jersey. She made all his clothes. The short corduroy knickers left his knees bare. They were grazed, and they had scabbed over quickly, he noticed. Then he would fall again, and there would be fresh blood and fresh scabs.

'Why don't you look where you are going?' Auntie Lucy had asked the last time she bathed his broken knees and smeared them with Zambuk.

''Cause I'm looking at things,' he told her. How could you watch where your feet were going when your eyes were searching the skies?

Once he told her importantly, 'I'm going to be a pilot when I grow up.'

'A pilot? I thought you were going to be a farmer. I thought you would stay with me at Russets? Oh Julian, love, it would break my heart if you went away.' Then she hugged him so tight he was smothered in her bosom, but he pushed her away and ran outside. Since he was seven, he hadn't wanted to be hugged and kissed. Since he was seven, he was not quite sure what he did want.

He carried the model aeroplane and tossed it skywards, but it travelled only a few yards then fell on the grass. He was beginning to feel a little bored with the Park when he heard the thudding of hooves. It was his Grandfather on the big black stallion he called Justin. All Grandfather's horses had names beginning with 'J'. He pulled up sharply to ask, 'Where do you think you are going, young fellow?'

'To the Big House, Grandfather.'

'Why?'

'Just to look.'

'I was coming to fetch you. Got some business to do over at Polegate. Hop up!' He leaned over and swung the boy on to the saddle. Only Grandfather ever attempted such a tricky operation, but then he was gentry and it made a difference. So Katie said.

'Do they know where you are?' he asked in his brusque manner.

Julian shook his head.

'Then we must trot back and tell them. We can't have them worrying.'

'All right.'
'What's that you're carrying?'
'An aeroplane. I made it all by myself.'
'Did you now? That's pretty good.'
'I'm going to be a pilot when I grow up.'
'At your age I wanted to be an engine driver.'
'Why didn't you?'
'They sent me off to boarding school.'
'Why didn't you go to my school in the village?'
'Wish I had. You don't know what you've escaped, young fellow. Thanks to your Auntie Lucy. She wouldn't hear of it.'

They trotted back to the farm and found her leaning on the gate, already anxious for his safety. After yesterday, she could hardly bear to let him out of her sight.

'Good morning, Lucy.' Grandfather swept off his hat with a flourish.

'Good morning, Sir Neville.' Justin pranced nervously when a pigeon flew past. 'Where did you find him?' she asked.

'I picked him up halfway across the Park.'

'Oh, Julian!' was all she said. She was looking up at Grandfather in rather a strange way. She seemed to asking a question with her eyes – like Uncle Tom and Carrie in the cow shed. Then she smiled and patted his grazed knee.

'Off you go. Take good care of each other.'

'We always do.' Grandfather always had the last word.

It would be many years before Julian fully realised what he had escaped by growing up at Russets – preparatory school, public school and university would be just names to which he attached no importance. To grow up at Russets was as natural to Julian as it was for Carrie to grow up in Richmond Row.

'It just happened,' said Carrie. 'It was the luck of the

draw. Because you happened to be Sir Neville's grandson, you came to live with us. There was nobody to look after you at the Big House, only servants. But when you were seven, you wanted an answer to so many questions.'

'Why haven't I got a mother and father like all the other children?' he had demanded that Sunday morning, as they walked to church.

Carrie hesitated. She believed in answering children's questions truthfully. 'Your mother went to Heaven when you were born, and we are not sure where your father went,' she explained, carefully.

'Did he run away?'

'It would seem like it.'

'Why?'

'I suppose he thought it was the most sensible thing to do. A man can't look after a baby, and you were such a tiny baby, you had to be kept in hospital in a certain temperature for several months. Then Auntie Cynthia brought you to Russets.'

'Did Auntie Cynthia know my father?'

'I don't think so.'

'Did she know my mother?'

'They were sisters. Your mother's name was Penelope. Everyone called her Penny.'

'Did she want to go to Heaven?'

'I'm sure she would rather have lived, then she could have looked after you. She was very young to die.'

Julian puzzled over these strange revelations concerning his parents. 'If my father comes back one day, will he know I'm Julian?'

'We shall tell him.'

'I expect he went to fight for his King and Country like all the other fathers. Then if he got killed by the Germans, he couldn't come back, could he?'

'That's probably the reason why you haven't seen him.'

'Jim Lindridge's father was blown to bits by a shell, so he couldn't to to Heaven, could he?'

Carrie was stuck. How to answer such a question? 'I honestly don't know, dear. It's a mystery.'

'Perhaps God can put all the little pieces together again like Humpty Dumpty?'

'You remember Humpty Dumpty?'

He nodded. 'I remember all the nursery rhymes you told me when I was a little boy, before I started school. I had a Noah's Ark once. What happened to my Noah's Ark?'

'You gave it to Katie for the Orphanage, and the other books and toys you had outgrown. Don't you remember?'

They were on to a safe topic at last, and Carrie sighed with relief as they went on their way.

Now, on this Easter Monday, riding across the Park with Grandfather, Julian suddenly asked, 'Did my father go to the War, Grandfather, to fight for his King and Country?'

'I doubt it. Why do you ask?'

'Because I would like to have a father and a mother, only I can't have a mother 'cause Carrie says she went to Heaven when I was born.'

'That's right.'

'Could you find my father for me?'

'I wish I could. A jolly good thrashing is what he deserves, and what he will get if ever I catch up with him!'

'Why?'

'Because he deserted your mother, and left you an orphan.'

'I didn't know I was an orphan. Katie says all the orphans go to the Orphanage.'

'Not quite all, Julian. Not my own grandson.'

'Grandfather?'

'Yes?'

'I'm hungry.'

'Cunning little devil! You know darn well I always carry a bit of chocolate. Help yourself. Left hand pocket. *Left*, boy, *left*! What do they teach you at school?'

'Reading, writing and arithmetic.'

'Can you tell the time?'

'Nearly.'

'Well, you'd best hurry up, for I thought of giving you a watch for your next birthday.'

'Thank you, Grandfather.'

'And don't tell your Auntie Lucy about the chocolate.'

'No, Grandfather.'

'Just between ourselves, you understand?'

'Yes, Grandfather.'

When they reached the farm on the outskirts of the estate, Julian was instructed to sit still and hold the reins. It was a proud moment to be left in charge. On the big black horse, he could pretend he was gentry, but it was only pretence because he was never allowed to forget that he belonged to Russets, not the Big House. The boys at school were not impressed by his relationship to Sir Neville Franklin.

'What do it signify?' Jim Lindridge had demanded. Jim liked using big words, but seldom knew their meaning. 'We ain't interested, see. And we don't want no flippin' snobs in this outfit,' he threatened.

'What's a snob?' asked Julian, innocently.

'Why don't you lay off the poor little bugger. 'e can't 'elp being related to the gentry.' Maudie Larkin was hanging over the wall, as usual. She was Jim's sweetheart, so they said, but you would never guess it was so by the way they abused each other.

'You shut yer mouth. Nobody asked for your opinion!' Jim retorted.

But the village school seemed a whole world away from Grandfather and the big black horse.

It was very quiet when they rode up to the stables at the Big House on this Easter Monday. The children had been taken to Hastings for the day by charabanc.

'Hetty!' bawled Grandfather, as they climbed the stairs to the flat.

'Yes, Sir Neville.' Hetty answered respectfully.

'Give this young shaver a glass of lemonade in the kitchen.'

'Yes, Sir Neville. Come along, Julian.' She would have taken his hand, but he tucked it behind his back. He was seven! Couldn't anybody understand the importance of being seven?

Ethel, the housemaid, seemed surprised to see him, as well she might, for it was the first time Sir Neville had brought his grandson to the flat.

Julian liked Hetty. She was a big, jolly woman, who often called at Russets for extra cream and butter when Sir Neville had unexpected guests. But he didn't like the look of Ethel. She had a thin face and small eyes, like little black marbles.

They all sat down in the kitchen. The lemonade was ice-cold and sweet, just like Auntie Lucy's.

'Would you like a scone, Julian?' asked Hetty.

'Yes, please.'

Still hot from the oven, she spread it with butter and it dripped down his chin. When he wiped his mouth with the back of his hand, she shook her head and handed him a clean napkin. It was one of several bad habits he had picked up at school.

'I shall make it messy. Does it matter?' he asked.

'That's what napkins are for,' she told him, with a smile.

'We don't have napkins at Russets. We use our

han'chiefs.'

'They answer the same purpose, anyway. How old are you, Julian? I seem to have lost count.'

'I'm seven.'

'Good gracious! Is it seven years since Miss Penelope died? How time flies.'

'She was my mother. Carrie told me. She went to Heaven when I was born, and my father ran away. Grandfather says he will get a good hiding when he's found.'

'Would you like to meet your own father?'

'Yes, I should. All children have a father, don't they?'

'Yes, but so many fathers got killed in the War.'

'Jim Lindridge's father was blown all to pieces by a shell.'

'How awful.' Hetty shuddered.

'When my father comes back, Carrie will tell him I'm Julian.'

'Do you expect him to come back?'

'I don't know. What do you think, Hetty?'

'I hope so, Julian, for your sake. Won't he be surprised to see such a fine big boy?'

Ethel sat there in sulky silence, but Hetty was used to her sulks. She was a good worker, clean and neat in appearance, and respectful to her betters. What more could be required of a servant? Hetty had to remind her from time to time, however, that she was lucky to have such a good home and an easy job. Not like the old days, when she was a housemaid, and had to carry cans of hot water upstairs and light fires for the governess and the nurse. Then all the meals had to be carried up three flights of stairs. Ethel never answered back. She knew her place. Hetty had trained her well.

When Julian had been collected, both servants stood at the window watching them ride away.

'Fancy Sir Neville still threatening to thrash that boy's father. After all these years he's not likely to get the chance, I'm afraid,' said Hetty.

'Why not? It's never too late. I should like to see him getting his desserts.'

'You? Why should it concern you?' Hetty swung round from the window. There was a silence. 'I asked you a question, Ethel, and I'm waiting for an answer? Why should it concern you?'

'Because I happen to know him.'

'What did you say?'

'You heard.'

'Don't be cheeky!'

'I'm not being cheeky. It's the truth. As a matter of fact, we both know him.'

'Who?' Hetty whispered.

'Master Charles.'

Hetty's hand was hard, and the stinging blow sent Ethel staggering back to clutch the kitchen table. Hetty stood over her.

'You dirty little slut! How dare you? They were brother and sister.'

'*Half*-brother and sister. It makes a difference. I tell you I *saw* them.'

'Then why have you waited all this time to mention it?'

Ethel closed her stubborn mouth.

'You've been bribed, haven't you? Tell me the truth.' The threatening hand was raised to strike again.

'He said he would pay me to keep my mouth shut. I've kept my part of the bargain. But not any more. I've not received a penny in the last twelve months.'

'Are you going to tell Sir Neville?'

'You bet I am! Or you can tell him. He might take it better from you.'

'What makes you think that? He'll be shocked and

disgusted. Master Charles, I still can't believe it.'

'A chip off the old block, if you ask me.'

'Nobody's asking you.'

Ethel shrugged her thin shoulders and straightened her cap. 'I'm leaving anyway. I've had an offer of marriage. That surprises you, doesn't it? You didn't even know I was going steady, did you? It's Frank Simpson. He's only been waiting for his old Mum to die. She always held the purse strings, the mean old devil. We are going to emigrate to Australia as soon as we're wed. It's all fixed up. Put that in your pipe and smoke it, Hetty O'Brien!'

Hetty slumped on the nearest chair, staring at the woman she thought she knew. She had never been more mistaken.

'Get out of my sight!' she hissed – and Ethel walked away with a bit of a swagger, closed the door quietly, and climbed the back stairs to her attic bedroom to start packing her tin trunk.

When Charles Franklin faced his father across the breakfast table that first morning of the holiday that had been arranged so suddenly by cablegram, he saw nothing unusual in that handsome, aristocratic face. The greying hair was distinctive, the dark eyes discerning. As for Sir Neville, he was looking at a replica of himself. Only the mouth was weak, and the hair as black and glossy as a raven's wing. Otherwise, it could have been the young Sir Neville Franklin, as portrayed by the French artist, during his student days in Paris.

It was not often that Charles was summoned by the parent who normally allowed his grown son even more liberty than he himself had enjoyed. Charles could only assume that his father had decided there was a limit to the time a young man could sow his wild oats, and that a career would be discussed. But what kind of career? Charles had never given it a serious thought! The War years had divided them, and when they met at the airport they were almost strangers and had nothing in common but their features, their cultured voices and their mannerisms. There was a restlessness about Charles that was typical of the post-War generation, and he was wondering how long he was expected to stay and how soon he would discover the actual reason for this rather abrupt summons to Marston Park.

They had skirted round the question of another bailiff for the estate over last night's dinner. The present bailiff would be leaving at Michaelmas to emigrate to New Zealand with his young family. There seemed to be an epidemic of emigration since the War. But Charles could not see himself tied to the estate, living permanently at Marston Park, so he made no comment. He had enjoyed living with Sylvia and her husband in Vancouver, but they were obviously relieved to see him on the plane, and no mention was made of his return.

'That young brother of yours is nothing but a parasite,' the Major asserted, as they made their way to their car.

'*Half*-brother, darling,' Sylvia corrected mildly. 'You are probably right. He has been rather presumptuous, but he is such marvellous company, we are going to miss him.'

'A good miss, sweetheart, as far as I'm concerned. I shall enjoy having you to myself again. I don't much care for sharing you.'

'We girls were partly to blame for spoiling him so outrageously when he first came to live with us at Marston Park. He was seven, and we adored him. So did the servants. He was not a goody-goody little boy, very naughty and wilful, but of course he was never punished. As for Papa, his pride and joy in his only son was quite pathetic. Sonja will be sorry to lose him.'

'Sonja's an old fool! You would think she would have more sense, but I suppose a wealthy widow is always fair game. Twice divorced and no children. Even before the poor old Colonel had drawn his last breath she was sharing her bed with young Bellamy. It was an open secret.'

Everything was an open secret in Army circles, so Sylvia made no comment. She liked Sonja. She was warm-hearted and generous, and she couldn't help being blessed (or cursed) with what the men called sex-appeal. It was something she herself had always lacked, and she had been so surprised and grateful to discover the Canadian captain had actually preferred her to the glamorous blonde during her war service as a VAD at Marston Park.

'I should never be surprised to see Charles settle down eventually with Sonja, if he decides to come back,' the Major was saying.

'But Sonja is old enough to be his mother!'

'What of it? She's still a handsome woman, and she's got what it takes to attract a chap like Charles – money and sex.'

'Aren't you being a little vulgar, darling?'

'Am I? Sorry.' He kissed her contritely. He loved her for her own sake. She was still the same sweet, unsophisticated girl he had married. Only that wretched half-brother they couldn't dislodge because Sylvia adored him had disrupted the harmony. All the women adored him, but he was not very popular with his own sex, for obvious reasons.

Driving back through the park with Sir Neville at the wheel of his Bentley, Charles was having some misgivings about meeting the housemaid, Ethel, and was relieved to discover she had left. The ever-faithful Hetty had cooked and served last night's dinner and this morning's breakfast. She was one of the old school of servants, loyal and respectful, and devoted to the family – or what remained of it. She often called at the little house in Tunbridge Wells on her free day, and took a walk with Ruby and little Wendy on the Common. They shared a cup of tea in the kitchen, then she waited to greet her Miss Cynthia on her return from the hospital, in the early evening. She was glad to see how happily they had settled down to yet another new chapter in their lives. Ruby was no longer haunted by the constant fear of having no permanent home in her old age. They needed her, and she served them with cheerful affection and gratitude.

Father and son rode out of the courtyard on that fine Summer morning followed by the admiring glances of the groom and Hetty, who was leaning on the sill of the kitchen window. The London children had already left to spend the day at Hastings – a treat enjoyed by each successive party of children and their teachers.

The groom kept the second horse exercised, and often wondered why Sir Neville bothered to keep a mount for Master Charles when he was so seldom home these days. Hetty thought it was a case of wishful thinking, and Sir Neville expected to see his son more often. She knew why he was here now, and she was afraid for him. Sir Neville had a violent temper, and he was only biding his time. When she had told him the truth about his son's part in the tragic death of his youngest daughter, his face had blanched and his eyes were so stricken, she wished she had allowed Ethel to do her own dirty work.

'I'm sorry, Sir Neville. Ethel should have told you years ago, but she's been collecting bribery money to keep her mouth shut, up till last year, the crafty little hussy!' she told him. Then she burst into tears.

'Don't cry, Hetty. It's not your fault. Thank you for telling me now.'

'Shall I get you a drink, Sir?'

'Yes – yes, a good idea.'

She watched him drain the tot of whisky at a single gulp, then he held out the glass for another. 'Leave the bottle. That will be all, Hetty,' he said.

So she left him alone, and closed the door with a sense of foreboding. She was a servant and he the master. After all these years of faithful service to the family, there was still a limit to the liberties a servant could take, and she must not presume on that limit. Had she made a mistake to tell him? If Ethel was going away, the secret would have been safe. Yet she could not trust that sly little bitch. Ethel could still make further demands for money from the other side of the world whenever they were in need of a few pounds.

When she tapped on the drawing-room door an hour or so later, to remind him that lunch was ready, she found him sprawled in the chair. The empty glass had slipped from his limp hand to the floor.

'Goo' ole Hetty!' He laughed at his own helplessness when she half carried him to the couch. 'Goo' ole Hetty!' He closed his eyes.

When she had removed his shoes and tie, she covered him with a rug and stood there, looking down at him with pity and affection. It saddened her to see him intoxicated, but it was not surprising under the circumstances.

Several weeks later, she was watching them ride away together and her heart ached for both. Whatever happened out there in the Park, it would be the end of a relationship between a father and his son. All the pride and joy in that only son to be forfeited for a few moments of sexual excitement between a boy and a girl. Who was really to blame? It could have been Penelope. Straight from the schoolroom into the wards, surrounded by officers who found her enchanting. It was too sudden. How she had enjoyed those years, and she looked so pretty in her nurses uniform. When it was all over, and the wards were empty and silent, she was lonely and depressed. Her sister Sylvia had married her Canadian captain, and Sir Neville was in London, having an affair with a young actress. Only Charles cared – or so it must have seemed.

Hetty was still a virgin, but she was no prude. Growing up in Richmond Row, the facts of life had been revealed at an early age, birth and death accepted as natural events. If she could speak her mind, as a woman who knew and understood the frailty of human nature, she would say, 'Forgive them, Sir. It was all so long ago, and they were little more than children.' But she couldn't speak her mind. She was still a servant, and she knew her place. That Master Charles would not only be punished, but banished from Marston Park, she had no doubt. Then the secret she would have kept for the rest of her days would be disclosed. Everyone would know.

This fresh scandal in the family would remind people of that other scandal, when Sir Neville Franklin had lain with the widow of a tenant farmer and a son was conceived. 'Like father, like son,' they said, and it was true. The little boy, Julian, so like his mother, would grow up at Russets. Would the sins of the fathers follow him into manhood, or would he escape the unhappy past he had inherited? He was such a dear little boy, and he loved his grandfather. But he was seven years old, and already curious about his parents. If he discovered the truth, at this tender age, it could ruin his chances of a normal childhood.

* * *

'Get down!' The stern command surprised Charles.

'Why?' he challenged, smiling that same disarming smile that so many women had found irresistible.

'Because I say so!'

As his father dismounted, Charles shrugged, laid his riding crop on the grass, and looped the reins. Then he did likewise. So it was not a career they were going to discuss. This was the showdown he thought he had escaped.

They faced each other now with nothing but their bare fists as weapons. In another age they might have settled it with pistols. But Charles was not prepared for the force of those two stinging blows. His ears were humming. The smile slid away. If his irate parent intended to teach him a lesson, he would soon discover his mistake. It was not so long ago when he could beat all his opponents in the boxing ring at the college gymnasium when he set his mind to it, but he was fundamentally lazy, and couldn't always be bothered.

'Dirty young swine!' The dark eyes were blazing.

Charles swung his fist. The jaw bone seemed to crack with the impact. Stunned by the blow, the older man staggered and fell in a crumpled heap on the grass. His heavy body twitched. Then he lay still.

Charles stood there, looking down on the prostrate figure with a sense of utter desolation. The chapter was closed. There could be no forgiving or forgetting. In his father's eyes he had committed an unpardonable offence, and he was condemned by its very nature. Kneeling on the grass, he slipped his hand inside the silk shirt and felt the steady beat of the heart.

'Sorry,' he muttered, choked with tears.

He tied Justin's reins to the nearest tree, remounted his own horse, and rode away in the direction of Russets. He must have money to get back to the States – back to Sonja.

His mother saw him coming and ran to meet him, like a young girl running to meet her sweetheart. When she saw his eyes, flooded with tears, and a trickle of blood on both cheeks, she gasped, 'What's happened? Where's your father? You've been fighting. Why, Charles? Why?' She had been expecting them both. Sir Neville had telephoned last evening to tell her that Charles had arrived, so she had stayed near the house. Tom, Albert, Katie, Carrie and Julian were busy in the hay-field.

'Where have you left him? Is he badly hurt?'

'No, just stunned. He will be all right.'

'But why? What happened?'

'He will tell you. Mother, listen. I've got to get away. Can you lend me some money?'

'Not again?' she sighed. She seemed to have been lending money to Charles since his prep school days, when he always wrote to her, not his father. But she never got it back, and it was not fair to the rest of the family to rob them of their dwindling capital.

'You'd better come in and I'll bathe your ears,' she said.

'It's nothing.' He dabbed his ears and wiped his cheeks with a clean handkerchief. 'I'm sorry, darling, but there just isn't time. I have to be on my way.'

She stared at him in utter disbelief. Was it really goodbye this time – the final goodbye? This was the son for whom she had forfeited her pride and her reputation. He was her darling, her best beloved, but for years she had seen less and less of him. To see him in tears, and to know he was in disgrace with his father, was unbearable.

'Will you hurry, Mother, *please*, darling.' He was looking over his shoulder, his swollen face was twitching. She hurried into the house, unlocked the cash box on the top shelf of the kitchen cupboard, and took out twenty pounds.

He wouldn't get far on that, but he had friends in London. She was not the only fool who would lend him money. He took it from her and pushed it into his pocket as though it had no value. 'Easy come, easy go,' she thought.

'Thanks, darling. I'll let you have it back.' He leaned over to kiss her. His mouth was soft and sensual – a weak mouth, not like his father's. She stroked his cheek.

'Oh, *Charles*! What have you *done*?' she asked, despairingly.

And again he answered, 'He will tell you.'

'Keep in touch, my dear. It will be all right. He will listen to me.'

'Not this time he won't,' Charles was thinking, as he rode away. When he turned to wave, she felt quite sick with the awful possibility that she would not see him again.

He was barely out of sight when she saw his father in the distance. He was walking stiffly, leading the horse. She went to meet him slowly, uncertainly. She loved them both. 'Like father, like son,' they said. If Charles had got a girl into trouble, it was not a crime, not by their standards, upper-class standards. Money could settle it. Then why all the mystery?

She smiled a welcome and took his hand. Everyone came to Russets to be comforted and healed. His chin was bruised, and he winced when he turned his head. She would bathe it with witch-hazel, and she always kept whisky in the house these days.

All the doors and windows were flung wide, and the sun streaming in. They used the front entrance to avoid being seen by the hay-makers. Justin pawed the ground impatiently when he was tied to a post, but Sir Neville soothed him and followed Lucy into the kitchen, where he sank gratefully into the rocking chair. While he sipped the whisky, she fetched witch-hazel and cotton wool, and knelt on the floor to examine the ugly bruise.

'Does it hurt?' she asked.

What a stupid question! 'Like Hell! I thought he had broken my bloody jaw!'

She took the empty glass, pushed his head back gently, and dabbed at the bruise with the soaked cotton wool. Witch-hazel dribbled on to his bare chest. Charles had not fastened the buttons after he tested the heart beat. He closed his eyes and gave himself up to her capable ministering hands. She asked no question. He would tell her in his own good time.

Since they had become lovers, both with grown-up families, there was no constraint between them.

'What should I do without you, my dear?' he asked, with a deep sigh.

She smiled at the question. Only rarely did the old arrogance assert itself these days, and then it was over some trivial misunderstanding. She knew he would always be masterful and would have his way with her, but she would not have him any different. When they were alone together, she called him Neville. Once he had actually suggested marriage, but it would have spoiled their relationship. There was no place for her at Marston Park. She belonged to Russets.

'Did Charles come here?' he asked, eventually.

'Yes. He was very upset.'

His eyes flew open. They were black as onyx. '*He* was upset? My God! I could have killed him!'

'What has he done?' she whispered.

'*Charles is Julian's father.*'

'No! Oh, *no*!'

'His own sister.'

'*Half*-sister. Who told you?'

'Hetty.'

'But why, after all these years?'

'The housemaid confessed to receiving bribery money from Charles to keep her mouth shut, but Charles had stopped sending money.'

'The housemaid? Ethel?'

'Yes, the little slut.'

'Where is she now?'

'Hetty sent her packing, then she told me. She was afraid the woman would talk. She will, anyway. The whole village will know now she has been sacked. It seems she actually saw it happen.'

'She could have been lying?'

'No. Charles is a silly young bastard, but he's no fool. He wouldn't have paid her money to keep her mouth shut if he was innocent.'

'My dear, it was eight years ago. They were little more than children. If they were just amusing themselves, it must have been an awful shock when they discovered Penelope was pregnant. And Penelope was a party to the deception. Is it fair to put all the blame on Charles?'

'Yes, it was cowardly and despicable to leave that poor child to her fate.'

'She probably insisted. She was a very strong-willed girl, I remember.'

'Nothing you can say, Lucy, will alter my opinion. As far as I'm concerned, it's finished. I never want to see him again.'

'But I'm his mother,' she insisted, tearfully. 'He is still my son. A mother doesn't stop loving her child, even if she discovers he has committed a murder.'

His mouth twisted in a wry smile. 'You're a very stubborn woman, Lucy. Supposing I threatened to walk out of here, *for good*, unless you promised me not to get in touch with Charles?'

She shook her head. 'I could never promise that, my

dear.'

'You know darn well I couldn't keep away. I need you. It's only you now, Lucy.'

'You won't tell Julian?'

'No, he is too young to understand the significance of such a relationship.'

'Supposing he hears at school?'

'We must take a chance on that. Where is he now?'

'In the hay-field.'

'With the rest of the family?'

'Yes. I shall be joining them later with the dinner basket, and a jug of tea.'

'I want you, Lucy.'

'Now?'

'Yes.'

Her blue eyes were tender with love as they climbed the stairs. 'Like father, like son.' She still thought he had been too harsh with Charles. A boy and a girl, exploring the limits of sexual excitement. It was natural.

It was the same old story, whatever the class of society. Hadn't she enticed Bert into the Dutch barn, all those years ago? She was sixteen when Harry was conceived. It seemed a long time ago, but she had stopped wishing to put back the clock. Life was good here, and now, and she savoured it with all her senses.

Part 3

Chapter 11

A little girl in a short print frock and a matching sun-bonnet hurried along the path to the Common on a hot afternoon in mid-Summer, with Grannie plodding along breathlessly a few paces behind.

Ruby was uncomfortably hot, but she had her eye on the bench under the stunted hawthorn bush, some fifty yards away. There was a time, not so long ago, when the child would have played quite happily in the garden, and Ruby could have enjoyed her forty winks. Not any more. An energetic three-year-old, with a puppy, needed more space to exercise, and the Common was just across the road. Ruby had always been plump, but she had put on a lot of extra weight of recent years. Her legs were enormous. Cynthia had bought elastic stockings for her varicose veins. She never complained. Living with her son Freddie, her favourite daughter-in-law, and the child, had solved the problem of her own security, and Cynthia's dedication to the nursing profession. They all were happy and content with this new chapter of their lives.

The puppy had been a present for Wendy's third birthday. She didn't care for dolls. She had it on a long leash, and it tugged at her hand as they set foot on the grass. She hung on, laughing gleefully, her long flaxen hair shining like ripened corn in the sunlight, her white socks slipping over her sandals. There was no need for Ruby to remind her about the seat. She was an obedient child, and would come when she was called.

Cynthia was strict about obedience, table manners, and politeness to grown-ups. Freddie had few hard and fast rules on bringing up children. They adored each other. She had been taught not to intrude on his privacy. The office was sacred to his work and his clients.

'Tap on the door. Wait for Daddy to call "come in". Turn the handle and walk in,' she had been instructed.

It was not always convenient, however. She would hear voices, and Daddy would call 'Later, Pet'. They all had different names for her. She was Daddy's 'Pet', Mummy's 'Darling' and Grannie's 'Little Love'.

For Ruby it had been a time of re-adjustment and obligation. Her own children, and her son Jack's children, had no fault to find with her dropped aitches. But it would not do for this child, she told herself. Her son Freddie had married into the upper class, against all the principles and objections of their working-class environment. Little children have no standards. They imitate. They are born mimics. To learn to 'talk proper' at her time of life was the most difficult thing Ruby had ever attempted. Neither Freddie nor Cynthia mentioned it, so there was no embarrassment. They knew, and understood, the reason for such a determined effort, and admired her dogged persistence. After nearly two years of careful enunciation, her speech was still a little stilted. For the child's sake, Ruby had sacrificed the rough idiom of Richmond Row, and the old, spontaneous gabble.

'Poor old Mum. It's pathetic,' Freddie would think. But he was wrong. It was plain commonsense!

Cynthia's cultured voice could not be ignored in that household, and her strong personality held undisputed priority. As Sister Simmons, she was respected by her subordinates, and she carried an air of authority quite unconsciously into her private world when she left the hospital. Freddie and his mother and the child all recognised this authority. When she was tired, they let her rest, and the child amused herself in the kitchen, making little men from odd scraps of dough, with currants to fasten their jackets.

'Your Auntie Carrie used to like making little men from my odd scraps when she was a little girl,' she was told.

Grannie had a fund of stories from what she called the 'old days' that were better than any found in her story books. Auntie Carrie was pretty and very nice. She had brought the puppy for her third birthday from a farm called 'Russets', and promised to show her all the animals as soon as she could manage the walk from the station.

'Next year, when you are four,' said Mummy, decidedly.

She would meet her cousin, Julian, for the first time, and all the animals in her favourite picture book – horses, cows, sheep and pigs. There were ducks on a pond, and hens in the orchard, and pigeons in the loft. Wendy liked the sound of it.

'Why don't we live there, Grannie?' she wanted to know.

'Because this is our home, my love. This is where we belong.'

'If we a'longed to Russets it would be better.'

'No place is better than *home*, lovey.'

The child accepted the fact. At the age of three she could only concentrate on one thing at a time, and arranging the currant buttons had all her attention. Her small pink tongue licked her lips. She was kneeling on a chair, and her cheeks were dabbed with flour. Grannie was putting on the kettle for another cup of tea. She had her own mug, and she liked her tea very sweet and milky. When Mummy was at home, she drank milk.

'Drink up, darling!' Mummy would say.

You didn't contradict Mummy. Daddy liked coffee for his elevenses, and tea in the afternoon. When he had clients in the office, Grannie would carry in a tray. The coffee had a lovely smell when it was brewing.

'Why can't I have coffee?' she asked one morning.

Grannie shook her head. 'Your Mummy wouldn't like it, my love.' 'Mummy knows best' was the code of conduct!

She was a happy, healthy child, and every day was a big adventure. Indoors and outdoors were two different worlds. Indoors always stayed the same. Outdoors was constantly changing. In one of her earliest memories, she was lying in her pram looking up at the sky. She couldn't bear it when somebody put up the hood and shut out the sky. There was a time for everything indoors – a time to be washed and dressed – a time to sit on her potty – a time to eat and drink – a time to play – a time to be read a story – a time to be bathed and put to bed. She made them understand as soon as she could talk and walk that she liked outdoors best. She had only to fetch her coat and bonnet. When it was Daddy's turn to push the pram, he would tease her and put the bonnet on his own head. They always went to The Pantiles because it was flat. The paths on the Common were too steep. They looked at everything and everybody, and shared a small portion of chocolate when they stopped to rest the iron leg called James.

'Don't tell your mother,' said Daddy, as he popped it into her mouth. 'To eat between meals is not done in the best circles. And don't tell your mother I took off your gloves.'

She couldn't bear her hands to be covered, even on the coldest Winter day. He understood about gloves being a nuisance, as he understood about most things. They always started out with the best intentions, for Grannie was fussy about pram-covers and starched pillow-cases, and the importance of being 'nice and tidy'. In the Winter months, her legs were encased in leggings, and she was wrapped in a tight cocoon under the pram-cover.

When they sat down on one of the benches to rest James, she was scooped out and set down to explore the ground beneath her feet. She picked up every leaf, and carried it back to Daddy who waited patiently till she had finished. The trees were so tall, she had to lean backwards to see the topmost branches, and once she toppled over she leaned so far back. She picked herself up, more than a little surprised, and went on her way to find more leaves. Sometimes they were stiff with frost, and crackled in her hands. Sometimes they were wet, and they smelled pleasantly of earth. That was Winter, when the branches of the trees were bare and she could still see the sky. There was a season called Autumn when The Pantiles was covered in leaves, and she scuffed along happily, scattering them with her small feet. But the men with their big brooms and barrows soon had them swept up. They were a darn nuisance, they said. There was a season called Summer, the best season of all, when her legs were bare, and Daddy took off her bonnet and she chased butterflies.

On Saturday afternoons they would hurry along to the far end of The Pantiles where tables and chairs had been carefully arranged outside the tea-shop, and they were served with strawberry ice-cream in little glass dishes. This was their Saturday treat.

'To do it every day would just become a habit,' said Daddy. He always talked to her as one grown-up to another.

The Spring was his favourite season, when all the branches of all the trees were covered in green shoots, yellow daffodils danced in the breeze, the swallows flew back to the nests, and a blackbird found his voice again.

Now she was three the pram was discarded, and they walked hand-in-hand down The Pantiles, keeping in step with James who wouldn't be hurried. They would stop for a little gossip with old acquaintances, and the puppy must be trained in good habits.

'I've got news for you, Pet,' said Daddy, one Saturday afternoon. 'Your mother has bought a second-hand car, and she is learning to drive.' She was always 'your mother', never Mummy: it made her seem very important. She *was* important, to each one of them, particularly to Daddy. 'Your daddy worships your mummy,' said Grannie.

'Will she take us for a ride?' Wendy wanted to know.

'She will take us to the seaside. We are having a holiday this year, Pet.'

'Can I paddle, Daddy?'

'You may.'

'Can I have a bucket and spade?'

'You may.'

'Can I ride on a donkey?'

'You may.'

She squealed with excitement and gave him a hug. She had seen pictures of happy children at the seaside, but it seemed beyond their reach in Tunbridge Wells, where you had the Common and The Pantiles, but no beach and no sea.

'What you never have you never miss, love,' Grannie always insisted.

'We shall take Grannie to the seaside, shan't we, Daddy?' she asked anxiously.

'Of course. Grannie has never had a proper holiday.'

'Why?'

'Because she was poor, and poor people have no money to spare for holidays.'

'Is Grannie rich now she's living with us?'

'So she says, bless her!' Daddy chuckled.

'Shall we take Julian? There is plenty of room in the car, and we could ask for a camp-bed, or he could sleep on the sofa in the sitting-room?' Freddie suggested the following morning over breakfast.

'*If* there's a sofa.' Cynthia was looking pale and tired after a hectic week in casualty, and she felt irritated by Freddie's suggestion. It was to be strictly a family holiday, and her young nephew was not included in her plans. 'It would be too big a responsibility,' she argued. 'You know the poor child is scared to death of the river, and it would be even worse at the sea.'

'Why?' Wendy interrupted.

'Empty your mouth before you speak.' Cynthia's voice was sharp. The child obediently swallowed a spoonful of boiled egg and repeated the question. Her mother sighed. 'When I was a little girl, we were not allowed to speak at the meal table. I am beginning to think it was an excellent arrangement.'

Wendy looked puzzled. 'How do you ask for more bread and butter?'

'We didn't. It was passed when we were ready.'

'Did you have to eat up your cabbage and bread and butter pudding?'

'We had to eat every scrap of food on our plates before we were allowed to leave the table.'

Wendy shuddered. She had two pet aversions – cabbage and bread and butter pudding – and when Mummy was sharing their meal she was obliged to eat a very small portion.

'Eat up, darling,' she would say. 'It's wicked to waste

good food when so many little children are hungry.'

'They can have my cabbage and bread and butter pudding.'

Daddy laughed, but Mummy hadn't thought it was funny.

'Were you 'lowed to spread your own jam?' This was a recent accomplishment, and afternoon tea had acquired a new importance.

'Not in the nursery. It was always spread for us, and there was a strict ruling that you ate the first slice without jam. If you made a fuss, you had no cake.'

It was a fascinating subject, and Cousin Julian was forgotten. It was not often that Mummy talked about the old days at Marston Park, only as a pattern of good behaviour for her own child, and not in any way suggesting it was preferable to the old days in Richmond Row. Freddie and Ruby were glad to have Cynthia's thoughts diverted. It calmed her nerves, and she forgot to scold.

When they had finished breakfast, she sent Wendy to wash her hands, and brought out the album of photographs. The child had seen them all a number of times, but never tired of looking at them. It was all so grand. The Big House had so many windows she had to be helped to count them, since she could only count up to twenty. She sat on the floor, spread the album over her knees, and turned the pages very slowly. She liked a lot of time to examine each photograph, especially the one with four little girls on the terrace, with a nurse and nursemaid in attendance. She knew their names – Beatrice, Cynthia – that was Mummy – Sylvia and Penelope. Beatrice and Cynthia were holding hoops, Sylvia and Penelope perched in a high pram. They were all dressed up in frilled frocks and floppy hats, but it wasn't their Sunday best.

She looked up from the album to ask a question, but Mummy was lying back on Daddy's shoulder, with her eyes closed, and he smiled at her and put a finger to his lips. So she contented herself with answering the question in a hushed whisper. She often carried on a conversation with herself now she was three.

'No, darling, we are not wearing our Sunday best. We were always dressed up even to bowl our hoops in the Park.'

Daddy smothered a laugh. The child was a born mimic.

She turned the page to find her grandfather mounted on a big horse, attended by a groom. She had not yet seen him on a horse, because when he came to lunch he always arrived in a big, important-looking motor car, and Grannie was not quite at ease with him either, and called him 'Sir'. They were all on their very best behaviour, and it was a great relief when he left and they could relax. The half-crown he gave her went into her money-box.

'Give Grandpa a kiss, darling,' said Mummy, always a little cross because she had to remind her. But Grandpa wasn't a kissable person, not like Daddy.

Their Mama was lying on a couch, draped in chiffon and lace, with a maid in attendance.

'Would you belive it, darling? We were waited on hand and foot. Ridiculous!' the small mimic told herself, and again Daddy smothered a laugh. They could hear Grannie in the kitchen, washing up the breakfast dishes, and the puppy barking at the boy delivering the Sunday papers. It was Grannie who had explained about Mummy being upper class.

'Born and bred, lovey. You can't mistake good breeding.'

'Is my Daddy upper class?' she had asked, innocently.

Grannie shook her head. 'Working class, me and your Daddy.'

'Am I upper class?'

Grannie considered the question carefully before she

answered. 'Blest if I know, my love. Best ask your Daddy,' she chuckled.

But Daddy didn't know either. 'Ask your Mother, Pet,' he told her.

It was all rather puzzling when you were only three.

'It's really quite simple, darling, only they will make an issue out of it,' said Mummy. 'When I married Daddy, I left the upper class behind at Marston Park. I had no use for it. I married Daddy because I loved him, and for no other reason. I want you to remember that, always.'

'Yes, Mummy,' the child had replied, obediently. But it still hadn't answered her question. She sat on the floor, turning the pages of the family album, wondering about the four little girls who had to eat up every scrap of food on their plates and were not allowed to spread their own jam in the nursery. It couldn't have been much fun in the schoolroom, either, for the governess was even more strict than the nurse, and rapped their knuckles when they touched the wrong note on the piano. The schoolroom piano was there, in the sitting-room, and Mummy played hymns after tea on Sunday. They sang 'Onward Christian Soldiers', 'Abide with Me', and 'All things bright and beautiful', because they were Grannie's favourites. Wendy stood behind the piano, watching her mother's hands on the keyboard. It was yellow with age, but it held an irresistible fascination for the child when the lid was left open.

'It's not a toy,' said Mummy, closing the lid with a firmness that was never disputed.

'I want to play the piano!' sobbed the child.

'Darling, what a fuss! You are much too young.' She was led away in tears. Could Mummy be wrong?

'Your mother knows best,' Daddy insisted.

But when she sat for a whole hour, listening quietly to one of his classical records on the gramophone, one wet afternoon, he was surprised and delighted. The golden rule that Daddy must not be disturbed when he played his records was no longer enforced. She sat in Grannie's armchair, her short legs stretched out, her cheeks flushed with excitement. The music caught her imagination, and held her attention. She was completely absorbed. So was Daddy, but he closed his eyes, and didn't speak a word till the music had finished. Then he let out a long breath and opened his arms. She slid off the chair and went to him, still entranced, still quietly submitting to his warm cuddle. She asked no questions, for her avid curiosity was satisfied by his simple explanation. One day she would want to know more, but not yet.

'You and your Daddy *has* got *high*-brow taste and no mistake, my love,' said Grannie, the first time it happened. Grannie had been closing the door. The golden rule had to be observed. She was still a little wary of her daughter-in-law and her golden rules.

'*Please*, Daddy.'

He couldn't resist that pleading little face. 'Let her stay. If she fidgets she will be sent out.'

Grannie shook her head. 'She's only a baby. What would you expect?'

'Let her stay.'

So she stayed.

For the child, that first holiday at St Margaret's Bay would be remembered with nostalgia for the rest of her life. It was an impressionable age for a bright, intelligent little girl who had hitherto explored no farther than the Common, The Pantiles, and Woolworths, to buy a bucket and spade.

Ruby had been washing and ironing every day for a whole week, and the house had been spring-cleaned for the second time that year, though Freddie flatly refused to have his office disturbed.

It was the second week of August when they set forth. According to Cynthia, every Dick, Tom and Harry took a holiday the first week of August. So they waited. The puppy had been well trained. It sat when it was told to sit, its ears cocked expectantly, its stubby tail wagging. It would never be a handsome dog, and it had no pedigree worth mentioning, but it had all the best traits of a long line of mongrels, and answered to the name of Rusty. The child's hair had been washed, and she had been bathed and put to bed early, smelling sweetly of Pear's soap. It was like Christmas Eve, without the stockings, and she lay awake, listening to the traffic of feet on the stairs, and the bumps and bangs of the luggage being piled in the hall, ready for an early start the next morning. Tense with excitement, she wriggled her small warm body in the clean nightgown, and peered repeatedly at the bedside chair, where the holiday clothes were laid out neatly, with her new bucket and spade. She could hear the thump, thump of James next door, where Daddy was doing his pacing. Then she heard a quick step on the stairs and Mummy's voice, sharp with irritation.

'Really darling, you *are* exasperating! Isn't it just like a man to leave everything to the last moment!

But Daddy answered her soothingly. 'Nearly finished, dear.'

The silence that followed was a very good sign that all was well. Daddy had a nice way of kissing Mummy. With his hands on her waist, he could lift her quite easily. She had a very small waist. Grannie had no waist at all.

'My darling, we have two whole weeks to make love. Don't spoil it. Be patient.'

The child could hear every word. The wall that divided the two rooms was not solid. A vague sense of uneasiness and the first pangs of jealousy disturbed the lovely anticipation of the morrow. Love was a word she understood.

She was surrounded by love. They all loved her in different ways, and she loved them in different ways. So how did you *make* love? Wasn't it always there, in every hug and kiss? The feeling that Daddy could make a special kind of love, just for Mummy, was hurting inside. She wanted to cry, but no tears came. When they stood in the doorway, whispering, she screwed up her eyes and pretended to be asleep. Then they were gone. They hadn't said goodnight. She wanted to call them back, but it was too late. She opened her eyes and sat up. It was still daylight because it was Summer. In the Winter, the curtains were drawn, and she had a tiny lamp standing on top of the chest of drawers because she was afraid of the dark. It was very comforting. Grannie filled the tiny lamp with paraffin every day, when she filled the big lamp for the sitting-room.

But now she was badly in need of comfort, and it was not there. Then she remembered the bucket and spade, and reached over to lift them carefully on to the bed. The red bucket and the little spade reminded her that Daddy had promised to help build a big sand castle, while Mummy and Grannie rested in their deck chairs. She smiled and lay down, cuddling them in her arms. It would be lovely.

'Wake up, darling!'

She stared at the pretty new Mummy in a bright blue dress and blue cardigan. What had happened to Sister Simmons in her uniform? Then her feet touched the bucket, and she squealed with delight, burrowed into the bed, and brought it out, then went down again to hunt for the spade. Starry-eyed, she asked breathlessly, 'Is it Holiday, Mummy?'

'Yes, it's Holiday, you funny little scrap!' She was scooped up and hugged. Now Mummy was not a hugging sort of person. This was something special because it was

Holiday. This new Mummy in the pretty blue dress smelled nice. Sister Simmons always smelled a bit like the lavatory when the floor had been scrubbed!

Freddie had washed and polished the car last evening. Wendy could see her face in the bonnet. She climbed on to the back seat and sat down, carefully arranging Rusty and the bucket and spade on her lap. Another anxious half-hour passed while the luggage was piled in the boot, and Grannie bustled about with baskets of provisions.

'Good heavens! One would suppose we were preparing for a siege!' said Mummy, who was supervising the whole operation.

Daddy had a little trouble with James in the front seat. 'He's just being awkward, Pet. There's plenty of room,' he told her.

The food baskets were stacked on the floor, under Wendy's feet, and covered with clean tea-cloths. Grannie had spent all day in the kitchen yesterday, and delicious smells of baking, roasting chicken, and boiling ham filled the whole house. They would have picnic lunches on the beach, and a high tea in the early evening at their lodgings.

'Move over, darling. Make room for Grannie,' Mummy instructed.

She wriggled obligingly, but when Grannie had settled herself with a bird-cage on her lap, there wasn't an inch to spare. Candy the canary had stopped singing. His cage was draped in a black cloth.

'I've got *him* covered, lovey, then *he* will think it's night time and go to sleep,' she explained breathlessly, still very conscious of those troublesome 'aitches'. When you have dropped them for more than sixty years, it is difficult to pick them up.

'Are you quite comfy, Mother?' her daughter-in-law asked solicitously.

'Yes, thank you, love.'

Then Cynthia climbed in behind the wheel, tossed a smile to the medley of passengers on the back seat, and let out the clutch. The car jerked forward. Wendy's tense little body sagged like a pricked balloon. They were off at last! Holiday had begun!

The miles slipped away, and with every mile her breakfast turned somersaults inside. She kept her mouth closed tightly, and Rusty licked her face. He knew something was wrong. But it was no use.

'I want to be sick!' she wailed – and there was no more time. Rusty barked indignantly, and scrambled off her lap. Grannie seized the bucket and held her forehead. Cynthia had braked, and the car slid to a halt. Freddie reached over to take the bid-cage.

'There, there, my poor little love,' said Grannie, soothingly. It was all over in a matter of minutes, but it took the combined efforts of all three grown-ups to comfort the child.

'My bucket! My new lovely bucket!' she sobbed.

Then Cynthia took charge. As always she was calm and efficient. She opened the windows, took the handkerchief Freddie proffered, reached for the bucket, and disappeared behind a bush.

'Would you believe it? We thought of everything but car sickness!' she said, briskly, handing back the clean bucket.

'She was so excited. Bless 'er little 'eart,' Ruby was too upset to pick up the aitches and nobody noticed.

'Shall we change places, dear?' Freddie suggested, anxiously.

Cynthia shook her head. 'No, darling. There's not enough room in the back. She will be all right now, and it's only another five miles or so. Sit on Grannie's lap, darling, and watch for the sea. Shush! Rusty, Shush!'

He was picked up by the scruff of his neck and planted firmly on the seat. The child flinched.

'Don't hurt him, Mummy.'

'It's the correct way to handle a puppy. Ask your Daddy.'

'Your mother's right, Pet,' he said.

The child sighed. Mummy was always right, but not nearly as comforting as Grannie. In her small world there was no more comforting place than Grannie's lap when you were feeling poorly. In five minutes she was asleep.

It was one of a row of tall terrace houses facing the sea. All were gleaming with fresh paint. Muslin curtains fluttered in the breeze. Towels and bathing costumes were spread to dry on all the upstairs window sills.

A neat little couple bustled out to welcome them. The Jacksons lived in the basement. Born and bred in Stepney, they had settled happily at St Margaret's Bay in 1920. The sea air was good for lungs permanently damaged by gas poisoning. Ex-seargeant Jackson's puckered face split into a wide grin as he relieved Freddie of the birdcage and helped him on to the pavement.

'Pleased to meet yer, Sir.'

They shook hands, and assessed each other kindly in the manner of men who had survived the holocaust of the Western Front. Mrs Jackson was lifting Wendy down, while the puppy yapped excitedly at a cat stretched in the sun on the basement steps.

'I was sick,' said the child, importantly. 'In my new bucket.'

Everyone laughed, and motherly Mrs Jackson adjusted the bow of blue ribbon on the long flaxen hair. 'Never mind, duckie. You got 'ere safe and sound. And this lidy will be your Grandma?'

'That's right,' said Ruby, stretching her cramped legs in the tight elastic stockings.

'Lean on me, luv,' Mrs Jackson invited.

Ruby smiled. She knew she was going to like May Jackson. After all, Stepney wasn't all that different from Richmond Row in the village, and she would probably discover she had picked hops at one of the farms before the war.

Cynthia had crossed the road after greeting their landlady, and snatched off her hat. The breeze ruffled her short hair, and lifted her skirt. Her slim, girlish figure had not changed in the past decade.

'My wife,' said Freddie, proudly, when she turned to walk back.

'How do you do, Mr Jackson.' Her smile was warm and friendly as they shook hands.

'I knew she was one of the nobs soon as she opened 'er mouth,' Ted Jackson would tell his wife later.

'A real nice lidy,' May would readily agree. In fact, they seldom disagreed. 'To 'ave my Ted back 'ome even with them poor lungs, was a miracle. I got a lot to be thankful for,' she would say.

'It looks as though you have a house full of guests who like to bathe?' Cynthia was glancing up at the draped window sills.

'Always full right up in August, Madam, and most of our visitors likes to bathe straight from the 'ouse, as you might say. It's so 'andy. They please theirselves.'

There was sand on the tiled path leading to the front door, and sand in the hall. Mackintoshes and sun hats draped the hallstand. The visitors were obviously prepared for all kinds of weather. Several little sailing boats and shrimping nets had been flung down carelessly when their owners discovered the tide was high. Rusty had found a bowl of water, and was drinking thirstily, splashing the sandy floor.

'You don't mind all the mess and muddle?' Cynthia was asking.

'We don't take no notice, Madam. It gets cleaned once a dye before breakfast. After all, it's their 'oliday, and they're paying for it. We like to see everybody enjoying themselves. We don't 'ave no rules and regulations, do we Ted?'

'That's right. Blimey! I 'ad enough of that in the bloody Army! Begging yer pardon, Madam.'

'You ought not to swear, love, not in front of little children,' May would chide him mildly when they were alone.

They were leading the way into the rooms they had prepared on the ground floor. A sitting-room, two bedrooms, washroom and lavatory, all smelling strongly of wax polish. It was noticed that Mrs Jackson was carrying the biggest and heaviest of the cases, and bustled away to bring in the baskets of provisions.

'The doctor said as 'ow Ted 'ad to take it easy on account of them poor lungs,' she confided to Ruby later.

'One of these dyes we thought of 'aving a nice little bathroom up on the first floor, but it don't seem all that urgent, do it, Sir, not when all our visitors is tyking a bath in the sea most dyes?'

Ted laughed at his own joke, then he realised it was not very tactful. But Freddie made no comment. At one time, when he was still very sensitive of his disability, he might have been embarrassed, but not any more. He pushed aside the muslin curtains, flung open the window, and lifted Wendy on to the sill. The sea was sparkling under a blue sky, the sun warm on their enraptured faces.

'There, what do you think of it, Pet?' he asked, hugging the small, wriggling body.

She was still clutching the bucket and spade. 'Can I fill my bucket two times, Daddy? Is it 'lowed?'

'As many times as you please. There's plenty of sea!' he chuckled.

Ruby had found a hook to hang the bird-cage. The canary was singing again in the bright sunlight.

And Cynthia was accepting the offer of a pot of tea.

Unlike the other families staying at St Margaret's, the small family on the ground floor had no bathing costumes draped on the window sills. Cynthia was too sensitive of Freddie's disability to enjoy a bathe on her own, though he urged her to do so that first day.

'But I haven't brought a costume, darling. To tell you the truth, I'm a bit of a coward,' she lied gallantly – and he believed her.

It would be a restful holiday, not an adventurous one, for all three grown-ups were greatly in need of relaxation, and the child content to play with sand and water. The Jacksons watched them making their leisurely way to their chosen spot on the beach.

'I'll be down later, Madam, with a fresh pot of tea,' Mrs Jackson called after them.

Soon the three deck chairs were lined up and all their belongings tidily arranged.

'Not like some, what spread theirselves all over the plyce,' Ted pointed out, that first day. They could see the little girl taking off her shoes and socks, and her Grannie tucking her frock in her knickers. Then she trotted proudly off with her daddy and her new bucket and spade. They never tired of watching their happy families, but there was work to be done, so they turned away from the window.

The Simmons family wore hats, but few of their visitors went bare-headed in this day and age. Cynthia would remove her own shoes and stockings discreetly, that first day. The ethics of her early training in the nurseries of Marston Park still clung in spite of all the years of hospital nursing. Cynthia would never be completely emancipated. It was one of her most endearing qualities that she recognised her womanly limitations, and allowed Freddie his moments of male superiority.

Ruby had waited for a signal from her daughter-in-law to remove her own shoes and stockings. She stretched her bare feet with a gusty sigh. They were ugly feet, with corns and bunions, but she had been promised a paddle when the tide was right, and had great faith in the beneficial properties of sea water. Ruby was not yet ready to relax, and sat heavily on the edge of the deck chair, watching her son busy with the tiny spade, and the child running back and forth to the water's edge with her bucket. Most of the water slopped out of the bucket as she ran, and only a trickle reached the moat around the castle, but it didn't matter. They had all the time in the world, it seemed. With the puppy at her heels, she was dodging all the children scampering towards the sea.

When Mrs Jackson arrived with a tray of tea and a bag of fresh rolls the baker had delivered, they were called up the beach for lunch. The home-cooked ham and cold chicken tasted so much better when it was eaten outdoors. There were bakewell tarts, sweet biscuits, apples and bananas, all spread out in a tempting array on a white cloth.

'Can I choose, Mummy?' asked the child, surprised and delighted by such a rare privilege. Rusty was not forgotten. He had his own bowls, one for the fresh water from a flask, and the other for his own special biscuits. Freddie was missing his coffee, however. Tea was all right at the proper time, he told Cynthia. Did all seaside landladies serve nothing but tea?

'My fault, darling. I forgot to mention it. Tomorrow I shall ask for a flask of strong coffee for my husband. Isn't it just like a man to want everything the same as he gets at home?' she teased him, affectionately. There was mischief in her smile that he hadn't seen for a very long time.

Wendy watched the castle anxiously, but it was quite safe, for the tide was going out, she was told. The tides would remain a mystery to the child for the whole of the two weeks. Every morning she would ask Mr Jackson the same question, 'Is the tide going out, please?' And he would know exactly what it was doing. She thought he was a very clever man, and told him so.

'Blimey! I was tickled pink. She's a rare caution!' he told May. It was another new word to add to her limited vocabulary, but not very popular with the grown-ups. As for that naughty swear word that popped out occasionally, she was threatened with the loss of her bucket and spade for a whole day if it was repeated, and there could be no harsher punishment.

The sun was hot, and her small stomach filled to capacity. Her head drooped, and her eyes closed. She was only partly conscious of being scooped up and planted gently on that familiar comfortable lap. There was sand in her toes, and sand in her hair, but it didn't matter. This was Holiday!

When she woke from her nap, her bright eyes sought the castle. It was still there!

Now it was Grannie's turn, and they went off together, hand-in-hand, to paddle.

'Don't be 'fraid, Grannie. I look after you,' they heard her say.

Ruby was choked with emotion. There had never been a child like this one. Never had she known such happiness, such pride and joy. Even her own children took second place now in her long memory. Could it be the mating of working class with upper class, she wondered? Had her favourite daughter-in-law been right to defy convention? Was this lovely, intelligent child proof of her rightness?

Children swarmed about them, splashing and squealing, but Wendy was completely detached. An only child, unused to playmates, she knew only the company of these three adored adults that made up her small world, and it was enough for the present.

When Ruby's feet were nicely soaked, she went back to her deckchair to keep guard over their belongings while Freddie and Cynthia walked on the sands with the child between them. They belonged together, and she was included in their conversation. There was no more jealousy.

After their 'high tea', Wendy was put to bed, and she lay awake, thinking of the castle, and the little shells she had found to take home to Tunbridge Wells. The castle would be washed away in the tide, but tomorrow they would build another. Tomorrow and tomorrow and tomorrow! She snuggled down in the big bed she was sharing with Grannie. She could hear her talking to Mrs Jackson on the front porch. They would sit there till the parents came back from their evening entertainment, listening for the cries of frightened or restless children, but all was quiet, and all the children slept soundly. Ted was washing-up the dishes in the back scullery, whistling tonelessly. When he had finished, he would brew another pot of tea for the Missus and the old lady, then disappeared for an hour or so to his favourite pub for a pint of beer. It reminded him of Stepney before the War. The smell was the same smell, only the beer was different.

Freddie and Cynthia slipped away for a quiet evening stroll. They had no taste for pubs or pierrots. This was their first holiday. It had been a struggle to make ends meet since the War, but they were lucky to have a home of their own, and congenial work, when so many were homeless and destitute.

'You are very quiet, darling,' Cynthia hinted, after a long silence.

Freddie yawned expansively. 'I was wondering if it was nearly time for bed?'

'You're tired?'

'No, my dearest girl. I want to make love to you.'

'Then shall we turn back, my darling?' she asked, demurely.

Chapter 12

Martha anxiously awaited news of Philip at the School House during that first week after his sudden departure with Harriet.

'He is busy at the Mission and can think of nothing else but preparing himself for the Congo. Your son has a one-track mind, and likes to concentrate on one thing at a time,' Andrew reminded her, bluntly. Hadn't he been the boy's unofficial, unpaid tutor during those early years, preparing him for Grammar School?

'But it would take only a few minutes to telephone, if he has not time to write a letter? It's not like him, Andrew. He has always been so thoughtful and considerate of his mother since he was a little boy.'

'And now you have to reconcile yourself to second place in your son's affections. It happens all the time.'

'But not so suddenly. I had no warning.'

'That's true. We both were taken completely by surprise. I must admit, it was the last thing I expected of Philip. I thought his mind was set on the Law. It does seem rather a waste of time and money, but what can one do when offered an ultimatum? We did know he was fond of Harriet, didn't we?'

Martha nodded miserably.

'She seems a strong-willed young woman which is all to the good with Philip.'

'But she is upper class, Andrew. Had you forgotten that?'

'In this day and age it hardly signifies. The War changed so many of our deeply rooted principles and prejudices. When one considers that successful marriage of Carrie's brother Freddie to a daughter of Sir Neville Franklin, it makes one realise how mistaken one can be about human relationships.'

'Yes, I suppose you are right. Carrie insists they are ideally happy, but it was such a risk, it could have been a disaster.'

'Isn't there an element of risk in every marriage? Your first marriage was a misguided misfortune, and what did you actually know about me, fundamentally, I mean? Obviously you recognised a certain status as the village schoolmaster. Why *did* you marry me, Martha?'

'What a question, dear, after all these years!' He could still make her blush, he noticed.

'Well, I am waiting for an answer.'

'Because I admired and respected you, Andrew.'

'Is that all? Nothing more?'

'You're teasing.'

'I'm serious. Never more so. I have to know where I stand, Martha, once and for all. Second best in your affections is not good enough. Philip has always come first, hasn't he? No, don't deny it. Now he is lost to you, even before he leaves for the Congo. It has been a shock, hasn't it, Martha? So what are we going to do with ourselves, you and I, for the rest of our lives? Do we keep up this pretence for the sake of propriety, or shall we be honest with ourselves and admit our marriage was a mistake?'

'A m-mistake? But I love you, Andrew. I've loved you

since I first took over the Infants all those years ago. It was not my fault that I had to marry Dick. He forced me to marry him because he was the father of my son. But you know all this. Have I ever made a secret of anything? Why do you say our marriage was a mistake? What have I done?' She was crying bitter tears. It was more than she could bear, after losing her son. It had been such a blow to her self-esteem. The young are so selfish, she had told Andrew. They think only of themselves. He had agreed that it was so, then reminded her of her own youth and the shame she had brought on her father's good name in the village, with a child born out of wedlock. They had argued and quarrelled over a number of issues since Philip went away, and it was not her nature to be so abusive. She was overwrought; her nerves were ragged with anxiety. Even her Infants were suffering from her sharp tongue.

'What have I *done*?' she wailed.

They were facing each other like strangers now – she with her bitter tears, and he with his frowning countenance and twitching eyebrows. This was no time to pick a quarrel, anyway, at 4 o'clock on a warm afternoon. Teachers and scholars had been hot and irritable all day.

'I am a jealous man, Martha, like that first husband of yours, and I have been patient for a very long time – too long. In every other aspect you are reasonable and sensible, but not where Philip is concerned. Even now you can't let go of him, can you, Martha? Well, the time has come for the truth to be told. I am sick to death of sharing you! I want all of you, Martha, not the crumbs you can spare from your precious son!'

She was appalled. Had she misjudged both her husband and her son? Had she seen them as two more children to be coaxed or scolded?

'I'm sorry! I'm sorry!' she sobbed, contritely. But he was still frowning. 'I love you, Andrew. You must believe me. A mother's love for her son is a different kind of love that only a mother can understand. I do love you. I truly do. How can I prove it?'

'By not taking me for granted any more. You didn't know I could be jealous, did you, Martha?' She shook her head. 'Still waters run deep, don't they, Martha?'

'Why have you waited so long to tell me?'

He hesitated, still frowning. 'I'll tell you why. Because I recognised myself in Philip. The umbilical cord was not severed during my mother's lifetime, and after she died, it was too late. Why do you think I waited so long to take a wife? The bond was so strong, her spirit still clung to me, even after death. It was the mother in you that first attracted me. I was a very lonely man after Mother died. I made no friends of my own sex, and the opposite sex were not attracted to me. Till I met Irene, Parson's delicate little daughter who gave me no peace till I took her. Believe me, Martha, I was no seducer. She seduced me. I never saw her again, for she died the next day. That was my initiation. My God!' He groaned, and his heavy body slumped in a chair.

She went over to him then, and knelt at his feet, still a disciple. They were no longer young, and she had never actually penetrated the depth of his reserve, or that secret place in the heart left empty by his mother's death. She had no weapon to fight the ghost of a woman long since dead, so she pleaded, humbly, 'It's not too late, Andrew, for a better understanding. We could try again, now that Philip has gone. Tell me what you would like me to do. You always say you can read me like a book, but that is not so with you, my dearest.'

'Your dearest? You mean it, Martha?'

She nodded tremulously, and pressed his grey head to her breast. Her woman's intuition was her only guide to the future, but there would be no more jealousy, no more of these distressing scenes. It was not her fault that her first husband had destroyed all her spontaneous sensuality, and the act of intercourse, even to this day, was an obligation, not a pleasure. Tonight, in the marriage bed, she would conquer her fear and reluctance. Dear Andrew!

Philip was lonely as never before in his young life, and he was desperately afraid. When Harriet boarded the bus for Marylebone Road and left him on the station forecourt, to make his way to Tottenham Court Road, he was sweating in a blind panic.

What was he doing here? He must have been more than a little mad yesterday. Being in love with Harriet, in the safe background of the School House, sheltered by the two devoted adults to whom he owed the security and comfort of a pleasant way of life, was a very different prospect to this bleak isolation. If only Harriet would be satisfied to serve her God in this country. Why go all the way to the Congo?

The more he considered it, the more outrageous it appeared. He stood there, long after her bus had disappeared. She had smiled and waved from the window, and he had returned the smile and the wave with forced bravado. She was so brave, so confident. He was shamed by his own inadequacy, and weak with uncertainty. To leave his mother had been a wrench, but not a calamity, because he had Harriet. But nothing had been arranged for their next meeting. It would depend on her off-duty at the hospital, and his own schedule of studies and obligations. The difference in their outlook and aspirations now seemed insurmountable, yet he had readily agreed to all Harriet's proposals as they travelled to London on the early train. Her enthusiasm and determination was so convincing. Now she was no longer there, he remembered she was no stranger to this Mission in the Congo, for she had spent all her early childhood there, under the strong influence of dedicated parents. Her father had left a deep and lasting impression on her young mind and heart. She had known she would return one day, and had never lost sight of her goal, all through the years of school and college. Her sister, Agnes, had almost forgotten those early years, and her mother had married again, but Harriet had remained faithful to her memories.

Philip's courage was slipping away as he was pushed and jostled by pedestrians who had no hesitation in boarding the buses to their particular destination. One bus had already left for Tottenham Court Road, but he let it go. There was no hurry. Harriet had telephoned to the Mission School and made an appointment with the Principal for 10 o'clock. She was familiar with the place, she had explained, because of her father's connections with this particular Missionary Society. She had kept in touch. He could understand that those early years would leave a lasting impression on a sensitive child, but his own youth had not inspired such dedication to duty and self-sacrifice. To emulate such an example was almost an impossibility at the outset of this strange and bewildering chapter. Tears flooded his eyes, and he blinked them away angrily. There was no escape. He was committed. The old way of life had already been abandoned, and he was not yet ready to adopt the new, or the Cause to which Harriet was so profoundly dedicated.

Was this love, this compelling urge to be united with Harriet for the rest of his days, coupled with the fear and hesitation? How could such conflicting emotions be reconciled? Of one thing he was certain. If he turned away and took the next train back to the village, he would lose

Harriet. She would never forgive him, or even attempt to understand the mentality of a grown man who relied on his mother's support and sympathy to make up his mind. No close bond existed between Harriet and her mother. She stood firmly and independently on her own two feet.

'I shall pray for you, darling.'

He was startled by the sudden reminder of her last words. The unfamiliar endearment was heart-warming. It had no place in his own environment. His working-class mother and intellectual step-father would be embarrassed by an endearment so essentially upper class. He had often wondered about this definition of class, and how it affected his own status when his mother married the village schoolmaster. Surely it must be a step up the ladder to be living in the School House? He had persuaded himself they were definitely middle class now, he and his mother, because of their relationship to Uncle Andrew. In a sense, it had isolated them from many of their former acquaintances in the village. Mother no longer visited the relatives of her first husband, still living in Richmond Row. Was he a snob to feel superior to the young men and women with whom he had shared a desk at the village school, and to avoid meeting them? His step-father held the sensible view that the War had broken down the barriers between the classes. He could be right. He was usually right.

When, at last, he boarded a bus, he found the passengers in holiday mood, and was reminded it was a Bank Holiday. Mother and Uncle Andrew would soon be enjoying their cycling holiday. Each day mother would pack a picnic lunch, and fill a flask with coffee. They would sit on a sunny bank, listening for the cuckoo. Mother would gather primroses. She loved to decorate the Infants' classroom with primroses and pussy willow. It all seemed so remote, so beautiful in retrospect, yet only a couple of days ago he had been impatient of the tedious business of gathering primroses to adorn the window sills in the church for Easter Sunday. They had spent all the morning gathering the flowers, and all the afternoon arranging them in the West aisle. Mrs Baker, the curate's wife, was responsible for the East aisle. Now he would give everything he possessed to be back in those quiet country lanes, and tea at Russets was always a treat, with Aunt Lucy's home-baked bread, farm butter, and his favourite blackcurrant jam. There would be a simnel cake for Easter, and all the time in the world to wander around with Carrie and young Julian. The Spring was a time of new birth on the farm – a new-born calf or a foal, tottering in the straw on its spindly legs; newly hatched chicks in the orchard, and lambs grown big enough to wander away from the ewes. He wondered if Julian had recovered from his frightening escapade of yesterday, and whether Sir Neville would manage to persuade Aunt Lucy the time had come for the boy to have his own pony. There often seemed to be some kind of undercurrent at Russets that disturbed the more usual atmosphere of quiet contentment. There was no answer to the problem of Tom and Carrie. For years they had tried to hide their attachment, but Philip knew about it. Even the child must soon recognise their feelings to be something more than cousinly affection. As for Aunt Lucy, she had seemed to be radiantly happy. Could this second youth be something to do with Sir Neville Franklin? Then there was the mystery of Charles. Why had he vanished again after spending only a few hours at Marston Park? Aunt Lucy was hiding something, and pretending an innocence of the whereabouts of her youngest son. Yet it was no secret that Charles had always been the favourite.

Such thoughts occupied Philip's mind on the bus journey to Tottenham Court Road. The holiday mood of the other passengers left him totally immune. In the nostalgic memories of the countryside and the farm he had known since early childhood, he was comforted, and he had found a small measure of courage by repeating, 'I shall pray for you, darling'.

Squaring his shoulders, he walked into the grim building that would provide a temporary refuge from the hazards of a noisy, unfamiliar world, and the disturbing doubts that only Harriet could banish. The elderly man who received him had a ready smile and a firm handshake for the nervous young man in the grey flannel suit. So this was Harriet's future husband. Whether or not he was missionary material would soon be proved. Candidates presented themselves from all walks of life and were normally recommended by a parson or minister of a church or chapel. There had been no time to contact the parson at Fairfields, but according to Harriet, Philip Martin had been a prominent member of the church choir since he was a lad. His home background and education could be called satisfactory. He trusted Harriet's judgement. She was her father's daughter, a dedicated Christian, and most unlikely to choose her life's partner carelessly. The fact remained, she could already speak the language, knew the customs of the people, had some experience in teaching, and was now on a course of study of tropical diseases. Her future husband would need to work hard on all these subjects if he was ready to accompany Harriet next year.

'Hang up your coat and hat, Philip, and draw up a chair. I expect you will be ready for a cup of coffee since you made such an early start?' Mr Bentley suggested, kindly.

'Thank you, Sir.' Philip was reminded of the headmaster of the Grammar School. Was he putting back the clock in this new venture? Harriet would say he was taking a step forward, a bold step, in a new direction, and all that was needed was courage and determination, but as he listened to the principal's quiet voice, expounding all the principles and objectives of the Society, and the compulsory subjects to be studied during the coming year, his heart sank.

A grey-haired woman brought in coffee and biscuits when summoned by the bell. He would not be alone, he was reminded as he sipped the coffee. Other candidates of both sexes would be boarded at the adjoining hostel, and receive their training accordingly. It was not the first time the principal had been confronted by a candidate as nervous as Philip Martin, and if he held doubts as to the young man's suitability, he gave no sign of it. Years of experience had taught him to be wary of passing a hasty judgement on a prospective student. It was not always the confident ones who made the best missionaries. Humility was also an asset.

When he had finished explaining the curriculum, Philip was invited to ask questions. He shook his head. 'No questions, thank you, Sir.'

Mr Bentley leaned on his desk and smiled at the grave young face. 'Cheer up, Philip! We won't work you too hard. Certain hours are set aside every day for recreation and social activities. Harriet tells me you have a good tenor voice. I can assure you that will be a great asset. Singing is a sure way of reaching the hearts of these people. Your voice could be a valuable asset in a community largely dependent on individual effort and enterprise. The gospel can be preached in a number of ways, Philip, as Our Lord demonstrated. There is a time to be serious, and a time to make merry. So make the most of your voice. It's a precious gift. Looking back over the years, I remember that Harriet's father had a good baritone. Has she told you much about her parents?'

'Only that it was love at first sight, and her mother

actually proposed marriage to her father!'

'That's true. A very determined young woman by all accounts. You've met Harriet's mother?'

'Yes, only briefly. She didn't strike me as being particularly interested in her daughter's intention to return to the Congo.'

'Perhaps she thinks it's a mistake. She has lost touch with us since she married again. I knew her in those early years of marriage, that is to say, by correspondence. Marion was a prolific letter writer. She had been greatly influenced by her father, as Harriet in turn was influenced by *her* father. Born and bred in an environment in which Christian values and service to the community takes priority over private aspirations is bound to make a lasting impression. They were well matched, Malcolm and Marion. Both had lively, intelligent minds, and a sense of dedication they have passed on to Harriet. Don't be afraid of her superior knowledge, Philip. She loves you, and love can smooth away all your doubts.'

Philip's shy smile lit his grave, boyish face. It was a charming smile, his companion was thinking, and much more likely to appeal to those black children of the Congo than a too serious approach to their hearts. The interview was over, and they shook hands cordially.

'I'll get Mrs Hawkins to show you to your room. You've brought your bag, I see, so you had already made up your mind?'

'To tell you the truth, Sir, it was Harriet who made it up for me!'

They both laughed. It was a relief to find a single room had been allocated at the hostel. To share a room with a stranger would have been the last straw on top of all the other strangeness. He had always enjoyed the privacy and privilege of his own room, as far back as he could remember, and had not been subjected to the crowded dormitories of boarding school.

It was a very small room, and sparsely furnished as a monk's cell. Was it intended to remind him that he too was a novice in a religious order?

When the housekeeper had left, after explaining it would be a cold lunch since it was a Bank Holiday, Philip threw open the window and leaned out. The heavy traffic on the Tottenham Court Road seemed unbearably loud to ears attuned to country sounds, and the happy shouts of the children in the playground adjoining the School House. His rare visits to London had been confined to Lincoln's Inn, and the Embankment Gardens, within easy walking distance of Charing Cross. He thought of Harriet with a wistful longing that they might have enjoyed this first day together, but she was back on duty at the hospital. She had renewed her acquaintance with Cynthia, but only superficially, since strict protocol provided little opportunity to speak freely with her superior.

A Bible had been provided on the bedside locker, and when he turned away from the window, he opened it at random, seeking comfort from its pages, but he was not yet familiar with the Bible, as Harriet would be familiar. It was all part of the strangeness. The lessons that were read in church by Sir Neville Franklin or another of the church wardens, had passed over his head unheeded in the choir stalls. Yet even without searching, the message was there, standing out boldly, in the *Book of Ruth* –

> WHITHER THOU GOEST I WILL GO, AND WHERE THOU LODGEST I WILL LODGE. THY PEOPLE SHALL BE MY PEOPLE, AND THY GOD, MY GOD.

'Harriet! Oh, Harriet!' He covered his face with his hands, and wept.

Letters were exchanged during that first interminable week, and a rendez-vous arranged for the following

Sunday evening, on a certain bench near the entrance to the park. Philip was there, waiting impatiently, a good half-hour before the time that Harriet had specified. He watched small children feeding the ducks, dogs of all shapes and sizes being exercised on leashes, elderly men and women walking slowly and sedately in the evening sunshine, and young couples, hand-in-hand, completely absorbed in each other. Flower beds were gay with tulips, the grass immaculate, the paths swept clean. Litter baskets had been filled with ice-cream wrappings, paper bags and cigarette cartons. Everything was neat and orderly. Even the small children, dressed in Sunday best, seemed to be observing the Lord's Day.

Philip's head was aching, and his throat was sore. He thought he was starting a cold, and had taken the precaution to dose himself with a Beecham's Powder, before leaving the hostel. Martha had profound faith in this particular antidote to the common cold, and she had slipped a packet into the rubber sponge bag in which he carried his razor, toothpaste and toothbrush. Martha had a remedy for all the common ailments, and some that were not so common, such as sprained ankles, bronchitis and migraine. She had two first-aid boxes, one in the Infants, and one in the house. Seldom a week passed without a minor accident in the playground. Bathing and binding up broken knees was a normal procedure for an Infants' teacher. Rolls of bandages were used and washed over and over again, and a tin of Zambuk could be replaced at the grocery, where a small stock of medicines and ointments was usually available. Martha had a soothing manner and a gentle touch for the injured child, and a boiled sweet helped to dry the tears. In a sense, Martha ministered to her husband and son in much the same way, whenever they showed signs of developing some ailment, but it had resulted in cossetting and fussing that was having repercussions on the son at this particular moment. He was feeling very sorry for himself, and missing his mother's ministrations quite dreadfully.

All the week he had known moments of such misery and loneliness he was near to tears. Even as he waited for Harriet he knew her manner would be brisk and cheerful, and she would boost his flagging morale with her own particular brand of humour. He had no sense of humour, unfortunately, and neither had Uncle Andrew. They were two of a kind, adopting a serious view of life in general, and sparing with their smiles.

A letter from Mother had arrived on the second day, but Harriet's brief note had not been received till the afternoon delivery on Friday. She may have been waiting to confirm the time of their Sunday rendez-vous, but even so, she could have written a decent letter. Mother wrote with sympathy and understanding, and concluded: 'We miss you very much, Philip, but I daresay we shall get used to it in time. We both sent our dearest love and best wishes for your happiness.' He had been waiting for exactly forty-six minutes when Harriet came in sight. He stood up and greeted her with a bleak smile as she hurried towards him.

'Sorry, darling. I was detained by Sister at the last moment, and one doesn't walk away from Sister!' she explained breathlessly.

'I was beginning to think you were not coming. I've been here ages.' He sounded peevish, and when she reached up to kiss his cheek, he turned his head away.

'Better not kiss me, dear. I think I am starting a cold.'

'Don't be silly, darling. Of course I am going to kiss you. If I was afraid of germs, I wouldn't be nursing!' And she planted a kiss on his cheek, took his limp hand and asked, 'Shall we walk?'

He shrugged indifferently, and muttered, 'I don't mind.'

'What's the matter – I mean, apart from the cold?'

'I'm sorry, Harriet. I can't go through with it.'

'Don't be an ass, darling. Of course you can. You haven't given it a fair trial. You *promised*, Philip. I won't let you give up. Let's sit down and discuss it sensibly. We can walk later.'

The bench was empty, and they sat down very close together, still holding hands. Harriet was bright-eyed and eager to do battle against his flagging resources. It was no too surprising, this temporary setback. Philip was no stranger, and he was a moody creature. They had been meeting at Russets for some years, and in his budding manhood the child was still in evidence. She blamed his mother. Changing circumstances had hastened her own maturity. There had been a time when she was completely dominated by her sister, Agnes. But not any more. They had gone their separate ways. She had discovered a new identity, and a kind of courage. Compelled to stand on her own two feet, it had been a rude awakening. She was sorry for Philip who had not yet explored the avenues of independence that she now enjoyed. Perhaps he never would? Perhaps he would always need a shoulder to lean on – a substitute for his mother? Perhaps she was a fool to be swayed by that one decisive action on Easter Sunday, when he had shown himself to be both brave and resourceful? It had taken courage to plunge into the river to rescue the child, and courage was a quality she most admired. For the rest of the day he had taken the initiative with a boldness that was totally out of character. But she had recognised her future husband when he handed her the living child on the river bank.

'What's troubling you, darling? Is it the language?'

'Yes.'

'But you have a whole year to master it.'

'I'm an absolute duffer at languages. My French is so

elementary it would sound more like Greek to the average Frenchman. Some people have a flair for languages, but I am not one of them.'

'It *is* difficult. I suppose I grew up bi-lingual. So did Agnes.' She wondered what his reaction would be when he discovered the natives spoke a mixture of tongues, according to their tribes. Poor Philip! She squeezed his hand reassuringly.

'It's like being back at school, only worse,' he grumbled. 'For one thing, I feel so inadequate. The majority of the students are so familiar with the Bible. A weekly Scripture lesson at school is no preparation for the mission field. I am not even sure that I am a Christian. Oh, Harriet, don't you see it's impossible?'

'Nothing is impossible with God, Philip. But you must have faith and courage.'

'I'm such a coward.'

'That's not true. Last Sunday you saved a child from drowning. That was courage.'

'It was instinctive. Not premeditated. Any man would have re-acted in the same way, given the same circumstances.'

'Then why didn't Tom? He was sitting there with the rest of us.'

'I don't know. I suppose he was too shocked to move.'

'Tom reacts slowly in an emergency. I have noticed it before. Darling, you must get your priorities right. How can you believe in God's purpose if you can't believe in yourself? There is a plan and a purpose for each one of us, though it's not always obvious. I was lucky. God's purpose was made plain to me as a child. I knew where I belonged. Father showed me the way. He lived what he preached. He really loved those black peoples. They were all God's children. That is what I was taught to believe. How can I convince you, Philip, that you *have* made the right decision?'

'You could marry me, Harriet.'

'*Marry you*? I thought we had decided to wait a year?'

'Had we? Why?'

'It just seemed sensible, under the circumstances.'

'I don't want to be sensible.'

She sighed. 'Now you are being difficult, darling.' It was not going according to plan. Her pattern for the future had seemed so neat and tidy. Now it was already frayed at the edges.

'Have you any money?' she asked, tentatively.

'More than enough. Mother has been saving in a post office account since I was born.'

'But wouldn't she be upset if you drew it out?'

'Why should she? It's my money.'

'Darling, are you quite sure you want to marry me, so soon after our engagement? We have only been engaged for a week.'

'My dear girl. I have been in love with you for years, but you hardly noticed me. I need to see you every day, Harriet, not once a week. If we were married, we could live in lodgings, not too far from our work.'

'Would it make it more agreeable? Would you feel happier?'

'Much happier.' He was smiling now. He had forgotten he was starting a cold. He kissed her tenderly.

'It takes three weeks to put up the banns,' she reminded him.

'We could get married by special licence without any fuss.'

'We could, but it wouldn't be fair to your mother, or to mine, and I would like a proper wedding at our own church in the village. The other way would seem rather secretive, as though we were ashamed, and had something to hide.'

'Would it? Well, you know best about such things, my dear. As for being ashamed, I shall be the proudest man on earth to be your husband.' His eyes were wet with tears. She had never seen him so emotional. He had always seemed so controlled. What did she really know of his inmost feelings, apart from the fact that he loved her, and was afraid to face the future without a shoulder to lean on? But wasn't that enough? Marriage was a lottery, Agnes declared. And if she couldn't have Charles, she would remain single!

'Shall I look for lodgings, or shall I leave it to you? It's going to be difficult to get time off together.'

He shook his head. 'I'll leave it to you. I wouldn't know what to look for. Whatever suits you, Harriet, will suit me.'

'I expect I shall be asked to pay a month's advance rent.'

'They wouldn't trust you?'

'This is London, darling, not Fairfields!' She was very conscious of being the practical partner, but it couldn't be otherwise. Somebody had to be practical. She still thought it was a mistake to get married until they had finished the year's course of study. All their concentration should be focussed on their public obligations, not divided by private indulgence. Besides, it was an additional expense. But Philip had taken out his wallet. He handed over five pounds.

'If you need any more, just let me know,' he told her, importantly.

'Thank you, darling.'

He patted her hand, sighing with satisfaction. He would have liked to put an arm about her waist, and have her head on his shoulder, but it seemed a little presumptuous on a bench in the park, and she might not approve. Decorum was expected of well-bred young ladies, and

Philip had been constantly reminded in the past by a snobbish Richard and Agnes, that they strongly disapproved of his association with their sister. They thought he was unworthy, and was taking a liberty. Grandmother Wellington had encouraged a sense of superiority in her grandchildren, as in her own children. If she had lived, she would strongly oppose the marriage. Doubts would inevitably arise from time to time regarding his birth. It was no secret that he was born out of wedlock. It had never been mentioned between them. Only Harriet could remove the chip on his shoulder. Bastard was an ugly word, and children were cruel. He shivered involuntarily.

'Are you cold, darling?' she asked anxiously.

'Somebody walking over my grave.'

'Don't!'

'I was only teasing. Shall we move? I seem to have been sitting around all the week.'

And she had been on her feet!

As they walked away from the bench, an elderly couple approached.

'Those two young people are in love, Dave. They didn't even notice us. Lost to the world. Bless their hearts,' she said, as he assisted her carefully on to the bench. She was crippled with rheumatism now, and their walks had become nothing more than a tedious shuffle with the aid of a stick and Dave's arm. But he was so kind and patient these days. Since his retirement, five years ago, they shared everything, even the washing-up. Yet Dave had never been a man to lift a finger with the chores. Not even when the children were small. It was a woman's work, he contended, rightly so. Two years ago they had been separated for the first time in their fifty years of marriage, and when she brought him home from the hospital after his operation, he noticed her own disability for the first time, and it was then that he paid her one of his rare compliments.

'I don't know what I should have done without you, Nell, all these years. You've been a wonderful wife to me, old girl.'

It was a lovely thing to say, and she choked with tears. 'Old girl' was the nearest Dave ever got to an endearment. In the early days of their marriage, she often wished he could be a bit more demonstrative, but when the children came along, she was too busy to worry about compliments.

'You warm enough, Nell?' he was asking.

'Yes, thank you, Dave.'

They exchanged a smile of complete understanding.

'Was you wishing you could put back the clock when you saw that young couple?'

Nell shook her head. 'We've had a good life, Dave, but I wouldn't want to live it all over again, especially the War years, when we lost our two boys.' She sighed wistfully, then reminded him how lucky they were to be blessed with four daughters, all married, and six lovely grandchildren.

'It's a nice feeling to know we can visit them without having to take any responsibility, and a week's long enough. I'm always glad to get back home.'

'Me, too,' Dave agreed.

'Just the two of us, jogging along quietly, pleasing ourselves. With your pension, Dave, and no rent to pay, we manage fine. We've got Frank to thank for buying us the house when it came on the market before the War.'

'That's right.'

They had been over it so many times, but the subject never paled. Frank had done well in his building and decorating business, but had not married, so he made certain his parents would always have a roof over their heads. Five hundred pounds was a lot of money, and they had never ceased to wonder at their son's generosity.

After a long pause, when both were remembering that precious document in the top drawer of the tallboy, Dave reflected quietly, 'I'm looking forward to a nice kipper for supper.'

Nell chuckled. Trust Dave to be thinking of the next meal!

'Why don't we look for lodgings now, instead of walking aimlessly in the park?' Philip suggested, anxious to get it settled in case Harriet changed her mind.

'All right.'

'Where shall we start?'

'We need to find a newsagents where they advertise vacancies. Let me think.' She was frowning with concentration, then her face brightened. 'Baker Street Station. Come on!' She tugged at his hand, and they hurried along.

They scanned the list, but found nothing suitable. A number of furnished flats were advertised, but the rents seemed quite exorbitant.

'We must make do with a bed-sitting-room, darling. All we need is a gas ring to boil a kettle for making tea and coffee. That is, if you can get your main meals at the hostel?'

'I don't see why not.'

'Neither do I. And I can eat in the canteen. Let's take a bus back to your area, in Tottenham Court Road. It's not so posh, so the rents should be more reasonable. Wait, I have a better idea. Buy a local paper, then we can pick out the suitable addresses and go straight there.'

Philip was full of admiration for such a practical suggestion. It would save a lot of time. The shop on the station forecourt was open for the convenience of travellers, and when he had paid for the paper, he insisted that Harriet selected a box of her favourite chocolates.

She was surprised to discover he carried his money in a purse, and hoped he was not mean. There is such a small margin between carefulness and meanness. It was not important. He wouldn't be carrying his money in a purse in the Congo!

They soon found several addresses, and boarded a bus with high hopes. Philip's spirits soon began to flag, however, when they were turned away from the first two addresses. The rooms advertised had already been booked earlier in the day.

'Cheer up, darling! Third time lucky.' Harriet was not so easily discouraged. Once again she realised how changing circumstances had made her so much more adaptable, while Philip's path had been smoothed by a devoted mother and kind stepfather. She could foresee a future when she would often be telling her reluctant spouse to 'Cheer up, darling!'

'Shall we ask Aunt Lucy if we can have our wedding reception at Russets?' she asked, irrelevantly.

Philip frowned. 'I thought we were looking for lodgings?'

'So we are. I just suddenly thought of it.'

He shook his head. 'Shall we concentrate on one thing at a time, dear?'

She giggled. 'I haven't got that sort of mind.'

A rather formidable landlady opened the door at Number 15. She was dressed in black alpaca, her hands folded over an ample bosom, her hair piled on top of her head with tortoise shell combs. Her smile was so forced, even Harriet was intimidated. It seemed almost a sacrilege to expect such an imposing figure to have a room to let. Nevertheless, she had advertised, and this was their first encounter with a London landlady, and they had not known what to expect.

'Good evening,' said she. 'You wish to see the room?'

'Yes, please,' Harriet murmured.
'Come this way.'
They followed her obediently, hand-in-hand. They came upon the stairs so suddenly, behind the front door, they stumbled on the bottom step. The top of the staircase was equally precarious, with a landing so narrow, one bedroom door seemed to open on to the top step. Harriet sighed with relief when it was by-passed, and they were led to the third door on the landing. With a sweeping gesture it was flung open, and they were ushered in importantly. The spartan bareness was so chilling, Harriet squeezed Philip's hand, and they stood there, listening to a catalogue of its amenities with sinking hearts. A tin kettle was provided on the gas-ring, and even a box of matches to light the gas. A tin tray, with an odd assortment of china, was balanced on the fender. Even soap was provided – a minute tablet that could have been lifted from the lady's room at Lyons! The brown linoleum shone with polish, and two small mats were placed strategically beside the bed and the marble-topped wash-stand. The bed was draped in a white quilt. A wardrobe, two wicker chairs, and a bamboo table completed the furnishing. A portrait of their Majesties held pride of place over the mantelpiece. A penny-in-the-slot gas meter was pointed out as the final amenity.
'Thank you. It's very nice,' said Harriet, politely.
'Ten shillings weekly. Four weeks in advance. When shall you be moving in?'
It was all being conducted with businesslike efficiency.
'Not till next month. We are not yet married.'
Their prospective landlady raised her eyebrows. 'Indeed, then this will be your first home.'
They exchanged names, Harriet handed over two pounds, they followed her downstairs, and they were shown out with the same formal politeness.

Philip had not opened his mouth, but when the door closed behind them, he muttered, miserably, 'What an awful woman'.

'Don't worry, darling. We are not going to live there.'

'But you paid the rent.'

'I know. It was worth losing two pounds to get away!'

He looked at her in amazement. Two pounds was a lot of money. She was giggling helplessly, and seemed to be enjoying a joke he could not share.

'Don't look so glum, darling. You have been saved from a fate worse than death!'

'But what do we do now?'

'Have another peep in the paper. There are dozens of addresses, and the night is young. Sorry about the two pounds. You shouldn't have bought the chocolates.'

He made no answer as they opened the paper on a convenient wall and pored over it. She was still feeling giggly, and he was puzzled and rather peeved by her lighthearted attitude.

'It's just a question of luck,' she was saying. 'I'll shut my eyes and jab. Number seven in this same road. That's our lucky number. Come on!'

He was not very convinced, but she smiled persuasively and they retraced their steps. This door was opened by a homely little woman wearing a coloured apron over what was obviously her Sunday-best dress. Her face shone from recent scrubbing with yellow soap, and her sparse grey hair was screwed into a bun.

'Good evening. 'ave you come about the room?' she asked.

'Yes, please,' said Harriet.

'I was beginning to wonder whether I was going to be lucky. There's so many widders what's letting rooms in the street since the War. I do 'ope you are going to like the room, Miss. It faces east, and it gets the morning sun, but then of course you'll be working in the morning and won't reap the benefit.'

They followed her into a small hall, almost completely occupied by an enormous aspidistra. A strong smell of onions floated up from the basement.

'My 'ubby likes 'is fried onions with 'is sausages and mash, but it do make a bit of a pong, don't it?' It was not an apology. She was just stating a fact, and both her prospective lodgers preferred it to the strong smell of polish. She was leading the way upstairs, and they stepped carefully over the worn carpet. She pushed open a door, smiling invitingly, and stood back. 'This was my lodger's room before the War. A lovely man. Never a grumble in all the seven years. Went 'orf to the War and got 'isself killed on the Western Front, like our own two lads. Not one of 'em came back.' Her eyes clouded for a moment. 'We all 'as our troubles, don't we Miss? Was it for yourself or your young man?'

'Both of us, as soon as we are married, Mrs . . .?'

'Smith. Easy to remember. Perhaps you would rather look around for something more suitable? I've only ever 'ad one lodger in this room, but the bed's big enough for two.' She paused. 'Sorry, Sir, 'ave I embarrassed you?'

'Not at all,' said Philip, who was blushing profusely.

'Things 'ave changed since the War for all of us. Lodgers nowadays come and go every so quick. Nobody don't stay for more than a few months,' Mrs Smith told them.

'I'm afraid we shouldn't be staying for more than a year. We shall be going abroad,' Harriet explained.

'That's all right, Miss. You must please yourselves. Will it suit you, then?'

Harriet had merely glanced about the room that was cluttered with heavy furniture, including two big armchairs and a sofa.

‘It will suit us very nicely, thank you, Mrs Smith. What do you charge?’

‘The rent’s ten shillings a week, Miss, but it don’t include the gas, I’m afraid.’

‘Will you keep it for us if we pay you a month’s advance rent?’

‘I’ll keep it, don’t you worry, only I can’t charge you ten shillings when you’re not living ’ere. That wouldn’t be fair. Shall we say five shillings a week till you move in?’

‘That’s very generous, isn’t it, darling?’

They both were smiling now, and when Harriet handed over the pound, Philip was thinking they still had enough left to pay for a good meal at Lyons and their train fare home as soon as possible to see their respective parents and explain about the early wedding.

They shook hands with the kindly little woman on the doorstep.

‘I think your onions are burning, Mrs Smith?’ said Harriet, tentatively, for she was still talking.

‘Now isn’t that just like a man? And ’im sitting there! Goodbye, and the best of luck!’

The door closed. The kiss was spontaneous and very loving.

‘You were right about number seven being our lucky number,’ said Philip, gratefully.

It was not the first time Marion had to explain that her husband was away on business, and that he had not left an address, but when her daughter Harriet arrived to arrange about the wedding, she was so distraught, she burst into tears.

‘I’m sorry, Mother. I thought you would be pleased.’

‘I am – I mean, I’m glad for your sake, but I haven’t any money, and it’s a mother’s duty to pay for her daughter’s wedding!'

'What do you mean, you haven't any money? You seem to be living in the lap of luxury these days?'

'We are, but the bills haven't been paid, and now Stephen has disappeared, and I'm pestered by all manner of people to whom we owe money.'

'Gosh!' Harriet exclaimed, snatching off her hat and gloves. This was a situation so unexpected, she felt completely at a loss. Stephen Grant's profession had always been a bit of a mystery, but it didn't concern his three grown-up step-children, who naturally assumed their mother had been fortunate in her second marriage. The house was situated in the most expensive area. The garden was maintained by a professional gardener, and the house lavishly provided with all the modern amenities.

Looking about the spacious drawing-room, with its elegant furniture, velvet curtains, and white carpet, Harriet was remembering the simplicity of their Mission home in the Congo, with a father who gave no thought to material possessions. Here, in this luxurious home, with a daily woman to do the chores, and no children or pets to spoil its perfection, her mother had the bored look of a woman who has too much time on her hands. She was not the same woman who had shared all the hardships and dangers with her first husband. But then, she had never really recovered from the shock of losing him, and to marry her boss was nothing more than a convenient peg on which to hang her uncertain future. It seemed to Harriet that at the moment she herself had to be a prop for all those people who tended to lean on someone. Having left Philip in a more optimistic frame of mind, she was now faced with a new problem.

A cup of coffee might help them both to get started on sorting things out. It was hours since her frugal breakfast at the hospital, and she had been anticipating a good lunch. There was no sign of any preparation for a meal, however; the daily woman had left the kitchen scrupulously clean and tidy – too clean. A kitchen should be lived in, like the one at Russets, Harriet was thinking, as she brewed the coffee. How did one cope with creditors and a husband who vanished when he was most needed? she wondered. A wry smile twisted her mouth, as she remembered she had been expecting a nice wedding cheque from Uncle Stephen. He had always been generous, but then it was easy when you had no scruples. Cheques were bouncing, Mother explained, tearfully, as she sipped the hot coffee. She had opened a curt letter from the bank manager addressed to Stephen, as well as other correspondence, all containing long overdue accounts.

The secretary had forwarded the post from the office after her telephone call. Perhaps the poor girl too had been paid by a cheque that bounced? Marion suggested, wearily. It was all too much in her present state of mind. Once she had been alert and intelligently occupied, but not any more. Gradually, with so much time on her hands, and her husband so seldom at home, she had succumbed to the apathy she had known in the early days of her widowhood, when her mother's cottage had been more of a prison than a refuge. Now there was no mother to bark – 'Pull yourself together, Marion!' – only a daughter who had overcome shyness with confidence, and weakness with courage. They had never been close. Now she looked at her daughter with new respect, and confided all the doubts and suspicions she had been harbouring for some time.

'It was foolish of me not to enquire more fully into these business deals that took him away from home so often, but he had a way of changing the subject, and he could be so charming and persuasive. "Why should you worry your pretty head, my darling?" he would say. "Put on your prettiest frock. I am taking you out to dinner." Or we would go to see a film. He knew my weakness for the pictures. Indeed, he knew all my weaknesses, Harriet. Look at my figure. Too many chocolates. It seemed so wonderful to be spoilt, but now I realise it was just a cover up for all his shady activities. When I was his secretary, before our marriage, he didn't confide in me, although I sometimes wondered where the money came from. I was there to type letters and take telephone messages. Nothing more. How could I have been so deceived?' she asked, plaintively. Then she broke off suddenly to complain, 'You are not listening!'

Harriet blushed guiltily. 'I'm sorry, Mother, my thoughts had wandered – I was wondering whether you had kept your wedding gown?'

'Of course I have kept it! Every bride keeps her wedding gown, and every mother keeps the gown in which her firstborn is christened for her other children, and her grandchildren. Cecily, Irene and myself were all christened in the same gown, and when I was married, Mother gave it to me so you three children wore it in turn. I shall give it to *you*, Harriet, for *your* children.'

'Thank you, Mother – but about the wedding gown. May I borrow it, *please*? I will take the greatest care of it.'

'You may, since I can't afford to buy new,' she sighed, impatiently, her mind still busy with her own urgent problems.

'What shall I do, Harriet? To whom can I turn for legal advice?'

'To Freddie, of course. We will go together, after lunch. I should like to see Wendy and Ruby. It's quite some time since I have seen their little girl. Cynthia is on duty at the hospital today. I caught sight of her on my way out.'

'I seem to have lost touch with them lately. I always feel so tired these days, and everything is an effort.'

Harriet made no comment. It was usually the women with idle hands who complained of tiredness, she noticed.

'What are we doing about lunch, Mother?' she prompted.

'I wasn't going to bother. I often have a boiled egg when I am on my own.'

'Why not an omelette?'

'I have never made an omelette, dear.'

'I'll make it. Have we any cheese?'

'Cheese? Yes, I think so.'

Harriet went back to the kitchen to investigate, found a near-empty larder, apart from a dozen eggs, a small portion of hard cheese, several tins of soup, and half a loaf in the bread bin. She wondered what would happen if the man of the house suddenly arrived home. She supposed they went out for their main meals, but had not enquired. On one of her rare visits to her mother they had lunched at an expensive restaurant, but that was out of the question today. She felt irritated by such poor housekeeping, and went back to the drawing-room to ask,' Mother, will you take soup as well as the omelette?'

'I don't mind, dear.'

'It will be ready in ten minutes if you will set the table in the dining-room.'

'Couldn't we have it in he kitchen? It would be less trouble.'

'All right.'

To eat in the kitchen in Grandmother's day would have been as unlikely as eating in the stable, Harriet was thinking as she opened a tin of soup. With two thick slices of bread, it would help to fill that void in her stomach. She really was famished.

The tidy kitchen was soon cluttered, for Harriet had

had little practice in culinary arts. The atmosphere was strained between them as they ate the simple meal, for their thoughts were so wide apart – the mother concerned with her husband's disappearance, the daughter with wedding plans.

When they had finished and Harriet had washed the dishes, they caught a bus going in the direction of the Common.

'I have never taken a bus since we came to live here. I always take a taxi,' Marion explained, as they waited at the bus stop for twenty minutes or so.

They found Ruby and Wendy just starting out on their afternoon walk with the dog, so Harriet joined them, while Marion consulted Freddie in his office.

'I wish I had known you would be in Tunbridge Wells today, love, and you could have joined us for a meal. We always have our main meal at midday, because it's better for Wendy. It was steak and kidney pie today, followed by chocolate blancmange,' Ruby was saying, as they followed the child and the dog up the steep path to the Common.

'You are making my mouth water, Ruby. We had an omelette.'

'An omelette? But that's a supper dish. Wasn't your mother expecting you?'

'No, it was not her fault. I came to tell her we are getting married as soon as the banns are called.'

'You and Philip?'

'Yes.'

'Well, what a nice surprise! I'm ever so pleased for you, love, and I hope you'll be very happy.'

'Thank you, Ruby.'

'You've changed your plans then? I understood from Lucy that you were going back to that foreign Mission.'

'We both are going, but not for a year or so. Philip has to

work hard on his studies at the Mission School in London, and I have to finish my nursing course at the hospital. We are both living in hostels at the moment, but we have found lodgings and we shall move in as soon as we are married.'

'Let's sit down on that bench over there, shall we, and you can tell me all about it. I don't often get farther than that bench these days, what with my poor legs and being so breathless. Must be old age!' she laughed.

It was good to talk to someone who had the time to listen.

They could see the small girl romping on the grass with the dog. 'I remember that wedding dress,' Ruby mused, thoughtfully. 'Your mother looked so pretty. Who would have thought you would be wearing it and going off to foreign parts just like your parents. Life is strange. I sometimes wonder if its planned up above, or if it just happens. What do you think, love?'

'I think there's a pattern, Ruby. A couple of weeks ago I hadn't thought of marriage. I was planning to go back alone to the Mission. It all happened so suddenly at Russets, on Easter Sunday. It's strange, but things *do* happen at Russets, have you noticed?'

Ruby nodded.

'I suppose you could say my eyes were opened and I saw Philip in a new guise – a person who actually acted promptly in an emergency and risked his own life to save young Julian. I always thought he was rather a weak character, but I was mistaken.'

'He takes a bit of knowing, does Philip. He's what you would call reserved, but I know all about that accident, and Lucy was full of praise for Philip. They all were. Carrie declared she wasn't surprised, but then she had known him since he was a little boy. Does his mother know he is getting married so soon?'

'Not yet.'

'She will miss him.'

'Yes.'

'It has to happen, love, in each new generation. That's life.'

The small girl had tired of her romping and ran towards them. She was scooped up on to the comfortable lap and smiled at Harriet without shyness, for she was a friendly child. Here was the perfect little bridesmaid, Harriet was thinking. She would mention it to Freddie later. It wouldn't cost very much and Ruby could probably manage to make a pretty little frock that would do for a party frock for her next birthday. Ruby was one of those useful women who could turn her hand to anything and make a success of it. There was a time when she dropped her 'aitches', but not any more! There was a time when she scolded her son Freddie for taking liberties with the upper class – but not any more!

'My Daddy gives me three pennies on Saturday. When I am four, I shall have four pennies. Does your Daddy give you pennies on Saturday?' asked the child.

'I haven't got a Daddy.'

'Why?'

'My Daddy went to heaven.'

'Why?'

'To live with Jesus.'

'I don't want my Daddy to live in Heaven. I want my Daddy to live in Tunbridge Wells.'

'I shouldn't worry about it, darling. Jesus understands.'

'My Mummy plays the piano. Does your Mummy play the piano?'

'Yes.'

'Does your Mummy play "Jesus wants me for a sunbeam"?'

'No.'
'I can sing it all by my own self. Shall I sing it for you?'
'Yes, please.'
Her voice was surprisingly pure and tuneful for such a young child.

Jesus wants me for a sunbeam,
To shine for Him each day,
In every way to try to please Him,
At home, at school, at play.

'Thank you, darling. That was lovely.'
'I know some more.'

Away in a manger, no crib for a bed,
The little Lord Jesus lay down his sweet head,
The stars in the bright sky looked down where He lay,
The little Lord Jesus asleep in the hay.

'Clever girl.'
'I know some more.'

All things bright and beautiful,
All creatures great and small . . .

She shook her head. 'I can't a'member'.
Harriet went on:

All things wise and wonderful,
The Lord God made them all.

'Sing some more. Go on, sing some more!'
'*Please*, Aunt Harriet,' Ruby prompted.
'Please, Aunt Harriet.'

Jesus bids me shine with a clear pure light,
Like a little candle burning in the night,
In this world of darkness, so we must shine . . .

'You in your small CORNER – and I in mine!' Wendy shouted gleefully.

When the dog howled, they all laughed.

'My Daddy plays the gramophone. I like it best. I sit quiet as a mouse and listen,' said the child.

'Yes, she does,' Ruby agreed. 'She loves all that highbrow music.'

'When my Grannie puts me to bed, I say "Gentle Jesus, meek-a-mild". When you was a little girl, did you say "Gentle Jesus, meek-a-mild"?' Wendy wanted to know.

'Yes, darling.'

'My Grannie lets me make a little pastry man.'

'That's kind of Grannie.'

'My little pastry man has currant buttons on his jacket.'

'What fun.'

'And jew know what?'

'What?'

'When he comes out of the oven, my Grannie says I can eat him.' She sighed ecstatically at the memory, and stroked Ruby's face.

This was Wendy's small world, Harriet was thinking – Daddy, Mummy and Grannie. Surrounded by love, she was loving. Her bright intelligence was encouraged, but she was not precocious.

'You will stay to tea, won't you Harriet?' Ruby invited, as they walked back with the child skipping along between them.

'Thank you, Ruby. That would be nice.' Ruby's teas were as satisfying and substantial as her sister's teas at Russets, and would compensate for the poor lunch.

They found Freddie escorting Marion round the garden. She was looking more cheerful.

'Freddie will get in touch with the bank manager tomorrow, and try to sort things out. Now I can stop worrying,' she told her daughter.

'Thank God for Freddie!' Harriet retorted. Now perhaps they could talk about the wedding.

'May I use your telephone, Freddie? I should like to speak to Aunt Lucy,' she asked, when she had explained about the arrangements.

'You may.' He was fond of Harriet. He remembered the plain, tearful child and her bossy sister, with the indomitable grandmother, when he was a patient at Marston Park. Who would have thought she would grow into the attractive, self-confident young woman? And who would have thought young Philip had the qualities of a missionary? It just goes to prove what love can do, he was thinking as he watched Ruby and Wendy busy with tea cups. They were having tea in the garden. Cynthia had painted the table and chairs a gleaming white in readiness for another Summer. She was the handyman about the place, not Freddie. It was Cynthia who mended a fuse, fixed a washer on a dripping tap, colour-washed the kitchen, trimmed the hedges, and pruned the roses. Nobody knew when and where she had acquired all these useful talents.

'Somebody has to do it. We can't afford to pay for such service,' she would say.

It was true. They would never be prosperous, and she would never again know the luxury she had taken for granted at Marston Park, but she had chosen her way of life with Freddie, and had found it satisfied all her senses. Being a wife and a mother had not been sufficient, however. She had to combine both the home and the hospital to feel completely satisfied. Without Ruby this would not have been possible. Ruby was the go-between, the steadying influence when tempers were frayed, and temperaments clashed, for no human relationship was perfect.

When Cynthia came home, tired and irritable after an

exhausting day at the hospital, or Freddie was moody, or the child naughty, it was Ruby who restored peace. She loved them all, and life was too short for quarrels, she contended. Even in the old days in Richmond Row, she had never crossed swords with her quarrelsome neighbours. Quite often now it was the child who caused the disruption, for she no longer obeyed automatically. She was growing into a child who questioned everything, and it was not always convenient. Cynthia's patience was limited, and Freddie was inclined to take Wendy's part, which made matters worse. There was a close affinity between father and daughter that was not uncommon. Had there been a son, this affinity would not have been so noticeable, since a mother invariably feels closer to a son than a daughter, so one would have balanced the other. The hospital discipline was strict, and Cynthia could see no reason why it should be relaxed at home. If Wendy was naughty, she must be punished, not excuses made for her naughtiness.

'She has a mind of her own, dear. She is nearly four,' Freddie reminded Cynthia, with quiet reasoning.

'And what do you suppose she will be like at fourteen if she is not corrected now?' she retorted. But Cynthia's hand was hard, and the small buttocks soft and sensitive. Freddie and Ruby could not bear to listen to the child's screams of pain and outrage. They both could think of a better way to punish a small girl, but they were not consulted. It was a mother's prerogative.

While Harriet had a long chat with Lucy on the telephone, Wendy was happily occupied carrying out a varied assortment of cakes, dainty bread and butter, jam, cheese, potted meat, salad, jelly and blancmange. She carried everything with careful concentration, her pink tongue licking her lips, and paid no attention to Marion's praise. She didn't like Auntie Marion, though she couldn't have explained why she didn't like her. It was different with Auntie Harriet. She was nice.

Lucy was surprised to hear about the early date for the wedding, but had no hesitation in agreeing to Harriet's request.

'It's some time since we had a party at Russets, and we shall all enjoy it. Just let me know how many to expect. If it's a fine day, we will have the wedding breakfast in the orchard, as we did for Carrie's wedding.'

'Thank you, Aunt Lucy. By the way, Aunt Ruby said to tell you she would come over and help with the baking, and bring Wendy if you could put them up overnight?'

'Of course.'

'I'm afraid Mother is not in a position to help financially. My step-father seems to have disappeared, and left her stranded, with very little money and a lot of creditors demanding payment. She has been talking to Freddie, and he has promised to try to sort things out.'

'I'm sorry to hear that, dear, but don't you worry, we shall manage. Will it mean the house will have to be sold?'

'I expect so. It's heavily mortgaged, apparently.'

'That's bad, and you all thought your mother was so comfortably provided for with her second husband.'

'Yes, we did.'

'Well, give her my regards, and tell her there is always room for one more at Russets.'

'Thank you, Aunt Lucy. What should we do without you?'

Lucy chuckled. 'That's what Sir Neville said only yesterday.'

'Sir Neville? He is not living at Russets, is he?'

'Almost. He's a lonely man now, Harriet.'

'Is Charles still in America?'

'Yes, and likely to remain there, according to the last letter I received.'

'What happened between father and son? It must have been something serious?'

'I have no idea,' Lucy lied.

'Will Sir Neville mind if Russets is invaded on the day of the wedding?'

'Why should he? I shall give him good warning, and he can please himself. Don't be surprised to receive quite a generous cheque, Harriet. Christenings, weddings and funerals, he remembers them all. Sir Neville is still very much the squire of his estate. The War did not change his attitude towards his tenants, though it changed his way of life quite drastically. Fancy, out of all those servants, only Hetty remains. She's lonely, too, but she knows she's always welcome here, providing she doesn't clash with Sir Neville, of course.' Her chuckling laugh was so infectious. Lucy was a happy soul, and like her twin sister, Ruby, a peace-maker in her own little world, so troubled by conflicting loyalties and frustration.

When Harriet had hung up the receiver she sighed with relief. Russets was a second home, and Aunt Lucy more of a mother than her own mother. When she told her, 'God bless you, Aunt Lucy,' she really meant it.

When Harriet had taken her mother home and tried on the wedding gown, she left her with a promise to keep in touch by telephone, and hurried to the station to catch a London train.

It had been a day of mixed emotions, but on the whole a successful day. She had settled the arrangements for the wedding breakfast with Aunt Lucy, and paid Ruby for the material and trimmings she would purchase to dress the little bridesmaid. Blue was the obvious choice for such a fair child, and Ruby was delighted to be entrusted with the task. A simple Grecian style had been suggested, on the lines of the child's nightgowns that Ruby had made. Freddie had already agreed, and Cynthia would have to be consulted, but Harriet was not expecting any opposition.

Marion had taken no part in the excited chatter between Ruby, Harriet and Wendy. She was wondering whether to offer to pay for Freddie's services, or whether he would be offended. It was all so difficult and distressing. How could she be expected to take an interest in her daughter's plans for the wedding when her own future was in jeopardy? In providing the wedding gown, she felt she had done her duty, and could do no more. It was a perfect fit. The veil, the orange blossom and the white gloves, all were there, as good as new, in layers of tissue paper, packed so carefully in the box that had travelled to the Congo and back to England. To see it spread on the bed after so may years, brought another flood of tears.

'Your father was my true love. I should never have married again,' Marion sobbed.

It was a pleasant surprise to find Philip waiting at the barrier at Victoria Station, and when his grave young face lit with the rare smile that was so disarming, Harriet felt a fresh surge of hope and happiness. She would love him as her mother had loved her father. It was a different kind of love, with a slow awakening, not the sudden flame of love at a first meeting. As for Philip, he might never have proposed, but for that accident at Russets on Easter Sunday. She would probably have gone off to the Congo Mission on her own, and eventually married another man. His shyness and reticence could be a hindrance in their work, but surely his voice would be an asset?

She hugged him as a mother hugs a child who has to be persuaded or bullied into shape. He kissed her tenderly, without passion.

'What have you been doing all day, my darling?' she asked, as they walked away together.

'Nothing much. Tell me about your day.

She told him everything that had happened, and he

listened attentively. To be a good listener was a quality too often neglected. They were compatible now, since she had acquired an outgoing exuberance of recent years. Providing his mother would let him go, all would be well. At the back of her mind, however, there lurked a suspicion that the umbilical cord could be a permanent bond between mother and son. She was not afraid, she had her own individual defence against such a possibility. They would have a child, quite soon, within a year if God willed. She smiled secretly and swung his hand.

On the crowded forecourt they waited for a bus, completely oblivious to the jostling throng. All the doubts that had troubled them since they last met melted away in the certain conviction that their love was unique, and the path they had chosen was ordained. If they regarded themselves with smug satisfaction, and not the humility such a calling demanded, they should be forgiven. Life has a way of correcting such youthful assumptions.

When Harriet slipped quietly into the nurses' hostel and Philip went on his way to the Mission hostel, they both reminded themselves of the homely lodgings that awaited them after their marriage. The following Sunday they had promised to visit Martha at the School House, and from henceforth till they sailed for the Congo, she would see her son only in the company of Harriet. Few mothers can accept a daughter-in-law with complete confidence, and Martha was no exception. She would see faults that should have been overlooked, and there was no sympathy between them. It was Lucy, with her warm heart, who would continue to welcome the young couple after their marriage, and their Sunday afternoon walk would invariably lead in the direction of Russets, while Martha begrudged every minute that Philip would spend away from the School House.

'Will you be back to tea?' she would ask, looking directly at her son.

'I expect so, Mother,' would leave her fretting in uncertainty, and Andrew reminding her to be reasonable. Their monthly visit would be spoilt and disappointing, and she could foresee the trend of events even before their marriage. Poor Martha! Her small world had already collapsed on Easter Sunday.

The day before the wedding, Martha purchased roses and carnations from the local nursery, and with Carrie's assistance, decorated the altar and the choir stalls and the chancel. They worked in silence, so emotionally disturbed they were choked with tears. For Carrie, it was a reminder of her own wedding – the wedding that should never have happened. It was cruel to keep her bound by her marriage vows for the rest of her days. Her youth had slipped away, and her natural gaiety had been lost in the demands of a marriage so lacking in the normal relationships of a husband and wife. Without children Carrie was sadly deprived, for she had inherited the maternal nature of the twin sisters, Lucy and Ruby. All her love had been lavished on Julian, but now he was a manly little boy, who preferred the company of men.

The scent of the flowers had an intoxicating effect on her strangled emotions, and she was torn with envy of Harriet, for there was nothing abnormal about Philip. As for Philip's mother, she was reminded that all the years of devotion, and her wretched marriage to Dick Martin, had still not eradicated the stain on her character, and her son still wore a chip on his shoulder. Away from the village, he could start a new life. This was the penalty she must pay – the second time such a high penalty had been demanded of her. She wondered if Philip had considered their parting a blessing in disguise. That hateful word 'bastard' had not been mentioned between them for many years, but it was still there, like a festering sore, that would not heal. Had Philip reminded his future wife that he was born out of wedlock? It was no secret, and country people have long memories. For some, like Charles Franklin, it was a joke, but not for her sensitive son.

The scent of flowers had made her head ache, and she urged Carrie not to linger over the final arrangement of white carnations and maidenhair fern in a handsome Grecian vase on the chancel steps.

'Come back to the School House, dear, and I will make a pot of tea,' she invited. So they carried away all the unwanted greenery in the basket, and took a last look from the porch as they went out. With their arms linked, their close companionship was very comforting.

For the last time, Philip would sleep alone in his boyhood room. For the last time, Martha would fold his pyjamas under the pillow, and lay out a clean shirt for the morrow. For the last time, she would kiss her son good-night, and leave him with a book. He had been taking a book to bed since he first started to read at the age of five.

On their monthly visits to the School House during the next twelve months, her new daughter-in-law would be sharing Philip's room. It was not a very big bed, but they would have to manage, for it would only be for one night, she assumed. It still seemed inconceivable to Martha that this was the last evening – she was expecting Philip in time for a late supper – and that her son was actually to be married on the morrow. He had all the fastidious habits of a confirmed bachelor. But then so had Andrew, and to this day he spent as much time in the bathroom over his toilet twice a day, as some men would spend in a whole week. He still glanced through the newspaper at the breakfast table, and was moody in the early morning.

They were much alike, her husband and her son, and she could foresee Harriet losing her patience. She wondered about their marital relationship, and whether her son was prepared to play the dominant role in the marriage bed? Supposing, in an acute state of nervousness, he should be impotent? She shivered at the possibility. For Harriet she had no fears, only for her son. She would never know whether he suffered or enjoyed such intimacy. After today, his mother would be of little consequence. It was a solemn thought, till she reminded herself she would still have Andrew.

Russets was bursting at the seams, but the old farmhouse loved its mellowed walls to echo to the voices and footsteps of men, women and children. It was built and intended for a large family, and when that family was depleted, the ghosts of Bert Blunt's forebears seemed to sigh on the creaking stairs and passages.

The warm smell of baking still lingered in the kitchen at day-break on the wedding morning, when Tom and Carrie drank their mugs of tea before milking, in a silence that was broken only by cock-crow. With their elbows propped on the table, they held their mugs in both hands, and fastened their gaze on the familiar features that had grown more dear with the passing years. Carrie's bright curly head had not lost its golden sheen, and her cheeks were glowing with health, but the sadness in the depths of the blue eyes had darkened the pupils. Tom had changed very little with the passing years, and his lean, tanned face and kindly eyes held, for Carrie, the very essence of love. All her senses were aware of him, and her sturdy body, still warm from sleep, yearned for fulfilment of the troubled dreams that so often disturbed her nights. The passion that had exploded on that Michaelmas Day so long ago had not been repeated, and although Tom's loins would occasionally hunger with desire, he did not seek out another woman, since only one woman could satisfy that hunger. Hard manual labour was the antidote at such times; then he would sleep, exhausted. Tom's sexuality had none of the perverted demands of his brother Albert's, but he was a normal, healthy man in the prime of life, in love with his brother's wife. Patient and gentle by nature, that one brief interlude of physical satisfaction had so filled him with loathing and disgust, it had not been repeated. For most of the time, his senses were lulled into acceptance of a situation that could not be altered. The only alternative was to go away, and he had faced that choice years ago, and lacked the courage to make a fresh life for himself without Carrie – and Carrie would not leave Albert. So they endured. He knew when her night had been disturbed by Albert's demands, and troubled dreams, for the early morning revealed the dark shadows beneath her eyes, and a soft mouth that trembled on the verge of tears. She could not hide her feelings, not from Tom. He knew every inflexion in her voice, every mood, every expression of that mobile face.

Carrie often found tears a relief from the burden she carried, and yesterday's preparations for Harriet's wedding were only the prelude to a day of emotional stress. All her determination would be needed to control this strong desire to weep. She must wear a false smile all the long day, but not yet, not for Tom. She hadn't to pretend with Tom.

When he laid his hand on hers, she could feel the tingling sensation like an electric current passing through every nerve in her body. It was a gesture of self-indulgence they seldom practised, and it spoke louder than words. But it was dangerous. Albert's movements were sly and unpredictable. He could walk in at any moment. They had no defence against such a threat, that had lessened only while Julian was small, and devoted to his Uncle Bertie.

Tom's lips formed the words 'Don't cry'. In the cowshed he would take her in his arms and comfort her, but not here. The house still slept, but soon the two children would be awake, ready for a new, exciting day. Little Wendy had taken a great fancy to her young cousin, and followed him everywhere. And Harriet was already awake on her wedding day, standing at the open window. She had shared a bed with her mother last night. Tonight she would share a bed with Philip, her husband, in their new lodgings. The start of a new chapter. Everything was new and very beautiful. She was not afraid. It was God's will, and His purpose made absolutely plain.

The scent of roses mingled with the farmyard smells. The roses trailed over the mellowed walls in rich profusion. She loved this old house, and all who slept under its roof. Freddie was here with Cynthia and Wendy, her little bridesmaid. Freddie would lead her to the altar, and Tom would be best man. Her own brother, Richard, could not attend, but her sister, Agnes, would be there at the church. She was staying overnight at 'The Three Nuns', and would spend a few days with her mother in Tunbridge Wells.

The village loved a wedding – especially a May Day wedding – when the children would collect on the churchyard wall, like swallows on the telegraph wires, to cheer the arrival of the guests, the bridegroom and bridesmaids, and finally the bride. They would be clutching paper bags of confetti, itching with impatience for the ceremony to be over. At the first glimpse of the newly-wedded couple, they would swoop down and pelt them unmercifully till they reached the shelter of the hired car with its fluttering white ribbons. All the children would be dressed in their Sunday best for the traditional crowning of the May Queen, and the Maypole Dance, still practised at Fairfields.

This was a very special wedding, however, and many of the women grouped about the ancient tombstones would remember the wedding of Old Parson's youngest daughter to that missionary fellow, who had taken his bride to some God-forsaken place in Darkest Africa. Now it was his grand-daughter repeating the saga of service and devotion to duty. The village applauded such worthy self-sacrifice, and turned out in force to wish them well.

When the bridegroom arrived, with his mother and step-father, the choir-boys shouted a greeting. This was the voice that led their shrill trebles every Sunday, and played the major role in all the religious festivals.

'Good old Martin! Give us a solo!' yelled the youngest recruit from Richmond Row. His irate mum, balanced precariously on a tombstone with her hair in curlers, shouted angrily – 'Give over, Nigel! You'll cop it from yer dad. I'm warning you now!'

Philip hurried down the path, his blushing face twitching with embarrassment. He was no match for these youngsters because he had never mixed freely with their older brothers and sisters during the five years he had attended the village school. The middle-aged women were remembering the scandal when the Infants' teacher was carrying a child – 'and 'er not wed!' The controversy in the ranks of the school governors when the schoolmaster actually allowed the baby in the classroom, set the gossiping tongues wagging for weeks. They remembered the wrath of Teacher's father, that much respected wheelwright, who gave up going to Chapel when his only daughter slipped from grace.

'The poor old bugger never went back, only in his

coffin,' they said.

But it was the Russets wagonette that everybody was waiting for, and the children climbed on the churchyard wall to get a better view as it came in sight. The two magnificent Shire horses stole the show, as they did on the occasion of Bert Blunt's funeral, when the wagonette was draped in black crêpe. Today it was draped in white ribbons, and the pretty little bridesmaid was smiling and waving, like a princess in a royal coach. It was Wendy's first big occasion, and she was making the most of it.

Tom was leading Duke, and young Julian, solemn with pride, was leading Prince. The twin sisters, Ruby and Lucy, sitting side by side in their Sunday best, with their straw hats freshly trimmed with new ribbons, caught the glad eyes of two old cronies standing on the forecourt of 'The Three Nuns'.

'They be a couple of bonny wenches, them two sisters and no mistake. I could fancy a bit of a tumble in the 'ay with either one of 'em!' chortled Henry, in his 82nd year.

'Aye? What's that you say?' Samuel was as deaf as a post, so Henry pointed his stick at the bonny pair.

'Oh, aye!' Samuel raised his cap in salute – a rare gesture that delighted the sisters, who waved their gloved hands. Katie was resplendent in flowered muslin with a borrowed hat. She was so excited, she would have to be reminded a dozen times of her duties by her long-suffering mistress. Katie was inclined to forget she was still a servant on these big family occasions.

Cynthia and Carrie had been shopping in Tunbridge Wells, and both looked charming. Albert had to be coaxed into his best suit and still looked sulky.

A few minutes after the party from Russets had disembarked on the forecourt of 'The Three Nuns' and hurried into church, Sir Neville Franklin rode up on his black stallion. He always seemed to time everything to get his full share of attention. Sir Neville was still a handsome figure on horseback, and he knew it. He had lent his car to Russets for the day. It was already on the way with a hired chauffeur, bringing Freddie with the bride. Willing hands reached out to hold Sir Neville's horse, as he swung to the ground. There was sixpence for the lucky lad who claimed to be first.

'Good day to you!' His Lordship strode down the path, doffing his grey topper. Two old retainers from Marston Park bobbed a curtsey as he went past. They were enjoying their retirement in the Almshouses. He acknowledged the curtsey with a smile and a bow.

'A proper gent, Sir Neville,' said the ex-housemaid, decidedly.

It was obviously the upper class who formed the biggest part of the congregation. Working-class women were shy of entering the church unless the wedding was a family affair, or a baby was being christened on a Sunday afternoon. Funerals were always well attended, and every penny of the insurance money would be spent on ornate wreaths and a coffin with brass handles. Funeral teas were lavish, and deep mourning would be worn for twelve months by close relatives. The whole village went into mourning when the old Queen died, on that day in January at the turn of the century. After those Sixty Glorious Years, her memory was revered by all classes of society. Yet it was during that era the barriers of class had been erected most strongly. It was here, in the village, on these festive occasions, that the working class seemed to revert to their pre-War status, for May Day had no particular significance for the upper class.

Ruby was proud of Freddie that day. To give the bride away was quite an ordeal. It was Cynthia who had persuaded him. But he soon forgot his nervousness in concern for his small daughter, who had been carefully coached by her mother, yet nobody could really predict what a little girl might do under the strain of so much emotion. It was all in the lap of the gods, Freddie was thinking, as he watched Cynthia fussing with her daughter's crown of flowers. Harriet waited calmly, and had no fears that her small bridesmaid might trip over her train. It was only a short train, and they had rehearsed in the passage at Russets. A kiss, and a whispered, 'You can do it beautifully, darling,' was all the encouragement she needed.

Now it was Wendy's turn to steal the limelight, with her cherubic face flushed with importance, and her pink tongue licking her lips. She followed Freddie and Harriet in slow procession down the long aisle. This was her debut. She would never be a debutante, or make her curtsey to the Queen like her Aunt Beatrice, for her mother had already broken with the tradition before she married the man from Richmond Row. All heads were turned in their direction now. The booming organ drowned the whispered admiration, and the rustle of petticoats. Every girl is beautiful on her wedding day, with a radiance all her own, and Harriet was no exception. Philip was aware of this radiance only when she stood beside him, and in that moment of revelation, he was also aware of her calmness. His own taut nerves were calmed when her cool fingers clasped his hot hand, and she smiled, reassuringly.

Now they were wrapped around in the aura of an age-old ceremony from which they would emerge as husband and wife.

'For better, for worse. For richer, for poorer. In sickness and in health. Till death us do part.'

He knew every word of the marriage service and its solemn implications. The parson was no stranger. They met every Sunday. He liked to be called 'Vicar'. His freshly laundered surplice crackled with starch, but the hem of the dusty cassock had come unstitched for a couple of inches or so, and it caught Philip's attention. His wife should have repaired it, but she was not a woman to concern herself with repairs. They said she had no time for the working-class parishioners, but was always sweet as honey to the upper class. They said she neglected her duties, and the poor man had to depend on volunteers to visit the sick and aged. They said she couldn't keep a living-in servant for all the tea in China, and had to depend on daily's. All this had nothing to do with Philip – only the drooping hemline offended his fastidious senses.

'Those whom God hath joined together let no man put asunder.'

The solemn pronouncement was interrupted by a slight scuffle. The little bridesmaid had dropped the bride's bouquet. Somebody stepped out of the pew and picked it up. Harriet was still incredibly calm. She was gazing at the flowers on the altar. Carnations and roses. They were so beautiful. Somebody had paid for them, but it wasn't Mother. Did Father know this was her wedding day, she wondered? It was sweet of Freddie to give her away, but her darling Daddy would have made the day perfect. She was glad Wendy hadn't cried when she dropped the bouquet. If they were blessed with children, they would grow up with the black children, and there would be no class distinction. She would pass on the Christian principles she had been taught. They were all God's children, the black and the white, her father had insisted. And when the Baby Jesus was black, it crowned his teaching with love and truth.

To the thunderous strains of the *Wedding March*, they paced the long aisle. Cameras clicked in the bright pool of sunlight at the open door. The children swooped, and they ducked their heads and ran, laughing hilariously.

The two mothers dabbed their wet eyes, and young

Julian crawled on hands and knees, scooping up confetti to pelt his little cousin. Who would have guessed they were destined for marriage, those two children, when another devastating War was shattering another decade?

Chapter 13

Back in the house in Tunbridge Wells, Marion faced the future with dismay, and her elder daughter, Agnes, did nothing to allay her fears. Her brusque manner was hurtful.

'You may as well face the truth, Mother. Your husband is a fraud, and will land up in jail if the police catch up with him. It seems to me you have been much too complacent,' she asserted. 'Surely a wife is entitled to know more about her husband's affairs? It's ridiculous! Bankruptcy is quite commonplace in this day and age, but I suppose it is a little disturbing when it affects you personally.'

'A little disturbing? – it's devastating!' Marion retorted, tearfully.

Freddie had broken the news as gently as possible. There was little that could be salvaged. The house and furniture must be sold to pay off the creditors. Marion was entitled only to her own small investments at the bank, the few personal possessions her mother had bequeathed in her Will, and her clothes.

During the weeks following the wedding, her thoughts had swung from hope to despair. Agnes was bored, and wanted to get back to London. Harriet was married, and Richard was teaching in a Jesuit College in Belgium.

Children were so selfish. She had completely forgotten her own young selfishness. She expected affection from daughters who had been robbed of affection since they left the Congo. It was too late to make amends. To have her own daughter tell her she was a fool was the last straw, however. They parted in anger.

When the taxi had driven away, the silent house closed about her, and she wept her bitter tears. But crying without a shoulder to cry on was poor consolation, and self-pity had already ruined her chances of sympathetic understanding with Harriet and Agnes. Empty of tears at last, she stumbled to the kitchen, brewed a strong coffee, and drank two cups. When the telephone rang some time later, she was almost ready to cope with the morrow. It was Cynthia calling. Freddie and Cynthia were not the only ones to be shocked by Marion's appearance at Harriet's wedding. They thought she was going to collapse.

'How are you feeling now, darling? Is Agnes still with you?' It was good to hear that clear, confident voice. Her ex-pupil was Sister Simmons now, and qualified to know all about the human anatomy.

'I am feeling much better, thank you, dear. No, Agnes is not still with me. She had to get back to London. She's a busy career woman now, you know, and her secretary phoned every day.'

'A pity she couldn't have spared you another week or so. I don't like to think of you on your own in that big, empty house. Had she any suggestions to make, about the future, I mean?'

'No, but she said she would keep in touch.'

'That's what Harriet said, didn't she?'

'Yes, how did you know?'

'I heard her telling you when she kissed you goodbye at Russets. It's too bad, darling. I'm very cross with them. I hope my daughter will be a little more considerate when she grows up.'

'It's my fault, Cynthia, I'm afraid. I have neglected them rather badly in the past, and they were upset when I married again.'

'Why shouldn't you, when you were still a young woman?'

'But I didn't love Stephen. It was just to escape from my own loneliness, and that's not a good enough reason, is it, dear?'

'I suppose not, but you have enjoyed being your own mistress again, and having such a lovely home?'

'Yes, I have, and I am going to miss it.'

'You know you are welcome to come to us until you have decided what to do.'

'Thank you. Everyone is so kind. Lucy invited me to stay at Russets, but I am used to living in a town now, and I like Tunbridge Wells. Besides, I have to find a job and earn some money. That's not too difficult, I suppose?'

'As a matter of fact, I had a suggestion to offer, but Freddie thinks it's too soon to bother you with it, and we should wait till you are feeling stronger.'

'Bless you both, but the sooner I start the better for everyone. What had you in mind?'

'There is a vacancy for a matron at The Firs. It's a preparatory school for small boys on the other side of the Common, and Freddie knows the Head. They met at the Convalescent Home in Worthing, and have kept in touch. The wife has been acting as Matron, since the War, but they are expecting their first child early next year, so they are looking for a replacement. It would be a living-in post, but you could afford to have your own little place, and feel quite independent for the long school holidays. And you would be near us, darling. What do you say? Does it appeal to you? We don't want to rush you into making a decision you might regret later.'

'Has the post been advertised?'

'Not yet.'

'May I think it over and phone you back in the morning?'

'Of course, and if you do decide on it, Freddie will arrange an appointment. I must hang up now. Goodbye, darling. Be brave. It's just a bad patch. It will pass. I should know.'

'You're a wonderful woman, Cynthia. I haven't your resilience. I went all to pieces when I lost Malcolm.'

'That was understandable.'

'But I shouldn't have, not with my background. Mother had to tell me to pull myself together. She was right, of course. Bless her.'

'Now it's Agnes. She's awfully bossy, isn't she?'

'Yes.'

'Never mind, darling, you still have us, and we love you.'

'Thank you, dear.'

The receiver clicked, and Marion sighed. Had she the courage to start another new chapter without Malcolm? There was no alternative. She could almost hear him say – 'Have ye no faith, woman?'

She squared her shoulders and climbed the stairs, to start on the packing.

The Firs was a rambling, Victorian house, sadly in need of fresh paint, and obviously suffering from the wear and tear of some twenty small boys. Set in several acres of garden, the overgrown shrubs and trees provided a happy hunting ground for the boys. The playing fields could be reached by climbing a gate or squeezing through the gaps in the hedge. But with all the boys on holiday, it was quiet and peaceful on this Summer afternoon. The informality appealed to Marion after the formal landscaped garden surrounding the house that was no longer a home. The front door stood wide open, but nobody answered the bell, so she wandered round the house and found Gerald Fairweather and his wife, Elizabeth, picking raspberries in a walled vegetable garden. When they glanced up to see her standing at the gate, they both exclaimed simultaneously, 'Mrs Grant!' and hurried to meet her.

'I do apologise. Have you been waiting long? We get carried away when we are picking raspberries, don't we Gerry?' Elizabeth explained, wiping her stained hands on Gerry's clean handkerchief.

'We do indeed,' he agreed.

She was a tall woman, taller than her husband, and her smile was warm and friendly. They both were dark, with sallow complexions, and would have passed for brother and sister.

'It's quite all right. I'm early. I was not sure how long it would take me to get here,' Marion told her.

'You walked?'

'Yes.'

'Oh, dear, and we asked Freddie to tell you to take a taxi and charge it up to us. Aren't men the limit?' There was no malice in her voice, however, only affection, as she took the basket from her husband so that he could shake hands. The grip of his left hand was firm and strong. The empty right sleeve was tucked into the pocket of his loose fitting linen jacket, and his flannels were baggy at the knees. Elizabeth was wearing a rather grubby print frock and sandals. Her legs were bare.

'We were going to change. Will you excuse us, Mrs Grant?' she asked.

'Certainly.' Marion could not have wished for a better introduction to her prospective employers. She had been dreading the interview.

'The raspberries look delicious,' she said.

'Yes, it's a good crop this year. We gave the boys a treat before they broke up for the holidays. Last month it was strawberries. They had strawberries and cream for tea on Sports Day. We had all the parents here. It's a very important event, isn't it, Gerry?'

'Very important.'

'Come and sit down,' Elizabeth invited. 'You must be exhausted. It's nearly 4 o'clock. I thought you could join us for tea. It breaks the ice, doesn't it?' She was a gentle woman in both senses of the word, and he was a dear. The liking was mutual.

'There is no ice,' said Marion, truthfully – and followed Elizabeth into the drawing-room. The bright sunlight picked out the thin patches on the carpet and the faded cretonne covers on the sofa and armchairs. There was no pretence to smartness. It was homely and old-fashioned.

To see Elizabeth Fairweather tugging at a Victorian bellrope was surprising in this day and age, and it was even more surprising when a grey-haired man entered the room.

'We will have tea now, Henry, please,' she said, with quiet authority.

'It's all ready, Madam,' Henry answered, respectfully.

'Will you give these raspberries to Cook, and ask her to serve enough for the three of us, with cream. We have a guest. This is Mrs Grant. We are hoping to persuade her to take over the post of Matron.'

'Good afternoon, Madam.' Henry inclined his head, took the basket and commented gravely on the quality of the raspberries.

'Help yourselves, Henry. There are plenty more. Tomorow we will pick for jam.'

'Very good, Madam.'

Mistress and servant exchanged a smile of complete trust and understanding, and Henry left the room. It was putting back the clock to pre-War days, Marion was thinking.

'Henry and Cook came to us after the War, with excellent references. We were lucky to get them. Both have been in service all their working lives. Cook started as a kitchen maid, and Henry as second footman, on a big estate in East Anglia. There were twenty indoor servants in those days, and eight outdoors. Times have changed, and well-trained servants are worth their weight in gold. We gave them the flat over the stables, had it decorated, and furnished it. So they have their own home where they can relax when they are off duty. We always insist they take a two-hour break in the afternoon. Next week they go on holiday to Brighton, so we shall have to manage without them. Gerry will help me, won't you?' Elizabeth appealed to her husband, and he grinned boyishly.

'I'll wash the dishes if you dry!'

'Thank you, darling.'

Then Henry pushed in the laden tea trolley, arranged a small, convenient table for his master, and went out, closing the door quietly. All his movements were quiet and his manner deferential.

Grouped about the open French windows, they could see across the garden. The smell of new-mown grass mingled with the scent of roses in a bowl on the piano. A marmalade cat stalked a bird, and a red squirrel darted along the lower branch of a massive oak tree, on which a swing had been tied for the junior boys.

'All the houses on this side of the Common had big families and a staff of servants at one time,' Gerald Fairweather explained. 'The War changed their style of living quiet drastically, but two of the owners had seen the red light, apparently, in the mid-twenties and sold their properties. One was converted into a Nursing Home, and the other into flats. We were told they went to live abroad in Southern Italy or Greece, where the sun almost always shines, and living is much cheaper. As for the servants, they were scattered all over the place. The younger ones emigrated, and the others were caught up in the shortage of trained servants after the War. We have an excellent gardener-groundsman, an ex-soldier, who comes three days a week, and his wife is here every week-day morning in term time to help Cook in the kitchen.'

'Do tell Mrs Grant about the extraordinary collection of servants who were working here after the war,' Elizabeth prompted. And while she poured the tea and played the hostess, he amused their guest with anecdotes of their early days at The Firs.

'They were refugees from Europe, and they stayed until they had earned enough money to return to their homelands. They all had picked up a little English during the War, but the temperamental Spaniards hardly missed a day in picking a quarrel with the Flemish-speaking couple from Belgium, or the housemaid from Marseilles. Fortunately we had an elderly university professor on the teaching staff who spoke four languages fluently, and sorted out the sparring partners! He is still with us, happily. It was Bedlam here some days. Yet with all these disturbing elements, Cook and Henry carried on quite calmly, and regarded the bunch of foreigners with condescending disapproval because they hadn't learned to speak the King's English!'

Elizabeth had heard it all before, but joined in the laughter. Marion would discover that he never bored his friends with War stories like so many of his contemporaries. Neither did Freddie. They had both lost a limb, and were very severely handicapped, but it was only mentioned in a light-hearted way. Marion was watching her host's deft movements with admiration, and her own self-pity was forgotten.

When they had finished tea, he asked, 'Would you like me to show Mrs Grant round, darling?'

'Yes, please. I'll sit here with my knitting till you come back, and I'm going to make a wish, Mrs Grant. You can guess what it is!'

'I think I can,' was all she said, although she had little doubt that she would accept the post. She liked small boys, and she liked what she had seen of Gerald and Elizabeth Fairweather. They all were on their best behaviour, of course, and she was still a little wary. The last time she had rushed impulsively into a situation it had turned out to be disastrous. Only a fool made the same mistake twice.

'Come and meet Cook,' her host was saying, and she followed him to the big airy kitchen. Cook was shelling peas at a table set in the open window. She was the exact replica of the old-fashioned Cook in the early days at The Parsonage – homely and buxom, draped in a starched white apron with rolled-up sleeves and her hair in a neat little bun. She greeted them warmly. She knew her place, but she also knew her worth.

'How is Madam?' she asked. 'I hope she hasn't tired herself picking all these raspberries?'

'She seems perfectly all right, thank you, Cook. She enjoys picking fruit. You know what she's like. She can't bear to be idle, and I am constantly reminded she is not an invalid. Anyway, we left her sitting in the drawing-room while I show Mrs Grant round the house, and we will take our time over it.'

'That's right, Sir. We have to be a bit diplomatic with Madam these days or she thinks she is being coddled, but we can't have her overdoing it.'

'Between you and me and Henry, she is unlikely to

overdo it!' he chuckled.

The tour of the house took the best part of an hour, for they stopped to chat in the comfortable bed-sitting-room already prepared for the new matron, adjoining the sick bay and the dispensary.

'Freddie has told us about your present unhappy circumstances, Mrs Grant, and we do hope you will join us here,' he said. There was sympathy and sincerity in his quiet, controlled voice – a voice that was never raised in anger, she would soon discover.

'How do you feel about it now that you have seen the place? Would you like to think it over and let us know what you decide?' Elizabeth asked, when they were back in the drawing-room.

'I have decided. I would like to accept the post.'

Elizabeth leaned over to clasp her hands. 'Thank you, my dear. It's such a relief. We have been a little anxious, I must confess, after what Freddie told us. We wondered if you would be able to cope?'

'I shall manage.' Marion was surprised at her own determination. Perhaps it had not been such a bad thing after all to have her bossy daughter, Agnes, telling her she was a fool.

'Would it be convenient if I moved in this weekend? Otherwise, I have to remove myself to an hotel?' she asked.

'But of course. I could come and pick you up any time tomorrow. We have a small bus. It's useful for collecting the boys and taking them to play football and cricket with other prep schools. If you have settled everything with my husband, I will run you back. How about the salary? Is it adequate?'

'Quite adequate, thank you.' Actually, it had been a little embarrassing, for she had to remind him. They both were embarrassed. Then he had led the way into the study, and made out a cheque for £10 – a month's advance salary.

It was only after Elizabeth had dropped her off at the front entrance, and she let herself into the silent house, that she fully realised her good fortune in acquiring a post without all the rigmarole of registering at an agency. With Freddie's kind recommendation they had accepted her, and all her misgivings that her inexperience would be a drawback had been banished by Elizabeth's promise to show her the ropes before the start of the new term. For all her strong resolve to put the past behind her and face the future bravely, she was crying quietly as she climbed the stairs to finish packing.

It was such a sudden, drastic end to a chapter in which she had enjoyed leisure and luxury for the first time in her life. To discover that such luxury had been enjoyed at the price of defrauding honest tradesmen and trusting dubious business associates was degrading. With her spartan and puritan background, it was unforgivable to revel in self-indulgence. Once she had been a strong-willed young woman with the courage of her convictions. Once she belonged to a society who put service before self. Was it too late to regain a measure of that discipline?

She pushed open the window to the poignant notes of a blackbird's evening song. She supposed it would still be singing on the morrow, but she would be gone. If only she could talk to Malcolm. But she had lost touch with Malcolm when she married Stephen, and no wonder. Malcolm's world had been dedicated to God's black children, and she had shared it, and wanted no other for the rest of her days. 'Woman,' he called her. It was his only endearment, yet it held so much more feeling and sentiment then the commonplace 'Darling'. She was all woman to her beloved Malcolm, but to Stephen she was just another possession, and he was an avid collector.

When the telephone rang on the bedside table, she picked up the receiver with trembling fingers, still expecting to hear that familiar greeting – 'Hello, darling. Missing me?' In the early days of their marriage, Stephen had phoned in the evening, but not for some time. She had wondered if his 'business' was with another woman?

But it wasn't Stephen. It was Freddie, enquiring about the interview. She sat on the bed and told him all that had happened in a tight voice. He thought she had been crying.

'That's fine, Marion. I'm glad you got along so well with Gerry and Elizabeth. What are you doing now?'

'Nothing much. I just have to finish packing, then I shall go to bed early.'

'Hang on a minute. Cynthia has just come in. It's her late night, and we always wait supper.'

Marion could hear the murmur of voices in the background.

'Cynthia says she will come and pick you up, and you can join us for supper. It's a cold supper, anyway, so it won't spoil.'

'Are you sure it won't be a nuisance?'

'Positive.'

'Thank you both. You are very kind.'

'By the way, Cynthia will run you back, so you can give her the keys.'

'Keys?'

'The keys of the house.'

'Yes – yes, of course.'

She hung up the receiver. It was so final.

The homely atmosphere of the little terrace house restored her spirits. It seemed strange to be sitting at the supper table with Ruby, who had once been her grandmother's servant, and servants had their meals in the kitchen. But of course she was Freddie's mother, and it was Cynthia who had brought about this change in their relationship with the tact and diplomacy that was inborn, not cultivated. Her gauche ex-pupil had come a long way since those early days in the schoolroom at Marston Park. Teacher and pupil seemed to have changed roles. It was Cynthia who had the courage of her convictions to sweep aside all the barriers of class. There was no constraint between them – the older woman from Richmond Row and the younger from Marston Park. This, to Marion, steeped in her mother's tradition, was still a little embarrassing. All the years with Malcolm had not completely eradicated that inherent distinction between mistress and servant. Richard and Agnes were snobs. Harriet was her father's daughter.

So there they were – Cynthia, Freddie, Marion and Ruby – gathered round the supper table for the first time since the wedding had brought them all together again at Russets. They avoided the topic that was uppermost in Marion's mind, and Stephen's name was not mentioned.

When Wendy called out for a drink of water, her mother called back sharply, 'Get it for yourself from the bathroom. I am not waiting on you now you're a big girl.'

They heard the patter of bare feet, water running in the wash-basin, the plug pulled, and the slam of the lavatory seat. Every sound was magnified in this small house. Freddie and Ruby made no comment. Their spoiling of the child was balanced by Cynthia's discipline.

Since her debut as a bridesmaid, Wendy had spent a whole week at Russets. Ruby had taken her by train, and she had absorbed the atmosphere of a new way of life with Julian as escort. She followed him everywhere on her short, sturdy legs, in much the same way as Carrie had followed Albert, in those early years.

'May I say goodnight to Wendy?' Marion asked, tentatively, when they had finished supper. You were never quite sure with Cynthia, but tonight she was being very agreeable.

'She knows you are here, Marion, and our small daughter cannot bear to be left out of anything.'

'Neither could you at that age, my dear,' Marion reminded her.

'I suppose not. I can't honestly remember much about those nursery days, only that we had to eat every scrap on our plates, and had no pudding until we had finished that horrid cabbage. At tea-time, there was a fixed rule that you ate the first slice of bread and butter without jam, and if you made a fuss, you had no cake. Disobedience was never allowed to go unpunished, but I suppose some of that discipline must have rubbed off on me because I am rather strict with Wendy, though I do try to be fair,' she added, in self-defence. 'There is no comparison, actually, for Wendy shares our way of life. We children were banished almost completely to the nursery wing, and played no active part in the rest of the house, only at Christmas. We were taught to respect our parents, but they were not terribly important to us, and I had no sense of belonging to them until I came under your jurisdiction in the schoolroom, Marion. The first thing you insisted on, I remember, was that we two girls, Beatrice and myself, had minds of our own, and should use them. When you forbade anything, you always gave a good reason for doing so. I know I admired you tremendously when you stood up to Papa on one occasion, and reminded him that his four daughters were separate entities, and should not be regarded collectively!'

'Did I really say that?'

'You certainly did. And what a rumpus it caused when you fell in love and gave notice,' she chuckled at the memory. 'You were never really dedicated to the job, were you, darling? I mean, it was out of character. I always knew you were a rebel at heart. It must have been your influence that gave me the courage to rebel against that awful system of presentation at court, and all the rest of the ballyhoo.'

'The marriage market,' Freddie murmured.

'The marriage market,' Cynthia echoed. 'What an escape!'

'Look what you got in exchange, you silly girl,' he teased.

'My darling,' was all she said, but her dark eyes were soft as velvet as she covered his hand with her own on Ruby's starched white tablecloth. They still were sweethearts, Marion was thinking. Their romance had met with every possible discouragement, but it survived. She herself had defied convention when she married Malcolm, but there was a difference. Cynthia had stayed to face the music. She had gone away, thousands of miles from her critics – and she hadn't been faithful to that first love, her dearest love. Now that she was freed of Stephen's influence, she would like to establish a closer relationship with Cynthia and Freddie. They were such an endearing couple.

She found the little girl awake, her long, flaxen hair spread over the pillow, her wide blue eyes eager for any diversion. With both parents dark, it was strange to produce such a fair child. Then Marion remembered Cynthia's mother at Marston Park – the child's grandmother, and saw the likeness.

Auntie Marion was not a proper auntie, and according to Julian, she liked boys best, but it was better than nobody. Julian said you could always tell by the size of the presents they brought you when they came on a visit – and Julian was *always* right.

Auntie Marion's hands were empty. Swallowing the impulse to ask 'What have you brought me?' – just in case there was a small present in her pocket – Wendy remembered her mother's punishment on a previous occasion, and asked, politely, 'Was it a nice supper?'

'It was delicious.'

'Did you have choclet burmange?'

'No, we had cheese and biscuits.'

'When I am married, I shall have choclat burmange for my pudding every day.'

'Goodness, what will your husband say?'

'He will say, "Thank you, Wendy, it's my favrit".'

Marion smiled involuntarily. It was so long since she had to sit and listen to the extraordinary chatter of a small child. It brought back memories of Agnes and Harriet, before she had started on their lessons.

'Daddy has a nartificial leg. It's called James,' Wendy confided. 'It comes undone when Daddy goes to bed.'

'Really?' This sudden plunge from chocolate blancmange to an artificial leg was a little disconcerting to a mother whose children had grown to maturity and had no further need of her. But she need not have worried, for Wendy had a fund of varied and interesting subjects, and loved an audience – usually Daddy or Granny. She sat up, flushed and starry-eyed, bursting with importance.

'I cut up my own meat with a small little knife, now I'm four, an' when we go to the shop, Daddy lets me ask for his abbaco. My Daddy smokes a pipe you see.'

'I see.'

'Mummy is learning me to play the piano. She plays doh ray me with this hand, and I play doh ray me with this hand.' She was demonstrating on the patchwork quilt that Ruby had knitted so laboriously. 'Then we play three blind mice an' sing a song of sixpence an' baa baa black sheep an . . . .'

'"Little Miss Muffet?"'

'How did you know?'

'Once upon a time I taught my two little girls to play the piano.'

'Where are they now?'

'Grown up, and one already married. Auntie Harriet was my litle girl.'

It was too much for Wendy's limited comprehension, and she liked to talk about herself.

'When I was four, I had four candles on my birthday cake an' I blew them out. When I am five I shall have five candles an' I shall blow them out. When I am six I shall have . . .'

'You will have six candles and blow them out!' Marion finished. 'Now I must go. Mummy is waiting to take me home.' It was not true, but this sort of saga could go on indefinitely.

'Goodnight, darling. God bless you.'

She bent to kiss the child, and was surprised to receive a throttling hug. A little girl of four can be very grateful for an audience when she has no brothers and sisters.

They kissed goodbye at Tonbridge and arranged to meet again in the late evening to catch a train back to Victoria. Much of the day would be taken up with travelling, for Philip had to change to the slow branch line, and walk a mile from the station the other end, while Harriet would disembark at Tunbridge Wells and take a bus to the other side of the Common.

This monthly visit to their respective mothers was more of a duty than a pleasure, since they both had to forfeit their only free day in the week, and Philip was inclined to sulk over an early breakfast. But Harriet insisted they must not be selfish, and the kindest way to settle a difficult situation was to split up at Tonbridge, and go their separate ways. It was useless to pretend that Martha enjoyed sharing her son with her daughter-in-law, and it was equally dishonest to pretend that Marion had suddenly developed maternal love for a daughter, or that she accepted a son-in-law with such a dubious history. 'Bastard' was a dirty word a governess avoided in the schoolroom – and sex was another. A married woman with three grown-up children should not be so sensitive to certain words, Marion reminded herself, but she was still a bit of a prude. Agnes and Harriet called it 'being stuffy', but they belonged to a younger generation, and she did not share their views. Harriet was adamant on the question of duty, however, and Philip was no match for her.

He sometimes wondered why he had been persuaded into being a student of theology, and a prospective disciple of Christ in the mission field. In the company of Harriet his doubts vanished, but on these particular Sundays, when they parted at Tonbridge and he went on alone to the village, they multiplied.

Nothing had changed at the School House. Everything in his room had been carefully preserved, even the teddybear and his first pair of shoes. It would have been so easy to slip into the pattern of his bachelor days, and he had to remind himself he was a married man, dedicated to a life of service and sacrifice, with Harriet. He parted from his mother at the end of the day with a heavy heart, that was only lightened by the sight of Harriet, waving frantically from a doorway on the London train, at Tonbridge Station. Then he ran down the platform with his bulky packages, climbed into the carriage, kissed her cheek, and muttered, 'Thank God that's over for another month!'

He was so young, she thought – like a little boy who had done what he was bid, and expected to be praised. But he did not confess the doubts he had known, or the tears he had shed, as he hurried back to the station, carrying a parcel of clean linen and a 'tuck box'. There were no facilities for washing clothes in their lodgings, and they couldn't afford the laundry, so Philip took home a parcel of soiled bed linen, towels and tablecloths, shirts, socks, pyjamas and underclothes, and collected the clean articles from the previous visit. Andrew did not interfere with this arrangement because he knew Martha enjoyed doing it. She would mend holes in his socks, sew on buttons, and turn frayed collars and cuffs, commenting a little acidly on Harriet's neglect. The 'tuck box' was packed with his favourite cake, sausage rolls, Cornish pasties, home-made toffee and coconut-ice. She did not enquire if Harriet had a particular favourite. She was concerned only for the health and welfare of her son. She thought he was losing weight, and slipped in a jar of Virol, which he detested, but their landlady always knew of some poor, undernourished child, so it was not wasted. If he sneezed, he was persuaded to take a Beecham's Powder, and if he complained of a headache, he lay on the sofa with closed eyes for an hour before dinner, and she crept about the house. Now that it was only one day a month, Philip enjoyed his mother's fussing. Harriet seldom fussed.

In the afternoon, they cycled to Russets, with Andrew pointing out the seasonal flowers, with their Latin names. Once a schoolmaster, always a schoolmaster! At Russets, Philip was warmly welcomed. It was like old times, with Aunt Lucy and Carrie, hugging and kissing, Tom and Albert avoiding each other, and young Julian a little shy of Teacher and the schoolmaster, and still regarding Philip a hero. The river was never mentioned, but that near tragedy would never be forgotten.

In the peaceful atmosphere of that valley farm, London seemed a thousand miles away, and he envied them now, though he hadn't envied them before. They were tanned and healthy, and they lived like fighting cocks. He was a poor thing in comparison, with his pallid face and nervous twitch. In his best suit and college tie, he seemed over-dressed. They all wore their sun-bleached, shabby clothes, without embarrassment. For a couple of hours or so, he could forget the mission school, the drab lodgings, and the noise and bustle of the London streets. He could even forget Harriet in the company of Carrie. Though a decade divided them and she had lost her youthful charm and gaiety, they still enjoyed the easy companionship of brother and sister while concealing their secret thoughts. Philip had no conception of Albert's cruel disability, or the frustration of a husband and wife who had never known a normal relationship. And Carrie was not burdened by the doubts and fears of her companion during those precious hours when they wandered about the farm together.

'Tell me about London,' she coaxed, on his first visit after his marriage.

But Philip was not very observant, and his world was still small, even in the vastness of a big city. It was Harriet who knew her London, and Cynthia, too, of course.

'Why don't you come up and see for yourself? You could stay at an hotel,' he suggested.

'I can't get away. They need me here.'

'Do you never get away?'

'Only to Tunbridge Wells occasionally, just for the day. I go to see Mum and Freddie, and I'm very fond of Wendy. But now Mum and Wendy come here more often, I suppose I shall have no excuse to take a day off.'

'Is it as bad as that? Can't they see you need a break?'

'Aunt Lucy and Tom wouldn't mind if I went every week, but Bertie likes to have me around the place.'

'That's selfish.'

'Aren't all men selfish, Philip?'

'I suppose so, and women pander to their selfishness.'

'It depends on the woman. Once I would have argued and made a scene, but not any more. It's not worth it – to stir up trouble, and it upsets Aunt Lucy. I suppose you could say I've mellowed.' She smiled whimsically and changed the subject. She could see Tom and Julian in the distance. They were driving in the cows for milking. The familiar scene was part of her life here at Russets. Morning and evening, seven days a week, through all the seasons of the year. During the week Julian was not home in time to 'help' Tom, who didn't need any help anyway. The cows came readily when they were called. They had been waiting with the dumb patience of their kind. Only in an emergency, when Tom was delayed, would one or the other raise a voice in protest, and the doleful reminder could be heard for miles.

'I must go, dear.' Carrie moved away. 'Are you staying for tea?'

'Yes.'

'Then I'll see you later.'

Philip was nervous of cows, so she did not suggest he accompanied her to the milking shed. She remembered her own nervousness in those early months at Russets, and her own fastidiousness. There was a time when she thought she would never get used to the stench of dung and silage, to the disgusting wallowing pigs, and the mud. The Winters were long, and it seemed that Spring would never come again. Her fingers were numb in the icy dairy, her feet were numb in the Wellington boots. It was a hard life, and she was not born to it like her cousins. Only Tom understood what she had suffered during those early months at Russets. Yet it was nothing to the suffering she had to endure from Bertie, home from the prisoner-of-war camp. They said there was a limit to a woman's endurance – and she was little more than a girl – when her way of life changed so drastically, almost over night. But she *had* to endure. There was no alternative. It was part of the heritage of the working class. 'Bred in the bone,' as her mother would say. Whatever came your way, you just put up with it, or lost your self respect. The upper class had their troubles, too. She had lived amongst them for several years. But they had servants to wait on them and money to buy the comforts and luxuries with which they were surrounded.

In this strange environment she had found a measure of peace and contentment. Then it was no longer strange. It was HOME. Tom was there. He stayed for her sake. And the baby Julian had come and had partly filled her empty arms. There were compensations in every difficult situation. This had been Aunt Lucy's sensible philosophy. They said she had lost her self respect when she lay with Sir Neville Franklin and carried his child, but she lived through it, and reclaimed her respect in later years when she fostered Penelope's child.

So Philip saw only the surface and not the depths of suffering behind their relationship, and his own endurance had still to be tested. On this mellow September day, he was still feeling his way as a newly married man. The marriage bed was not something to be discussed on these monthly visits, but he was dying to know whether his step-father played the leading role in the act. He would never know whether his own clumsy performance was common among the uninitiated. Harriet had not complained about his fumbling, so he supposed with a little more practice, he could turn out to be a most satisfactory lover.

It was a sober thought to occupy his mind as he strolled back to the house. He could see their bicycles propped against the wall, and he didn't need to be told his mother would keep his machine carefully oiled when he went away. It would be yet another of her son's precious belongings to be preserved for all time. Nostalgic tears would be shed. Poor Mother. Dear Mother.

To see her mother in a starched white coat, looking very capable, shooing a group of noisy small boys upstairs was quite surprising to Harriet. The last time she had seen her had been distressing for both.

The Firs was swarming with boys, all in their best suits, for they had been to church, and were on their way to the dormitories to change their clothes. Their lively young voices echoed about the house. Doors and windows were open, and the savoury smells of roasting meat and potatoes reminded Harriet she was hungry. A young master was herding a group of older boys like a flock of sheep. He had escaped the War by being still at public school, and had joined the staff in 1922. The grey-haired, bearded professor was drinking coffee in the dining-room. He was off-duty today, but since he had no relatives or close friends to visit in England, there was no urgency to get away before lunch. Next Sunday it would be his turn to escort the boys to church, but they were allowed to leave before the sermon, so it was not too tedious. He was feeling a little sad today, but he would not inflict his sadness on the headmaster and his wife, who had always treated him with the utmost kindness. It was the anniversary of their marriage, a day which evoked many memories of past happiness, and emphasised the loneliness of his days without his beloved Lydia. This afternoon he would walk across the Common and sit on his favourite bench. An elderly woman would talk to him, while a little girl chased a dog around the bushes. The woman reminded him of Lydia, who had also been plump, with blue eyes and a warm smile. This woman was much older, with a faded prettiness, but still the likeness was there.

When he looked up to see a young woman hesitating in the doorway, he bowed and with old-world courtesy, bade her enter.

'All the doors were open, so I walked straight in,' Harriet explained. 'My mother is Matron here,' she added.

'Then we are delighted to welcome you, my dear.' He always assumed full responsibility in the absence of the headmaster. It came naturally. The younger man would have been embarrassed. 'She was here a moment ago, drinking coffee with me. She will be supervising the younger boys while they change their clothes.'

'Yes, I caught a glimpse of her on the stairs as I came in.'

'You will have coffee while you wait for her, yes?'

'Thank you.'

'Black or white?'

'White, please.'

Henry had left a percolator of coffee and a jug of hot milk on the hot plate. He was back in the kitchen, helping his wife to prepare the vegetables. The kitchen-maid was free on Sunday. She was a married woman, and her own family expected a hot roast for dinner. Only one daily woman was willing to work on Sunday, and she was a widow who came in for two hours to make beds and clean bathrooms and lavatories.

It seemed very informal, Harriet was thinking. She could hear the boys laughing and talking excitedly. They were lucky boys. Her own memories of boarding school were most unpleasant – home-sickness, bilious attacks – and bitchy prefects! Ten minutes later, the boys were clattering down the stairs and out into the garden, where they would play till the lunch gong brought them racing back to the house to wash their hands in the cloakroom.

Once in the dining-room, however, they had to behave, and table manners were strictly enforced. There was no corporal punishment at The Firs, but there was no bigger punishment for a small boy than to be kept indoors when his mates were kicking or batting a ball in the playing fields.

The young master had snatched a quick cup of coffee and followed the boys into the garden. One daring boy could lead the whole lot into mischief if they were left to their own devices. Introduced to Harriet, he had been surprised to discover she was Matron's daughter. He hadn't known she *had* a daughter. There had been little time to get to know one another once the new term had started, and Marion was too tired to be sociable when the boys had bathed and settled down for the night. Her new role was exacting and exhausting; she had not fully recovered from the shock of the bankruptcy, and finding herself without a home or a husband.

The professor was surprised at the coolness of the greeting between mother and daughter, but then he had never grown accustomed to the unemotional mannerisms of the English upper class. Generally speaking, they did not wear their hearts on their sleeves, and boarding school, from the age of seven or eight, was a hard training ground for the adult world. The system was so firmly established, not even the War and the tragic loss of thousands who had barely grown to manhood had permanently disrupted the system. The small boys, here at The Firs, had quickly adapted to a disciplined routine, and the shared dormitory, though the majority had not shared a bedroom since infancy. The herd instinct was stronger than the home influence, and only a rare child would assert his identity and isolate himself from the rest.

'You shouldn't have much trouble with their health in this first term,' Elizabeth had told Marion. 'It's after

Christmas, with all the coddling and over-eating, when you get the feverish colds and bilious attacks. But a couple of days in bed for the bilious lads, on dry toast and weak tea, will work wonders. Minor accidents can be expected almost any time, and we seldom get through a term without a broken arm or leg. Don't let it worry you, Marion. It's off to hospital in the ambulance, and the parents notified.'

'But I *shall* worry,' Marion confied to Harriet as they sat in the garden after the boys had been marched off for their Sunday afternoon walk. 'I shall never have a moment's peace till the end of term.'

'Yes you will. It's because it's all so new and strange. You managed beautifully at the Mission. Small boys are much the same anywhere, whether they are black or white.'

'But I had your father, and I was so much younger.'

'You'll manage, Mother.' Harriet was already glancing at her watch. She would walk across the Common and have tea with the little family in the terrace house. It was all arranged.

Harriet had developed a surprising flair for organising people. In this self-confident young woman there seemed no trace of the shy, sensitive child. She hardly mentioned Philip, and her mother wondered if her sex life was satisfactory? Since the facts of life had never been disclosed in adolescence, it was utterly impossible to ask such an intimate question of a married daughter!

She watched Harriet's hurried departure wistfully. Sunday was a long day. She had too much time on her hands – time for church – but she hadn't the slightest inclination to make the effort. It would come later, Elizabeth had told her kindly. (It was Gerry and Elizabeth when they were alone.) She had only to mention it to one or the other, and she could have accompanied Harriet and stayed to tea at the little house on the other side of the Common, but she had a very strong feeling that she would be intruding. Whenever she called there, she was drawn into some discussion on her fluctuating affairs, and Harriet had heard enough of bankruptcy and creditors.

'You know you are always welcome, darling,' Cynthia had insisted.

She was grateful to Freddie for handling the business so efficiently, without charge, and grateful to her ex-pupil for her warm friendship. She envied them their contentment and security. If Cynthia was on duty at the hospital, and Freddie engaged with a client, she could sit in the kitchen with Ruby, drinking tea, and listening to her fund of stories about her previous employment. The little girl would sit at the table, turning over the pages of a favourite story book. She was learning to read, and her index finger pointed to each word in turn. One day, in the near future, for she was an intelligent child, that pointing finger would not be necessary, and she would discover she could read without its guidance. In the same way, when she started to skip, the rope would pause automatically till she suddenly discovered the rhythm. Such small discoveries were wonderful to a child, and always her Daddy and her Granny would be there to share the excitement of each new achievement.

The slight embarrassment of drinking tea in the kitchen with Ruby, an ex-servant of the family, would soon be overcome. The child was the go-between, growing up in a classless society, because of her mother's courage and foresight. Ruby always had news of Russets. The twin sisters kept in touch by telephone between visits.

'Lucy was telling me only yesterday,' Ruby would begin, then settle down to a long and detailed account of the human and animal activities – Tom had been sitting up all night with a frightened cow in the throes of labour –

Katie had a new boy-friend – the clumsy old sow had rolled on three of her newly-born piglets – Albert's headaches – Carrie's success with a new recipe – and so on and so forth. The latest bulletin had contained the surprising information that Sir Neville Franklin and Lucy – who had the last word on Julian's welfare – had decided to send the boy to The Firs as a weekly boarder. He was getting into rough ways at the village school, and was too easily persuaded into playing truant. It was not what Lucy had intended, because it would inevitably lead to public school and separation, but she recognised the good sense of his grandfather's proposal. It was not an ultimatum, as it had been with Charles, but just a tentative suggestion.

'I won't go! I shall run away!' Julian had threatened.

Marion was not the only one to notice the child had developed an extraordinary likeness to Charles, not only in appearance, but mannerisms and temperament. The hair had grown darker, and was thick on his shapely head, only the eyes were different. He had his mother's eyes and his mother's smile. At the age of eight Julian Neville Franklin was a strong, sturdy boy, with the self-importance of an only child. His grandfather shared Lucy's anxiety that more of Charles's reckless nature might develop as he grew older if he was left to the influence of the village boys, who had grown up without the order and discipline of an earlier generation. The War could be blamed for robbing so many families of fathers and older brothers.

Albert had long since lost interest in Julian, who was cheeky and aggravating. To keep the peace had always been Lucy's main objective, and Tom, her dear, unselfish Tom, was the go-between, as always. Once there had been a time when she thought he would have to leave Russets, because of his love for Carrie, but it seemed that his love for Russets was as deep and enduring as his love for his pretty cousin. The danger was past, the years had slipped away, and the young, impetuous girl had grown into a quiet, mature woman. These two had a good influence on Julian, for they were consistently even-tempered and kind.

It was easy to slip away. He had finished his breakfast of egg and bacon and fried bread, and left Tom and Carrie sitting at the table. Aunt Lucy was in the dairy, Katie upstairs making beds, Albert still in bed. The hop-picking season was in full swing, the shop-keepers and the publicans cleaning up their premises after the invasion of pickers last night. A barricade of wire netting protected the boxes of sweets on the counter in Mrs Penfold's sweet shop, but Julian was past the age of aniseed balls, sherbert bags and humbugs, and with his grandfather's birthday half-crown he could afford a slab of his favourite Cadbury's nut milk chocolate, and still have money left for the Big Adventure.

Mrs Penfold was sweeping out the shop and seemed surprised to have a customer at that early hour. She put the broom aside, and greeted the child with a toothless smile.

'Good morning, Julian. You be up bright and early.'

He nodded.

'You don't grow no 'ops down at Russets no more, does you?'

'No, we don't.'

'Lucky for you, luv, or you would be out in the gardens picking like all the rest of the youngsters.'

'Yes.'

'Is all the family well, then?'

'Yes, thank you.'

'Give my respects to your Auntie.'

'All right. Can I have a big bar of Cadbury's nut milk chocolate, please?' He held up the half-crown.

'My! My! That's a lot of money.'

'It was a present from my grandfather for my birthday.'

'Sir Neville?'

'Yes.'

'A lovely gentleman, Sir Neville.'

'Yes.' He took the chocolate and the change, thanked her politely, and backed away from the counter. He could see through the door a fat tabby cat curled on a hearth-rug in front of the stove. It was a cosy, familiar scene, the cat and the stove. The kitchen at Russets was the nicest room in the house.

For a brief, uncertain moment he hesitated in the doorway on the brink of the Big Adventure. Then he shrugged, pulled open the door and walked away along the highway, with a nonchalant air.

To walk along the highway was in itself an adventure, for he hadn't ever been beyond the High Street, the church and 'The Three Nuns'. He had been to London with Carrie, to see *Peter Pan*. It was exciting, but it was not a Big Adventure. All his short life had been spent at the farm, and he knew every yard of those familiar acres. Going to school, he always met up with other children. He was a friendly child, not a loner, and to be alone was a new experience. It was unlikely that he would meet any of the village children on the highway. They would be picking hops, and the hop-gardens were tucked away in quiet lanes, near the farms and the oast houses.

A farm wagon rumbled past, and a man wearing a battered straw hat lifted his whip in salute to the small figure. He was not a very intelligent person, and his mind worked slowly, so it was some time before he got around to wondering what the boy was doing on his own. When he turned to look back, there was no sign of him, so he shrugged and muttered, 'What do it matter? T'ain't my business,' and went on his way to the station to collect a new threshing machine.

At the crossroads, Julian had stopped to examine the signpost – 'CRANBROOK 4 miles'. He understood all about acres, but was rather vague about miles. What was 4 miles, and what did it matter? He had all the time in the world to do exactly as he pleased. It was a heady thought.

The highway still attracted him, so he followed the sign to Cranbrook, and did not venture down the byways. He was not exactly *afraid* of those narrow winding lanes, but he liked to see where he was going. The opposite arm of the signpost had pointed back to 'FAIRFIELDS 1 mile'. Surely they had made a mistake? He seemed to have been walking for ages. The sun was climbing high in the sky, and he was hot in his jersey and short corduroy knickers. His legs were bare, and he could feel the hard surface of the road through the rubber soles of the old canvas shoes he wore about the farm in the Summer holidays, to save his leather shoes for school. Aunt Lucy insisted that he wore a jersey in the early morning, because of the heavy mist that covered the valley in September. Later in the day he would change into a cotton shirt. Aunt Lucy was fussy about his health because he had been a delicate baby. Now he was eight he resented all the fussing. Couldn't she see he was strong and healthy?

The chocolate was melting and sticky in his hot hand, but it still tasted good, sitting by the roadside like a tramp. Tramps were lucky people, free to come and go as they pleased, and they didn't have to wash. They often called at the farm in the Summer months to ask for a drink of water, and Aunt Lucy filled the can with lemonade from the earthenware crock in the cool larder. In the Winter months, she filled the can with hot cocoa. With a thick chunk of freshly baked bread, and a slice of cheese, they went on their way. No wonder they came back, year after year.

Thinking of that sweet, cold lemonade, he licked his dry lips and sighed for something that he had always taken for granted. He had only to ask, and it was provided. When he went on his way the jauntiness had gone from his step, and the next couple of miles was a test of endurance and he was near to tears, remembering the lemonade. It was lonely. The Big Adventure would be fun if he had the company of Sandy Butcher or Dusty Miller – or both.

When he next sat down for a short rest, he was feeling a little sick and didn't fancy any more of the sweet, sticky chocolate, so he dropped it in the ditch. It was uncannily quiet. Everyone would be busy in the hop-gardens. Had they missed him at Russets? Were they searching all over the place, calling his name? 'Julian! Julian!'

'Have you found the little bugger?' Uncle Albert would be mad!

Wiping his wet eyes on the sleeve of his jersey he grinned, and felt better. To aggravate Uncle Albert was fun because he got so mad. The scars on his brown face were white, and he always limped because he had been wounded in the War.

'Show me then – show me where you were wounded,' he had demanded, some time ago – and got his ears boxed for being cheeky!

Grandfather was the most important person in his small world. Would he be angry? Would he take his pony away as a punishment? Uncle Charles had been punished and sent away. It must have been something bad, but nobody would say why he had to live in America and not at Marston Park. Grandfather had told him there was no mystery. Uncle Charles preferred to live in America. When you were a grown man, you pleased yourself where you lived. Aunt Lucy told him it was not his business, and Carrie said she had no idea. If she knew, she would tell him. Next to Grandfather, he liked Carrie best. She was old enough to be called 'Auntie' but she liked to be called Carrie. Perhaps she hadn't *quite* grown up. She would swing on a branch, pick wild flowers, and even climb a tree. Carrie would be sad. She would cry, and blame Aunt Lucy. But it was not Aunt Lucy who had decided about boarding school. It was Grandfather who still had the last word on the most important issues. As if he didn't know! Clever old Grandfather!

He had fallen asleep under a hedge by the roadside, and was rudely awakened by a rough hand on his bare leg and a gruff voice demanded, 'Wake up, boy! Wake up!'

He looked up into a pair of black eyes in a thin brown face. A gypsy caravan, drawn by a scraggy horse, had halted nearby. Julian was a little afraid of gypsies. They had a bad reputation for stealing children as well as chickens, but there was nothing sinister about this particular gypsy, or the woman who sat on the shafts with a baby at her breast. Two little girls were peering out of the doorway, eating bread and jam. They were dirty, and their cheeks were sticky with jam, but they were pretty, with their black eyes and tangled black hair. Julian's stomach rumbled, and he looked longingly at the bread and jam.

'What you doing here, boy? You lost?' the man was asking.

There was no time to make up a story, so he told the truth.

'I'm running away. They want to send me to boarding school.'

'So! – and where you running to, ugh?'

'Cranbrook.'

'Me, too. We go also to Cranbrook. My boy, he's sick. You come with us, yes? Too far to walk.'

'Thank you,' said Julian politely.

The woman leaned down to grip his hand and pulled him up beside her. The man clambered up easily, flicked the reins, and the scraggy horse moved forward, its head hanging dejectedly. It was such a small horse to pull a loaded caravan. The horses at Russets were giants in comparison, and the mare that pulled the milk float was fat. There was a sour smell about the woman and the baby, but there were more sour smells than sweet at Russets, so it did not bother him. The little girls ate the bread and jam, too shy to speak.

'You hungry, boy?' the man asked kindly.

Julian nodded.

'Marie, get the boy a slice,' barked the man, and the elder girl obeyed instantly. The thick slice of bread was spread thinly with the cheapest 'plum' jam from the grocer. Aunt Lucy could have told you it had never seen a plum – but it looked good to a hungry boy.

The poor horse ambled along at a slow pace – clippety, clop, clippety, clop – the baby had stopped suckling and fallen asleep. It was a fat baby, but all the rest were thin – the man, the woman, the two little girls, and the horse. It was fun sitting up on the shafts, squeezed tightly between the man the the woman, eating the bread and jam. The woman fastened her blouse over her breast. Aunt Lucy and Carrie were modest, but Katie had to be reminded to cover herself decently. He was surprised to discover Cranbrook was such a small town. It was not much bigger than Fairfields, with only one street, but more shops and more people.

The man called out to the greengrocer to ask where the doctor lived, and was directed to the other end of the town, near the old mill. Once again he handed the reins to the woman and climbed down. He was quickly back, shaking his head.

'Doctor not there. Called away to accident on one of the farms. The girl said not to come to the surgery, to wait in the field behind the mill. Doctor would come there later.'

The woman spoke for the first time. 'Doctor don't bother with gypsy child.'

'We wait in the field. If doctor don't come, I fetch him. We have money to pay,' the man answered her sullenly.

The church clock was striking 3. They had been a long time on the way, but it seemed they had plenty of time to squander. Time was precious at Russets, and there was a time for everything – a time to milk the cows and feed all the animals – a time for ploughing, sowing, hay-making, and harvest. Spring, Summer, Autumn and Winter, time was precious at Russets.

The man took the bridle and led the horse off the road and up a narrow track into a field, surrounded by trees. He seemed to know the place. He lifted Julian down, but the woman clambered down with the fat baby slung in a shawl, and the two little girls swung down like monkeys, ran a few yards, and squatted to pee, holding up their skimpy frocks. Their bottoms were bare, and their feet were bare. They ran about, gathering sticks for the fire, while the woman collected a saucepan, a frying pan, a bucket of water and a bag of shopping from under the caravan. The man gave the horse a bag of oats, then sat down to watch.

'Sit down, boy,' he said, and Julian obeyed.

It seemed that only the woman and the little girls were expected to work. And all the time the baby slept, while the woman made a fire, and brewed tea. Marie fetched mugs from the caravan. The tea was strong and smoky. The younger girl was sent to fetch a tin opener to open a can of Nestlè's milk that was spooned into the tea. When the tea had been served, the woman peeled onions, and fried them in the pan, then she fried the sausages. The two girls climbed back to the caravan to fetch tin plates, knives and forks. The younger girl carried another mug. Her brother wanted a drink of water, but nothing to eat. He was not hungry.

'Let him be. He's got a fever. Nobody don't want to eat when they got a fever,' said the woman.

Julian sat beside the man, in the same attitude, hugging his knees, savouring the smell of the onions and sausages. The woman sliced a loaf of bread. Then she served the man and the boy with the food, finally the two little girls and herself. They sat apart, and the fat baby still slept. The only sound was the scratching of knives and forks on the tin plates, and the munching of oats. The church clock struck 4, then 5, but still the doctor did not come. The man had stretched out on the hard earth, and slept soundly after the meal. The woman boiled more water and washed the plates and cutlery and the frying pan in a bowl. Then she took away the bag of oats, and gave the horse a drink from the bucket. When the bucket was empty, she sent the little girls to the nearest house to get it refilled. They came back staggering under the weight.

Julian had asked permission to look inside the caravan He was fascinated by the way they lived, and wished he could be a gypsy. There would be no boarding school, and no village school to worry about, and he could live on bread and jam, fried onions and sausages quite happily. He stood at the 'stable' door and gazed wide-eyed at the crowded interior. A boy about his own age was lying on a bunk, covered by a dirty blanket, his tangled black hair damp with sweat. He had vomited into a bowl and it smelled sour. Julian said 'Hello', but the boy made no answer. It seemed a very small place to house a family of five, and most of the space was taken up with the four bunks, a table, a dresser and a stove that was used only in the Winter. After a few minutes, Julian said 'Goodbye' and climbed down.

The two little girls were playing 'tag' under the trees, the woman squatting like a tailor, nursing the baby, the man snored. The fire was dying. Without the fire, it would soon be cheerless, for the sky was overcast, and it looked like rain.

'Shall I find more wood for the fire?' Julian asked the woman. She nodded, but did not speak or smile. He had never known such a silent, solemn family, but they were kind. Thy had offered him a lift and given him tea and food. They seemed not to mind that he was still with them, so he gathered sticks and kept the fire blazing till the doctor came – a young man in a crumpled linen suit and straw hat, carrying a black bag.

The woman got up and woke the man. They both were nervous of the doctor, not knowing what he would say. It was not often they had to call the doctor to the children. They were healthy enough, and the woman had her own remedies. His manner was brusque. He was a busy man, and still had evening surgery. They could hear his raised voice giving instructions, but he was quickly finished, and climbing down. He spoke to the woman in a kinder tone. The two little girls were clinging to her skirts.

'The boy has scarlet fever. We must get him into the Isolation Hospital as soon as possible. It's very contagious. I will telephone for an ambulance. Where are you picking?'

'Loaders Farm, Doctor.'

'Well, wait here till the boy has been collected, then get back to the farm. I shall have to report it, and the farmer may ask you to move on. If you are allowed to stay, keep these two children away from the rest.'

'Yes, Doctor.'

Then he turned to Julian, who was obviously not a

gypsy, and asked, 'What are you doing here, young man?'

'I am running away from home, Sir,' came the prompt reply.

The doctor's tight mouth twitched with amusement. 'Then you had better run back, unless you want to catch scarlet fever. It's not much fun being cooped up in the Isolation Hospital for six weeks. Where do you live?'

'Russets Farm, Fairfields, Sir.'

'Can you find your way back?'

'Yes, Sir.'

'Good.'

He lifted his hand in salute and hurried away, his mind on an epidemic. It was always the same in the hop-picking season, one damn thing after another!

'Get along then, boy. You heard what the doctor said.' The man's voice was surly.

'Goodbye, then – thank you for having me.' Julian walked away slowly. When he turned to wave, they were standing there, staring after him, but they did not return the wave.

By 6 o'clock the town was crowded with shoppers, and the shop-keepers busy with their customers. Hop-picking finished at 5 o'clock on all the farms, and the women were buying provisions for the following day, with swarms of lively children. Outside the bakery, customers were queueing, for bread was still the staple diet. Nobody took any notice of a small boy in short knickers and a jersey, wandering disconsolately about the town. He was feeling lost without the gypsies, and not yet ready for the next stage of the Big Adventure. The doctor had told him to go home, but he hadn't known about the threat of boarding school, and it was too soon to go back. The gypsy man had asked no further questions, and shown no surprise in a boy running away from home, but local people would soon put him in charge of the police constable, and that would be an end to it.

He hung around the town for some time because he liked being with people, but the lonely highway still had to be faced. It was raining steadily now, and he sheltered in a shop doorway, jostled by the customers, all anxious to get back to the shelter of their huts on the farms. Noisy Cockney children chased each other in and out of the shops with coats over their heads. The irate mothers, tired after the long day in the hop-gardens, shouted and slapped, and threatened awful punishment that fell on deaf ears.

Julian could see a little group of gypsies, the women all carrying babies slung in shawls, and big flat baskets filled with loaves of bread. Their children stayed close to them, sly as little foxes, with furtive glances at the Cockney children. They avoided each other deliberately, like two strange tribes, speaking a different language, and Julian belonged to neither. He still had money in his pocket. It was a novelty to buy a pound of apples. At Russets, he had only to help himself. It was strange the way his thoughts kept drifting back to Russets.

Munching an apple in the shop doorway, he thought of Aunt Lucy, in her starched white apron, rolling out pastry for a pie. When he was little, before he started school, she always gave him a piece of dough to make little pastry men with black-currant eyes and buttons. Hot from the oven, they tasted good. Those were the days when she spared half-an-hour in mid-afternoon to read him a story. He sat on her lap in the rocking chair. It was a long time ago, and when he started school, he learned to read, and did not sit on her lap.

Standing there in the shop doorway, with the rain dripping off the sun-blind, surrounded by strangers, he thought how nice it would be if he could see just one familiar face from Russets – Aunt Lucy, Carrie, Uncle

Tom, Uncle Bertie, or even funny old Katie. They all had their own particular smell, and even with his eyes closed, he would have known who was there. When he was seven, he had pushed Aunt Lucy away, no more hugging and kissing. Now he would like it very much, just at this moment. Her arms were so warm and comforting. She was such a comfortable person to think about. And what wouldn't he give to see Grandfather riding down the street on Justin – to be swung into the saddle and to ride away, back home to Russets?

The families were drifting away now. The rain had stopped. He followed a group of Cockneys through the town to the highway. It was his first encounter with children from the East End of London. The boys were still racing about with old coats draped over their heads. They were free to run wild, while the girls were holding the hands of younger brothers and sisters, and helping to carry the shopping.

When two of the boys suddenly started a fight and rolled in the road, the rest gathered round, cheering and jeering, and a woman shouted angrily, 'Give over, nah, you two! I've 'ad just abaht enough of you for one day! Jew 'ear me? Give over, else you'll get the back of me 'and across yer chops!'

Nobody took any notice. The women and girls plodded on, leaving the boys behind. 'They calls this an' 'oliday. Blimey!' grumbled a woman with two small children dragging at her skirts.

'Cheer up, Maud! You'll soon be dead!' she was told, and they all laughed – gusty, raucous laughter, as natural as breathing.

Julian had caught up with them, and was watching the fight.

'Aw, come on Bert, else we get left be'ind and lorst,' urged Bert's younger brother.

When Bert's opponent was seen to have a bloody nose, it was all over, and they scrambled to their feet, picked up the coat, draped it once more over their heads, and appeared to be the best of friends.

''ullo, kid. Where you come from then? You lorst or something?' a boy called Sykes enquired, and they all peered out from under their coats to inspect the newcomer.

'I'm not lost. I'm running away,' said Julian, stoutly.

'Garn! You're kidding!' jeered Sykes.

'It's true, I tell you!' Julian insisted.

'What jew running away for then?'

'Because they want to send me to boarding school.'

'Boarding school? Blimey!' They looked at him with fresh interest and respect. 'You come along with us, kid. We'll look after you,' Sykes invited, draping his coat over Julian's head.

'Thank you very much,' said Julian. 'Have an apple.'

They went on their way, their heads close together, munching the apples. They had to run to catch up with the women and girls before they turned off down a narrow lane, leading to a farm and the hop-pickers' camping site. Now the boys kept close to the others, for the peace of the countryside was frightening to these city-bred children. They all were singing a popular song of Marie Lloyd's that was not familiar to Julian, but he had a shrill whistle, and he was soon joining in. It was his latest accomplishment, and he was rather proud of it, but Sykes wasn't very impressed. The voices echoed across the silent fields.

Julian was sweating under the smelly old coat, and a blister had rubbed on his heel, but he plodded on. He was not lonely any more. He had found a friend.

''oo you got there then, Sykes?' his mother asked casually, when she discovered they had collected an extra child.

'A kid what's running away from 'ome cause they want ter send 'im ter boarding school.'

'What a bloody shime. Still, you ought ter do what yer ma wants, ducks. What's yer name?'

'Julian Franklin.'

'Where yer from?'

Julian told her.

'Well, you're welcome ter stop with us, my ducks, just for the night. Termorrow you must go 'ome ter yer ma.'

'Thank you,' said Julian, gratefully. Tomorrow was another day. Anything could happen.

It was pandemonium at the camp when they all arrived back. Babies cried, dogs barked, and everyone seemed to be shouting. Grandmothers had been preparing rabbit stew, with plenty of onions, in the cookhouse.

'Come and see our canary,' Sykes invited, leading the way into one of the huts. A canary was singing cheerily in a cage suspended from a hook on the wall. 'That's our Joey. We 'as ter bring 'im, see, 'cause all the neighbours is dahn 'ere picking 'ops, an' we can't leave the poor little bugger by 'isself,' Sykes explained. 'We all 'as ter bring our pets, see? Bert's brought 'is 'amster, an' George 'as brought 'is dawg.'

This was another strange new world, as strange as the gypsies' caravan – this hut where a Cockney family lived, ate, and slept, for six weeks in the year – and brought their canary! Rolls of bedding were stacked along one side of the hut. A trestle table and benches took up most of the space. Clothes were hanging on hooks round the walls, and a hurricane lamp was suspended from the ceiling on a chain.

'We 'as this same 'ut every year. We been coming 'ere since me Gran were first married, an' she 'ad a big fambly. Me ma was one of 'er kids, see?' Sykes explained. 'They all come dahn 'ere picking 'ops. That's me Gran over by the cook'ars. The one in the sacking apron and button boots. She's a proper caution, me Gran. You ought ter see 'er on a Sat'dye night, outside the pub, doing knees up Mother Brahn. You'd bust yerself laughing!'

'Where's your father?'

'Killed in the War. Me sister Rosie, she's eight. Me Ma only 'ad us four kids. There wasn't no more time, see? Ma says if Dad 'ad lived, there would 'ave been a big fambly, one every year she reckons, for me Dad was 'ot stuff.'

Julian looked puzzled, but asked no more questions.

'Was your Dad killed in the War then?' asked Sykes, conversationally, as they waited for Gran to serve the rabbit stew.

'Nobody knows what happened to my father. He just disappeared. It's a mystery. Grandfather told me he would get a good thrashing when he came back, but it was a long time ago, and Aunt Lucy says he ought to be forgiven.'

'Where's yer Ma then?'

'She died when I was born.'

'That makes you a n'orphan, then?'

Julian nodded.

'What does it feel like to be a n'orphan?'

'It doesn't feel like anything special. I'm just me, aren't I?'

'You're a funny kid. Shall I tell yer somethink? I reckon you could be a little bastard.'

'What's a bastard?'

'Your Ma wasn't proply married, so when you was born, that makes you a bastard, see?'

'But my mother died when I was born.'

'Don't make no difference, kid.' At the age of ten, Sykes' superior knowledge left eight-year-old Julian feeling very ignorant.

'Bastard,' he repeated, and shrugged his small

shoulders. 'I shall ask Aunt Lucy,' he said.

For the second time that day, Julian was sharing a meal with strangers, but this time the family were seated all together at the table, crowded on the benches, all talking at once. Gran served the stew on to tin plates, while Sykes's mother sliced a new loaf of bread. Gran was a scraggy little woman, with a face as wrinkled as a raw prune, and no teeth, but she ate her share of the stew and the crusty bread without any difficulty. The eldest girl made a pot of tea and filled the tin mugs, while her sister collected a can of skimmed milk from the farm. There was plenty of sugar.

'What's for afters, Ma?' Sykes demanded, mopping up the gravy with a chunk of bread.

'Doughnuts and jam tarts,' said Ma, emptying two paper bags.

''elp yerself, kid,' Sykes invited.

When they had finished the meal, the women dragged the benches outside the hut, to sit with their neighbours while the girls washed up. Babies were handed round, small children climbed on to laps and went to sleep. Several old men sat on a bench, smoking clay pipes. It was a warm, friendly place. They laughed and joked and sang till it was time to spread out the bedding in the huts. The lamps would be kept alight all night, for they all were scared of the dark. One of the farm labourers had been made responsible for filling the lamps and trimming the wicks. A good supply of paraffin was kept at the farm, and piles of faggots, for the cook-house and the wash-house copper. It was a rough way to live, but they were not accustomed to luxury.

The hut was hot and stuffy, and the smell of sweaty, unwashed bodies a little distasteful to the boy from Russets, but he slept soundly on the straw mattress, wrapped in a dirty Army blanket close to Sykes.

He was wakened by the clatter of the teapot and the tin mugs on the table, and rolled over to see Gran pouring tea. Nobody wanted to move from the warm beds, but she poked and prodded and swore till she had them all sitting up, yawning and grumbling, drinking the hot, strong tea. It was only a little after 6 o'clock, but the foreman would be calling 'ALL TO WORK!" at 7 o'clock in the lower hop garden. Few of the Cockneys would be there to answer the summons.

It was Gran who sorted out the scattered clothes and sent the reluctant children to the wash-house, where they fought for a place at one of the sinks. Sykes's mother, who had been the life and soul of the party last night, was still heavy with sleep, and her temper was short. Rosie got her ears boxed for treading on her corns!

But the indomitable old woman soon had the girls busy with their early morning duties. While Molly and Rosie scuttled off to the farm for more milk and eggs, Maudie was rolling up the bedding. It was Gran who was first in the cook-house with her frying pan, and soon the savoury smell of eggs and bacon and fried bread was a signal for the eldest girl to lay the table and slice another loaf of bread.

Sykes and Julian splashed their faces in the cold water, and stood around with their hands in their pockets, waiting for their breakfast. Other grandmothers were waking their families. They seemed to be the only ones with any energy or enthusiasm for another day of hop-picking.

Now the camp was coming to life again, with crying babies, barking dogs, shouting mothers and quarrelsome children. It was damp and chilly in the early morning mist, and the children shivered in their poor garments, but were dragged off down the lane with the little ones wailing 'I wanna go 'ome!'

Sykes and his family had eaten their breakfast in gloomy silence, then Sykes muttered, 'So long, kid', disappeared through a gap in the hedge, and was gone for ever.

Soon only Gran was left, to wash the dishes, feed the canary, tidy the hut, and have a little gossip with the old men, who waited till the women and children had finished with the wash-house and the privies. They would take their time. They were old and privileged, and if they felt disinclined to pick hops, they would stay in camp, smoke their clay pipes, and wander up to the 'Rose and Crown' for a pint of beer, with bread and cheese and pickled onions.

It was quiet and peaceful in the camp with Gran and the old men, and they did not want the strange boy hanging around.

'Get along 'ome, lad. Yer Ma will be worred sick,' said Gran, tersely, lighting up a Woodbine.

'Goodbye, then. Thank you for having me.' He walked away, and she stared after him, shaking her head. 'Runned away from 'ome, the silly little bugger. I 'ope 'is Dad gives 'im a good 'iding,' she told the men. They nodded agreement.

'Kids is spoilt these days. You don't 'ardly see a Dad using 'is belt to a kid,' mused one old Grandad.

'The War changed all that. Not many of the men come 'ome dahn our way, and the women was too busy earning a living to control their kids. Nothing more than a clip round the chops if they caught the little perishers!' She pushed a strand of lank hair out of her eyes, took off the sacking apron, and smoothed her hips with a gesture as old as Eve. Who would believe she had once been a good-looking girl, with jet black hair and flashing dark eyes?

Julian went on his way, feeling a little puzzled and sad.

The gypsies and the Cockneys had welcomed him, but were glad to get rid of him. He belonged to neither. He belonged to Russets. Now he was ready to go back, and he quickened his pace. He had only to keep on walking along the highway and he would see the tall Elizabethan chimneys of the old farm house down in the valley. The blister had broken on his heel, and he was limping badly, then he remembered the handkerchief. Aunt Lucy provided a clean one every day. He sat down by the roadside and bandaged the broken heel, rather clumsily, but it was the best he could do. It still hurt, but he marched on – left, right, left, right. He was a wounded soldier now, coming home from the War. The Big Adventure was forgotten. He whistled shrilly as he marched along.

'Is Julian with you, Hetty?' asked Lucy, anxiously, when they had searched all the out-houses and called his name repeatedly in the wood.

'No, I've not seen him, Mrs Blunt.'

'He hasn't gone out with Sir Neville?'

'Not to my knowledge.'

Lucy sighed. 'He's probably hiding somewhere, just to give us a fright. He's a naughty boy!'

'I expect he will turn up when it's time for dinner, Mrs Blunt.'

'I expect so. I've never known Julian to miss a meal. You will let me know if you see him?'

'Right away, and I'll send him back.'

'Thanks, Hetty. Goodbye.'

'Goodbye, Mrs Blunt.'

'No luck?' Albert had been listening.

Lucy shook her head.

'I'll tan his backside when I do get hold of him!'

'You'll do no such thing. I won't have him whipped!'

'Spoilt little brat!'

'And who did most of the spoiling when he was little?'

'Me, I suppose.'

'Yes, you idolised him.'

'Not any more. He's just a bloody nuisance.'

'It's just mischief. Charles was the same at this age, and Julian is getting more like him as he grows up.'

'More's the pity. Anyway, Charles was sent off to boarding school when he was seven. The sooner we get that young scamp to The Firs, the better for everyone. Nothing like boarding school for strict discipline. They all have to toe the line or get a good thrashing.'

Lucy looked at her son and wondered, not for the first time, why he always had to be so aggressive. It was seven years since the end of the War – seven long years of putting up with Albert's bitterness and frustration. It was inconceivable that so little was left of that lovable younger son; he was hardly recognisable as the same person. His whole personality had changed, and his mind was distorted. That was the tragedy. They could have coped with the physical disfigurement, but not one of them could cope with his black moods and vile temper. He had to be left alone. Yet Freddie had suffered and survived. Freddie was still fundamentally the same person. But then he was still a whole man, even without the leg. He had lain with his wife and conceived a child. No, there was actually no comparison between the two men, and she loved this poor, disfigured son of hers, excused and defended him. She helped to carry his cross on her own sturdy shoulders, and acted as go-between for the two brothers and Carrie.

If only she could put back the clock. Time had not healed. Time had only destroyed their separate relationships. The eternal triangle. She could only watch and deplore a dangerous situation that was cloaked in deceit and distrust. They did not confide in her any more, not

Tom and Carrie, so she did not know if they had intercourse. She blamed herself, for she could have prevented the marriage and sent Carrie away. The girl had been sacrificed to her son's desperate need. It was too late to make amends. They all had to suffer and endure, in their own separate ways.

Her own life would hold little joy or hope without Sir Neville. He loved her now with both passion and tenderness. Since Charles went away, he needed her. A sad and disillusioned man, he found comfort in the arms of the mistress of Russets.

They sat down to dinner and tea without Julian, but only Katie was hungry. Now it was dusk, and there was still no sign of him. It was no longer a question of a mischievous prank, but a much more serious issue.

'He has run away, Aunt Lucy,' Carrie had insisted.

'Why? Why?' Lucy asked, chokingly.

'The threat of boarding school.'

'She's right,' said Tom.

'But The Firs would be different. The principal is a friend of Freddie's, and Julian would be a weekly boarder and come home at week-ends.'

'It's still a boarding school. Do you remember young Harriet? She cried for days before the start of a new term,' Tom said, remembering how he had tried to comfort the child, but she was inconsolable. 'Harriet hated boarding school, and went on hating it till her sister Agnes had left.'

'Then it could have been the fault of the domineering sister and not the school?' his mother suggested, looking from one to the other.

Both Tom and Carrie were against it, and Lucy was beginning to think it had been a mistake to mention it so early. The child had too much time to build up a hatred of the place he had not yet seen.

'But where would he *go*? I have phoned the Home

Farm, the School House, and the Forge, and he hasn't been seen at any of those places.'

'Did he have any money?' asked Tom.

'He had the half-crown from his grandfather.'

'Then he could have got as far as Tunbridge Wells?'

'On the train?'

'Yes.'

'But surely Ruby would have phoned?'

'You could check on it.'

Lucy put down her cup and saucer and hurried to the phone. She had lost count of the number of times one or the other had brewed a pot of tea during this interminable day. She was back in five minutes.

'He hasn't been there,' was all she said, but now her eyes were flooded with tears, and she slumped into a chair and covered her face with her hands. It was Tom who went to her and draped an arm about her shoulders.

'Don't cry, Mum. We'll find him,' he told her quietly.

It was so seldom that they saw her cry. She was the strong, indomitable maternal figure, always ready to listen to their troubles, or to find a remedy for their aches and pains. She had weathered the storms of family disharmony, scandal, death and sickness, as well as every farmer's perpetual anxiety over the weather that could ruin the harvest, or the dreaded foot-and-mouth disease among the cattle. She was hurt and baffled by the disappearance of the small boy she had fostered so lovingly for eight years. Her own boys had often been troublesome and careless accidents had happened that could have been prevented, but not one of them had wanted to run away from Russets.

'We must notify the police,' Albert was saying.

'The police?' It had an ominous sound. The police constable was a stranger, for they had never required his services. He was a busy man in the hop-picking season, and would have little time to organise a search for a missing child. What with farmers reporting thefts, publicans claiming his assistance at closing time, and drunken revellers to be removed from the tombstones in the churchyard, he had more than enough to contend with.

'I'll do it.' Albert was already on his feet, and Lucy nodded agreement. It was time to accept help and advice. But before he could reach the phone, it rang, and they all started towards it with mixed feelings of hope and fear. Albert waved them away impatiently and picked up the receiver.

'Hullo?' The voice that answered was easily recognisable.

'Hullo? Is your Mother there?'

'Yes, Sir.'

'I should like to speak to her.'

'I'll get her.'

She was already there, beside him, trembling and blushing, and he handed over the receiver.

'Is that you, Lucy?'

'Yes.'

'Is Julian back?'

'No.'

'Have you notified the police?'

'We were just about to do so.'

'Leave it to me. I'll attend to it.'

'Very well.'

'Don't upset yourself, my dear. We shall find him. He can't have gone far.'

'He had your half-crown. He could go a long way with half-a-crown. We thought of Tunbridge Wells, but I phoned my sister, and he hasn't been there.'

'Try not to worry. I will get in touch with you again later. Goodbye, Lucy.'

'Goodbye.' She hung up the receiver and stood there

for a long moment. She was still trembling and blushing. His voice always affected her this way.

The darkness deepened over the valley, and Lucy stood in the doorway with a prayer on her lips. Julian was afraid of the dark, and she always left his door open and a night-light burning. Albert declared it was time he had outgrown such silly nonsense, but she saw no reason why a child should be frightened into nightmares when it could be avoided. Darkness and the river, these were the two abiding fears that beset the child, but she had no remedy for the river – only, knowing his fear, to keep away. She had expected to see him back before dark. One by one the others had drifted away to bed after supper, but she had banked up the fire, and made herself comfortable in the old rocking chair that had witnessed so much sadness in the passing years. It was here she had sat, dry-eyed, on the evening of Bert's funeral, for she had no more tears to shed. It was here she sat in lonely isolation when her sons had discovered she was pregnant – and her husband dead for more than twelve months. It was here she sat and mourned for Harry, her firstborn, who went to fight for his King and Country and never came back. It was here she had settled her poor disfigured Albert, with his first cup of tea, that day he arrived back from the prisoner-of-war camp in Turkey. And here she had found Tom, slumped in sleep, with the cat on his lap, the morning after Michaelmas Day. Something had happened between Tom and Carrie coming back from the Michaelmas Fair, but they hadn't confided in her. Yes, it was mostly sadness the old chair had witnessed, till Julian arrived; then they all had shared in the joy that a baby brings into a home. Their lives had been brightened by this small scrap of humanity. Another boy-child to replace Charles. She loved her boys.

Now she was back in the rocking chair, drowsy with

memories, when the latch lifted, the door opened, and Sir Neville walked in, carrying a lantern.

'I couldn't sleep,' he grumbled, petulantly. It could have been any one of her boys standing there. He put down the lantern, and she stood up, swaying with exhaustion. He caught her in his arms and she went limp. After a moment, he dropped into the chair and pulled her on to his knees. It was a heavy load for the old chair, and the rockers creaked as they swung to and fro. They had no thought of intercourse. All their thoughts and senses were directed towards the missing child. The lover was an anxious grandfather who had lost his grandson. He held her close, the woman who had mothered the child that Charles had deserted. She was also a grandmother, but few people were aware of this close relationship.

Tonight they felt their age, and the burden of their joint responsibility. Without saying a word, they had arrived at the same conclusion. It had been a mistake to change their minds about boarding school. It had been right for Charles, because he was the only son and the heir to the estate, but not for Julian. If the village school had been good enough for Harry, Tom and Albert, it was good enough for Julian. It was the home environment, not the school, where a child's character developed, Lucy contended – and Home, for Julian, was Russets, not Marston Park. There was no comparison. It was not only a question of size. It was something unique in the very walls of the old farm. Bert's forebears could actually claim a longer pedigree than the Franklins. The Blunts had earned their inheritance by the sweat of the brow, while the Franklins had merely passed it on from father to son.

It was Bert himself who had reminded her of this one day – her dear, devoted, hard-working Bert, who never took a holiday and liked his sex as regular as his Saturday night visit to 'The Three Nuns'.

It was not often that she thought of Bert these days. This man, in whose arms she was cradled like a child, had become a part of her. Their need of each other was greater now than at any other time. Charles had betrayed them both, but it was his father who suffered most. The breach would never be healed between father and son, but a mother could forgive, and *did* forgive. That was the fundamental difference.

When the clock struck 3, they stretched and yawned. They had slept for nearly a couple of hours.

'I must go,' he said. 'There could be a message from the constable.'

'Yes, you must go.'

He cupped her face in his hands and kissed her. Then she slid off his knees and watched him take up the lantern and open the door. She was not yet ready to face the new day, and the scene had a dreamlike quality as he went on his way, the light bobbing between the trees. Then it was gone. She shivered and closed the door.

Mid-morning, and Lucy was changing the beds. It was a job she could do automatically, with her thoughts wandering and her heart aching. From time to time she went to the window, to gaze across the Park. She could hear Katie scrubbing the kitchen floor; Carrie was busy in the dairy, Tom mending a broken fence, and Albert in the orchard. Life went on. Albert was the least affected by Julian's disappearance. He had eaten a good breakfast, and told his mother bluntly, 'I'm not wasting any more time. It's a job for the police,' and gone off as usual with a flask of tea and a slice of cake for his elevenses. The poultry had become quite a profitable sideline of recent years, since Albert took it over completely. It was his one absorbing interest, and it kept him busy most of the day.

Although he still liked to see a few hens hatching out their chicks, his main concern was the incubator, where he reared the batches of day-old chicks he bought in the market. Everything was scrupulously clean. He had a little hut in the orchard where he kept the grain and the meal in bins, plucked the fowls for the market stall, and graded the eggs. It was his favourite place. He liked the smell of it, and he liked to be alone in his small domain.

Lucy had been surprised at his methodical bookkeeping. He knew exactly how much profit had been made month by month; where to expand, and where to curtail expenditure. She had no fault to find with his methods, and they left him alone with a sense of relief that he had found such an absorbing occupation.

Lucy had not mentioned to anyone that her night vigil had been shared by Sir Neville. They wouldn't understand.

She was standing at the window of her own bedroom, gazing wistfully across the Park, when she saw the small figure dwarfed by the giant trees. He was limping. She leaned out of the window, calling excitedly, 'Julian! Julian! I'm coming! I'm coming!' She flew downstairs, out the front door, and down the path. Then she was running across the grass, and he was standing there, waiting, his head hanging. She fell on her knees, gasping for breath and choked with tears, and gathered the small, limp figure to her breast.

'Where have you been? We've been worried to death.'

He shook his head, too tired to speak. He had walked all the way – a hundred miles in his eight-year-old reckoning. He was pale, and his face was streaked with tears. His clothes were dirty, and his canvas shoes worn out. A grubby handkerchief was tied clumsily round one heel.

She scooped him up, and staggered towards the house. In the kitchen, she dropped him gently into the old rocking chair.

'Tom! Carrie! Albert!' she cried from the doorway. 'He's back! Julian's back!'

Tom and Carrie came running. Albert followed more slowly. Katie had moved the pail of soapsuds, and stood there, gaping, the scrubbing brush dangling in her red, roughened hand.

'Where you bin? We bin looking all over.' She wagged her hand at him, but he took no notice. He was on Lucy's lap now, with Carrie on her knees hugging and kissing him. Tom and Albert said 'Hello' but got no answer.

'Fetch a bowl of warm water, Carrie, and bathe his foot, and bring the Zambuk,' said Lucy.

'Where have you been? You're a naughty boy,' Albert scolded.

Lucy frowned. 'Let him alone. Can't you see he's worn out?'

'Serves him right!' he retorted, and went back to the hut in the orchard.

The broken blister had stuck to the grubby handkerchief.

'I'll do it very gently,' Carrie promised, and Julian winced as it came unstuck.

Tom had picked up the discarded shoes. 'He's done a fair amount of walking by the look of these,' he told them.

'Make a pot of tea, will you Tom? We could all do with a cup,'said Lucy.

Tea, always tea! he was thinking, as he waited for the kettle to boil. Carrie emptied the bowl and refilled it with fresh water. The child lay passive, his eyes heavy with sleep while she washed his face, hands and legs. Then she held the cup to his lips, but after a few sips, his head lolled and he was asleep.

'Give him to me. I'll carry him upstairs.' Tom led the way, Lucy and Carrie followed. He did not wake when

Lucy took off his clothes and pulled on his clean pyjamas. Tucked under the bedclothes, they stood looking down at him.

'Poor little devil. Wonder where he's been in the past twenty-four hours?' mused Tom as he took Carrie's hand, and they followed Lucy down the stairs.

He slept for more than twelve hours. They had all gone to bed, but Lucy lay awake, and when she heard him whimpering, she got up and went to him.

'Well, my love, how are you feeling after that lovely sleep?' she asked.

In the faint glow of the nightlight his face looked small and peaked.

'I'm cold,' he grumbled.

'Come into my bed. It's nice and warm.' She gathered him up, carried him to her bed, climbed in beside him, and cuddled his shivering little body in her warm arms.

'You've caught a chill,' she said.

'I feel poorly.'

'Never mind, you will soon be better.'

But she had no sooner dozed off than he was whimpering again.

'I feel sick' – and his vomit was sour on his clean pyjamas and her own nightgown.

'Bless me! You really are poorly,' was all she said, for it was not the first time she had a sick child in her bed, and it wouldn't be the last. She found clean garments in the airing cupboard, gave him a drink of water, and they settled down again. But he was restless, and she slept fitfully.

When Tom and Carrie crept downstairs at 5 o'clock, she followed them down, to share the pot of tea they would be making. In the old blue dressing-gown, with her flushed cheeks and her hair hanging loose on her shoulders, she looked more like Carrie's sister than her aunt. They kissed her affectionately, and Tom poured a mug of tea. She told them about the disturbed night.

'He's proper poorly. I shall keep him in bed,' she said. 'If he is no better by tonight, I'll get you to move his bed into my room.'

They left her sitting there.

'Mum can always cope, bless her,' said Tom, as they hurried across the yard to call the cows to the milking shed.

'She's wonderful the way she just accepts everything that happens. I wish I had her mentality,' Carrie sighed.

He squeezed her hand. 'You haven't done so badly yourself, my love,' he reminded her, gently.

But Julian was feverish and tearful, so Tom carried him downstairs after breakfast, and made him comfortable in the rocking chair where Lucy could keep an eye on him. It was baking day. She wondered if Julian was sickening for something, but he had measles and chicken-pox during his first year at school. So had Harry, Tom and Albert.

From time to time she sat down and nursed him, then he fell asleep in her arms. It was so strange to see him so dependent on her when for more than a year he had been pushing her away. Now he couldn't bear her out of his sight. She still didn't know where he had spent those interminable twenty-four hours. Time enough to ask questions when he was feeling better. He was safely back, and that was all that mattered.

She had sponged him down in bed in the early morning, and she would sponge him again when Tom carried him back to bed. The house seemed to revolve around this one small boy who was sick. He had eaten nothing all day, and drank only lemonade. Lucy had no need of a thermometer to tell her the child had a temperature. It was obvious. She still thought it was a feverish chill until she discovered bright red spots on his chest. Then she phoned the doctor. She had no option. Now she put him in bed, clean and sweet-smelling in freshly laundered pyjamas. A doctor liked to find a patient in bed.

There was no hesitation in his diagnosis. 'Scarlet fever,' he told Lucy.

'Scarlet fever!' she gasped, and Julian's eyes were wide with fright.

'Have you been with the gypsies, young man?' the doctor demanded.

'Yes . . . Sir,' the child confessed, haltingly, and started to cry. 'Don't send me to the fever hospital. I don't want to go to the fever hospital,' he sobbed.

'It's not compulsory, is it, Doctor?' Lucy asked.

'No, but it's better in the long run, for you I mean. It's a matter of three weeks in bed, and another three weeks convalescence. How will you manage?'

'We shall manage.'

'He must be kept away from other children. That's important. We don't want another epidemic. So far it's confined to the gypsies.'

'I understand, Doctor.'

Julian stopped crying. Aunt Lucy wouldn't let the doctor send him away. He loved her best in all the world, and Grandfather next best. Wiping his hand across his wet eyes, he listened to the stern voice attentively.

'I want you to stay in bed, Julian, until your Aunt Lucy says you may get up. You must be a good boy and do as you are told. Three weeks is a long time for a boy to stay in bed, but you won't feel much like running about, anyway. It's a nasty complaint. You have to put up with it because it's your own fault.'

'I'm sorry, Sir.'

'So you should be. Running away from home was a stupid idea. Why did you run away?'

'I – I don't want to go to boarding school.'

'I see. Where did you spend the night? In the gypsies' caravan, I suppose?'

'No.'

'Where then?'

'In a hut.'

'Whose hut?'

'Hop-pickers.'

'Londoners?'

'Yes.'

'And they fed you, I suppose?'

Julian nodded.

The doctor's mouth was twitching with amusement. 'You won't do it again, will you?'

'No, Sir.'

'Good.' A pat on the head and he was gone. Aunt Lucy followed him out of the room, but she was quickly back.

Sitting on the edge of the bed, she smoothed the damp hair from his hot forehead and told him, quietly, 'Well, that settles it – no boarding school.'

He was choked with tears again, weak tears of relief that poured down his cheeks. He lifted his arms and hung them about her neck. Even this was an effort. Her bosom was soft and comfortable. The clock had been put back several years, when his world was small and safe.

'There now. Have a nice drink of lemonade and you will soon feel better,' coaxed Aunt Lucy. A sick child was pathetic, she thought, as he lay back on the pillows and clung to her hand.

'Don't go away. Stay with me,' he begged.

'I won't be far away, love. I will leave the door open, then you can hear me. Have a little sleep.'

He nodded, and closed his eyes. 'No boarding school – no boarding school – no boarding school.' It was beating in his head like a little drum. He sighed, and slept.

Part 4

Chapter 14

It was surprising how quickly Julian adapted to enforced isolation, and after the first week, when he felt too ill to bother about anything, he began to take an interest in the parcels that were piling up on the chest-of-drawers. To receive presents when it was not his birthday or Christmas was a novelty, but then everything was a novelty when you were kept in bed.

The threat of boarding school had been removed, and he had been forgiven for running away. Uncle Bertie was kind again, and came up every afternoon to sit with him for a couple of hours, while Aunt Lucy had a rest on the sofa in the parlour. He was teaching him to play chess, and helping to build the intricate models in the new Meccano set. Uncle Tom and Carrie waved from the doorway, but did not come into the bedroom because of infection, though Julian could not imagine the cows would catch scarlet fever. Aunt Lucy said she was glad of the afternoon rest. With a sick child in her bedroom, her nights were disturbed.

But it was not only the rest she enjoyed. It was a good opportunity for her lover to slip in quietly for a little cuddle. A short briefing on the telephone earlier in the day would ascertain whether the rest of the family would be engaged elsewhere and they would not be disturbed. Albert could be relied upon, but he was no fool, and he always knew when his mother had been entertaining her lover. She was not clever enough to hide the pleasure and excitement in her bright eyes and flushed cheeks when she carried up the tea-tray. Sir Neville was a frequent morning visitor to the sick room, and his breezy manner swept away the stuffy atmosphere. He seldom stayed for more than twenty minutes, but he always brought a present. These were second-hand, but good as new for a small boy confined to bed. Hetty had discovered toys and books that had belonged to Charles in the old toy cupboard, and persuaded Sir Neville that the gifts would be more appreciated separately, not wrapped together in one big parcel. She was a sensible woman and fond of the boy. Julian was a Franklin, and the Franklins had dominated her small world since she first arrived at Marston Park at the age of thirteen. Birth and death, marriage and separation, joy and sorrow, and the changing fortunes of the family were meat and drink to Hetty. She had sometimes wondered vaguely what would happen when Sir Neville died, but when it actually happened, on a sparkling October day of that same year, she was too shocked and stunned to speak.

They carried his body home on a hurdle, and she stood transfixed at the window, watching the sad little procession making its way across the Park. Then she groped her way downstairs to wait in the courtyard. The groom was the first to speak as they gently lowered their burden. His face was ashen.

'Something must have frightened the horse. It bolted,' he explained, jerkily.

The gardener nodded. Tears ran unchecked down his withered cheeks. These three were the only survivors of the original servants' hierarchy, and they stood looking down at the master they had served with loyalty and affection for so many years. They knew it was the end of an era, and they were not yet ready to face the future.

'Best phone the doctor, Hetty,' the groom reminded her.

She went back upstairs, like a woman walking in her sleep, and had no recollection of making the phone call, or the doctor's arrival. Her movements were automatic. She obeyed his instructions in every precise detail, because it was as natural as breathing. 'Yes, Sir–No, Sir.' Of course she understood that her master was dead. He had been thrown from his horse and broken his neck. She knew her place. The doctor must be offered a drink. She took up the decanter of whisky from the sideboard with a steady hand, and asked, 'Soda water, Doctor?'

'No, thank you Hetty. I'll have it neat,' he answered her.

After he left, she brewed up a pot of tea for the three of them, and they sat in the kitchen, still numbed with shock. The two men would have welcomed something stronger, but it did not occur to Hetty to offer it, or the men to ask. The squire was lying dead on his bed, and the door stood open, but his authority had not diminished. He was still very much alive, and they knew their place.

'I had better start phoning the family. Somebody has to break the sad news,' Hetty told her two silent companions. 'Where do I start? I feel proper flummoxed.'

The groom looked up from filling his pipe. Hetty was never flummoxed. Her stricken face was quivering.

'Steady on, old girl. You don't have to phone them all. It's not your place. Just phone Miss Cynthia at Tunbridge Wells. She will do the rest,' he reminded her, kindly.

She nodded. He was right, of course. But she would have to let them know at Russets and the other farms on the estate. She left the two men in the kitchen, smoking their pipes. The smell of the tobacco was homely and comforting. She wished she had their capacity to comfort themselves. Men were funny creatures. She knew they were already anticipating the important role they would soon be playing. Their wives would be told, then they would be on their way to 'The Three Nuns' where the customers would crowd around the bar, astounded by the tidings that Sir Neville Franklin was dead. It would spread through the village like a prairie fire.

As she picked up the telephone in the little alcove that had once been a housemaid's cupboard, she was choked with tears. The operator must have wondered what was wrong, but she would soon know when she listened in to the conversation. The telephone exchange was another extension of the grape vine.

'Hello?' It was Freddie's voice. She could never bring herself to call him Mr Simmons, and he didn't expect it. After all, they had been neighbours in Richmond Row, and spent their childhood in that rat-infested slum.

'Hello, Freddie,' she began haltingly. 'Is Miss Cynthia there?'

'Hello, Hetty. No, she's not yet back from the hospital. Is anything wrong?'

'Yes, terribly wrong.'

'What's happened? Has there been an accident?'

'Yes.'

'Sir Neville?'

'Yes.'

There was no need to ask if it was fatal. Hetty was sobbing.

'Oh, Freddie. What shall we *do*?'

'Was it a heart attack?'

'No, he was thrown from his horse. The doctor said he died instantly.'

'Where is he?'

‘Here, at Marston Park.’

‘Thank God. I’m glad for his sake. Had he lived he could have suffered brain damage, or been a permanent cripple. But it’s an awful shock for those who are left. Cynthia will be broken-hearted. They had drawn very close of recent years, since Charles went away. Try not to worry too much, Hetty. Leave everything to us. We shall be over this evening.’

‘Will you notify Miss Beatrice and Miss Sylvia, and Charles?’

‘Yes, of course.’

‘Thank you, Freddie.’

‘You will let Aunt Lucy know?’

‘Yes.’

‘Poor Aunt Lucy. She is going to be very upset.’

‘Yes.’

‘Life is strange, Hetty. She lost Uncle Bert in a similar accident. You remember the day he fell off the hay-wagon and broke his neck?’

‘I remember the lovely funeral.’

‘Yes, I suppose you could call it lovely. It was certainly very impressive.’

They both knew that Sir Neville had coveted his tenant’s pretty wife, and envied Bert Blunt his three healthy, good-looking sons. It was an open secret on the estate, and with Bert out of the way, there was no need for caution. It was inevitable that the squire would eventually claim her. Yet a whole year had passed before he bedded her, and then only once.

As they put down their receivers, Freddie and Hetty were both remembering that humiliating situation. With three healthy sons, it seemed a safe bet that Lucy would produce a fourth. Lucy had wanted a daughter to complete her own family – Bert’s family. A girl would have changed the fortunes of both families, but Charles was born, and her status established. As the mother of Sir Neville's son, she must have thought herself worthy to be his mistress, but almost immediately he took another mistress to satisfy the demands of his virile body.

Poor Lucy! The years had brought such heartache, but she had survived to know at long last that she was loved for her own sake.

Lucy was not the only one to watch Sir Neville Franklin ride away that October afternoon. Julian's illness had provided a golden opportunity for Tom and Carrie to meet and make love. In the shelter of the beech wood, they were safe from prying eyes. Albert was amusing the child, and it was Katie's half-day holiday. They could forget the rest of the world, and their nagging consciences.

They had waited a long time, and this unexpected opportunity seemed like a gift from the gods.

When the squire rode along the bridle path and tethered his horse to a tree, they were standing still as statues only a few yards away. The pungent smells of Autumn were all about them, and the sun's golden rays filtered through the branches. They were no strangers to the wood, or to each other now, and their mating had none of the desperate urgency of that night so long ago, when Tom had seduced his brother's wife, on the homeward journey from the Michaelmas Fair. They still went to the Fair, but they took Julian, and he sat between them in the trap. They belonged to each other, these two, and to Russets. This was their world, and the earth was their bed. They were so close in spirit, each was aware of the other's thoughts and unspoken words. Their love had a depth and a permanence that nothing could destroy.

So the scene was set, for Lucy and Sir Neville, and for

Tom and Carrie, when Julian succumbed to scarlet fever, and unwittingly provided a golden opportunity. But caution had been their watchword for so long, Tom and Carrie practised it automatically.

Carrie was the first to slip away to the wood, and Tom followed, discreetly, ten minutes later. He found her leaning against the grey-green bole of the tree, and in her tweed skirt and hand-made blouse, she matched her surroundings. He stood there for a long moment, gazing adoringly at the plump little figure. There was no need to hurry. Every precious moment must be savoured to the full. They both felt the same way, for she made no move towards him. Across the sun-dappled space that divided them, her blue eyes held a mischievous invitation. This was the young Carrie he thought he had lost, and when she opened her arms, he went into them. She was so like his mother, she might have been his sister, and once upon a time, before the War, he had regarded her with brotherly affection. It had been a slow awakening to the reality of their relationship. Like his mother, Carrie smelled of sweat and earth, and it was sweeter to his senses than perfume. Her short, curly hair was damp, and her mouth was damp. There was no sound in the wood but the soft rustling of the leaves as they lay together.

When Tom unfastened her blouse and pressed his lips to her breast, she trembled and smiled, while her hands rumpled his stiff, sun-bleached hair. There was no yesterday and no tomorrow, only the sweet ecstasy of surrender to that lean, hard body.

The phone was ringing as Lucy carried the tea-tray downstairs. That would be Ruby or Martha, she thought, ringing to enquire about Julian. They had phoned every day, and Martha had also sent a parcel of books that had once belonged to Philip. It was a kind gesture because they valued books at the School House, and were disinclined to part with them. Both women had shared the anxiety when the child was missing, and the joy and relief when he returned. Marion and Harriet had also phoned, so had the principal of The Firs, to acknowledge her letter. It was a pity, he said, to decide so quickly against sending Julian as a weekly boarder. Why not wait till after Christmas, and give the matter second thoughts? She had thanked him politely, but insisted they all had agreed unanimously to keep the boy at home. They had not realised he was so unhappy at the thought of boarding school, and it had been a shock when he ran away. She knew, by the tone of his voice, that he disagreed with such foolish pandering to an eight-year-old child, but she was not concerned with his disapproval. All her protective maternal instincts had been aroused, and now she would not part with her youngest until he was grown a man. He belonged to Russets.

As she put down the tray and took up the receiver on this bright October day, she was a happy woman. They had made love on the parlour sofa, and her lord had complained that it cramped his style! He was an impatient lover, but she did not keep him waiting, for her own strong body trembled with desire, and he entered her almost immediately. She had always been a sensual woman, but when she was deprived of sex – as her lord had deprived her, once she had borne his son – then she had found a certain satisfaction in maternity. Though not entirely. There had been so many nights when she could not sleep, and her tortured body had craved for a man who was not her husband.

'Why have I wasted so many years with other women when you were here? Not one of them could hold a candle to my Lucy,' he told her, as he kissed her goodbye.

Why had she no premonition that would be his last kiss, and those his last words? she would ask herself repeatedly in the days and weeks and months that had no meaning and no purpose now her lord was dead.

Hetty had not meant to blurt it out with such devastating suddenness, but the poor woman was sobbing and distraught.

'Is that you, Lucy? There's been an accident . . . Sir Neville is dead.'

She could not answer. No words came. She hung up the receiver and hugged her plump, warm body, moaning with unbearable anguish.

'What's the matter, Mum? What's happened?'

It was Albert, standing over her, his hand on her shoulder. She shook her head. Her eyes swam with tears.

'What's happened? Tell me.'

She stared at him as though he were a stranger. It was the child's voice that captured her stunned senses. He was calling her.

'Aunt Lucy . . . Aunt Lucy.'

But she could not go to him, not yet.

'Tell him . . . tell him I'm feeling poorly. I'll be up later.'

'You were all right a few minutes ago. Who was that phoning? What's upset you?'

She gave him a little push. 'Go back to Julian, *please*.'

'Not till you tell me what's wrong.'

'That was Hetty. There's been an accident.'

'Sir Neville?'

'Yes.'

'Killed?'

'Yes.'

'My God!'

For years he had hated Sir Neville, and blamed him for the split in the family. His half-brother, Charles, had been a constant reminder, and he was jealous of the child who had supplanted him in his mother's affections. It was not his nature to forgive, and he couldn't pretend to grieve for that arrogant man at the Big House. Born into the privileged society, he had had no conception of the deprivations of the tenant farmers and the working class. They said he was a good landlord, but his tenants had not dared to speak a word against him.

Now his own mother was weeping for her lover, and Albert was nauseated by her tears. He could not comfort her. He turned away, and went back upstairs.

When Carrie came away from the wood and left Tom to take another path back to the milking shed, she met Albert, laboriously climbing the steep bank, and her heart raced with fear. What was he doing here? Had they forgotten the time and stayed too long? He was scowling, and he greeted her with the surliness that was usually the prelude to a black mood.

'Where have you been?' he demanded. 'I've been looking all over for you.'

'Just walking in the wood. It was such a lovely afternoon.'

He was staring at her suspiciously, but if he noticed her crumpled blouse and flushed cheeks he made no comment.

'I've got news for you,' he said, blocking her path. And he told her, with a kind of sadistic pleasure, as though he enjoyed the telling.

'Dead?' she echoed, her eyes wide with shock. 'Oh no!' It couldn't be true, yet why should Bertie lie? 'Does Aunt Lucy know?'

'Of course. She told me.'

'Where is she?'

'In the kichen, crying her eyes out for that bloody arrogant bastard!'

'How can you talk that way? She loved him.'

'Love?' he sneered. 'He took what he wanted, when it suited him.'

'You always hated him, didn't you?'

'You bet I did!'

'I must go to her.' She pushed past him, scrambled down the bank, ran across the yard, and into the kitchen. Lucy was huddled in the rocking chair. Her hands covered her stricken face. She was distraught and sobbing wildly. Carrie flung herself down and buried her face in her lap. She wept for the woman who had given so much, and received so little. And she wept for the man who had wasted so many years in a restless search for happiness when it was here all the time, at Russets.

'What's the matter? Why are you crying?' asked a small voice. Julian was standing in the doorway, a forlorn little figure in flannelette pyjamas, with eyes too big for his peaky face.

Lucy choked on a sob and sat up. 'Come here to me, my love,' she said, holding out her arms.

Carrie was on her feet, heading for the door. They must not forget the quarantine period was only half way through. She waved and smiled wanly, then she was gone.

Julian cuddled into the warm, comfortable arms, forgetting he was a big boy of eight. Julian was the go-between in the family. He had played the role, unwittingly, since he first arrived at Russets, and Albert had claimed him. Later there were the two brothers and the antipathy between them, yet both adoring the child. Recently, almost without knowing what he was doing, he often warned Carrie and her dear, devoted Tom of Albert's whereabouts. It was a game he played only partially aware of the danger to Carrie, but always on her side. According to Katie, Uncle Bertie was a devil, but he could be quite nice when he felt in a good mood. Staying in bed wasn't such a punishment when an uncle kept you company every afternoon, and played chess. But suddenly the mood had changed. What had happened to upset everyone? He wanted to know.

'Grandfather has promised to take me to the Zoo when I'm better,' he told Aunt Lucy, conversationally.

She made no answer, and when he looked up, her eyes were brimming with tears again, and her mouth quivering. It was always a shock to see a grown-up crying, and a little embarrassing.

'You can borrow my hankie if you like,' he offered.

She smiled through her tears. The handkerchief smelled strongly of plasticine. Grandfather had brought the box of plasticine only this morning. 'It belonged to your Uncle Charles, like all the rest of the stuff I've been bringing over. He's messed it up, I see, but I expect you can sort it out. Too many toys, too much of everything when he was your age, Julian. A spoilt little brat, that son of mine. Spare the rod and spoil the child. I should have given him a good thrashing,' he growled.

'Like my father when he came back, only he didn't come back, did he, Grandfather?'

'No, he didn't come back,' he lied, and wondered how soon the child would learn the truth.

'Have you caught the scarlet fever, Aunt Lucy? Is that why you are crying?' Julian asked innocently.

How did one tell a child that his beloved grandfather was dead?

'No, It's not that, love.'

'What, then?'

'I've had bad news.'

He waited. He was looking very puzzled. It must be very bad, he thought, for so much crying. It must be someone very important – as important as Grandfather?

'It's Grandfather, isn't it?'

She nodded tremulously.

'I don't want Grandfather to be dead,' he whispered.

She hugged him to her breast and rocked gently, to and fro, to and fro.

'Julian.' It was Tom calling quietly from the doorway. He was holding a squirming little puppy, and he set it down on the kitchen floor. It ran straight to Lucy, and she scooped it up and gave it to Julian. Gulping back a sob, he asked, 'Can I keep it, Uncle Tom?'

'Yes, you can keep it.'

'What's its name?'

'It hasn't got a name. You think of one.'

The puppy was licking the child's wet cheeks. It had a white blob of a nose, a black body, and four white paws. The bitch, Ruby, had given birth to a litter of four pups the day Julian ran away.

'Is it a boy or a girl?' he asked Uncle Tom.

'A boy.'

'Then I'll call him Jasper. He looks like a Jasper, doesn't he?'

Tom agreed. He was glad to see the child diverted. An animal, especially a young animal, could often succeed where a human failed.

'He won't catch my scarlet fever, will he?' Julian asked anxiously.

'No, dogs don't get scarlet fever. He's really too young to be taken away from his mother, so you must take good care of him.'

'What does he like to eat?'

'Bread and milk, and you could try him with a little mashed potato and gravy. Only a small amount because he's only a baby. I think he is ready for his tea.'

'Thank you, Tom,' said Lucy gratefully, as Julian slid off her lap. She could always depend on Tom.

'Carrie has started on the milking. See you later, Mum.'

'I'll have tea ready when you are finished.'

'Thanks.' They exchanged a sad fleeting smile, then he was gone.

When she had poured the warm milk over the fragments of bread in a deep saucer, she gave it to the child, and he knelt on the hearthrug, watching the puppy. He looked very small and defenceless, kneeling there, and she was worried that he had lost so much weight during his illness. Children soon picked up again once they are back on normal food, she reminded herself. But she went upstairs to fetch his dressing-gown and slippers, for she couldn't risk a chill at this stage. He did not mention his grandfather again. All his attention was focussed on the puppy. They played together on the floor, but Julian quickly tired, and they settled down in the rocking chair. When it was time to get tea for the rest of the family, Lucy sent him away upstairs. It had always been a strict ruling at Russets that no animals were allowed upstairs.

'You mean I can take him to *bed*?' The child was puzzled.

'Just for a treat while you are poorly. He can keep you company. I shall be busy this evening. Off you go. I'll be up later with your supper.'

'And Jasper's supper?'

'Yes.'

He was deceived into thinking she was feeling better, but it was not the first time she had had to control her own distress for the sake of a sensitive child. He went obediently back to bed, and she could hear him talking to the puppy. Now she went to close the parlour door. It would be a long time before she could bear to rest on that sofa. A long time before she would forget her lord complaining that it cramped his style.

Life went on. He was gone, but she was not alone. She still had Tom, Carrie, Albert, Julian and Katie, all needing her, all dependent on her. No, she was not alone. Only so desperately lonely. There was all the world of difference.

She had no time to set the table, however. The phone was ringing, and it went on ringing, intermittently, all the evening – Ruby, Martha, Marion, Harriet, Cynthia and Philip. She spoke to Ruby and Cynthia, but left Carrie and Tom to cope with the rest. Then, in the early hours of the morning, as she lay dry-eyed and spent with her grief, the phone was ringing again. It was Charles. He had received Cynthia's cablegram. His voice was so like his father's, she was choked with emotion, and could only answer him briefly. He told her he was terribly shocked and saddened by the tragedy. He had spoken to Sylvia on the phone, and they would be travelling over together for the funeral.

'It's the end of an era, Mother. I wonder what will happen to Marston Park?'

'I don't know, Charles. We must wait and see.'

It did not seem to matter. It was Russets, not Marston Park that had become the focal point of the estate since the War, and it was at Russets, not Marston Park, where the squire had enjoyed a measure of happiness.

'Goodbye, darling. Take care,' her son was saying.

'Goodbye, dear.'

She hung up the receiver. The sense of irretrievable loss was accentuated in this brief reminder of a breach that could never be healed. It was too late.

It was the first time in years that the three Franklin sisters had met. And there would be no grandchildren to pay their respects. Beatrice had refused to bring her own daughters because of the danger of infection. Wendy would be kept at home with Ruby for the same reason, and Julian was still in quarantine.

Charles arrived with Sylvia and her husband the day before the funeral. He was very quiet and subdued. With this sad gathering in the old home, Hetty was very conscious that it could be the last occasion when she served the Franklins at Marston Park. Lucy saved the strained situation by keeping an open house and a warm welcome at Russets. The farm kitchen was a homely place where they could sit and chat and drink tea.

With the main part of the Big House closed and shuttered, and only the flat to accommodate the visiting members of the family, it seemed very strange and restricted. There would be no more country holidays for the children from the East End of London. It was indeed the end of an era.

It had been left to Cynthia and Freddie to arrange the funeral, and they arrived, as promised, that same evening, so Hetty was not alone. She was kept busy catering and cooking for the family, and serving refreshments to the stream of callers.

In his own small world, Sir Neville Franklin had been the uncrowned king, and his sudden death had an impact on the whole village and all classes of society. Shops would be closed on the day of the funeral, and the school children marched to church to join the rest of the mourners in the packed congregation – the boys wearing black arm bands, the girls black hair ribbons. Farm labourers, servants, tradesmen and housewives, all would be there in their respective places. The sidesmen, acting as ushers, would know where they belonged and there would be no confusion. The upper class had their reserved seats in the centre aisles, as always, and visiting gentry would be accommodated according to their status. The choir had been instructed to attend in clean, starched surplices, and the organist informed of the special hymns and anthem.

The bishop would officiate, assisted by Parson. The flag would fly at half-mast on the flagpole, and the church bell tolled all day, as it tolled at the passing of the old Queen in the early days of the century. The cortege would make its slow and solemn way across the Park and through the village, flanked by tenants and the surviving servants. At the rear of the procession, the groom would lead Sir Neville's handsome black stallion. Nothing had been forgotten. It would be a memorable occasion, an impressive reminder of a day and age lost for ever in the changing world.

Young Julian, confined to the bedroom with his puppy, could hear all the comings and goings down below. From time to time someone would climb the stairs, call a greeting, and leave a package outside the door. It was fun to tear off the wrapping and see the puppy tossing it about the room. Aunt Lucy had changed his pyjamas and brushed his hair. The visiting aunties would have liked to give him a cuddle, but it was not allowed. He hardly recognised Aunt Lucy in the black clothes, smelling rather strongly of moth-balls, and Uncle Tom in his best suit and bowler hat. Only Albert would remain behind, but then he had no wish to attend the funeral.

From the attic window, Julian could watch the cortege crossing the Park. It was hard to imagine Grandfather in a coffin piled with wreaths. He was not that kind of person, and he would hate all the fuss. Grandfather should be riding the big black stallion.

'I don't want him to be dead,' he told Jasper, with a lump in his throat.

'Julian! Come on down! You'll get cold up there.' Uncle Bertie was calling, authoritatively.

Julian came down slowly, carrying the puppy. He was wondering if his uncle was in a better mood and whether they would play chess. 'You mustn't worry your Uncle

Bertie,' he had been reminded again and again.

A fire was blazing in the small grate. A pot of tea and a plate of buttered toast stood waiting in the hearth. There was a lovely smell of apple wood and toast.

'Surprise, eh?' Uncle Bertie was grinning cheerfully. He was still wearing his old clothes, and had no intention of changing. Nobody had been able to persuade him to pay his respects to a man he positively disliked and despised. It would be hypocritical to pretend, he maintained stubbornly. And nobody could be more stubborn than Albert.

'Is it tea-time, then?' Julian wanted to know.

'Any time is tea-time. We suit ourselves.'

It was a strange sort of day, with no regular meal times, and no proper dinner, only scrambled eggs and a small dish of jelly. Now they were having tea in the middle of the afternoon, and a fire in the bedroom on a warm October day. Uncle Tom called it St Luke's Summer, but couldn't explain why it was St Luke's. Why not St Matthew's or St Mark's?

They squatted together on the hearth-rug. Uncle Bertie poured tea into two mugs, and filled Jasper's saucer with milk. It was very cosy, and the toast was nice and buttery, but Julian was still thinking of Grandfather.

'Uncle Bertie, what does it feel like to die?' he asked.

His uncle frowned thoughtfully. 'I guess it's just like going to sleep and not waking up,' he hazarded.

'Could I go to sleep and not wake up?'

'You could, but you won't.'

'Why?'

'Because you are young, and your heart is strong.'

'Did Grandfather know he was going to die?'

'That's a difficult question to answer. It happened so suddenly, in a split second. Nobody will ever know what frightened the horse.'

Julian sighed. 'Grandfather promised to take me to the Zoo when I'm better.'

'I'll take you if you like.'

'You?'

'Why not? We could take Carrie.'

'Thank you.'

'You're welcome.'

It was settled. Everyone said 'You're welcome'. Well, not quite everyone. Grandfather, Auntie Cynthia and Auntie Harriet said 'It was a pleasure'. That's because they were gentry. He remembered how Hetty had answered his question one day.

'Am I gentry, Hetty?'

'Not exactly, Julian. Sort of half and half.'

He was puzzled. 'Why?'

'Because we know for certain that your Mother was gentry, but we don't know about your father,' she had explained carefully. It made Hetty feel uncomfortable when the child questioned her about his parents. She wished the truth had never been divulged.

'If I was all gentry, and not half and half, I would have to go to boarding school, wouldn't I?'

Uncle Bertie turned his scarred face to grin at the child.

'You're a funny kid,' he said. 'What do you mean by half and half?'

'My Mother was gentry, wasn't she?'

'Yes.'

'But nobody knows who my father was?'

'That's true.'

'Well, then?'

'It doesn't signify.'

'What does that mean?'

'Your Uncle Charles was only half gentry, but he didn't escape the system so easily – prep school, public school, university, the lot.'

'Nobody ever told me Uncle Charles was only half and half. Who was his mother then?'

'Your Aunt Lucy.'

'*Aunt Lucy*?'

'Yes, I thought you knew.'

Julian shook his head. 'Grandfather was married to Aunt Lucy? She was his wife?'

'No, they were not married.'

'Why?'

'Because your Aunt Lucy is working class.'

'If Aunt Lucy *was* married to Grandfather, then she would be my Grandmother, wouldn't she?'

'That's right.'

'It's such a muddle, Uncle Bertie.'

'Not really. It's quite simple. If I were you, I wouldn't worry about the gentry part. You belong here, at Russets. You belong to the working class. Get your priorities right when you are young, and there won't be any confusion. Your Uncle Charles made a hash of it, with a foot in each camp, but he wasn't to blame. Your grandfather had the last word on everything, and his word was law. It was cruel to take his son away from Russets at the age of seven, and from thereon he had to regard Marston Park as home. It broke your Aunt Lucy's heart. I could have killed him for making her so unhappy.' He threw another log on the fire and it blazed afresh. The puppy climbed back into Julian's lap, watching the sparks fly upwards.

'It was a long time ago, but I have never forgiven your grandfather, and I never will,' Uncle Bertie insisted.

'Aunt Lucy cries every night now Grandfather is dead. It makes me feel sad,' said Julian, cuddling the puppy.

'I know what you mean,' Uncle Bertie agreed, sympathetically. 'I felt the same way when my father was killed, and I heard your Aunt Lucy crying in the next room. I was a big boy then, much bigger than you, but I crept into her room and got into bed with her. We both cried together, then she felt better, and she went downstairs to make a cup of tea. Then we went to sleep. She told me I was a great comfort to her at the time. So you take my advice, Julian, and get into bed with her tonight, for she's going to be very upset after the funeral. Now, put the puppy down, and get out the chess-board. You beat me yesterday, so I have to take my revenge!'

Julian nodded. The time slipped away quite pleasantly, till they heard the car returning, and voices in the courtyard. A few minutes later, Aunt Lucy came upstairs and seemed pleased to find them still engrossed in the game. She kissed them both, took off her hat, and smoothed her hair.

'Did everything go according to plan?' asked Albert, quietly.

'Yes.' Her eyes were bright with unshed tears, and her mouth trembled, but she braced her shoulders bravely. 'I must go,' she told them. 'Life goes on, doesn't it? And all these people have to be fed.'

'Have they all come back here?'

'No, the family have gone back to the Big House to hear the Will read. It shouldn't take long. Hetty will give them tea, and they will join us here later in the evening. All our neighbours are here, as anxious as we are to know about the Will.'

Their farming neighbours on the estate were worried about the future. Lucy had said her last goodbye to her lord. It seemed like a bad dream, but her commonsense reminded her it was no dream, but cold, stark reality. She smiled at her son and the child, a sad, wistful smile, and repeated, 'I must go. Katie goes all to pieces in any emergency. She can't help it, poor thing. It's all ready in the pantry, and Martha is putting on the kettle. Tom and

Carrie have slipped away for milking, and the men are putting out the trestle tables and benches in the yard. It's too warm in the kitchen.'

'Can I help?'

Lucy was surprised at the question. Albert never volunteered to help in any other job but with the poultry, and it wasn't expected.

'We shall manage, thank you, dear. Finish your game, Will you join us later?'

He shook his head. 'There's a job waiting for me in the orchard.'

'As you wish.' She collected the tray, gave the child a warm hug, and left the room.

When they had finished the game, Albert crept down the back stairs. Katie was crying in the scullery. He slapped her fat buttocks with a hard hand, and growled, 'Stop snivelling, Kate. Get into the kitchen and help your mistress. Do you hear me?'

'Yes, Mister Albert.'

She remembered a time when he liked to lift her skirts. He was a very sexy man, and she was a sexy woman, so she could never understand why he hadn't lain with her in the barn, or in the wood. She was willing, all those years ago, and she was still willing. She could always find a man on market day, however, and a place to lie together. It hadn't been a very comfortable position, hanging over the scullery sink!

She was giggling at the memory as she mopped her wet eyes on her clean starched apron.

In the glow of the lanterns, all the faces had a strange, earthy beauty, Cynthia was thinking, as Freddie pushed open the farm gate. Apart from Martha and Andrew, Harriet and Philip, these people were her father's tenants

– 'the salt of the earth', he had called them, for he was sentimental over his own people, and regarded them as a sacred trust. Only the men and women were here tonight. The children had been kept away because of infection. Measles and chicken pox could be expected in most families in all classes of society, but scarlet fever was a scourge, usually confined to the poorest of the working class.

All the tenants were dressed in their Sunday best, and they gave the cobbled courtyard an air of unreality. It was like a scene from a play or a film, and the solemn faces and gestures were reflected in the lantern light as in a mirror. The tenants rose from the table in a body, respectful but not subservient in the presence of their betters. It was instinctive, and as natural as breathing, this respect. Martha and Andrew, Harriet and Philip stood up for politeness' sake. Their sense of belonging to the Marston Park estate was developed over the years by their love for Russets, not inherited. Only two were missing – Albert and Charles. The one had chosen to be absent from the gathering because of a stubborn resentment of the archaic system – the other, because he could no longer claim the privilege of belonging, so he went away, shamed and saddened.

'Good evening,' they said, gravely, one to the other, and shook hands, with little nods of recognition and a few well-chosen words. The tenants remained standing till the daughter of Sir Neville Franklin bade them be seated, and when they had closed ranks, there was room for all on the benches. The visitors were served with tea or home-brewed cider, according to taste, and all were remembering the man who had ruled their lives.

A law unto himself, arrogant and domineering, but just and honourable in his relationships with his own people.

After a while, when all had been said regarding the

funeral, a brief silence was broken by Cynthia, who stood up and glanced about the familiar upturned faces with a warm smile. Beatrice was the eldest, but almost a stranger now. She was her mother's daughter, enjoying her role as a semi-invalid, and so she left it to her younger sister to speak on behalf of the family. Sylvia, too, was almost a stranger, but her shyness and her quiet manner had an endearing quality. As for the young Penelope, also in their thoughts tonight, she had not lived to see her child growing up at Russets. Julian's father had never been traced, so they said, but there were ugly rumours in the village that the bitter quarrel between Sir Neville and his son had some connection with the affair. Be that as it may, the child had inherited the breeding and distinction of the Franklins.

All eyes now turned to the slim, girlish figure in her tailored suit of grey gaberdine, and a neat matching hat.

'My friends and neighbours,' she began, in her clear, cultured voice, 'I know you are waiting anxiously to hear how my father's Will reflects on your own individual lives. I can put your minds at rest, here and now. In due course you will be hearing from the solicitors, and all the legal formalities will be observed. In the meantime, I am happy to tell you that all tenants on the estate, both farmers and cottagers, become the freehold owners of their rented properties as from today.'

A great sigh of relief and a heartfelt 'Thank you' burst spontaneously from a dozen throats. Once more they were on their feet shaking hands, and now they were smiling and happy, their eyes bright with fresh hope and the promise of continuity for their children, and their children's children.

Freddie kissed his wife's cheek and took her hand. It was a wonderful moment. Then Lucy asked the question they all were dying to ask.

'What happens to the Big House? Who will be living there?'

Cynthia answered her quietly. 'It will be sold, together with the acres of parkland, the outbuildings and stables. It will probably be converted into a school, for it's too big for any other purpose.'

'It will seem strange.'

'Yes, I'm sorry, but changes are inevitable.'

Lucy nodded mutely. For her, the promise of continuity for Russets and her sons was marred by her own personal loss.

When they had split into small groups, and were talking amongst themselves, she spoke to Cynthia again, privately.

'Where's Charles?'

'He left soon after the Will was read. There was no mention of him, and it must have been a shock. Perhaps you did not realise I knew? The others were astonished. You see, it had always been assumed that Charles was the heir.' Cynthia lowered her voice. 'Beatrice and Syliva have no idea what the quarrel was about. As far as I'm concerned, and you and Hetty, they need never know. The chapter is closed. Charles seems to enjoy living in the States, and he is obviously not short of money, so I shouldn't let it worry you too much.'

Lucy smiled, wanly. How could Cynthia understand the feelings of a mother who had lost another son? Only by the merest chance would she see him again. If he behaved himself, he would inherit a sizeable fortune from the wealthy mistress who was old enough to be his mother – according to Sylvia's husband. But would he tire of her, or she of him? Life was so unpredictable with Charles.

'We three surviving daughters and the grandchildren are the joint beneficiaries. The grandchildren will receive their legacies at the age of twenty-one,' Cynthia explained. 'The three servants still in the Franklin employ, that is Hetty, the groom and the gardener, each receive an annuity of £200. The retired servants, including our old nurse, already have annuities. There's a donation of £500 to the church, and smaller donations to the British Legion Club, the Village Hall, and the Village School. That's all. It was very concise, and no complications, so it should be settled reasonably soon. The villa in France and the shooting lodge in Scotland were sold some years ago, apparently. Father didn't mention it, but then he was not very close to his daughters as you know, so I suppose he thought it was not our concern. Poor darling.' She was struggling to control her tears. A Franklin does not cry in public. That strict nursery training made a lasting impression. She could see her sister Beatrice was wilting. It had been an emotional and exhausting day. They must get her to bed as soon as possible.

For the third time they all were shaking hands. The formality was customary with the upper class. The tenants, who had recently acquired the status of property owners, were not demonstrative. They met and parted with nothing more than a brief 'Hello there' and 'So long'. Sir Neville Franklin had always shaken their hands whenever they met, and his little daughters had been trained to offer their tiny hands, since nursery days.

Lucy hung over the gate with Tom and Carrie. Cynthia and Freddie kissed her affectionately. Martha and Harriet had started to clear the tables, a drowsy Katie was sent off to bed. The men cleared the courtyard of tables and benches, then the tenants dispersed gradually in their traps or on foot.

Martha and Andrew, Harriet and Philip were the last to leave on their bicycles. The lights flickered between the trees, then they were gone, and the sudden silence was eerie and infinitely sad.

Albert had gone to bed, and Julian had fallen asleep hugging the puppy. While Tom extinguished the lanterns, Carrie made another pot of tea and they sat there together, talking quietly, Lucy in the rocking chair, and Tom and Carrie holding hands, till the grandfather clock struck 12.

In the early hours of the morning, Julian was awakened by muffled sobbing. Still drowsy with sleep, he crept across the room and climbed into Aunt Lucy's bed. Warm arms received him gratefully. Their tears mingled on their hot cheeks. So they comforted each other, even as Albert had predicted.

Chapter 15

For Hetty O'Brien, the day of the auction at Marston Park was a personal indignity. Hordes of strangers – and most of them out of sheer curiosity – had been viewing the previous day, and she shuddered at the desecration of the beautiful furniture she had polished with such diligence and energy in the years as housemaid, the years when her superior would remind her brusquely, 'A little less polish and a lot more elbow-grease, my girl!' Valuable pictures, porcelain, china and silver, she knew every precious piece.

Spring-cleaning had lasted for six weeks every year, an orgy of cleaning by housemaids and footmen. When the house was converted into a convalescent home for officers in the early days of the War, most of these valuable objects had been put into store, and had remained there when the Association for Country Holidays for Deprived Children took over the house at the end of the War. The flat had been carefully and tastefully furnished for the family, and the three daughters had each selected their favourite pieces for their own homes. Hetty had been invited to choose a memento from the flat, and had selected a pair of Grecian vases, much prized by her late Ladyship but despised by the rest of the family.

'I'm glad to see the back of those hideous monstrosities!' Cynthia confided to Freddie.

Hetty was amazed at the cool manner in which Miss Cynthia inspected all the various 'lots' that had been prepared for the Auction.

'It has no value for me now, my darling, without the family, and it's no longer a home,' she overheard.

But Mister Freddie was quietly deploring such a sad ending to the Franklin estate. As for Hetty, her small world had collapsed on that bright October afternoon when they carried home the body of her master on a hurdle. She had moved through the days with the automatic precision of a well-trained servant attending to the comfort of the family. In spite of the annuity – and £200 a year for the rest of her life was generous and totally unexpected – the future was bleak. 'Service' had been her way of life since she left the village school, and she had expected to serve the Franklins till her own retirement. A number of old retainers were living in cottages on the estate, and had always paid a small rent of half-a-crown weekly because it gave them a sense of independence. Now they had become the proud owners of their cottages, and Hetty envied them. She was not yet forty, young enough to start a new chapter with a new family, but she had no heart for it. The War had changed everything. The gentry was a dying race, and the new rich the ruling class. Hetty would find them vulgar and ostentatious. The good old days were gone for ever.

The two Franklin daughters, Miss Beatrice and Miss Sylvia, had departed for their respective homes, leaving Miss Cynthia and her husband to cope with agents and auctioneers, and all the paraphernalia of disposing of the house and its contents. Miss Cynthia had always been her favourite, and when she had married into the working class, Hetty had been shocked, for Freddie Simmons had been a close neighbour in Richmond Row, and a fellow pupil at the village school. But it was a happy marriage with no regrets.

With the house open to the public the day before the auction, Hetty stood by in her kitchen, waiting to serve drinks and make tea and coffee to prospective buyers. Mister Freddie sat on the terrace, working on some papers for most of the day. It was a mild November. Hetty had served an early breakfast in the dining-room, and when she went back to clear the table, she was invited to sit down.

'We were wondering, Hetty, if you had made any plans?' Miss Cynthia asked, kindly.

'No, Miss Cynthia. That is to say, Lucy has suggested that I stay at Russets until I find another situation, but I think it might be better to stay with my friend in Tunbridge Wells, then I could visit the public library and look for vacancies in the local papers. I wouldn't want to go right away. I should feel lost.'

'If we had a bigger establishment, Hetty, you would not need to look elsewhere. You would come to us. But we are perfectly happy in our little house at Tunbridge Wells, and of course we have my mother-in-law living with us. Yes, it would seem to be a sensible plan to stay with your friend. We could keep in touch. I will give you our phone number, then any prospective employer could contact us for a testimonial.'

'Thank you, Miss Cynthia.'

'There *is* an alternative to domestic service, Hetty, that might suit you, and that would be to open a domestic agency in Tunbridge Wells.'

Hetty looked puzzled.

'All you need is a small office, a telephone, a filing cabinet, and several chairs, and an advertisement in the weekly press. With all your experience, Hetty, you would know exactly what qualifications to look for, and who to recommend. We would back you, my husband and I, and help you to find suitable premises. What do you say? Does it appeal to you? It's just a suggestion. We don't want to interfere.'

'But it's not interfering, Miss Cynthia. It's very kind of you and Mister Freddie to bother. To tell you the truth, I do feel rather depressed at the thought of working for another family.'

'That's understandable, Hetty. It has been a long time, hasn't it?'

'Since I was thirteen, Miss Cynthia, when the housekeeper engaged me as fourth housemaid. I was proud as Punch!'

They smiled at her with affection. Hetty was almost the last link with the days of the servants' hall and the strict protocol of the servants' hierarchy.

'Only the new rich can afford residential servants these days, Hetty,' Cynthia explained. 'They have to offer high wages and plenty of free time. You will find your agency catering for a new type of servant called "daily helps" and "Mother's helps" and "*au pairs*".'

'What's that, Miss Cynthia?'

'Foreign girls who wish to perfect their English, and are willing to help with the children and light housework. They are allowed a work permit for twelve months. Girls from Switzerland and Sweden are the most popular, I understand. If they registered at your agency, you would find them suitable employment.'

Hetty still looked a little dubious. 'Could I manage it, Miss Cynthia? Do *you* think I could manage it?'

'Yes, I do. Think it over, Hetty.'

It had been arranged for a team of women from the village to clean through the empty house. They would be transported by lorry, paid by the hour, provided with a substantial dinner, and as many cups of tea as they could drink. Hetty would supervise the whole operation. Her brother Lennie arrived, unexpectedly, one morning to collect all the 'junk' thrown out in the stables.

In the intervening years since they had last met, Lennie had prospered in his own particular sphere. He now employed two Cockney lads with the gift of the gab, one for the market stall in Soho, the other for Petticoat Lane, while he personally collected the junk from all over London in a horse and cart. He often found valuable articles among the junk that fetched a good price on the stalls.

The immaculate Hetty was ashamed of the scruffy looking individual who greeted her in the rough language of Richmond Row, and revived many old memories. She did not intend to introduce him to the village women, but he was quickly recognised, so she felt obliged to invite him to the kitchen to share the dinner she had prepared. In her own sphere among high-class servants, Hetty was a snob, and she listened to the lewd jokes and raucous laughter with a straight face and disapproving manner that only added fuel to Lennie's glib tonguc. She had lost touch with her family, and there was no sense of loyalty to her own blood relations. She liked to feel she belonged to the Franklins, not the O'Briens, and she had risen through the ranks of servants to the coveted status of housekeeper solely by her own dedicated application to her duties, her cheerfulness and politeness.

'Who told you about the auction at Marston Park?' she demanded.

'Wouldn't you like to know, old girl!' he teased. He was cunning as a fox, her brother Lennie. Even as a boy at the village school he knew how to make money. Little girls, like Carrie Simmons, who couldn't bear to have him fiddling under their drawers, were obliged to pay a halfpenny for the privilege of being unmolested.

She watched him drive away in the piled cart on the first stage of the long trek back to London, with a sigh of relief, and went back to her kitchen to brew more tea for the women.

Only the kitchen and Hetty's bedroom were still furnished, and Cynthia had telephoned from Tunbridge Wells with a further inducement to start the domestic agency. They would find suitable premises so that she could furnish a bed-sitting-room and a kitchen adjoining the office. It would be more economical, and she would enjoy complete independence.

For a woman who had never known independence, it was rather overwhelming, and she still needed some assurance from her own kind before embarking on such a venture. By the time she had finished chatting to Ruby on the telephone that evening, Hetty was almost convinced that she would be a fool to turn down such an exciting project.

'Your evenings would be free, love, and all your weekends. Your friends could visit you in your own little home, and Tunbridge Wells is a lovely town,' Ruby had pointed out sensibly.

During that long dreary week, listening to the clatter of buckets and inspecting the freshly scrubbed floors, Hetty turned the project over and over in her mind. It was a challenge, but would she find such a challenge beyond her scope? In her formal black dress and starched white apron she was at ease. It was impossible to visualise such a future. No more 'Yes, Madam', 'No, Madam', 'Certainly, Sir.' It was true she had not worn a cap of recent years, but she could well remember a time when she had curtsied to her betters. This new chapter in her life would be revolutionary.

She was still undecided when the women had finished

their work at the end of the week, and departed, well pleased with their wages, in the crowded lorry. She was watching them drive away when the telephone rang, and she bustled into the hall and picked up the receiver.

'Hello, Hetty here.'

An excited voice answered her. 'We have found the ideal premises for you, Hetty. You must come over and inspect it right away. It's the top floor of a business establishment adjoining The Pantiles. A perfect situation, and so convenient for everyone. There's a lift and three good-sized rooms and a bathroom. We came upon it quite by chance. My husband and I were taking a stroll after our morning coffee at the tea-shop in The Pantiles. It's my free day, and if we can get this settled, it won't have been wasted.'

When she paused for breath, Hetty managed to inject a single word – 'But –' and was cut short impatiently.

'Now don't quibble, Hetty!'

'No, Miss Cynthia.'

'Phone for the station taxi, take the next train to Tunbridge Wells, and I'll meet you with the car at the other end. Hurry, now!'

'Yes, Miss Cynthia.'

'You see, you are still a servant: "No, Miss Cynthia, Yes, Miss Cynthia,"' Hetty told herself, severely, as she hung up the receiver.

It seemed such a simple operation, to press a button, step into the lift, and ascend to the top floor, but Hetty was petrified. She knew she would never use it if she came to live here. Three flights of stairs was no problem to a servant from Marston Park. She had been climbing stairs with buckets of coal and cans of hot water for several years, until she was promoted, to head housemaid. Her stomach seemed to drop into her shoes, but she held on to her dignity, and stepped out on the top landing with a sense of relief.

Miss Cynthia was still enthusing over the premises, but Hetty could not see herself behind a desk, interviewing prospective servants. There was another big drawback that had to be reckoned with, apart from the lift, and even more frightening. When all those other offices and her own office were closed, she would be alone in the building, alone in a strange world, until 9 o'clock the following morning.

'You don't seem very enthusiastic, Hetty?' Miss Cynthia was saying.

'Do I have to decide right away, Miss Cynthia? Could I think it over?'

'I thought you *had* been thinking it over? The agent won't wait indefinitely, Hetty, for you to make up your mind. These premises are much sought after. The day after tomorrow is the deadline, I understand. Other applicants are waiting. If you are worrying about the rent, you can forget it. We should settle it for the first twelve months. After that, we should expect you to stand on your own two feet. Why do you hesitate, Hetty? Is it the rent that is bothering you, or the responsibility? You're an intelligent woman, and I am certain you could manage it.'

How to explain her doubts and fears to a Franklin born of the ruling class, married into the working class, but still a lady? Before she could frame the words to answer, Miss Cynthia was speaking again, and her voice was brusque with irritation.

'Come along, then. I'll run you back to the station. You can phone me tomorrow evening, after 7 o'clock. That gives you one more day to make up your mind.'

'Yes, Miss Cynthia.'

She was pressing the button. Going down was even worse than coming up. Hetty knew she was annoyed by the strained silence between them, and when they parted at the station, Hetty had to wait over an hour for a branch line train and the buffet was closed.

Back at Fairfields station, she hired a taxi to take her to Russets. Lucy would be expecting her. The warmth of the welcome and the warmth of the farm kitchen did much to restore her flagging spirits. She had shed a few tears in the privacy of the empty carriage on the homeward journey. It was late, and the rest of the family had retired for the night, but Lucy's hospitality took no account of time. The kettle was boiling, and the tea brewed in a matter of minutes, and Hetty was in the rocking chair, unburdening all her doubts and fears to this wonderful woman who had known more sorrow than joy in her own chequered life. She bore no trace of her suffering other than a few grey hairs among the gold, and a lurking sadness in the gentian blue eyes. They shared the secret of the bitter quarrel between Sir Neville and his son, and they shared that sense of belonging to the Franklins that no outsider could understand.

Lucy Blunt had survived a scandal that had rocked the village, and held her head proud while her name and reputation were dragged through the mud. And why should she be ashamed when she had borne a healthy, handsome little boy to the squire, who was blessed – or cursed – with four daughters?

Hetty admired Lucy tremendously. She had the looks and the personality, as well as the courage, to battle on through all adversity. Now, with this latest shattering blow, she had already picked herself up from the ruins of a middle-aged romantic odyssey and carried on.

'What would *you* like, Hetty?' she asked kindly, as she poured a second cup of tea.

'I want to stay in service. I know I have to start all over again with another family, and I'm dreading it, but not half as much as the thought of plunging into the business world.'

'Then why not get in touch with an old-established domestic agency in Tunbridge Wells. You could find the phone number in the telephone directory. If they haven't a vacancy for a housekeeper on their books, leave your name and address – give them this address – and ask them to get in touch with you.'

'What will Miss Cynthia say?'

'It's your life, Hetty. It's for you to decide. Make a firm stand and don't be persuaded into something you are not suited for.'

'It's easier said than done, Lucy, when you have always taken orders from your betters since you were thirteen years old.'

'I know,' Lucy smiled affectionately at the homely figure with the pallid complexion of one who spends her life indoors. This was the biggest decision Hetty O'Brien might be called upon to make in her whole span of life. Poor Hetty!

'When do you expect the caretakers at the Big House?' she asked.

'Tomorrow.'

'That's good. It releases you from any further obligation and you are welcome to stay here till you get fixed up in another job.'

'Thank you, Lucy.'

'Let's get to bed now, shall we? You are looking tired. I always find it's a good idea to sleep on it. Tomorrow is another day, and every day is a fresh beginning.'

The couple who had been engaged as caretakers at Marston Park arrived early the next morning, and Hetty was there to welcome them, make tea for them, and the removal men. They had brought everything they needed to furnish their modest apartment, and were hoping to settle permanently. They would offer their services to the new owners, they told Hetty.

The Larkins were a very respectable couple, and Cynthia had chosen wisely from a number of applicants. Jack Larkin had been employed as a bailiff for the past twenty years on another big estate in the Cranbrook area, and the last surviving member of that prominent local family had recently died.

When Hetty had shown them round the house, she was free to concentrate on her own affairs, and she put through a call to the Ambrose Domestic Agency with a sense of desperate urgency. The empty house had been getting on her nerves, and she had cried a lot. She was not normally an emotional person. It was time she pulled herself together. If Lucy Blunt had managed it, so could Hetty O'Brien.

She was surprised at the prompt reaction to her enquiry. An experienced housekeeper was exactly the person they had been looking for, but had not yet found a suitable applicant to satisfy their client. They had already recommended several, but they had been turned down for various reasons.

'We had to admit they were not very suitable, but it's getting more and more difficult to find someone willing to live in. You are quite sure you would not mind?' the clear young voice inquired eagerly.

'I have always been resident. I can't see there is any alternative, especially for a housekeeper. Servants have to be supervised, not left to their own devices. I should know, for I started at the bottom of the ladder as fourth housemaid here at Marston Park at the age of thirteen.'

'You poor thing! How awful!'

'Not at all. We were well fed, and well trained. Those were the days when the butler and the housekeeper ruled over the servants' hall. The good old days when servants curtsied to their betters, and knew how to behave!' Hetty was quite carried away by her own eloquence, and the young woman was listening attentively. Here was the type of old-fashioned servant so rare as to be almost extinct since the War, but her superior was making signs of impatience, and she had to interrupt, politely but firmly.

'Thank you, Miss O'Brien. It sounds quite fascinating. Now, I will give you the name and address of our client, and you can telephone to make an appointment to suit your own convenience. By the way, I hope you like children, because this is a preparatory school for boys, but you do get long holidays. The address is The Firs, The Common, Tunbridge Wells, and you ask to speak to Matron, because she is doing the interviewing on behalf of the headmaster's wife who is indisposed. Perhaps you would be kind enough to phone back to let us know if you have accepted the post?'

Hetty smiled, involuntarily. It was indeed a revolutionary change if the servant and not the mistress could decide, though in this particular situation the matron was not so easily persuaded to take an unsuitable applicant. Hetty promised to ring back, hung up the receiver, then put through a call to The Firs.

'Hello, this is The Firs. Matron speaking. Can I help you?' It was a brusque, cultured voice – the voice of a person who would stand no nonsense.

Hetty took a deep breath. 'Good morning, Madam. I am enquiring about the vacant post for a housekeeper. The Ambrose Agency gave me your name. I should like to make an appointment to call and see you, if you will tell me a convenient time.'

'Who is calling, please?'

'Miss O'Brien.'

'Hetty O'Brien, from Marston Park?'

'Yes, Madam.'

'Hetty! Bless my soul! You mean you are actually free, now, at this moment?'

'Yes, Madam.'

'It's not Madam any more, Hetty. It's *Matron*. Do you remember me from the old days at Marston Park, when I was governess to Miss Beatrice and Miss Cynthia?'

'Miss Marion Wellington?'

'Exactly. It does seem a long time ago, doesn't it. Hetty?'

'Yes, Miss – Madam.'

'I caught a glimpse of you occasionally during the War, when I was living with Mother in that cottage on the estate.'

'Did you Miss?'

Marion chuckled. 'You know, Hetty, you must practise calling me Matron if you are coming to live here, and you *are* coming, aren't you? That stupid agency has been sending me the most unsuitable people, quite impossible people. I am afraid I lost patience. I mean to say, they were not the least bit interested in the job, only in the wages and the free time. Now, how soon could you get here, Hetty?'

'I could come today. I've finished my work here.'

'Bless you. Listen, I must explain the situation. Mrs Fairweather, the headmaster's wife, is expecting her first child in March, and something has gone wrong. She has been ordered to rest in bed, and her doctor has told her husband he will not be responsible for the consequences if she disobeys his instructions. So that's the position. We have an excellent couple – cook and handyman – and several dailies, so it shouldn't be too arduous with the long school holidays. You could stay here during the holidays, or you might prefer to stay at Russets on board wages. We will discuss it later. Just pack your bag and come along, there's a good girl! We will refund your taxi and train fares right away. And cook will have the kettle boiling for a nice cup of tea.'

'Thank you, Miss – Matron.'

'Thank *you*, Hetty.'

It was not yet 1 o'clock. Time enough to make several more phone calls, pack her bag, clear out the larder – the Larkins could use the food and groceries – brew another pot of tea and eat a sandwich. Her methodical mind was working again, and she felt she had been given a new lease of life.

When she had phoned the Ambrose Agency, she put through another call to Tunbridge Wells. Miss Cynthia would not be at home, and it would be so much easier to explain to Mister Freddie. He would understand because his roots were buried deep in the working class, and they had shared the squalor of Richmond Row. Lucy and Ruby were delighted to hear the excitement in her voice, and wished her luck. Ruby reminded her she would be among friends, and she must call at the little house on the other side of the Common on her first free afternoon. Lucy reminded her she would always be welcome at Russets. She promised to send Katie over to collect the soiled linen and blankets from Hetty's bed. It was typical of Lucy to offer such practical help. Soon the flat would be stripped and bare like the rest of the house. Nothing would remain of the old life, but Hetty would never go back. It must be a complete break, she told herself as she climbed into the station cab. The Larkins waved her on her way. She dare not look back. Her throat was tight with tears as they circled the Park. Autumn leaves were strewn on the grass. Her nostrils twitched with the acrid smell of a bonfire. They passed the spot where Sir Neville Franklin had been thrown from his horse, the spot where father and son had parted, and the spot where the young school teacher had been strangled all those years ago. These tragic events were part of the history of Marston Park.

Hetty looked straight ahead. This new chapter of her life would depend entirely on her own ability to adapt, her willingness and respectful regard for her betters. Circumstances had changed, but not the pattern. She was still a servant.

Cynthia was tired and irritable when she arrived back from the hospital, and in no mood to listen to Freddie's soothing explanation. Hetty was a stupid, ungrateful woman! She had thrown away a splendid opportunity to better herself.

'Perhaps she doesn't wish to better herself?' Freddie suggested, mildly.

'Then she's a fool!'

'Not necessarily.'

'Why must you always have a different opinion?'

'My dear, that's not true, and when I do agree you accuse me of weakness, and just wanting to keep the peace.'

'I'm sorry. It's just that I am so disappointed. Why didn't she tell me she was scared of the lift, and scared to be alone in the building when the offices were closed? Why couldn't she be honest with me, darling?'

'I think Hetty is normally a very honest person, but you may have been a little over-persuasive, for you do like to organise people, and sometimes it's resented.'

She sighed. He stood there so quietly, smiling his gentle smile. Then she moved into his arms, and he held her close.

'I'm a domineering bitch!' she insisted.

'You're not a domineering bitch. You're my darling girl.'

She lifted her head to look at him, astonished by the endearment.

'What did you say?'
'You heard.'
Yes, she *had* heard. Freddie had called her darling! It was a word she had used indiscriminately all her life, but not Freddie. She had often wished he would be a little more demonstrative, but it was not his nature. She loved him dearly, and would not have him different. Her dark eyes were soft as velvet now, and all her irritation had vanished. She kissed him with a fierce pride and joy. Hetty was forgotten. Here, in this little house, was a husband who waited for her, who understood all her moods and forgave all her faults. Together they had battled through the years of mental and physical suffering. Together they were building a brighter future for their child. And when that child ran into the room, they smiled at her, and took her hands, and she was happy again. When she saw them kissing, she felt left out, and it was a horrid feeling.
'Mummy . . . Daddy,' was all she said as she turned to look at each, but they understood.

It was Christmas Eve of that eventful year – 1925. Julian Franklin had been enjoying one of the happiest periods of his young life. Fully recovered from the scarlet fever, he was allowed to run wild at Russets with his lively puppy, for it had been decided he would not go back to school until after Christmas. It was fun to be so free, to come and go as he pleased, providing he was back in time for meals. On wet days he played in the Big Dutch barn, and watched Betsy and Bella with their newborn calves. The sweet-smelling hay was stacked high, but a passageway was cleared to their stalls. They were separated one from the other by fences, and clean straw covered the floors. Carrie called it the maternity ward.

Cows were timid creatures, and Uncle Tom often sat up all night in the stall when a calf was due. They did not seem to mind Julian leaning on the fence, and they stared at him with their placid bovine faces while the calves suckled. Their conception and birth was no mystery to Julian. He knew all about the bull. It was natural. Everything was natural to a child growing up at Russets.

Earlier in the year a foal had been born in one of the stalls, a pretty little creature that had struggled to stand on its spindly legs as soon as the mare had finished her licking. He had seen it born. He had heard the pitiful moans of pain, and Uncle Tom's soothing voice. Nothing was hidden or secret. He was always included in everything, and his questions answered truthfully. Breeding was a common topic of conversation in the farm kitchen, and there would be no inhibitions about sex as he grew older. In his final year at the village school, sex would provide an interesting subject, but it would never take on the same importance as aircraft. Flying was his one passionate ambition, and he had built up a fleet of model planes in his bedroom. The walls were plastered with photographs. He studied the different designs, and read avidly of the men who designed and the men who flew the aircraft. But he was alone in this passionate interest in flying, for nobody shared it, and there was no opportunity to meet anyone who had actually flown.

Grandfather had promised him a visit to an airfield on his next birthday, but Grandfather was dead. It still seemed strange not to see him riding his big black stallion. He had his own pony, and was allowed to ride as far as The Home Farm, but not across the Park. Marston Park did not belong to the Franklins any more, and that was strange, too. He had promised never to run away again, but he had no wish to do so. Once was enough.

Aunt Lucy had provided a comfortable basket for the

puppy in his bedroom, and she may not have been too surprised to find it curled up in his bed. They were inseparable companions, day and night. The white mice had been exchanged for a catapult. Uncle Bertie had threatened him with a good hiding if he caught him in the orchard, so he practised in the wood. He wondered what it would actually feel like to kill a pigeon. So far he had killed only slugs, snails and caterpillars because he disliked creepy, crawly creatures. He would never kill a butterfly, or catch it in a net. That would be cruel. But he *did* collect birds' eggs. 'Boys will be boys,' Aunt Lucy shrugged, but Carrie was upset.

When he saw Uncle Tom kissing Carrie he was afraid. Would Uncle Bertie kill Uncle Tom one day, if he caught them kissing? It was a gruesome thought.

It was difficult to stay awake. There were no voices after 10 o'clock, only noises – the whistle of the wind down the chimney, the rattle of the window, and the creaking boards of the old house, as though the ghosts of their forebears had come back to share in the Christmas festivities. The night light was comforting, and it was tempting to fall asleep with the puppy's warm little body curled in his arms. Curiosity would overcome that temptation, however, and he was waiting for the hand of his new watch to move round to ten minutes to midnight. The watch was not exactly new, but it was very precious because it had belonged to Grandfather.

When the grandfather clock struck 11, he whispered to Jasper, 'The next time it strikes will be midnight, and we shall see whether it's true that the cattle kneel to worship Baby Jesus.'

The puppy yawned, and licked his face. He would have to take Jasper because if he left him behind, he would yap and disturb Aunt Lucy. She was a very light sleeper. He had practised avoiding the creaking stairs, and was rather proud of the way he had managed to smuggle a candle and a box of matches to his room while Katie was busy polishing the furniture in the parlour.

Christmas had been building up gradually since November, when he helped Aunt Lucy stone the raisins for the pudding, and cakes, and ate the sticky lumps of sugar in the candied peel. Today he had helped Carrie gather the holly to decorate the pictures, and he and Katie had made all the paper chains that were strung across the kitchen and the parlour. Uncle Tom had dug up the Christmas tree from the garden. Every year, as far back as he could remember, they decorated the tree, he and Carrie, with the same coloured baubles and little Chinese lanterns. When the candles were lit, on Christmas Day, they would sparkle, and look very pretty.

And every year, Aunt Lucy would remind them, with tears in her eyes, that these same baubles had decorated the tree since Harry, Tom and Albert were little boys. Only two had been broken. The memories brought sadness at Christmas, as well as joy. For Julian's sake, nothing must be changed. For Julian's sake, a row of old stockings would be hung on the kitchen mantelpiece, bulging with apples, oranges and sugar mice while their proper presents would be stacked under the tree in the parlour, to be opened after dinner. They all would lend a hand with the washing up to get it done quickly, for Katie was slow. Before he started school and discovered the truth about Father Christmas, a bulging stocking would be hanging on the end of the bed. Carrie and Uncle Tom sat on the bed and shared his excitement before they went out for milking at 5 o'clock.

Katie was like a child at Christmas, and so excited she was not allowed to handle the best china tea service that had been in the family for more than a hundred years.

It was the longest hour that Julian could remember,

and he picked up the watch a dozen times and held it to his ear to make certain it had not stopped. Once upon a time, when he was very small, he stood between Grandfather's knees when the watch was held to his ear. It seemed a long, long time ago. Grandfather's present had always been the biggest and the most expensive, but Aunt Lucy had reminded him every year that a small, handmade gift should be even more appreciated because so much effort had been put into the making. Be that as it may, Katie's clumsily knitted muffler or mittens could not be compared with Grandfather's clockwork toys from Harrods! There would be no more. It was a solemn thought.

He sighed and looked at the watch for the last time. It was exactly ten minutes to midnight.

In his dressing-gown and slippers, clutching the puppy, and the lighted candle, he crept downstairs. He could see the row of bulging stockings, one for each person, dangling from the kitchen mantelpiece. The stove and the fender shone in the candlelight. Katie would boast proudly, 'You can see your face in them, Ma'am!'

He looked about the bright, warm kitchen, and was tempted to linger for a few minutes. It was the nicest room in the whole house, and his earliest memories were here, cuddled on a comfortable lap, in the old rocking chair. He was too small then to want to explore, too young to be curious. Aunt Lucy had warned him only recently, 'Curiosity killed the cat'. But he was not a cat. He was a big boy, and before he went back to school, he would know the truth about the strange behaviour of the cattle on Christmas Eve.

Fortunately for his midnight escapade, the back door was not bolted, and he could slip out quietly. Aunt Lucy would have told him the doors at Russets were never bolted, had he asked her.

The east wind cut across the yard, took his breath

away, and blew out the candle. He stood there, shivering, his heart pounding, till the moon crept out from behind a cloud, then he hurried towards the barn. A small door was snugly fitted into the massive doors of the barn. A man could slip through easily in the night. He climbed through, re-lit the candle, and stared about him in wide-eyed astonishment. It was a *huge* place. It seemed to be ten times larger than it did in the daylight, when the doors were flung wide open. He could not see the roof, it was too high, and the stack of sweet-smelling hay was tall as a mountain in the small circle of light when he lifted the candle.

Trembling and hesitant, he dare not move another step until he found his courage again, and that urgent sense of curiosity that could not be abandoned at the last moment. To wait a whole year would be an eternity. It was so far removed, he could not visualise such a time, and looked no further ahead than the Boxing Day treat. He and Carrie would meet Wendy and Aunt Ruby in Tunbridge Wells. They were going to the pantomime.

Now he could hear a faint rustling in the straw, and he knew he had disturbed the cows in their stalls. He moved forward cautiously, step by step, until he could smell their breath and see their dim shapes, first one pair, then another in the small circle of light, but not both together. They were not kneeling. They were lying in the straw, gazing up at him in drowsy contentment, the calves sleeping. They showed no sign of homage – that was the word Carrie had used. Nothing was going to happen. He was nearly crying with disappointment. The puppy was slipping under his arm, and clawing his chest to save himself from falling. Suddenly he lifted a paw and sent the candle flying.

For a brief second they were plunged into darkness, then the hay was alight, and the flames spreading quickly.

He could only scream and scream till his lungs were bursting. The acrid smoke blinded his eyes and closed his throat. Choking and gasping, still clutching the puppy, he fainted.

It was not the screams that wakened Lucy. The walls of the old barn were too thick for a child's thin cries to penetrate. It was the collie dog, straining at the chain that fastened her to the kennel. She was barking furiously. Lucy always slept with an open window. She was wide awake now, sniffing the tang of smoke in the cold night air.

Tumbling out of bed, she pulled on her dressing-gown and slippers, ran down the passage, and threw open the doors, calling urgently, 'Tom! Albert! Carrie! Wake up!'

Julian's door stood wide open, and the room was empty.

'Julian! Julian! Where are you?' Now her voice was frantic with anxiety. There was no answer. Carrie and Albert were so soundly sleeping, she had to shake them awake.

'What–what's happened?' Carrie was yawning, Albert muttering.

Lucy had flung open the window, and they were shivering in the blast of cold air. 'It's the Dutch barn! It's blazing! – and Julian's missing!' she told them.

Albert was pulling on his trousers, Carrie her dressing-gown and slippers. They were fully awake now, and ran downstairs. She found Tom had turned over and gone to sleep again. She stripped off the bed-clothes and shook him into wakefulness.

'Tom! Wake up!'

Then he, too, was shivering in the blast of cold air from the open window.

'Get into these and hurry!' She flung his trousers and slippers on the bed.

'What?' he yawned.

'The barn's alight, and Julian's missing. Hurry!' Her voice was sharp with authority. She left him and followed the other two downstairs and out to the yard. She could see Carrie at the pump, and Albert disappearing through the little door with a bucket of water. It seemed a futile attempt to stop the fire from spreading, and she hurried indoors to call the fire brigade. Back in the yard, she was just in time to catch the child, flung into her arms by the irate Albert.

'Bloody little fool! I'll tan his backside when we've finished here!' he growled.

'Where's Katie? Why isn't she here?' Carrie gasped.

'Let her sleep. She would only be in the way. You know what she's like in an emergency.' Lucy's voice was still sharp, but now that Julian was safe she could think clearly. As she carried him to the kitchen and dropped him gently into the rocking chair, Tom ran downstairs.

'Will he be all right, Mum?' he asked, jerkily.

'He'll be all right. I'll be back in a minute. Get those barn doors open, Tom, and get the cows and the calves out.'

'Yes, Mum.' He was dazed with shock, and not fully awake.

As soon as she was satisfied the child was breathing normally – the puppy was whimpering with fright – she hurried back to the yard. Tom and Albert were shouting at one another and almost coming to blows.

'Don't be such a bloody fool! If we open those doors, the wind will rush in and fan the flames!' Albert shouted.

'And if we don't open them, the cows and calves will suffocate!' Tom shouted back.

'Open them!' Lucy ordered, authoritatively. 'We can afford to lose the barn and hay, but we can't afford to lose the cattle. Tie these wet cloths over your nose and mouth.

Take care!'

A few minutes later, they were leading the cows and calves across the yard to an empty stable. Now they could concentrate on the fire. While the two women manned the pump, the two men raced back and forth with the buckets of water. But their puny efforts had little effect on the blazing hay. The flames were licking the beams, and the heat was suffocating. For every bucket that Tom handled, Albert handled two. He was like a mad creature, cursing his wife and mother for their slowness, snatching at the buckets, choking and panting. Tom was flagging. He kept going only because of his brother's untiring efforts. If he gave up now, Albert would torment him for the rest of his days. Carrie watched his stumbling steps with an aching heart, and a throat tight with tears. Lucy could hear the fire engine in the distance. They would probably be too late to save the barn.

When Katie blundered into the yard, wide-eyed with terror, Lucy sent her back to the house, to stay with Julian.

Both brothers were together in the barn when a beam cracked. The women screamed. The fire bell clanged, and the engine raced into the yard. The four men manning the engine, including the butcher and the grocer, had been working hard all day, and summoned from their beds after barely a couple of hours sleep. But they were well schooled in fire fighting, and took control of the situation with calm efficiency.

'Tom and Albert – they are both in there,' Lucy sobbed, clutching at the butcher in his steel helmet.

'Don't worry, Mrs Blunt. We'll get them out,' he told her, and put her gently aside. They worked as a team, two men manning the hose, the other two, quickly masked, plunged into the barn.

Lucy and Carrie, with their arms wrapped about each

other, were crying quietly now. They hadn't long to wait. A limp form was carried out. The face was blackened, the hair singed, and blood was pouring from a nasty gash over one eye. It was Tom. They carried him into the parlour and left him with Carrie. She was on her knees beside him, stemming the blood with a clean cloth she had snatched from the kitchen in a matter of seconds. Her face was streaked with dirt and tears, and she was murmuring endearments. The men thought it was a little odd that she had not mentioned her husband.

'Albert?' Lucy was asking, anxiously.

'We have to get him out very carefully, Mrs Blunt. He's trapped by both legs, but he is unconscious, so he's not feeling anything. We'll get him out, never fear, but it's a job that can't be hurried. I'm afraid the hay is a write-off after all that soaking. I'm sorry.' It was the butcher speaking again. The gleaming helmet sat on his huge head like a child's toy, and the buttons of his uniform jacket were bursting over his fat stomach.

'The hay has no value if I lose my son,' she told him.

'You could phone the doctor while you're waiting, Mrs Blunt. Albert is going to need medical attention when we get him out, and that gash on Tom's forehead needs stitching,' he reminded her kindly.

And she hurried to the phone, feeling better now that she had something definite to do.

The doctor said he would be there within half an hour. The fire bell had wakened him as it would waken the whole village. When she had put down the receiver, Lucy lingered in the kitchen to comfort Julian and Katie. They were very frightened, and Julian had been sick.

'Why did you go to the barn in the middle of the night, my love?' she asked the child.

'To see if the cows and the calves were kneeling.'

'Kneeling?'

'Yes, kneeling to Jesus.'

'Who told you they would kneel?'

'Carrie. Well, she didn't 'zactly say they would, she said it was a legend that all the cattle paid homage to Jesus at midnight on Christmas Eve, and legends are sometimes true, aren't they, Aunt Lucy?'

'Sometimes.'

'Well, it wasn't true, and nothing happened. Then Jasper knocked the candle out of my hand, and set the hay alight. I was scared.' He shivered at the memory of that awful moment, and was near to tears again.

Lucy knelt on the floor beside the rocking chair and held him close. She was reminded of that Easter Day when he was nearly drowned in the river. A small boy seemed to have as many lives as a cat.

'I'll let you know when to brew the tea, Katie. You can set out cups and saucers, sugar and milk in readiness, and put more coal on the fire,' she reminded her, kindly.

'Yes, Ma'am,' sniffed Katie obediently. She was wearing an overcoat over her flannel nightgown, and her house shoes.

'I must get Ruby to buy her a dressing gown and slippers in Tunbridge Wells,' she was thinking. But Katie had always dressed before coming downstairs, so it hadn't seemed a necessary expense. Neither the child nor the servant enquired about Tom and Albert, but Julian wanted to see the fire engine, so she carried him to the door and he watched the two men manning the hose in fascinated silence.

When her second son was carried out of the barn, she left Julian in the kitchen again and gave all her attention to Albert. He looked so ghastly she thought he was dead, but the men assured her he was still breathing. Tom was lying on the sofa in the parlour, holding a blood-stained cloth to his head, Carrie beside him. They seemed completely absorbed with one another till they saw Albert. Tom slid off the sofa and went to sit in a chair, and they laid Albert down. Only then did Carrie seem to remember her husband, and she hurried away to fetch fresh water and a clean towel, and knelt beside him, gently bathing his face.

Lucy left her there, holding Albert's limp hand, and went back to the yard. The two men were still playing the hose on the smouldering remains of the hay. One end of the roof was sagging. The stench was horrible, and the devastation was heart-breaking. But her loved ones were safe, and she was thankful.

While Katie brewed tea, she poured hot water into a bowl, and laid out a clean towel. With their helmets on the kitchen table, and their blackened faces clean, the butcher and the grocer resumed their own identities.

The grandfather clock was striking 2 when the other men put away the hose and joined them in the kitchen. Lucy poured more tea and offered to make sandwiches, but nobody wanted to eat. It was tea they wanted, strong, sweet tea, to clear their parched throats. Katie was instructed to take cups of tea to Carrie and Tom in the parlour, where she took a quick, fearful glance at poor Mister Albert and hurried back to the kitchen. Now the danger was past, she was enjoying the presence of four hefty men in the kitchen. She had not fastened her overcoat, and George Sanders, a railway ganger, was feasting his bloodshot eyes on the heavy body in the tight flannel nightgown. 'Like a bitch on heat,' he thought, and swallowed the hot tea, anticipating their next meeting. It could be easily arranged at 'The Three Nuns'. Katie had quite a reputation in the village, and his own reputation was no secret!

When all four men had refreshed themselves with three mugs of tea, they donned their helmets and climbed back on the engine. They met the doctor's car speeding across the Park. The headlights dipped, and they raised their hands in salute. It was Christmas morning, and the church bells were pealing as they hung up their helmets in the fire station.

'Happy Christmas, lads!'

The butcher went on his way, dragging his feet with weariness.

'Happy Christmas, Chief!' they echoed.

'We must get him to hospital as soon as possible, Mrs Blunt,' the doctor told her, brusquely, after a brief examination. 'Both legs fractured, and internal injuries. His pulse is weak. I'll give him an injection.'

'Yes, Doctor.' Lucy turned to her daughter-in-law to ask, quietly, 'Will you go with him, Carrie?'

'Yes – yes, of course. I'll get dressed. What about the milking?'

'We shall manage.'

'I shall be all right when this cut stops bleeding,' Tom interrupted.

'Just hang on a minute, Tom, while I phone the hospital and get that ambulance moving. Twelve miles is a hell of a long way, but there's nothing nearer, so we shall just have to wait.'

Carrie hurried away. Would she be spending Christmas Day in hospital? she wondered. She was not leaving Bertie till he was out of danger.

When the doctor had put through the call to the emergency service in the Tunbridge Wells hospital, he asked Lucy to hold Tom's head steady while he stitched the deep gash. She thought Tom was going to faint. He had lost a lot of blood, and his face was grey with exhaustion. But she had the bottle of whisky handy, a Christmas present from the Home Farm. Even Carrie, who had never tasted anything stronger than elderberry wine, was persuaded that it was good for her under the circumstances.

'Good stuff this, Mrs Blunt. I must admit I was feeling a bit low myself. Had a difficult birth last night. Didn't get to bed till after 11, then that confounded fire bell woke me up.'

'I'm sorry, Doctor,' said Lucy, sympathetically. She had been so engrossed with the family, she had not noticed his weariness. His tired eyes smiled at her concern.

'It's all part of the job, Mrs Blunt. It's what we are here for. I'm sorry this had to happen. Try not to worry. Albert will be in good hands.'

'How soon shall we know, Doctor?'

'Difficult to say. It's almost certain that an emergency operation will be necessary, and those legs must be put in plaster. Some hours, I'm afraid, but Carrie will keep in touch with you, won't you, Carrie?'

'Yes, Doctor.'

It seemed an eternity that they waited for the ambulance. Katie had been sent back to bed.

'Can I have my Christmas stocking now?' Julian had pleaded, and gone back to bed quite happily, clutching the puppy and the bulging stocking. For the child's sake, Christmas Day must not be allowed to pass unheralded, but for Lucy and Tom it would be a travesty without Carrie and Albert.

Carrie had packed a bag with immediate requirements for herself and Bertie. She kissed Lucy and Tom, and climbed into the ambulance. Holding Bertie's hand, she wept quietly, deeply conscious of her relief that it was Bertie, not Tom, who was lying there. It was cruel and selfish to have such thoughts. Poor Bertie. There had been no love between them, only pity. They said pity was akin to love. They said, to do your duty was all that mattered. They said, you would get your reward in Heaven. Dear God! She was so tired, so frustrated. Her youth had been drained away in doing her duty. Only Tom's love and devotion had saved her reason.

She had forgotten the ambulance attendant who was sitting there so quietly, watching his patient.

'Won't be long now. Your husband will be all right. Don't you worry.'

'I'm sorry we had to bring you out on Christms Day.'

'We were on duty, anyway, Stan and me. I don't mind if I get back in time to see the kids open their stockings.'

'Kids? Your're married? You look so young.'

'Married at eighteen. Got three lovely kids, two girls and a boy. You got a family?'

'No.'

'Pity. Nothing like kids for a really happy marriage. That's my personal opinion, of course.'

Carrie smiled wistfully. 'I'm sure you're right,' she agreed.

A doctor and a nurse were waiting to receive their patient. He was wheeled away, and Carrie was invited to sit down in a waiting room with comfortable chairs and a settee. A gas fire hissed faintly in the hearth. The room was warm and stuffy, and smelled faintly of embrocation. The usual out-dated magazines and children's comics were spread neatly on the table.

'I'll bring you a cup of tea, Mrs Blunt. It's going to be a long wait, I'm afraid. Let me help you off with your coat. You won't need it here.' The nurse was young and pretty, and very efficient, in her starched uniform.

When she came back with the tea, she found Carrie perched on the edge of a chair, and explained quietly, 'Your husband is being prepared for the theatre, Mrs Blunt. Why not make yourself comfortable on the settee when you have finished your tea, then you can catch up on some sleep?'

'Thank you, nurse.' The quiet voice and soothing manner were comforting and reassuring. Everything was under control. Bertie had been taken away. He didn't belong to her, here, in this place. It was a relief to curl up on the settee and close her eyes. She drifted into troubled sleep almost immediately, and woke to the touch of a hand on her cheek. A doctor had drawn up a chair, and was sitting beside her.

'That was a good sleep,' he said quietly.

'What's the time?' She was dazed, and her head ached. What was she doing here?

'It's a little after 10 o'clock.'

'*10 o'clock*! My – my husband?'

'He slipped away. I'm sorry, my dear. He didn't regain consciousness.'

She frowned. 'You should have wakened me. Bertie would be so frightened of dying without having me there.'

'He wouldn't know. Your husband was in a deep coma,' he explained patiently, as to a backward child.

'How can you be sure he didn't need me? You should have called me.' She shook her head, still frowning and troubled.

'We let you sleep. There was nothing you could do.'

'I could have held his hand.'

'But he would not have known you were there. Do not distress yourself on that account.'

'I must telephone. I promised to keep in touch. They must be so worried.'

'They know. Your mother-in-law telephoned a couple of hours ago. She said not to disturb you, but when you awoke, to ask you to phone back. I'll send nurse with a cup of tea, then you can use the phone in Sister's office.'

'Thank you, Doctor.'

He patted her hand. 'You would like to see him?'

'Yes.'

'Nurse will bring you after you have telephoned.'

There was no sense of reality. She was functioning in a dream world that had no substance. Aunt Lucy was crying while she herself was dry-eyed and numb with shock. She listened to the choked voice, explaining carefully, 'I have been on the phone to Cynthia. She will collect you at the hospital and bring you back here. Just let her know when you are ready.'

'Thank you, Aunt Lucy,' was all she said. She seemed to be incapable of saying anything else. 'Thank you, Doctor' – 'Thank you, Nurse' – 'Thank you, Aunt Lucy,' till she was looking down on that calm, scarred face.

Then she whispered, 'Goodbye, Bertie,' kissed his cold cheek, and turned away.

Cynthia walked into Sister's office and wrapped her arms about Carrie.

'Poor darling. Leave everything to me,' she said. She had no shyness with Sister or the surgeon, for she had introduced herself, and they accepted her as one of their own kind, a member of their dedicated fraternity.

Carrie sat down where she was told to sit, and listened while they discussed the nature of Albert's injuries and arranged for the body to be removed to the hospital mortuary till the day of the funeral. Albert Blunt would join his forebears in that special corner of the churchyard, almost cheek by jowl with the Franklin vault, in which Sir Neville had been laid to rest only a few weeks ago. Carrie listened to their conversation in numb acceptance, and took no part in it. What had a mortuary and a funeral to do with Bertie? She would find him waiting for her at Russets. It was inconceivable that he would not be there.

'Where have you been?' he would demand, truculently. 'I've been looking all over for you.'

'Did you want me, dear?' she would ask.

'I always want you. You should know that. You're my wife.'

She could hear him speaking and herself answering while she sat there, waiting to be taken back to Russets.

'Did you want me, dear?'

'I always want you. You should know that. You're my wife.'

Over and over, like a bell tolling in her head. More than seven years had passed since that agonising discovery on her wedding night. Seven years of fear and frustration, and pity for a man's crippling deformity that could never be healed.

Back at Russets, wrapped in Aunt Lucy's comforting arms, she was still dry-eyed. And she shrank from Tom as though she could not bear to be touched by Bertie's brother. The stockings had been removed from the hearth, and nobody had dared to light the candles on the Christmas tree. It was another fear that would haunt young Julian Franklin for many a long year – the fear of the river – the fear of darkness – and now the fear of a falling candle, spreading flames.

They could smell beef roasting in the oven, and the plum pudding boiling on top of the stove. Only Julian and Katie would be hungry, but the others would eat automatically to keep him company. Presents would be handed round in the afternoon before milking, but Lucy had hidden Albert's packages. She had knitted warm jerseys for Tom and Albert, and Carrie had knitted scarves. There were socks and ties and handkerchiefs, the usual gifts for men. Only the child and the servant would expect to be surprised by their gifts.

Cynthia could not stay. She had to get back to her own family, but she hadn't forgotten the promised treat for

Boxing Day.

'Children must not be disappointed. If you will put Julian on the train tomorrow morning, Tom, in charge of the guard, I will meet him the other end. Just let me know which train to meet. Ruby can take both children to the pantomime in the afternoon. Pack a small case, Aunt Lucy. Let him stay for the rest of the week. Wendy will love to have him,' she told her.

'Can I bring Jasper?' Julian asked as she hurried away.

'Why, of course, darling.' She kissed them all affectionately, and shot off across the Park in her little car. She left behind a gap that could not be filled. Her dominant personality, so accustomed to organising, had arranged everything so effortlessly.

Carrie moved through the days still numb with shock. She slept in Lucy's bed, and Lucy slept in the marriage bed.

'Why is Carrie avoiding me, Mum?' Tom was hurt and saddened by her strange behaviour.

Lucy had taken over the milking since Christmas, for Carrie slept late, and spent most of the day in the rocking chair, her idle hands lying in her lap.

'Be patient, Tom,' his mother advised. 'It's a natural reaction after such a terrible shock.'

'I don't understand. I thought she would turn to me for comfort. I love her, and she loves me.'

'Perhaps she needs a holiday, Tom. A change of scene.'

'But where could she go at this time of the year?'

'Perhaps they would have her at the School House for a week or two? Philip and Harriet sailed last week, and Martha will be missing them sadly. She was always so fond of Carrie.'

Tom shrugged. 'You could try.'

It was only a short distance away, but it was another

world, and Martha welcomed Carrie with open arms. In Philip's bedroom, she slept late and was wakened by the shouts and screeches of the children in the playground. Then the whistle blew, and all was silent.

She remembered the drill as though it were yesterday. That first whistle brought the children to a halt, instantly, wherever they happened to be, so that the two playgrounds, one for the girls, one for the boys, became a tableau with children standing, kneeling, lying motionless as statues. Little girls would be caught running from the lavatory, their drawers round their ankles, and boys fastening their fly buttons. At the second whistle, the statues came to life, and raced towards the doors to form into line in orderly fashion, and march into school.

When the sound of shuffling feet had died away, Carrie got out of bed, sponged her face in the bathroom, and went downstairs in her dressing gown and slippers. Her breakfast had been laid ready, and a kettle was singing on the hob. She had only to brew a pot of tea, boil an egg, and make toast. She could take her time. There was no hurry and no sense of guilt at her idleness.

As she toasted the bread at the glowing fire, she could hear the children singing the hymn that preceded lessons. Nothing had changed here, in this small world. In retrospect she was back in the Infants with Teacher writing on the blackboard with white chalk. The letters were bold and easy to copy. CAT – BAT – MAT – PAT – FAT – HAT – RAT – SAT. She copied them on her slate. Half the class were copying the letters and the slate pencils scratched and squeaked. The rest of the class sat reading quietly to themselves, their fingers pointing to each word separately, their voices hushed. She was four years old, the youngest child in the classroom. They called her 'Teacher's pet'. She smiled at the memory. It was the beginning of their long friendship.

The troubled years had drawn them closer. There had been more sorrow than joy, more tears than laughter. Now they both were sad again, with a different kind of sadness. Teacher had said goodbye to her adored only son, and five years would pass before she saw him again. As for herself, she had lost Bertie, and now she was tortured by a guilty conscience. Hadn't she lain with Tom in the beechwood on those pleasant afternoons of late Autumn, when Bertie was amusing the child in the bedroom? Now Bertie was dead, and she was ashamed. Her thoughts were confused. Shame and sadness mingled with relief that could not be denied. She had shed no tears, not even on the day of the funeral. She was empty of tears, and so tired.

The days passed and the weeks slipped away. She was not yet ready to go home, and nobody urged her to do so. On Saturday and Sunday afternoons, they left Andrew reading by the fireside, put on boots and tied scarves round their heads, for a walk round the quiet lanes. With their arms linked, the two saddened women found a measure of comfort in their isolation. The snow was crisp under foot, and the hedgerows draped in white blankets.

But their relationship was so close, Andrew was already disturbed by the twinges of jealousy and resentment he had known with Philip. Would there never be a time when he had Martha to himself? he wondered. He was tired of sharing her.

The long month of January had slipped away. The snow had melted and early crocuses were blooming in the School House garden. The time had come to take Carrie home. *She was three months pregnant*!

It was a Sunday afternoon, and Martha had telephoned Russets in the morning to warn Lucy to expect them for tea. Andrew pushed Carrie's case on his bicycle, and Martha pushed her own bicycle so they could cycle back after supper. They stopped on the way for Martha to pick catkins to fill the empty jam jars in the Infants' classroom. Next month there would be primroses and celandines. Then it would be Spring again.

Two children were racing down the cart track to the farm gate on the borders of the spreading acres of Russets. A puppy yapped excitedly at their heels. They ran hand-in-hand, and the legs of the little girl were too short to keep pace with her companion. She stumbled into potholes and puddles, and he dragged her out with the normal impatience of an eight-year-old boy.

Carrie pushed open the gate and they ran into her out-stretched arms.

'Why did you stay away so long? I wanted you. Don't ever go away again!' Julian insisted.

Wendy was too breathless to speak for herself.

'She's staying here for the week-end with Aunt Ruby,' Julian explained.

They were reminded to say 'Good afternoon' to Aunt Martha and Uncle Andrew. It was embarrassing for a boy to greet his schoolmaster as a member of the family on Sunday afternoon when on Friday afternoon at 4 o'clock he had stood to attention with the rest of the school and joined in the chorus of 'Good afternoon, Sir'. The schoolmaster was strict on such matters as politeness and respect for your elders, but he wasn't such a bad old geyser, and not too free with the cane!

The children were full of importance to show her everything, and she hurried with them to the yard gate, and stood there, staring at the Dutch barn. It had been repaired rather clumsily, with new slates and timber. The scarred doors stood open and bales of hay were stacked neatly along one wall.

'They brought it over for us from the other farms because we lost all our hay in the fire, and they all helped Uncle Tom to mend the broken barn,' said Julian.

'Come and see the small little calves.' Wendy was tugging at her hand. The stalls had been rebuilt and whitewashed. Both calves were suckling greedily.

'The littlest one is mine. It's name is Rosemary,' said Wendy, proudly.

'Rosemary's a soppy name for a cow. I've called mine Polly,' Julian told her, scornfully.

'But she's not a cow. She's only a small little calf,' Wendy protested.

'Calves grow into cows, silly! You're such a baby. You don't know anything!'

There were times when his little cousin was a bit of a nuisance, and he felt smothered by her adoration. And other times when he was quite fond of her. She was always a willing slave, and never cried when she was hurt.

'Come and see the baby chicks.' She had seen enough of the calves, and seldom stayed for more than a few minutes in any one place. Carrie could see herself at the same age when she first came to spend a day at Russets. Brimming over with mischief and curiosity, her twelve-year-old cousin, Albert, had followed her round.

'Keep an eye on Carrie,' Aunt Lucy had instructed.

They went out of the door at the back of the barn and into the orchard, with Wendy skipping ahead. Scores of brown and white hens trod daintily in the grass, and the incubators were crowded with tiny chicks.

'I've been helping Uncle Tom with the poultry since Uncle Bertie died, but he said you would help when you came back. I don't mind helping with the feeding and collecting the eggs, but I don't like mucking out the chicken houses. It's a messy job,' Julian explained.

They left Wendy on her knees at the incubator, talking

to the chicks, and went on a tour of inspection. Nothing had been neglected. How strange it seemed to be back here without Bertie. They had always known where to find him. This was Bertie's domain, and he allowed no interference. The hut had always been tidy, and the bins clearly marked.

Carrie was listening for another familiar voice, but there was no sign of him. He knew she was coming home this afternoon. Why was he not here to meet her?

She left the two children to collect the eggs in a bucket, and hurried across to the house. But he was not there. The twin sisters smiled a welcome.

'Hello, Mum. Hullo, Aunt Lucy.'

They wrapped their arms around her. It was good to be back. Why had she stayed away so long? She knew the answer to that question, and she was nervous as a kitten, moving restlessly about the kitchen.

Martha and Andrew were drinking their first cup of tea, and Aunt Lucy was pouring another cup. She stood there, sipping the hot tea, very conscious of their watchful eyes. Andrew had carried her case upstairs. Why did she feel so embarrassed and shy? Embarrassed to talk about something that would soon be obvious?

'I'll just take a look around,' she said when she had finished the tea.

Out of sight of the house, she leaned on the gate of the twelve-acre field to watch the frisking lambs. She was choked with tears.

When he came, at last, to lean on the gate beside her, she did not turn her head to look at him.

'Hello, Carrie,' he said.

'Hello, Tom,' she answered.

'You're crying,' he said.

She nodded.

His roughened hands were gentle on her shoulders.

'What's troubling you, sweetheart?' he asked.

'I'm expecting.'

He took her face in his hands and kissed her trembling mouth.

'I know. Martha told me.'

'You don't mind?'

'Mind? – I'm the happiest man in the world! My dear love. My dear, sweet love.'

Then she was in his arms.

They were married at Easter. It was a very quiet wedding, attended only by the family and close friends.

The villagers were shocked that Carrie Blunt had taken a second husband with the first not yet cold in his grave.

'She do be expecting, the shameful hussy!' they said.

'They make their own laws at Russets,' they said. 'Lucy Blunt never knew no shame when the squire bedded her and young Charles was born out of wedlock,' they said.

'That were a fishy affair with young Julian not knowing who was his father. Another little bastard,' they said.

But they were too far removed from the village to be disturbed by spiteful tongues. The seasons ruled their lives – Spring, Summer, Autumn, Winter. The land was their heritage.

Tom and Carrie were busy with milking at 5 o'clock on their wedding day, and again in the early evening.

The child that stirred in the womb had been conceived in the beechwood. A new generation of children would grow up at Russets, no longer beholden to a powerful landlord, but the proud possession of the descendants of a brave woman who had trespassed beyond the barrier of class.

THE VILLAGE
by Sarah Shears

Part one of the Fairfields Chronicles

Set in the heart of the Kent countryside and spanning the period from the turn of the century to the end of the Great War, THE VILLAGE introduces us to the inhabitants of Fairfields Village, whose lives and loves become irrevocably entwined over the years. Richly evocative of Edwardian village life – from the brutal poverty of the slum dwellings of Richmond Row, to the grand splendour of Marston Park – this superb saga, with its wonderful cast of characters, depicts the changing pattern of English country life, portrayed by one of our best-loved novelists.

0553 40161 7